The Adventures of Kennedy Ryan and Friends

Alicia Layne Thomason

Illustrated by Amber Disney, Joyce Caberto, and US Illustrations

Acknowledgments

Thank you to my parents, Dennis and Michelle, for their support of my writing throughout my life.

Thank you to my cousin Amber Disney for working on the illustrations for the novella "Escape From Under the Mendenhall Glacier". Thank you to my dear friend Joyce Caberto for working on the illustrations for the novella "A Necklace Lost Deep in the Mine." Thank you to US Illustrations for working on the rest of the illustrations.

Thank you to my editor, Julia Hilton, for her edits on each of the novellas.

Special thanks to Tom Webb, my classmate in my Creative Writing 310 class, for sharing with me information about mining operations for the novella "A Necklace Lost Deep in the Mine", and to the rest of the class and my teacher, Tami K. Haaland, for their input on the novella.

Special thanks to the Billings Writers' Group members Virginia Duke, DS Ford, Alison Bohne, and CJ Christensen for sharing their editorial input and ideas for the novella "The Case of the Vanishing Painting."

And thank you to God and Jesus Christ my Lord and Savior for giving me the wonderful gift of imagination.

The Adventures of Kennedy Ryan and Friends

Table of Contents

The Lost Treasure of the Innocents

KENNEDY RYAN PRESSED her nose against the window of the van. As she gazed at the snowcapped mountains beyond the green hills in the distance, she felt like every breath she took was desperate to escape her lungs. Those mountains touching the blue sky were more beautiful than she had imagined.

"You sure are enjoying the view, aren't you?"

Kennedy looked over at Felicity Weston, who was sitting in the driver's seat in front of Kennedy.

"Yeah," Kennedy said. "Do you know which mountains those are?"

Felicity shook her head. "I'm sorry, hon, I can't remember. It's been a little while since I've studied Montana geography. Maybe Marilyn here knows."

Kennedy turned to her stepsister, Marilyn Wilson, who was sitting in the passenger seat. But Marilyn shook her head.

"I can't remember either," she said.

Kennedy felt a hand grasp her shoulder. Her sisters, Victoria and Jessica, leaned over her.

"That's the Greenhorn Range," Jessica said. "It's part of the Rocky Mountains."

"How do you know that?" Victoria asked.

Jessica smiled. "We've been studying orogeny in my summer geology class," she said. "We touched on Montana's mountains."

Kennedy bit her lip. If she was anywhere near as smart as her younger sister, she might not be struggling in her own summer chemistry class.

I should've stuck with my archery and music lessons. Why did I even think that taking on chemistry was a good idea? I'm so behind all the other kids!

"Well," Victoria said, "we're not gonna be able to sightsee sitting in this van driving around! Virginia City's calling my name!"

Felicity laughed. "Patience, Vic," she said. "We're not stopping until we find that gift shop."

"We'll find it in no time, right?"

"Oh, I'm sure." Felicity turned to Marilyn. "Speaking of which, I'm still going the right way, aren't I?"

"Yep," Marilyn said. "And actually, if you turn right on that street just ahead, you should find my uncle's gift shop easily."

Felicity turned onto a smaller street. She pulled the van alongside a curb in front of a small, square-shaped building made of wood.

"Is this the place?" she asked.

"It sure is!" Marilyn's smile matched the eager tone of her voice. "My uncle's gift shop and café!"

"Sweet!" Victoria said. "Let's get out!"

She flung the door open and jumped out. Holding up a pair of binoculars, she looked at the mountains in the distance.

"This is really different from Arizona!" Victoria exclaimed. "I've always associated the Wild West with the sandy, bright orange hills and the saguaro cacti of the desert, all under a blazing hot sun, but this place sure does give me some good Wild Western vibes!"

Kennedy had to agree with her sister. Everywhere she looked, she saw mountains and grassy hills. Hardly any sandstone bluffs in sight. Kennedy breathed deeply; the air smelled of pine trees and old wooden buildings.

"Sure is nice out," Marilyn said as she stepped out of the van.

"Yeah, cooler than it is in Arizona," Victoria said. "This will be a nice break from the heat back home."

And a nice break from chemistry, Kennedy thought gloomily. *Why does everything have to revolve around science, math, and technology these days? Not sure how art, music, and history are gonna do me much good when I graduate.*

"Come on, let's go in," Marilyn said. "I'm sure my cousin's waiting for us."

Kennedy looked up at the gift shop. A wooden sign that read WILSONS' GIFT SHOP AND CAFÉ in fancy writing hung above the front door. Toward the back of the building, Kennedy could make out what appeared to be a stone chimney.

Marilyn opened the door of the gift shop, making the little bells tied to the handle ring. Kennedy looked around the shop as she entered. The brown wooden floors matched the hues of the walls, pillars, and even the ceiling and shelves. A wooden staircase led up to a second floor. The checkout counter, which was also made of a light-brown wood, stood near the center of the room. The only area that looked remotely modern was the café, which was adjacent to the gift shop. The café had a black tile floor, a counter with pastries behind a glass display, and a single glass door next to a large trash can. Kennedy smiled; this little store reminded her of the gift shops back in her own hometown of Pine Lodge. Kennedy saw a few people looking at the shelves. One person was sitting in the café, drinking a soda.

"So, Marilyn," Victoria said, "where's your cousin?"

"And shouldn't Sierra and her cousin be meeting us here too?" Jessica asked. "I hope they didn't get lost."

Marilyn turned her head in different directions. "I'm not seeing anyone," she said. "I'll run upstairs. My cousin might be up there."

"Right," Victoria said. "We'll watch for the Hamiltons."

Marilyn ran up the stairs. Kennedy crossed her arms. She wondered what Marilyn's cousin would be like. When Felicity had first suggested taking Kennedy, her sisters, Marilyn, and their friend Sierra Hamilton on a girls' trip, Kennedy was more than happy to accept. After convincing their parents, Caitlin and Isaiah, that they would be alright with Felicity watching over them, all that the girls needed to do was decide where they would go. Initial suggestions had included the Grand Canyon or Monument Valley, but then Isaiah had suggested that they visit his brother, Marilyn's uncle, in Virginia City, Montana.

"You girls haven't met my brother yet," he had said to Kennedy, Victoria, and Jessica. "And frankly, I reckon it's about time you did."

Marilyn completely agreed with her father's idea. "Oh, yes!" she said. "You will love my cousin Darcy!"

Kennedy remembered those timid feelings washing over her while the other girls agreed to visit Marilyn's uncle. She had felt even more shy when Victoria suggested that Sierra bring her own cousin, whom none of the girls had met. Despite her timidity, Kennedy had also agreed.

And here she was now, waiting in the gift shop to meet her stepcousin for the first time.

Kennedy walked over to a bookshelf. Several magazines and books about Montana's history and geography stood on one side.

One magazine caught Kennedy's eye. Its front cover had a black-and-white photograph of a stocky, unruly looking man wearing a black cowboy hat and a beady look in his eyes. Kennedy picked up the magazine and read its title aloud to herself.

3

"'The Not-So-Innocent Innocents.'"

Kennedy smiled; she remembered studying about the Innocents, an infamous gang of road agents who robbed stagecoaches in the 1860s, in her Western Civilization class the previous spring. She picked up the magazine and flipped through its pages.

"Here's something for you, Jess," Victoria's voice said from the other side of the shelf. "A book on Montana geology. You might even get some extra credit when school starts up again next month."

Jessica laughed. "I'll check it out, thanks," she said. "I also found a book on Montana's flowers and birds."

Kennedy bit her lip. She was about to place the magazine back on the shelf when she noticed a young woman with long, dark brown hair in a ponytail walking briskly down the stairs. She was followed by an older gentleman who appeared to be in his early fifties. They went over to the counter.

"Please don't worry, Dad," the woman said in a cheerful voice, "our family's been through rough times before. We can handle this. Just look at my cousin!"

The man sighed. "Hon," he said, "I know you like looking on the bright side of things, but the truth is the gift shop's finances are looking very grim."

"But this building is a historic building. Been here since Virginia City's founding."

"Yes, I know. And that's probably why it's beginning to fall apart."

"You got that beam upstairs fixed up."

"Yes, and it became more debt for me to worry about."

Kennedy gave the man a sorrowful look. Just then she heard the bells ringing behind her. She glanced over her shoulder. A stocky man with black hair had entered the gift shop. He went over to the counter.

"Sorry I'm late," he said.

"It's fine," the first man said. "Give any tours today, Hugo?"

The black-haired man, Hugo, shook his head.

"Well, anyway," the woman said, "I was just about to say that maybe we should look for that lost treasure of the Innocents and use it to save the shop!"

Kennedy looked straight at the woman. Despite her smile, Kennedy could see a glint of worry in her light blue eyes. She also noticed a glint of worry in Hugo's eyes.

The first man chuckled lightly. "Provided it's even real," he said.

Kennedy's eyes fell back to the magazine in her hands. She flipped the pages and grinned when she spotted the word "treasure" on a page near the middle of the magazine. What also caught her

5

eye on the same page was the name CHESTER MORRIS. Kennedy had never heard of Chester Morris before. She read through the first paragraph:

> BORN JULY 1ST, 1821, CHESTER MORRIS
> GREW UP ON A FARM IN KANSAS.
> HATING HIS LIFE AS A FARMER, INSTEAD
> DESIRING A LIFE OF ADVENTURE AND
> RICHES, MORRIS TRAVELED TO THE
> NEWLY ESTABLISHED VIRGINIA CITY IN
> LATE JUNE OF 1863 AS A PROSPECTOR.
> MORRIS FORMED A CLOSE PARTNERSHIP
> WITH HENRY PLUMMER, WHO WAS THE
> LEADER OF THE INNOCENTS, THE GANG
> OF ROAD AGENTS WHO TERRORIZED
> VIRGINIA CITY IN 1863. BUT MORRIS'S
> MEMBERSHIP WITH THE ROAD AGENTS
> WAS BRIEF; HE WAS RUMORED TO HAVE
> STOLEN TREASURE FROM THE GANG
> THEMSELVES AND HIDDEN IT FOR
> HIMSELF. EVEN AFTER THE HANGING OF
> PLUMMER AND OTHER AGENTS, THE LOST
> TREASURE OF THE INNOCENTS REMAINED
> A RUMOR, AND MORRIS'S INVOLVEMENT
> WITH THE GANG HAS REMAINED OBSCURE.

Kennedy closed the magazine. Before she could approach the counter, a lanky man carrying a few books and a magazine rushed in and stood in front of the counter. Kennedy raised her eyes in surprise.

Sheesh, somebody needs a lesson in good manners, she thought irritably. She shrugged; she would just have to wait her turn.

A woman with dark blonde hair up in a bun approached the man. "Shawn," she said, "you do realize that you just cut in front of this young lady, don't you?"

The man, Shawn, looked over his shoulder at Kennedy. His face turned red.

"Oh, golly," he said, "I am so sorry, miss. I just got a little overexcited, I reckon. I didn't notice you."

"It's alright," Kennedy said. Her eyes rested on the stuff he was carrying. She noticed that his magazine was the same as hers.

"Wow," she said, holding up her own copy, "we're both buying magazines about the Innocents."

Shawn grinned. "I guess so," he said. "My sister Lydia here and I have been waiting for this magazine to come out for a year. I'm hoping that it'll have some good info on Chester Morris and his lost treasure!"

Kennedy lifted an eyebrow. The woman, Lydia, just smiled.

"Are you ready to check out?" the woman at the counter called.

Shawn went over to the counter. Hugo frowned when he saw Shawn and Lydia.

"You're back, eh?" he said. "Where's your third treasure-hunting comrade?"

"Outside, probably waiting impatiently for us," Shawn said.

The brown-haired woman scanned the magazine. "You know, Dad," she said, turning to her father, "even if we did find that fabled treasure of the Innocents, we'd probably have to turn it into the authorities."

Her father chuckled. "I'm sure we would," he said. He walked through the counter's swinging doors. "I'm gonna run up to the office, hon."

He went up the stairs. Hugo followed him.

"You thinking about looking for that missing treasure?" Shawn asked.

The woman chuckled. "I'd like to," she said, "but digging up these lands for it would get the law on my back. Not to mention that I'd have to beat you to it."

Shawn laughed. "The race is on," he said.

As soon as his purchases were stuffed into a brown paper bag, Shawn and Lydia left the shop. Kennedy stared after them as she approached the counter.

"Hello," the woman said, "did you find everything okay?"

"Yes, thanks." Kennedy gave the woman an encouraging smile. Her eyes fell on the woman's silver name tag. Kennedy raised an eyebrow when she read the name: DARCY.

"Hey," she said, "are you—I hope you don't mind me asking a random question, but are you Darcy Wilson?"

"Yeah, that's me," the woman said. She grinned. "Are you one of the gals with my cousin Marilyn? Did she finally get here?"

Kennedy nodded. "Yeah, she ran upstairs looking for you," she said quickly. "Uh, hold on a second."

She turned around and scanned the store for Victoria and Jessica. She spotted them sitting in the café with Felicity. Kennedy

7

raised her hand to wave at them, but then two other girls entered the café. Kennedy immediately recognized the brunette as Sierra Hamilton.

"Ooh!" she murmured. She turned back to Darcy. "Um, our other two friends have just arrived, it seems. Sorry, sorry, I'll go get them."

Darcy chortled. "No worries," she said. She placed the magazine to the side. "I'll just follow you over there."

Kennedy turned and began to make her way to the café when she heard Marilyn's voice.

"There you are!"

Kennedy looked over her shoulder. Marilyn was skipping down the stairs, followed by Darcy's father, who Kennedy now guessed was Marilyn's uncle. Marilyn ran up to Darcy and wrapped her arms around her.

"Hey, little cousin!" Darcy said. "So glad you and your posse could make it!"

"Me too!" Marilyn said. She glanced at Kennedy and her grin broadened. She let go of Darcy. "I see you've already met Kennedy."

"Oh, that's Kennedy?" Darcy said. "She's the stepsister with the detective skills, right?"

Smiling shyly, Kennedy walked over to Marilyn and Darcy. "Hi," she said.

"Hello there," Darcy's father said. He held out his hand, and Kennedy shook it.

"Nice to meet you, Mr. Wilson," she said.

"Oh, hon, just call me Uncle Edward."

Kennedy's smile grew. So did Uncle Edward's.

"So," he said, "I've heard from Isaiah that you've been leading my niece to chase criminals. On two separate occasions!"

Kennedy tried not to let her smile falter. She was relieved when she saw that Uncle Edward was still grinning.

"Well," she said, "Marilyn, Sierra and her cousin just got here. They're in the café."

"Sweet!" Marilyn said. "Let's run over there."

Kennedy followed Marilyn, Darcy, and Uncle Edward to the café. Jessica and Felicity were talking to Sierra.

"Oh, there you guys are!" Victoria said. "We were just wondering where you ran off to. Sierra and her cousin are here."

"I see," Kennedy said. "And Marilyn found her cousin and uncle."

"Oh, good!" Felicity said. She gave Darcy a pat on the back. "Remember me? Felicity? I reckon it's been a long time since you've visited Pine Lodge."

"I reckon so," Darcy said. "But yeah, I remember you, Felicity."

She turned her gaze to the other girls. "Nice cowgirl posse," she said. "Now, I've already met Kennedy. Marilyn, didn't you say you had three stepsisters?"

A flurry of giggles erupted from the girls.

"We're the other two," Victoria said. "Me and Jessica here. And that's our friend Sierra and her cousin."

"Rachel," Sierra added.

She motioned to the girl standing next to her. She was a slim girl who appeared to be around Kennedy's age, but she had a more petite figure. She wore a flower garland in her long and sleek, light blonde hair. The blue flowers seemed to match her blue eyes and rosy cheeks.

Smiling, Rachel held out a hand. "Hi," she said. "You must be Kennedy. It's nice to meet you."

"Likewise." Kennedy shook Rachel's hand. "So, you're Sierra's cousin?"

Sierra nodded proudly. "She sure is," she said, grasping Rachel's arm. "Sorry we're late. It took Rachel here forever to pick me up. She probably got to my house long after the rest of you left Pine Lodge."

Rachel rolled her eyes. "Girl, it took me forever just to get out of Prescott. There was a lot of construction on the highway."

Kennedy looked over from Rachel and Sierra to Darcy and Marilyn. Why was she so worried about meeting her stepcousin? They had gotten off to a good start so far.

"How was your trip, girls?" Uncle Edward asked.

"It was fine," Marilyn said. "How's Aunt Nora?"

"She's good. We've been looking forward to your visit."

"So were we. How's the gift shop business coming along?"

Uncle Edward's smile faded a little. "It's . . . fine," he said. He quickly smiled again. "Come along, we shouldn't keep your aunt waiting."

"Oh, yes," Darcy said, "but first, Kennedy, let's go pay for your magazine."

Everyone went to the counter, where Kennedy was finally able to purchase her magazine.

"Alrighty, now to clock out," Darcy said. "Say, Mary, you should ride with me and Dad to our house."

"I'd love to!" Marilyn said.

Kennedy looked down at her magazine, hoping that nobody would notice her frowning. She followed her sisters and Felicity out to the van. She watched Marilyn climb into the backseat of a small blue car.

"Kinda feels weird not to have Marilyn with us, eh?" she said as she got into the passenger seat.

"I don't blame her for wanting to ride with her cousin," Jessica said. "We'll be back with her soon."

"As long as Felicity here doesn't lose sight of Darcy's car," Victoria said.

Felicity chuckled. "I'm sure I won't. This isn't a big town. And Rachel will be following me."

Kennedy glanced out the window. Rachel and Sierra were getting into a white Grand Prix.

Felicity followed the blue car. The ride was shorter than Kennedy anticipated; in just five minutes, the blue car turned onto a dirt road and drove up a small hill. Felicity followed it to a small house. As soon as everyone was parked out front, they got out of the cars.

Kennedy looked at the house. Judging by the ground-level windows, the house had a basement. Its siding was a light-blue color, and the trim around the windows was white. The house also had a wide front porch and a fence around the backyard.

"Well, here we are!" Darcy said. "Home sweet home and overlooking Virginia City!"

"Oh, yeah," Rachel said, "you've got a gorgeous view of the town from here!"

Kennedy gazed down the hill. Rachel was right; the buildings sitting in that little valley, surrounded by green hills, trees, and mountains, made for a very picturesque scene.

"You coming, Ken?" Felicity asked.

Kennedy followed Felicity onto the porch. Uncle Edward opened the door to let everyone in.

"Nora!" Uncle Edward called. "We're here!"

A woman, who looked to be the same age as Uncle Edward, appeared from the kitchen. She grinned when she saw everyone.

"Hello!" she greeted, her arms wide open.

Marilyn ran up and hugged her. "Good to see you again, Aunt Nora!" she said.

"And you as well, dear," the woman said. "Did you have a good drive from Pine Lodge?"

"We did. We stopped at a hotel in Salt Lake City. Come on, you should meet my stepsisters."

"Oh, I've been looking forward to meeting them," Aunt Nora said.

"And so have we!" Victoria said eagerly. She grabbed Aunt Nora's hand and shook it. "I'm Victoria!"

Aunt Nora chuckled, even though she looked a little bit startled. "Is this one of them, Marilyn?" she asked.

"Yeah," Marilyn said with a smirk. "That's Victoria."

"I already said so!" Victoria said. She let go of Aunt Nora's hand. "Don't mind me, Aunt Nora. May I call you Aunt Nora?"

"Of course, dear. You're family now. Oh, we wanted to come to your parents' wedding in November, but we had a really bad snowstorm, and we couldn't get out of Virginia City. We were so disappointed."

"Oh, well, at least we're here now! And those are my sisters, Kennedy and Jessica."

Aunt Nora turned to Kennedy. Kennedy smiled, only to let it fade a little when Aunt Nora's smile faded.

"So you're Kennedy?" she asked.

Kennedy nodded. She held out her hand.

"It's nice to meet you, Aunt Nora," she said.

Aunt Nora hesitantly shook her hand. "I heard from Marilyn that you are quite the amateur detective," she said. "Led my niece into a couple of dangerous mysteries, huh?"

Kennedy chuckled, only to notice that Aunt Nora did not. She didn't seem to have the same reaction that Uncle Edward had when he had commented on Kennedy's past adventures.

"Oh, Aunt Nora," Marilyn said, "we got out of those situations just fine. Kennedy here is very lucky."

"Yes, I'm sure," Aunt Nora said. She turned to the other girls. "So I see you've brought Felicity Weston and Sierra Hamilton with you. And who's this young lady?"

Marilyn introduced her aunt to Rachel. Kennedy stared at Aunt Nora longingly. A few butterflies fluttered in her stomach. Did her aunt not approve of her?

11

"I'm happy to meet everyone," Aunt Nora said as she shook Rachel's hand. "I do wish I had enough space in my house for the three of you."

"Hey, we'll be fine in our cabin," Felicity said.

Kennedy glanced at Felicity. She was not sure that she would be fully comfortable without Felicity, who was basically an older sister to her.

"Well, why don't you girls hang up your coats and get settled in?" Aunt Nora said. "I'm almost done cooking dinner."

Uncle Edward helped the girls hang up their coats in the front closet, then Darcy led everyone downstairs to the basement.

"Hey, Kenny," Marilyn whispered, "don't worry about my aunt. She's really nice, but she's a bit of a worrier and can be a little overprotective. She'll warm up to you."

Kennedy could only nod and silently hope that Marilyn was right.

The den in the basement was cozy. A sofa stood against the maple-colored wall. There was a dartboard and some pictures of rural settings hanging on the other walls, and an ornate rug of Indian design lay on the carpet at the foot of the stairs.

Darcy went over to the sofa. She pulled off its cushions and pulled out a bed.

"Alright," she said, "who wants this pull-out bed?"

"I'll take it," Kennedy said.

"Sweet," Darcy said. "Marilyn, you'll sleep in here."

She went over to a door and opened it, revealing a studio apartment. It had a kitchenette with an earthen-colored tile floor. The carpeted area to the right made up the living room. It had a small sofa, a cat tree, and a bookshelf. A desk stood next to the brick fireplace. A fluffy gray cat slept on top of the cat tree.

Darcy pulled out another bed under the sofa. "This is Marilyn's bed," she said. "We've got a guestroom upstairs for Victoria and Jessica."

"So, wait a sec," Rachel said, "Darcy, do you have your own apartment in your parents' basement?"

Darcy laughed. "One of my biggest life blessings," she said. "Mom and Dad were more than happy to let me live down here when I finished college. Now all I have to do is finish paying off those student loans, then I'll try to get my own place."

"Your parents must love having you live with them again," Sierra said.

"Mom did say it helped with her empty nest syndrome."

"Where's your room?"

Darcy pointed to a bedroom just across from the kitchenette. "Over there," she said. "The bathroom is just across from my room, but there is another door to it on the other side."

"What's your cat's name?" Rachel asked, pointing up at the cat tree. The cat lifted his head and looked down at the girls.

Darcy smiled. "That's Earl Grey," she cooed. "He's my baby boy."

She went over to the tree. Earl Grey stepped down onto a lower level of the tree and headbutted Darcy's hand. Rachel went over to pet the cat. He instantly soaked up her attention. He even let Rachel scoop him into her arms.

Darcy went over to the door. "I'll take Victoria and Jessica upstairs," she said. "Kennedy and Marilyn can get settled in."

She led Victoria and Jessica out of the apartment. Kennedy went into the den and put her suitcase on the floor.

"This is so nice!" Rachel said. She was still holding the cat. Kennedy could hear him purring. "I almost wish I was staying here instead of at the cabin."

"I haven't been here in ages," Marilyn said. "Last time we saw each other, they had come down to Arizona."

"I don't remember that," Sierra said.

"We went to the San Francisco Peaks then. We wanted to have them stay in Pine Lodge, but it didn't work out."

"I hope you don't mind me saying so, Marilyn," Kennedy said, "but I noticed that your uncle seemed a little hesitant to talk about his business earlier?"

Marilyn frowned. "He did," she said. "I hope everything's alright. I could try to ask him later."

"Oh, maybe we shouldn't," Kennedy said. She didn't want Aunt Nora to think that she was a snoopy young lady who meddled in other people's business.

The girls finished unpacking and went upstairs. The cat was right on their heels. The girls met Darcy, Victoria, and Jessica in the dining room. They had just finished setting the table.

"Oh, good, you're here!" Darcy said. "Dinner's almost ready. Let's sit down."

"Well, does Aunt Nora need any help in the kitchen?" Kennedy asked.

"I don't think so, but we can check."

Kennedy and Darcy went into the kitchen, only to stop in the doorway. Uncle Edward and Aunt Nora were whispering to one another. Both had nervous frowns on their faces.

"I'm just not sure how long I can keep up," Uncle Edward said. "I could barely afford my electric bill last month."

"What about your other bills?" Aunt Nora asked quietly.

Uncle Edward shrugged. Just then he noticed Kennedy and Darcy in the doorway, and he quickly put on a smile.

"Well, you two must be hungry!" he said.

Aunt Nora could only give Kennedy a slight frown.

"No, no!" Kennedy said, trying not to make eye contact with Aunt Nora. "We were, uh, just wondering if you needed any help."

Aunt Nora shook her head. "No thank you, we're doing fine," she said. "You two go take your seats."

Kennedy rushed to the table and sat between Felicity and Rachel. She hoped that her face was not blushing too red with embarrassment.

In just a few moments, Aunt Nora brought a steaming chicken dish to the table. Uncle Edward carried a salad bowl and a plate of biscuits. As soon as the pair sat down and Uncle Edward prayed over the meal, everyone began serving.

"So, Jessica," Aunt Nora said, "I've heard from Marilyn that you are a bit of a young scientist."

Jessica chuckled. "I like studying science stuff," she said.

"She's a brainiac," Victoria said. "I don't know how she does it!"

Kennedy kept her eyes on her plate. The only thing she felt like she was enjoying right now was the tender, buttery chicken.

"So, Kennedy, what's life like on your uncle's ranch?"

Kennedy looked up. Rachel was smiling at her.

"I love it," Kennedy said. "I enjoy working there. And riding there. My mare Sunshine is my best friend on the ranch. She's a golden palomino. We bonded the moment we met."

"Aw, that's so sweet!" Rachel said.

"So you're from Prescott?"

"Yep. I work in a coffee shop. Mom is a general manager for a hotel. Dad's the pastor of our church. We have a few horses on our land, but we don't run a big farm or anything."

"But you do ride?" Kennedy asked.

Rachel nodded. "All the time."

"I didn't see you at our hotel in Salt Lake City," Kennedy said.

"Since Sierra and I started driving late, we stopped at a nice little bed-and-breakfast in a small town in Utah."

"And your mom is okay with you and Sierra traveling by yourselves?"

Rachel sniggered. "Well, I did graduate from high school this past spring. But even so, Sierra and I called our parents to let them know we were fine."

Kennedy and Rachel continued talking as they ate dinner. Kennedy felt glad to have Rachel's company.

"Dinner was really good, Aunt Nora," Victoria said. "If Mom were here, she'd be asking you for the recipe."

Kennedy picked up her plate and stood up. "Do you need any help cleaning?"

"No, Edward and I can do that," Aunt Nora said. "Thank you, though."

"It's getting late," Felicity said. "Rachel, Sierra, and I should probably go to our cabin."

"I really do feel bad that you have to pay for your own cabin," Aunt Nora said.

Felicity chuckled. "Oh, it's fine, Mrs. Wilson. It was a good price."

"Sierra and I put our stuff downstairs," Rachel said. "We'll grab it."

The girls went down to the basement. Kennedy went over to the sofa bed and picked up a small suitcase and handed it to Rachel.

"This one is yours, right?"

"Yep." Rachel took the suitcase. Her eyes rested on the magazine on the sofa bed. "A magazine on the Innocents, eh? I remember studying them with Mom."

"You studied with your mom?" Jessica said. "Were you homeschooled?"

Rachel nodded. "I loved it," she said.

Kennedy frowned a little. She and her sisters used to be homeschooled. That is, until her family moved to her uncle's ranch shortly after the death of her father. Kennedy liked her private school back in Pine Lodge, but sometimes she still missed being homeschooled.

Darcy grinned. "I bet you girls don't know about Chester Morris," she said.

Kennedy looked at Darcy. Her curiosity was aroused.

"I know I've never heard of him," Victoria said. "Who was he?"

"Only one of the most obscure members of the Innocents."

"I've always thought that the Innocents was the most sarcastic name for a gang of stagecoach robbers."

Darcy laughed. "Can't argue with you there, Victoria. They were led by Henry Plummer."

"Oh, yeah, now Henry Plummer, I did learn about. He was that infamous sheriff of Bannack."

"A crooked politician who joined a bunch of robbers?" Sierra said. "Sounds a lot like Maurice Carr."

Kennedy bit her lip. She hated to be reminded of Maurice Carr. He was once part of Pine Lodge's city council, and a father figure to Kennedy, until she discovered that he had secretly joined a gang of bank robbers.

"Anyway," Darcy said, "Chester Morris was one of the Innocents. He was rumored to have gathered a bunch of gold coins, jewelry, and such stolen from the victims of the stagecoach holdups and put them in a single chest. He told Plummer that he would share the contents with the rest of the gang. But he double-crossed the sheriff! Imagine that. Morris was too greedy for his own good, that sly fox. He hid the chest. And not one of any of those road agents was able to find it, not even with Chester's code."

"Chester had a code?" Felicity asked.

"Well, he was rumored to have had some sort of secret code for his own use. But if he did, none of the road agents figured it out. And if the treasure story is true, I'll bet that Plummer would not have been happy about being crossed."

"Do you believe in the lost treasure?" Victoria asked eagerly.

"I certainly think it's possible. It's not a super well-known story, though. Morris did defect from the road agents. Whether it was because of a stolen treasure or not, I'm not sure. Morris fled from Virginia City the same day that Plummer and those other guys were hanged. He was pursued by the Vigilantes."

"I remember learning about the Vigilantes!" Victoria said. "They were basically a bunch of guys who took the law into their own hands, right?"

"Yep," Darcy said. "The Vigilance Committee of Alder Gulch was organized in December 1863. The Vigilantes got the best of Morris in a shootout not far from Bannack."

Darcy's grin broadened and her voice fell to an excited whisper.

"It's said that Chester Morris's ghost haunts Hotel Meade in Bannack. Same with Henry Plummer's ghost."

"Cool!" Victoria said in a hushed voice. "Have you ever seen either of them, Darcy? Caught a glimpse of those guys?"

"Oh, I wish, girl."

Kennedy could only stare at Darcy with wide eyes. Smiling meekly, she turned to Marilyn.

"Your cousin must be a very interesting storyteller for the tourists," she whispered.

Marilyn sniggered. "She does enjoy a bit of dramatic flair."

"I just hope we'll be able to sleep tonight," Sierra said.

"Hey, I love a good ghost story," Rachel said. "Ghost stories make Western Civilization even more fun to learn."

Kennedy's smile grew. "I really enjoy studying Western Civilization," she said.

"Me too!" Rachel said. "I just love cowboys and cowgirls and vigilantes and showdowns!"

"We can probably tell more ghost stories at the cabin," Felicity said. "Do you have everything?"

Rachel picked up her purse. "I do now."

"Same," Sierra added.

Just as Felicity, Rachel, and Sierra turned to go up the stairs, Marilyn ran over to Darcy's side.

"Hey," she said shyly, "I hope you don't mind me asking, but . . . that is, I couldn't help but notice that Uncle Edward and Aunt Nora seemed a little on edge earlier."

Darcy's smile vanished. So did the enthusiasm in her eyes, which she lowered.

"To tell you the truth, Marilyn," she said, "Dad's gift shop has seen a few financial hardships recently."

Marilyn put her hand over her lips. "Gosh," she said, "I hope it's not too serious."

Darcy just shrugged.

"Well," Rachel said, smiling, "I reckon your folks will figure something out."

"I hope so," Darcy said. "The place that houses our shop is a historical building. We're proud of it."

Kennedy looked at her feet. She remembered the time when her mother's bakery back in Dallas had closed. It had not been long after her father's death.

"Well," Darcy said, her voice suddenly cheerful again, "we should let our friends go to their cabin so they can get their beauty sleep! I've got big plans for tomorrow!"

Felicity, Rachel, and Sierra wished everyone goodnight and headed upstairs. Kennedy's thoughts were still on the gift shop as she prepared for bed. She thought of how her mother's then-supervisor had been unable to save the bakery due to financial issues. She hoped that the gift shop would not face the same fate.

"Here we are!"

Darcy got out of the driver's seat and slammed the door. "Welcome to Bannack!"

Kennedy stared at Bannack. Even for a ghost town, it was the tiniest town she had ever seen. Just a bunch of old wooden buildings surrounded by hills and mountains. She opened her magazine and flipped through its pages until she found a map of Bannack.

"Well, what are we waiting for?" Victoria exclaimed. She ran ahead. "Let's explore and try to find some ghosts!"

Marilyn laughed. "We still need to wait for the others!" she called.

"Oh, it won't be long," Darcy said. "They've just arrived."

Kennedy turned around. Sure enough, Felicity's van was parking next to Darcy's car. Felicity, Jessica, Rachel, and Sierra climbed out. Kennedy followed everyone to the wooden boardwalk, where Victoria was waiting.

"This will be so much fun!" she said. "I've never been here before!"

"My magazine has a map of Bannack," Kennedy said. "The most famous building might be the Hotel—"

"Those trees are really pretty!" Sierra said, pointing beyond the buildings. "What are they?"

"Those are alder trees," Jessica said. "And if you listen, you can hear Grasshopper Creek flowing near here."

Kennedy turned her gaze to her magazine. She pretended to focus on the map as she followed everyone inside the first building. The rusty smell of old wood met her nostrils.

"This place is tiny," Victoria said. "It literally only has three rooms!"

"Yeah, this was normal back then," Darcy said. "Come on, you should see the other buildings, like Skinner's Saloon and Hotel Meade."

They left the old house. Kennedy lagged behind, still trying to focus on her magazine.

"Hey, you okay here? You're awfully quiet."

Kennedy looked up. Rachel was walking next to her.

"Yeah," she said, "just fine."

"Then why the scowl?" Rachel asked.

Kennedy shrugged. "It's nothing."

"Really? I don't think it's just nothing."

Kennedy sighed. "You got me," she said. "I worry about my future. I'm mildly autistic. And my sister Jessica is such a science prodigy. If I were as smart as her, and Victoria, I'd do better in my summer chemistry class."

"You shouldn't think like that," Rachel said. "Sierra was telling me last night about your skill in music and art. I've actually been meaning to ask you if I can look at your drawings."

"Yeah, I can show you," Kennedy said. "But while music and art are certainly good hobbies, they're not big money-making careers like technology and science and stuff like that. I'm not good at those kinds of things. Unlike Jessica."

"Girl, you should focus on the gifts that God gave you," Rachel said, "instead of envying your sister. Besides, you were the one who solved those mysteries of that politician who joined the bank robbers, and those cattle rustlers!"

Kennedy shrugged. "I didn't really mean to get involved in those cases," she said. "I don't intend to become a detective. That would be too much of a hassle for me. Believe it or not, I'm actually not super good at dealing with people."

She looked ahead at Victoria and Jessica, who were talking with Darcy and Marilyn.

"I also hope I can bond with Darcy like my sisters," she said.

"Well, what's holding you back?" Rachel asked.

"I dunno. Maybe I'm too shy. For one thing, this is the first time I've met Darcy since Mom married Isaiah. I also don't think

Aunt Nora likes me all that much. I know Darcy's nice. I just hope I can build a good relationship with my stepcousin and her family. Kinda like what you have with Sierra."

Rachel smiled. "I reckon you can," she said. "All you gotta do is step out of your comfort zone."

Kennedy smiled meekly. "I guess you're right," she said.

She turned her gaze to the hills. And she spotted a strange marking on the trunk of an alder tree.

"Hey," she said, glad to have an excuse to change the subject, "look at the mark on that tree over there."

Kennedy pointed to the tree. Rachel put her hand on her brow.

"I see it," she said. She grinned. "Gosh, Kennedy, do you think it could be a symbol used by the Innocents?"

"Dunno. Let's get a closer look."

Kennedy ran past Hotel Meade. She paused to look up at it. With its two stories and balcony over the front deck, Kennedy imagined it to be one of the bigger and fancier buildings in this tiny ghost town.

"Did you know that some people say that Hotel Meade is haunted?" she said. "I think Henry Plummer's ghost is supposed to be haunting it."

"I think I've heard of those stories," Rachel said. She smiled nervously. "Sure hope we don't meet any ghosts."

Kennedy sniggered. "Come on, let's check out that tree and keep our minds off ghosts."

The two girls approached the tree. Kennedy scraped her fingers over the symbol etched on the trunk. It was composed of a half circle with a capitalized letter *M* under it. Underneath the *M* was a tiny circle with two lines sticking out on either side and passing through the *M*.

"Wonder what this means," Rachel said.

Kennedy flipped through her magazine. "I'm not seeing it on any of these pages," she said.

"So maybe it's not a symbol used by the road agents?"

"Guess not."

Rachel took a picture of the symbol. "Well, that's kinda disappointing. Imagine if we had seen one of the Innocents' secret symbols."

Kennedy glanced over her shoulder. "We should probably catch up with the others," she said.

She and Rachel ran to Bannack's main street. Kennedy
spotted Darcy and Marilyn entering one of the buildings. She and
Rachel raced over and rushed inside. Marilyn, Victoria, Jessica, and
Sierra were walking around rows of desks, and Felicity and Darcy
were looking at the chalkboards on the wall.

"Oh, there you are!" Felicity said, smiling at the two girls. "We were wondering where you gals ran off to."

"Ah, we just spotted some weird marking on a tree," Rachel said. "I took a picture."

She showed her phone to Darcy and Felicity.

"I don't recognize that symbol," Darcy said.

Kennedy looked at the chalkboards. A bunch of sentences were written all over the board in white chalk.

"Can you believe these were the rules for the teachers?" Darcy said.

"Oh, yes, the rules that schoolteachers had to follow back in the day were very strict," Kennedy said. "They couldn't be away from home between the hours of seven in the evening and six in the morning."

"What, they couldn't go on evening outings?" Victoria said. "Golly, I wouldn't wanna be a schoolteacher in the nineteenth century."

"That's not all," Kennedy said. "Look, the teacher had to come to this place early to clean and prepare for class. And she had to wear two petticoats."

"Sheesh, that must've been uncomfortable!"

"Yeah. And she couldn't get married or leave town without permission. And if she hung out with other men, it had to be either her father or her brother."

"When you said strict, Kenny," Jessica said, "you weren't kidding."

Kennedy chuckled. Rachel gave her an encouraging smile.

After thirty minutes of exploring Bannack, the girls agreed to return to Virginia City.

"So, what now?" Marilyn asked as she buckled her seatbelt.

"Can we go back to the gift shop real quick?" Kennedy asked.

"Sure thing," Darcy said. "I wanna pop in there anyway."

She drove out of the parking lot. After an hour and a half of driving, they arrived at the gift shop. Felicity's van drove up just a moment later. Kennedy ran inside the shop and went straight to a bookshelf.

"Golly, Kennedy," Victoria said, walking up to her, "what's the rush?"

"I'm just looking for something that might tell me what that symbol was," Kennedy replied. "The one Rachel and I saw."

"Well, good luck, I mean, Darcy didn't know what it was. I'm gonna grab a snack."

Kennedy looked over her shoulder at the café. "I think I will too," she said.

She and Victoria went to the café. Kennedy stared at the pastries behind the glass display. She could hardly decide which one she wanted; all those cookies, cupcakes, muffins, and bagels looked so good.

A teenage boy came out of the kitchen. He ruffled his black hair and straightened out his apron. When he noticed Kennedy and Victoria standing at the counter, he sighed and went over to them.

"Hey, what can I get for you?" he asked.

"I haven't decided yet," Kennedy said.

"Well, take your time." The boy pulled his phone from his pocket.

Victoria pushed past Kennedy and leaned over the counter.

"Hey there," she said with a smile. "Beautiful day, isn't it?"

The boy just shrugged. "I guess, after a cold and cloudy morning," he said.

"I know, right? So, what's your name?"

The boy fingered his silver name tag, which read ANDREW.

"Nice to meet you, Andrew. I'm Victoria. Me and my sisters are visiting from Arizona."

"Oh?" Andrew said. "Lucky you. You get to spend the final weeks of your summer having fun. I'm spending them working here so I can make money to pay for college."

Kennedy picked up an apple juice and set it on the counter. "I'm ready now," she said. "I've got this juice here, and I'd like to buy two cupcakes."

Andrew took the juice and scanned it.

"Where are you going to college?" Victoria asked.

"Bozeman," Andrew said. "I almost regret it. Living in the dorms cost almost as much as the tuition."

"What are you going for?"

"Tourism business. My brother is a local deputy. A pretty boring job if you ask me, being a deputy in a tiny tourist town, but he makes good money. Better than me. I'm studying Western Civilization and Montana geography and, of course, those useless gen eds."

Kennedy held in a sigh. "How much do I owe you?"

"Hold your horses," Andrew said, "I haven't gotten your cupcakes yet."

"My sister Kennedy here loves learning about Western Civilization," Victoria said.

"Same here," Andrew said. "That's much better than math and geography. I suck at those. I gotta know Montana geography if I wanna work in tourism here, but science and I don't seem to get on."

"I know the feeling," Kennedy muttered. She tapped her fingers on the counter, staring at the glass display and wondering when Andrew was going to open it up. She shot him an impatient glance; she almost doubted that he really wanted to work with tourists.

"Andy, I hope you're not complaining about college to the tourists again."

Kennedy and Victoria turned around. A young man who appeared to be in his twenties was walking toward the counter. He wore a pair of jeans, dusty cowboy boots, and a brown vest over a gray shirt. A gold star reading BRANT MITCHELL, DEPUTY was pinned to his vest.

"Hey, don't arrest me, Brant," Andrew said. He quickly opened the display and took out two cupcakes. "Alrighty, that'll be ten dollars even."

Kennedy opened her wallet. She handed a ten-dollar bill to Andrew, then she grabbed the cupcakes and sat down at a table with Victoria.

Brant went over to the counter. "Andy," he said in a quiet voice, "how many times do I have to tell you not to whine about your college woes to the tourists?"

Kennedy and Victoria eyed one another.

"Hey," Andrew said defensively, "forgive me for being a vocal kid who is worried about my job here. This gift shop is going down the drain."

Kennedy thought of what Darcy said the previous evening.

"Well, you shouldn't keep the tourists waiting," Brant said, "like you did with that young lady."

"She seemed pretty impatient, eh?"

Kennedy covered her face with her hands.

"I don't blame her," Brant said.

"Well, I'm not going to progress past working in this café even if the gift shop doesn't close," Andrew grumbled. "What good is teaching history to the tourists?"

"But that's what you want to do. And I think you should."

"Your job is better. It earns more income."

"That doesn't matter."

"It will when the student loans bite me in the rear."

"You shouldn't be grumbling about the future yet, Andy," Brant said. "I'll bet you that you'd find success if you wouldn't be so pessimistic."

Andrew just sighed. "Do you want your usual coffee with two creams and two sugars, Brant?"

"Sure. Why not?"

Andrew turned away from Brant. Kennedy looked at Victoria. They shrugged. Kennedy glanced back at the counter.

Man, I know how you feel, Andrew, she thought.

Brant paid for his coffee and left the café. Kennedy stood up. "I'm gonna look at the books," she said.

"Wait for me," Victoria said. She stuffed the rest of her cupcake in her mouth, then she followed Kennedy away from the café.

"Well, that was awkward," Victoria whispered.

"Tell me about it," Kennedy said. "But let Andrew deal with his own problems. I wanna see if I can find that symbol."

"What does it look like?"

"Well, it was like a half circle on top of the letter *M*. Rachel took a picture of it."

"I saw her going upstairs just a minute ago. Let's find her."

Kennedy and Victoria ran up the stairs. The second floor of the gift shop was filled with racks of clothes such as caps, jackets, sweatshirts, and T-shirts. A few women were looking at a jewelry stand next to the checkout counter, which had a glass display filled with more jewelry. An elegant shelf filled with figurines stood next to the fireplace.

Kennedy's eyes searched the area for Rachel. They rested on Shawn and Lydia. The two of them, along with a tall, broad-shouldered man with spiky, sandy-colored hair, were standing in front of the bookshelves, flipping through pages of books and whispering to one another.

Victoria tugged on Kennedy's sleeve. "Hey, she's right over there."

Kennedy turned her head. She saw Rachel standing in front of a bookshelf near the fireplace.

"Hey, Rachel, we were looking for you," Victoria said. "Wanna show me that tree mark you took a picture of?"

Rachel smiled. "I figured Kennedy would still be looking for it," she said. "But who am I to talk? I'm still looking myself."

She pulled her phone out of her pocket. She tapped the screen a few times and handed her phone to Victoria.

"Darcy didn't recognize the symbol," she said.

Kennedy looked over Victoria's shoulder at the phone. "I wonder if we could try asking someone else," she said. "Maybe Uncle Edward can tell us something."

"Or Andrew," Victoria suggested.

Kennedy frowned. "I wouldn't," she said.

"Who's Andrew?" Rachel asked.

"Some kid who works in the café downstairs," Kennedy said. "Seemed more interested in complaining about college than serving me and Vic."

"Hey, don't be so judgmental, he's just worried about his future," Victoria said. "Kinda like you."

Kennedy scowled at her sister. "Let's find Uncle Edward," she said. She turned around.

"Hey, look at that brick. It's really loose."

Kennedy looked over her shoulder. Victoria was toying with a loose brick around the rim of the fireplace.

"Better leave that alone, Vic," Kennedy said. "The last thing Aunt Nora and Uncle Edward need is for us to be messing—"

Two bricks suddenly collapsed. Kennedy gasped as she watched the bricks and dust fall to the floor.

"Oops." Victoria smiled sheepishly at Kennedy. "I'll just put this back."

Kennedy sighed. She tried not to think of what Aunt Nora would say if she were ever to learn of this.

"Might be too late for that," she said. "I just hope this won't be too much of an added bill for Uncle Edward."

"You'd think they'd have these loose bricks fixed up," Victoria said.

"Maybe they couldn't afford it," Rachel said.

Victoria bit her lip. Kennedy picked up the fallen bricks and attempted to slide them back into their holes.

But something in one of the holes caught her eye.

26

"There's something in here," she said.

Kennedy gingerly stuck her hand into the hole. She felt a crinkled paper brush against her fingertips.

"Well, pull it out," Victoria said.

"I am," Kennedy said. She grasped the paper and pulled out a rolled-up piece of parchment. Kennedy gingerly unrolled it. Thick gray dust covered her fingers.

"What is it?" Rachel asked.

"Not sure," Kennedy said. She stared at the parchment. It had little tears near the top corners and the handwriting was somewhat faded. Kennedy blew on the parchment.

"Wow, it's really old!" Victoria said.

"Duh, look at it."

"No, no! Look at the year!"

Victoria pointed to the bottom right-hand corner of the parchment. Kennedy stared. The year was 1863.

"Whoa," she said, "this is from the time of the Innocents!"

"What?" Rachel said. "Are you being serious, Ken?"

"Yeah, she is!" Victoria said. "Come on, Kenny, let's see what these drawings mean."

"No way," Kennedy said, "it's too faded. All I can make out are some initials down here. They look like, uh, *C* and *M*."

"Well, alright, what could *C* and *M* mean?"

Kennedy let out a gasp. "Perhaps they stand for Chester Morris?" she said in a hushed voice.

"Don't look now," Victoria said, pointing to a spot near the bottom left-hand corner, "but that looks like an *X* right there."

Kennedy looked up at her sister. "Do you suppose this could be Chester's map?"

Victoria grinned.

"I wouldn't say it out loud," Rachel whispered. She pointed her thumb over her shoulder. Kennedy glanced at the crowd that was beginning to gather. She spotted Shawn, Lydia, their friend, and even Hugo staring at her, all four of them with wide eyes. Kennedy knew what Rachel was thinking; if word got out about this map, who knows what might happen?

She folded the paper gingerly. "We need to find Uncle Edward."

"I know where his office is," Victoria said. "Follow me."

She led Kennedy and Rachel to a door with a sign that said EMPLOYEES ONLY. Kennedy knocked on the door. Darcy opened it.

"Hey, there," she said. "What's up?"

"Hi," Victoria said, smiling sheepishly, "you wouldn't mind if we pop in here for a private chat, would you?"

Darcy held the door open wider. Kennedy, Victoria, and Rachel went in the office. It was a small room with a thin, navy blue carpet and one window. Uncle Edward was sitting at an L-shaped desk covered in stacks of papers and envelopes. He turned around in his chair and smiled at the three girls.

"Howdy," he said. "What brings you in here?"

Victoria closed the door behind her. "You won't believe what we found!" she said excitedly.

Kennedy handed the parchment to Uncle Edward. She told him about the loose bricks in the fireplace and how she had found the parchment within the hole.

"Sorry about the fireplace, by the way," she said after she finished her story.

"Oh, I'm sure it'll be fine," Uncle Edward said. He laid the map out on the desk. "So you're telling us that this could be Chester Morris's fabled treasure map?"

Darcy clapped her hand over her mouth. "Oh, Dad!" she exclaimed. "Imagine if it is! Found in our very own gift shop! If we found it, imagine what we could do with it!"

Uncle Edward chuckled. "We wouldn't be able to legally use the money to save the shop, honey."

"I know. I meant turn it in and get some reward money."

A wistful look filled Uncle Edward's eyes as he gazed at the old paper. "I suppose it's worth trying," he said. "Darcy, can you call Brant, please?"

"Sure thing, Dad!"

Darcy whipped her phone from her pocket and stepped out of the office. Uncle Edward pulled out his own phone and snapped a few pictures of the paper.

"I guess X marks the spot," he said.

"Hey, wait a moment," Rachel said, looking over Uncle Edward's shoulder, "Kennedy, see that symbol right there? Isn't that the same symbol that we had seen on the tree in Bannack?"

Kennedy looked at the spot where Rachel was pointing. She was right; that strange symbol that had been on the alder tree was on the paper.

"Well, we found it at last," she said. "Uncle Edward, do you recognize that symbol?"

"No, I don't." Uncle Edward picked up the parchment. It allowed Kennedy to see the handwriting on the back.

"Hey, look!" she said. "Turn it around!"

Uncle Edward did so. "Well, would you look at that," he said. "We've got some sort of riddle."

He read it aloud.

"'Where I bury my love, locate my mark above, on the tall wooden post, which has hair that falls most, when it changes colors, nearest a fine alder, at the boot of the hill, I find my treasure fill.'"

Everyone exchanged confused looks.

"Okay, did that make any sense to anyone here?" Victoria asked. "Because it didn't to me."

"Chester Morris was known for his love of riddles," Uncle Edward said.

"Darcy mentioned last night that he was rumored to have his own secret code!" Kennedy said. "Maybe this riddle is the code?"

"Let's figure this out," Rachel said. "So, buried his love? Did Chester have any wives or girlfriends?"

"I read in my magazine about a saloon girl Chester was dating," Kennedy said. "Claudia Stone. She acted as his spy while he was a member of the Innocents. The Vigilantes chased her out of town after Plummer and others were executed."

"Did she ever try to return? Was she caught and executed?"

"Nobody knows what happened to her," Uncle Edward said.

"Maybe we're looking for this lady's grave!" Victoria said.

"Well, before we jump to any conclusions," Kennedy said, "I read that Claudia and Chester broke up shortly before Plummer was hanged. Though I guess it's possible Chester still loved her."

"I can tell you that she wasn't buried in Virginia City or Bannack," Uncle Edward said. "She has no gravestone here."

"And I don't suppose there are any wooden posts around, are there?" Kennedy asked.

Uncle Edward shook his head.

"And what does this riddle mean by hair that falls most when it changes colors?" Rachel asked.

"There's a lot to unpack here," Kennedy said. "Oh, Uncle Edward, mind if I take a few pictures myself?"

Uncle Edward laid the map on the desk. "Have at it."

Kennedy took a few pictures of the map just as Darcy came into the office.

"Brant said he'll be here shortly," she said.

"We'll keep it in here until he comes," Uncle Edward said.

"Sure thing, Dad. Oh, Kennedy, Rachel, and Victoria, the others are just outside the office, wanting to know what's going on."

Kennedy, Victoria, and Rachel followed Darcy out of the office. They were met by Marilyn, Jessica, Sierra, and Felicity.

"We got a gist about a map," Marilyn said in a hushed voice. "What's the scoop?"

"Yes, tell us, what's the scoop?" a new voice said eagerly.

Kennedy looked behind her to see Shawn, Lydia, and their friend approaching them. Shawn was grinning from ear to ear.

"We saw everything," he said. "Didn't take much to put things together. Was it really the old map of Chester Morris in that fireplace?"

"What?" Marilyn said. She, Felicity, and Sierra exchanged surprised looks.

"We've been searching for that map for a long time!" Lydia said.

"You should let us see it," Shawn added, "and tell us all about it. Treasure hunting is our specialty!"

Kennedy hesitated. "Uh, we're not exactly at liberty to say much," she said.

"Well, why not?" Shawn asked.

"Dude," the sandy-haired man said, "can't we just let them be? They're just not ready to say anything yet."

"Let's show them our card," Lydia said.

"Good idea!" Shawn reached into the pocket of his jacket and pulled out a business card. He handed it to Felicity.

"The three of you are from Bozeman Treasure Hunters, Incorporated?" Felicity asked.

"Yep," Shawn said. "I'm Shawn Hudson. This is my sister Lydia and our friend Trent Ross."

"Well," Darcy said, smiling, "you've finally come to Virginia City at the right time, it seems."

"Who knew that Chester's map was right here in your family's gift shop!" Lydia said.

"I know, right?" Darcy said. She then frowned. "But look, I'm sorry, Kennedy here is right. We probably shouldn't make this big news yet."

Shawn's face fell. "Aw, come on," he said, "can't we talk to your manager? I mean, your father?"

"Please, I'm certain. We'll call you."

Shawn sighed. Trent tugged at his sleeve. "Let's not bother them anymore, man," he said. "Come on, let's head out."

Shawn and Lydia reluctantly followed Trent downstairs.

"Gosh, I feel bad," Darcy said.

"Ah, don't," Kennedy said. "We really shouldn't let this news get out yet. Give your dad time to let Brant see the map."

"But it's really the map itself?" Marilyn asked eagerly.

"We'll explain later," Kennedy said.

"You can tell us while we get dinner," Felicity said.

"Good idea, I'm getting hungry," Victoria added. "Where to?"

"Mom's making dinner at home. You girls run along."

"Are you coming?" Marilyn asked.

"My dad and I will meet you at the house," Darcy said. "It's almost closing time. I should wait for Brant so I can give him the map."

"Alright, we'll see you then."

Kennedy followed her sisters, Marilyn, Rachel, Sierra, and Felicity out to the van. Kennedy explained everything from seeing the weird symbol on the alder tree in Bannack to finding the paper in the fireplace.

Felicity whistled. "That's amazing!" she said. "Oh, Billy will be so disappointed that he wasn't here to experience this!"

"Well, this is a girls' trip," Sierra said with a smirk.

"And you think it's Chester Morris's old treasure map?" Marilyn asked eagerly.

"We'll find out soon," Kennedy said.

In a few minutes, they arrived at the Wilsons' house. As soon as they jumped out of the van, Victoria, Rachel, and Sierra dashed for the front door.

"I don't see Darcy's car," Jessica said.

"She's probably still waiting for Brant," Kennedy said. "And I reckon we would've seen her driving on the way here."

The girls entered the house and went into the kitchen. Judging by the excited chatter of Victoria, Rachel, and Sierra and the surprised look on Aunt Nora's face, Kennedy guessed that Aunt Nora had already heard the story.

"So you claim to have found the old treasure map of one of the Innocents in my husband's gift shop?" Aunt Nora said, looking at Rachel.

Rachel nodded. "Darcy might have something to say when she gets back!"

The girls helped Aunt Nora set the table. They sat down just as Aunt Nora and Marilyn set dishes of lasagna, biscuits, and salads on the table.

"Darcy and her father are late," Aunt Nora mumbled. She sat down next to Marilyn.

"Darcy might still be talking with Brant," Kennedy said. "Victoria and I met him and his brother Andrew in the café earlier. Andrew seemed worried about college."

Aunt Nora frowned. "Was he complaining about college?"

"Yeah, he was."

"But I'll bet that when he learns about us finding the map," Victoria said, "he'll be happy! I mean, think of the reward you'll get for us finding it!"

"We sure can use it," Aunt Nora said. Kennedy gave her an encouraging smile.

Just then, Marilyn's cell phone rang. She excused herself from the table and answered it.

"Hey, Darcy!" she said. "What's . . . hey, calm down, I can't hear you . . . what? Oh, uh, yeah, she's right here."

Marilyn turned to Kennedy. "It's my cousin," she said. "She wants to speak with you."

Kennedy cringed at the frown on her stepsister's face. She stood up, took the phone, and went out to the living room.

"It's Kennedy, Darcy."

"Oh, good!" Darcy said. "Kennedy, something awful has happened!"

Kennedy's heart leapt.

"Dad's office was broken into. The map is gone!"

Kennedy gasped. "Stolen?" she said.

"Most likely. Brant's here, but . . . oh, Kennedy, with the sheriff out of town . . . the thing is, Marilyn's told me all about your detective skills. Would you be willing to step in? I mean, the map was found in my family's gift shop. That discovery alone has the potential to save our shop. We need that map back, Ken. Call me desperate, but even if you kept an eye out for clues that might help us get the map back, that'll be great."

Kennedy glanced back at the dining room. "Well," she said slowly, "I can try."

"Sweet. Brant agreed to let you look at the office."

"Okay. We'll be there as soon as we can."

"Oh, thank you, thank you!"

Kennedy hung up and went back to the dining room. She handed the phone back to Marilyn.

"You got our undivided attention when you said 'stolen,'" Marilyn said. "Does Darcy really think the map had been stolen?"

Kennedy nodded. She winced at the grim look on Aunt Nora's face.

"Darcy wants me to come and look at the office," she said.

Aunt Nora stood up. "I'm not sure that's a good idea," she said sternly.

"But, Aunt Nora," Marilyn said, "Kennedy has great detective skills. She's solved a couple of mysteries before. And Brant and Uncle Edward will be there."

Aunt Nora still didn't look convinced. Kennedy lowered her eyes.

"How about this, Mrs. Wilson?" Felicity said. "I'll take the girls to the gift shop. We'll just peek around for a few minutes. I'm sure we'll be okay."

Aunt Nora hesitated. "Well, since Kennedy already said that she'll look around," she said, "I don't suppose it could hurt. But let's finish dinner first."

Everyone seemed rushed to finish eating. Kennedy put her plate in the sink and went to the living room to grab her magazine. As she passed the kitchen, though, she noticed Marilyn and Aunt Nora whispering to one another.

"Marilyn, please be careful out there," Aunt Nora said. "All of you. Don't let your stepsister lead you into any danger."

Kennedy held in a deep breath.

"Don't worry," Marilyn said, "Kennedy's smart, Aunt Nora. We'll be fine."

Kennedy stepped away from the kitchen. Her eyes fell past her magazine and at her feet. She kept them lowered as she walked out to Felicity's van.

It only took five minutes for Felicity to drive to the gift shop, but it seemed like forever to Kennedy. As soon as Felicity parked, everyone jumped out of the van and ran inside. Darcy, her father, Brant, and Andrew stood in front of the counter.

"Oh, good, you're here!" Darcy exclaimed. She gave Kennedy a hug. "Thank you for coming, Ken."

"No problem," Kennedy said. "So, uh, what's going on?"

"Um, wait just a minute," Andrew said, raising his hands. He turned to Brant. "Are you seriously okay with a bunch of tourists looking at a crime scene?"

Brant shrugged. "I'm sure it'll be fine," he said. "I mean, the sheriff's out of town. And I've heard some pretty neat things about Miss Kennedy here."

He smiled at Kennedy.

"Oh, guys," Darcy said quickly, "this is Brant Mitchell, local deputy and my boyfriend, and his brother Andrew."

Kennedy raised her eyebrow. Darcy was dating Brant?

"Well, Kennedy," Andrew said, "if Brant thinks it's cool to let you in on a crime scene, don't let me stand in the way."

"Alright." Victoria playfully pushed Andrew aside.

"Oof!" Andrew gasped. He gave Victoria a wry smile. "That's not exactly what I meant."

"Alright, enough fooling around," Brant said. He turned to Darcy. "Tell Kennedy what you told me, hon."

Darcy faced the girls. "After you left this afternoon, I decided to wait for Brant and give him the map myself. Then I heard this loud crash here, downstairs. Dad and I checked it out. One of our bookshelves was lying flat on the floor, its contents all over the place."

Kennedy's eyes widened.

"I helped Dad and Andrew clean up the mess. I left the map in the office and locked the door, but when Dad and I went back to the office after we cleaned everything up, we found the door open. I just about had a heart attack. Dad and I found some drawers open, and a few things scattered on the floor, but the only thing missing was the map."

"May I check out the office for myself?" Kennedy asked.

"I think it'll be fine," Brant said, "as long as you're careful not to disturb anything."

Darcy led everyone upstairs to the office. Kennedy went inside with Brant. The office did not look too ransacked, although papers were scattered all over the desk and the floor.

"I've already dusted for fingerprints," Brant said. "And the lock looked like it had been picked."

Kennedy peered at the doorknob. Tiny scratches covered the gold lock pad.

"I wonder if that bookshelf had been deliberately knocked over to create a diversion," she said. "Were there any witnesses to this?"

"Only the security camera," Darcy said.

"Well, Kennedy, what you said does make sense," Uncle Edward said. "I mean, knocking down an entire shelf, even just a small one? It took us quite a while to clean everything up and put the shelf back up."

"Exactly. Have either you or Darcy noticed any suspicious characters recently?"

Darcy shook her head. "Not me. I didn't notice anybody go upstairs while we were taking care of the fallen shelf."

"Neither did I," Uncle Edward said. He sighed and sat down. "Though I probably should've had someone up here. The last thing my shop needs is a robbery."

"It'll be alright, Mr. Wilson," Brant said. "We'll get to the bottom of this."

"Is there anything else?" Kennedy asked. She turned her gaze to the open window. "Perhaps the thief escaped through that window?"

"I wondered that too," Brant said, "but I can't figure out how. The window was open when I came in to investigate, and Darcy said that it hadn't been open before then. But how did the thief get out of here from the second story? I highly doubt that he would've been able to scale down a wooden building, but there's no evidence of rope marks."

Kennedy poked her head out the window. She grinned when she saw the large tree branch.

"Perhaps he used the tree?" she said.

Brant's eyes widened. He lightly slapped his forehead.

"Why I did not think of that, I'll never know!" he said. "Let's go outside! Maybe we'll find footprints!"

Everyone ran downstairs and out the door. Uncle Edward and Darcy led them behind the gift shop. Kennedy was ready to turn on her phone's flashlight. But when she saw the gravel on the ground, disappointment gnawed at her stomach.

"Ooh, I don't think we'll find any footprints," she said.

"I think you're right," Brant said. He sighed and crossed his arms. "Guess there isn't anything else to be done tonight. I suggest the rest of you head on home."

He wrapped a comforting arm around Darcy. "I'll keep at it," he said, "and keep you and your parents updated."

Darcy nodded. "Thanks, Brant."

Felicity, Rachel, and Sierra said goodnight to everyone and left in Felicity's van. Kennedy got in the passenger seat of Darcy's car. The drive back to the house was silent. Kennedy stared out the window. She hoped that she would be able to help Darcy sort out this mess soon.

A few rays of sunlight shined through the window of the den. Kennedy huddled in her blanket. Even though her eyelids were heavy, she had a hard time falling asleep. For most of the night, her thoughts wandered back to the map.

Who could've stolen the map, though? Or, wait . . .

She thought of those three treasure hunters, Shawn, Lydia, and Trent. Shawn had seemed really disappointed when Darcy had refused to let them meet with her father. And that was shortly before the office had been broken into.

Kennedy sat up and grabbed her phone from off the floor. She looked at the pictures she had taken of the map. But most of them looked slightly blurred. And she still had no idea what that riddle could mean!

She heard footsteps upstairs. Then Darcy's voice.

"Good morning, Mom." Darcy did not sound as cheerful as she usually did.

"Good morning, honey," Aunt Nora's voice said. "Did you sleep well? Are you hungry?"

Kennedy stretched. *Might as well get up too.*

After she showered and dressed, Kennedy went upstairs. Darcy and Aunt Nora were in the kitchen, which smelled of pancakes, eggs, and sausages.

"Hey, look who's awake!" Darcy said.

Kennedy smiled. "Morning," she said. "Need any help with breakfast?"

"Nah, we've got the table set and everything."

Kennedy sat down just as Victoria, Jessica, and Marilyn came into the dining room. Darcy and Aunt Nora placed the food on the table and sat down themselves.

"Where's Uncle Edward?" Marilyn asked.

"He went to the gift shop early," Darcy said. She sighed. "I'd like to apologize for all the drama from last evening. I don't want our girls' trip to go down in shambles."

"Hey, it won't," Victoria said. "I mean, I hope things work out for you, Darcy, but are we still going to hang out today?"

"Of course. There's plenty of stuff that we can do. There are some museums in town, we can go on the Virginia City Shortline Railroad, and we can take rides on the stagecoach and the historic fire truck."

"Ooh," Jessica said, "that all sounds like fun!"

Kennedy barely listened to her sisters and Darcy talk. She looked down at the sausages sitting on her plate. How could she have fun knowing that some selfish thief had the map, was working to decipher it, and was searching for the treasure to take for himself? And all at the Wilsons' expense?

"Hey, Kennedy," Felicity said, "we need to get going. Our railroad ride is going to start soon."

Kennedy reluctantly put the book back on the shelf. She had initially been looking forward to visiting the museums. But after looking at the exhibits and artifacts in three museums, she had not found anything that could give her useful information on Chester Morris's map or a possible interpretation of the riddle. Nor did she find anything in the library of the Thompson-Hickman Museum.

Kennedy followed Felicity, Victoria, and Jessica to her van. In a few minutes, the girls met Darcy, Marilyn, Rachel, and Sierra at the station of the Alder Gulch Shortline Train. Kennedy stared at the train. It was small and red. She noticed Darcy waving at the man sitting in the engine car at the front. Small wonder; that man was Hugo.

"What's Hugo doing there?" Victoria asked.

"He's a part-time driver for the Alder Gulch rides," Darcy said.

The girls bought their tickets and took their seats near the front of the train.

"Hey, hey, Darcy!"

Kennedy whipped her head around. Shawn, Lydia, and Trent were running toward the train. Darcy frowned a little as the three of them climbed into the aisle behind her and Kennedy.

"Darcy," Shawn whispered, "I really hope you don't mind us asking, but is it true?"

"Is what true? Oh, you heard about the map, haven't you?"

Lydia nodded. "We went to your father's gift shop this morning to talk to him more about it," she said. "He told us what happened. That's just awful! We had such high hopes too!"

Trent shrugged. "It's not like we haven't found old treasures before," he said. "We just missed one because of a thief."

"Yes, Trent," Shawn said irritably, "but this treasure would've been one historic find!"

"And with the sheriff out of town, things look bleak," Lydia said.

"Well, our local deputy is working on the case," Darcy said.

Shawn just sighed. Kennedy felt like doing the same. She saw Hugo set his phone down and look over his shoulder.

"Alright," he called in a loud voice, "is everybody ready?"

Cries of affirmation erupted from the tourists. Kennedy smiled a little as the train began moving.

"As many of you are aware, the Alder Gulch Railroad takes you in between Virginia City and Nevada City," Hugo said, "and you will have the opportunity to see beautiful scenery and learn about the areas."

Kennedy's smile grew. She wondered if Hugo would say anything about Chester Morris and the Innocents. He might even mention the lost treasure!

"You can see alder trees all around us," Hugo said. "That's how Alder Gulch got its name."

"They're gorgeous!" Jessica whispered to Sierra.

"I know!" Sierra said. "Look, what kind of trees are those?"

"Those are Douglas firs, and those are Rocky Mountain junipers. Oh, I see some aspens, narrow leaf cottonwoods, willows, and chokecherries!"

"Whoa, slow down, girl, I can't keep up!"

Kennedy turned her eyes to her feet. She wondered when Hugo would start talking about the history of the area. But he only talked more about the trees, then he moved onto the geology of the mountains.

"I remember reading a story in my magazine about Chester Morris escaping from the Vigilantes in early January of 1864."

Now Hugo had Kennedy's attention. Her smile returned. Finally, Hugo was talking about Chester Morris!

"Morris was too slippery for those guys. He wasn't caught, ergo, he wasn't among the road agents who had been hanged along with Henry Plummer. Morris eventually ran out of Virginia City altogether. But the Vigilantes did catch up with him. Morris died in a shootout with the Vigilantes."

Kennedy's face fell. Disappointment turned her eyes back to her feet. Any smile she had was thanks to the beautiful landscapes before her. And all further hopes of hearing Hugo say anything more about Chester Morris were dashed. He mentioned Henry Plummer and how the Vigilantes had caught him, but that was it. Soon the train returned to the station.

"So, girls, what did you think?" Darcy asked.

"It was great!" Jessica said. "The scenery was gorgeous!"

Kennedy smiled. "It was," she said, "but, well, I guess I was hoping that Hugo would talk more about Chester Morris."

"You still pining over the lost map?" Victoria said.

"I agree with you, Ken," Darcy said. "Hugo usually talks about Morris and Henry Plummer and the Innocents and the Vigilantes. He's even mentioned Morris's treasure on some rides."

"Really?" Kennedy said.

"Oh yeah. But he didn't talk a whole lot about Morris. He didn't even mention the treasure. But it's fine. What would you girls like to do now?"

"I'd like to visit Boot Hill Cemetery," Jessica said.

Kennedy's eyes widened. She grinned at her sister.

"Uh," Jessica said, "why are you smiling at me like that?"

"Oh, nothing," Kennedy said quickly. "I'd love to go to Boot Hill Cemetery."

"Let's do that, then," Victoria said. "But, uh, after we get a snack. I'm hungry."

"After that big lunch we had just an hour ago?" Felicity said with a chuckle.

"Ah, I can use a snack myself," Darcy said. "Let's visit the Cousin's Candy Shop, then we'll go to Boot Hill Cemetery."

The girls agreed with Darcy's plan. Kennedy pulled out her phone and looked at pictures of the riddle on the back of the map.

She stared at the words *boot of the hill*.

"There it is!"

Felicity pulled the van over. "Here we are at the famous Boot Hill Cemetery!"

Kennedy opened the door. She felt a few twinges of those butterflies in her stomach. They were fueling her eager impatience to check out the area.

Darcy and Rachel's cars pulled over behind the van. Darcy, Marilyn, Rachel, and Sierra jumped out.

"Alright, the gang's all here, let's begin exploring!" Victoria said. She ran ahead, only to stop in her tracks almost instantly. "Uh, what's with all the holes around the area?"

Kennedy looked up. Her eyes widened; there were several holes in the ground around the gravestones.

"Golly!" Darcy said. "These holes weren't here yesterday!"

"Ah, I'm sure it's nothing," Victoria said. "Come on, let's check out these graves."

She led Jessica, Rachel, and Sierra to the graves while Darcy and Marilyn went over to look at the holes. Kennedy felt like she was the only person who lacked any enthusiasm. She kneeled by the grave with Henry Plummer's name and looked at the ground.

"You okay there, Ken?"

Kennedy looked up at Rachel.

"Yeah, doing just fine."

"Even after what happened last night? I mean, you've been so quiet all day."

Kennedy shrugged.

"I wish we knew who could've stolen the map," Rachel said.

"Well," Kennedy said, "I've thought of those three treasure hunters. You know, Shawn, Lydia, and Trent?"

"Oh, yeah, that does makes sense. But they're from that company in Bozeman. Don't you think taking the treasure for themselves would be too risky for them?"

"Maybe they just want the glory of finding the treasure. But, then again, they did seem surprised and eager to know what had happened when we met them at the Alder Gulch train."

Kennedy turned her gaze to the holes. She glanced at Rachel, then she stood back up and went over to Darcy and Marilyn.

"Do those holes look freshly dug to you?" Kennedy asked.

"Sort of," Darcy said. "I've taken a few pictures and sent them to Brant."

Kennedy's eyes wandered over the holes. "None of them look like they could've held a chest recently."

Darcy shook her head.

"Hey, look at this!" Victoria's voice called. "It's a miniature grave site for mice!"

Kennedy and Rachel walked over to the spot where Victoria and Jessica were standing. Kennedy smiled feebly at the tiny gravestones, which were made of little pieces of cardboard. Below them laid a small pile of tiny sticks, a few pennies, and little dried-up wildflowers. Kennedy read the writing on one of the cardboard graves:

CHESTER MOUSE, TRAPPED MAY 1ST, 2013
FOR SCARING CUSTOMERS AND STEALING
CRUMBS OFF THE FLOOR.

"Hey, hey, fancy meeting you ladies here."

Kennedy turned around. Andrew was walking up the hill toward them.

Victoria smiled and went over to him. "What brings you here?" she asked.

"Just wanted to pop by and snap a few pics of this historic gravesite for a history assignment," Andrew said.

"You're doing homework in August?"

Andrew chuckled. "Just getting ready for when I go back to college," he said. "You gals notice the mouse gravesite?"

Victoria grinned. "We sure did!" she said.

"It was my idea," Andrew said. "The café was having mouse problems at the time. We set the mousetraps where we needed to. When we caught them, I suggested that we put together that little gravesite. We called the mice the Rodent Agents."

"The Rodent Agents!" Victoria said with a laugh. "I love it!"

Andrew smirked. "Glad you do."

The girls followed Andrew over to the actual graves, where Darcy and Felicity were standing. Andrew raised his eyebrows in surprise when he saw the holes.

"Uh," he said, "what's all this about?"

"That's what I'm trying to figure out," Darcy said.

"I see. So, Darcy, how's your family doing?"

"We're okay. I don't suppose Brant has any updates?"

"Not that I know of. This has got to be the worst thing to happen in Virginia City. The cruel irony. A map to Chester Morris's fabled hidden treasure might've been found, and it gets stolen. My brother's dealt with people digging around here for the treasure, but not with a theft like this."

"People have dug here before?" Kennedy asked curiously.

Andrew nodded. "On this very hill."

He squatted in front of a hole next to a gravestone.

"Looking for the treasure, I'm guessing?" Kennedy said.

"Yep. The story of Chester's lost treasure isn't a very well-known legend. But Brant used to tell me about some riddle that mentioned something about the boot of the hill."

Kennedy crouched down next to Andrew.

"And people who have also heard of the riddle have tried digging around here," Andrew added. "Which they shouldn't be doing, of course."

"Do you think that the treasure could be buried here?" Kennedy asked eagerly.

Andrew narrowed his eyes. "Highly doubt it," he said. "The folks who were dumb enough to dig up this hill never found anything. You aren't up to something, are you?"

Kennedy frowned at the suspicious look in Andrew's eye. "No, of course not," she said.

Andrew shrugged. "Well, you gals enjoy wandering around," he said. "I've got to get started on my history."

"Alright, since you insist on doing homework even before school begins," Victoria said. "We'll see you around, I'm sure."

Andrew smiled at her. He turned around and walked over to the other gravestones. Kennedy watched him warily. Was he really just at the cemetery to do homework? Or did he have something else in mind?

"Alright, Kennedy, let me guess," Felicity said, interrupting her thoughts, "you're looking for the lost treasure, aren't you?"

Kennedy smiled. "Hey, I just had a hunch about the phrase *boot of the hill* in the riddle," she said.

"Not a bad hunch," Rachel said. "Boot of the hill, Boot Hill Cemetery?"

"Don't get excited," Kennedy said, "Andrew doesn't seem to think that this cemetery's hiding the loot. And I didn't have explanations for the rest of the riddle."

Kennedy pulled up her photo gallery on her phone and stared at the picture of the riddle on the back of the map. She looked back at Andrew, who was taking pictures of the gravestones and the signs. Her heart skipped a beat.

Could Andrew be the thief? But he had been at the gift shop with them when they met Brant, Darcy, and Uncle Edward there the previous evening. Then again, maybe Andrew just didn't have time to get out of the shop and had to play dumb. He was paranoid enough about his future to complain to random tourists about college, after all.

She heard a car driving up the dirt road. Looking over her shoulder, Kennedy saw a police car pull up. She recognized the driver as Brant. He got out of the car and went over to Darcy. Andrew turned around briefly, then turned his attention back to the graves. The other girls gathered around Brant, Darcy, and Kennedy.

"I got your texts," Brant said to Darcy. His eyes wandered over to the holes. "Yeah, this isn't good. Tourists digging here again, I see."

"Uh, Brant," Kennedy said, "I was thinking, what if these holes aren't from tourists? I think it's weird that this has happened so soon after the theft of the map."

Brant blinked. "Are you saying the thief was digging here for the Innocents' treasure?" he asked.

"Maybe. We do have the riddle. And part of it mentioned the boot of the hill. Perhaps the thief misinterpreted the riddle?"

Brant nodded slowly. "I suppose," he said.

"I have some pictures of the map." Kennedy handed Brant her phone. "We don't know what to make of the map. Maybe you can try?"

Brant looked at the pictures. He stared at them for several minutes. Then he smiled. He pulled a notepad from his pocket and began drawing on it.

"What are you doing?" Darcy asked.

"You'll see, honey," Brant said. He finished his drawing and handed it to Darcy.

"I just thought," he said, "that if our thief had been digging around here, he was digging in the wrong place. It's very hard to tell at first glance, but with a little careful study and a good eye, well, I can tell you gals that this map is a map of Bannack."

Kennedy gaped at Brant. She and Darcy looked at one another. Kennedy wondered whether she or Darcy looked more surprised. Darcy burst out laughing.

"Gosh, I feel so stupid now!" she exclaimed. "I thought that the faded design on the original map looked familiar, but it didn't occur to me that it was Bannack!"

Kennedy frowned. Such a thought had not occurred to her, either. *Guess I should be studying my history a little better before I flunk it like I'm flunking chemistry.*

She then noticed Andrew looking at them intently.

"Well, at least we know now," Rachel said, "but what if the thief has already found the location?"

"I doubt it," Kennedy said. "If he's been digging here, then he probably hasn't figured out the map and its riddle yet."

Brant cast a worrisome look at the holes. "He may soon," he said.

Kennedy frowned. Brant was right.

45

"We need to get to Bannack right away," Kennedy said.

"I'm not sure about that," Darcy said. "It's late in the day. Bannack is over an hour's drive from Virginia City."

"Then I'll plan on going there tomorrow morning," Brant said. "I'm sure I can at least call the ranger station and tell them what's going on and to keep their eyes open."

"We'll be there too," Darcy said.

"Say what now? Hon, it could be dangerous."

"But I did ask Kennedy to help find clues. She's really good at it, you know. We'll stay together, or at least stay in groups. Besides, with other tourists in Bannack, we should be safe."

Brant shrugged. "Okay, then, if you say so."

Andrew ran over. "I'm going,too!" he said.

"You are?" Victoria smiled playfully. "Are you following us or something?"

"Well, I wasn't trying to follow you, but all this talk of a treasure hunt sure appeals to me!"

"I thought you had some studying to do," Kennedy said.

Andrew rolled his eyes. "Homework can wait when there's a treasure hunt happening. Besides, like your sister said, it's summer."

"Well, if you insist," Brant said, "I'll let you come, but all of you better watch your backs."

"Great!" Darcy said. "Come on, ladies, we should head back to my house. Mom's bound to have dinner ready soon."

Kennedy walked to Darcy's car. She stared at Andrew from the corner of her eye until she climbed into the back seat.

"You're quiet all of a sudden, Ken," Marilyn said. "I was expecting you to be excited about this new clue."

"Just thinking of suspects," Kennedy said.

"You mean like those people from the Bozeman treasure hunting company?" Victoria said.

"I thought of them," Kennedy said, "but don't you guys think it's strange that Andrew came here just after the map was stolen and we found these holes?"

Marilyn gasped. "Do you think Andrew could be another suspect?" she asked.

Darcy frowned. "Andrew?" she said. "Hardly. I know that young man. He'd never steal. I mean, yeah, I know he complains about college a lot, but he knows to make an honest living."

Victoria stared at Kennedy. "You can't really think that Andrew stole the map and was digging for the treasure," she said.

"Hey, it's just a theory," Kennedy said. "I just know that Andrew has a motive, and he could've had the opportunity."

"Oh?" Victoria said testily. "And what would his motive be?"

"Money to secure his future that he is so neurotic about," Kennedy said.

Victoria still frowned. Holding in a sigh, Kennedy turned to the window. She stared at the cemetery until it was out of sight.

Kennedy jumped out of the car. She could feel her heart pounding with anticipation as she stared at the familiar wooden buildings of Bannack.

"Well, what are we waiting for?" Victoria said. "Let's find ourselves a buried treasure!"

With a chuckle, Darcy gripped Victoria's shoulder. "Not so fast, girly," she said. "And keep your voice down, we gotta be inconspicuous."

Felicity's van and Brant's car steered into parking spots. As soon as everyone gathered together, Brant led the group to the ghost town. Kennedy frowned a little when she saw people walking in and out of the old buildings. There were more tourists than she expected to see. Kennedy hoped that nobody would notice what they were up to.

Victoria ran over to Andrew's side. "I gotta agree with what you said yesterday," she said. "Treasure hunting is so much more fun than homework."

Andrew laughed. "I reckon anyone would agree."

Kennedy stared at Andrew from the corner of her eye. She made a mental note to watch him closely.

"So, where exactly are we going?" Brant asked. "Is there a certain spot marked on the map?"

"Oh, yes," Kennedy said. She held up her phone. "On the map, there's an—"

A scream pierced the air. Kennedy looked up in surprise. So did everybody else. Just ahead of them, a woman was pointing up at Hotel Meade.

"I saw him!" she screeched. "I saw him!"

People began gathering around the woman. Kennedy ran ahead.

"Kennedy, wait up!" Felicity called.

Kennedy did not slow down. She approached the crowd, which was growing larger by the second. She felt like the loud, excited chatter of all the people was going to pop her eardrums.

Rachel ran to her side. "Golly, what's with all this commotion?" she asked in a loud voice.

"That's what I'm trying to find out," Kennedy said.

Two men and a woman ran out of Hotel Meade. Kennedy immediately recognized them as Shawn, Lydia, and Trent. The moment they spotted Kennedy, Brant, and Darcy, they ran over to them.

"Good thing you're here," Trent said to Brant. "You should do something about crowd control."

"What, sir?" Brant asked loudly. "Hold on, let's get away from the crowd so I can hear you better."

Brant led everyone further away from the crowd. Even so, Kennedy still thought the commotion behind her was loud.

"Alright, what's going on?" Brant asked.

Shawn grinned. "You won't believe this," he said, "but we saw the ghost of Henry Plummer in the hotel only minutes ago!"

Victoria gasped. "You have got to be kidding!" she said. "No wonder that lady was screaming! Come on, let's go check it out!"

She turned and took a step ahead, but Andrew grabbed her elbow.

"Not so fast, wannabe ghost hunter," he said.

"I agree," Lydia said. "I heard Plummer's moans just moments before the three of us entered the hotel. I think he wants people to stay away from that old place."

"This doesn't make any sense," Brant said. "People have visited that hotel for a long time with no issues. Why would some random ghost show up now?"

Kennedy nodded slowly. Yes, indeed, why would a ghost show up in Hotel Meade, and now of all times?

"I've heard ghost stories about Hotel Meade," Darcy said, "but this is the first time I'm witnessing one myself."

"Alrighty," Brant said, "can you three show me where you saw this ghost?"

Trent hesitated. "I suppose we should," he said, "but I think we should all get out of here. I've had enough of this crazy hunt for this road agent treasure."

"I do need to find out what's really going on," Brant said.

"Oh, very well, Deputy."

Shawn, Lydia, and Trent led everybody back to the hotel. A few rangers had shown up and were trying to calm the people. One ranger was talking to the woman who had screamed. Other people were holding up their phones and taking pictures of the hotel.

Kennedy looked up at the second-floor windows of the old hotel. Nothing looked suspicious. Only the sunlight bouncing off the windows made her wince and squint her eyes.

Kennedy's attention was drawn away from the windows when she noticed Andrew inching his way toward the porch of the hotel. She lifted her eyebrow. What was he up to?

"Andy," Brant said, "hold up, don't go in there yet until I inspect it."

Andrew scowled at his brother, but he didn't say anything. Brant, Shawn, Lydia, and Trent went into the hotel.

Time seemed to slow down for Kennedy. She pulled out her phone and stared at the pictures of the map. She grasped a curly strand of her hair. Why hadn't she thought of Bannack before?

"I hope they're not in there for long," Marilyn said.

"Hey, I wouldn't mind seeing a possible ghost," Victoria said.

"I don't think it's a ghost," Marilyn said, "but who knows what's going on in that building?"

"I totally agree, Marilyn," Kennedy said. "I highly doubt any of these recent circumstances are coincidences. You know, the map to a lost treasure of the Innocents was found in the past couple of days, the map was stolen, the treasure's supposed to be hidden here in Bannack, and now there's a ghost haunting Hotel Meade?"

"Look!" Jessica screamed. "Up there!"

Kennedy looked up at the window that Jessica was pointing at. She gasped.

In that window was the silver apparition of a man.

Kennedy's heartbeat accelerated. She recognized that man from the pictures in her magazine.

It was Chester Morris.

Almost immediately people started screaming and pointing. Kennedy heard the snaps of cameras going off.

"That's Chester Morris!" Andrew yelled. He turned his frightened look to the door of the hotel. "And my brother's still in there!"

49

He dashed into the hotel. Victoria and Sierra were right on his heels.

"Hey, get back here!" Kennedy screamed, but she only took a few steps forward before Marilyn pulled her back.

"Please, Kennedy, don't go in!"

"You just said you didn't believe those are ghosts!" Kennedy said.

"And I still don't," Marilyn said fiercely, "but whoever's in there probably does not want anybody poking around!"

Kennedy jerked herself out of Marilyn's grasp. "I'm going in anyway."

She ran toward the steps but stopped when Brant, Shawn, Lydia, Trent, Victoria, Sierra, and Andrew came dashing out of the hotel. All of them had horrified looks on their faces.

"We saw them!" Victoria shouted. "We actually saw the ghosts of Henry Plummer and Chester Morris!"

Kennedy's heart skipped a beat. "Yeah, they're upstairs, aren't they?"

She dashed past them, up the porch, and inside the hotel. It seemed as though the moment she entered, all noise outside diminished, replaced by an eerie silence that quickly filled the atmosphere of the old hotel. Kennedy became still herself. Her eyes wandered over to the stairwell to her right, then to the hallway.

She took a step forward. A creak beneath her foot made her freeze on the spot. But she guessed that it was probably just the floor underneath her own foot. She took a few more steps.

"Kennedy?"

Gasping, Kennedy spun around. She smiled in relief to see that it was only Rachel and Marilyn.

"How did you two get past Brant?" she asked.

"We just ran up like you did," Marilyn said. "Come on, we should get out of here."

UUUUUHHHHHH!

The three girls squealed and huddled together. That ghostly wail nearly made Kennedy jump out of her skin. She gazed at the stairs, hardly daring to move an inch. The only thing making any movement at all was her heart pounding against her chest. She took a deep, silent breath to keep herself calm.

"We need to look upstairs," she said.

"Are you kidding me right now?" Rachel said.

Kennedy ignored her. She went up the stairs. Rachel and Marilyn followed her.

"So what are we looking for, exactly?" Rachel asked.

"Uh, anything unusual, I guess," Kennedy said.

The stairs creaked loudly under the girls' feet. Kennedy's heart beat faster with every step she took. The silence was almost as frightening as that wail had been.

The threesome arrived at the top of the stairs. Kennedy gazed at the empty corridor that lay in front of them. The silent emptiness made the hallway seem creepy. Kennedy tried not to imagine any ghosts floating out one of the rooms. She took a tiny step forward. The floorboard creaked. Kennedy's stomach churned.

"Come on, Ken," Marilyn hissed, "can we go back down?"

"Just give me a few minutes," Kennedy said. "I wanna check these rooms."

"Well, at least let us accompany you. Safety in numbers."

"Hey," Rachel said, "what's that?"

Kennedy turned around. Rachel was pointing up at the window that looked outside at the main road. Kennedy spotted a tiny piece of white cloth on a nail in the wall. She reached up for it and pulled it down.

"Really, Ken?" Marilyn said. "Highly doubt you're supposed to pull off remnants of old curtains in an old, historic hotel."

"This isn't old," Kennedy said. She held out the cloth. "Look, it's not the type of fabric you'd expect to find on a curtain. It's like a transparent sheet. And way too new to have belonged to this hotel."

Kennedy stuffed the cloth in her pocket.

"Say," Rachel said, "isn't this the window that the ghosts had been spotted through?"

Kennedy studied the window. "I think it is," she said. She turned back toward the hallway. "Let's check out these rooms."

The three girls headed down the hallway. With every room they entered, Kennedy expected to see either the ghosts of Chester Morris or Henry Plummer. But every room was empty.

"I wish we'd find something," Rachel said as the girls searched their fourth room. "Call me crazy, but finding something would relieve those unwelcome, irrational, and anxious thoughts in my mind telling me those ghosts might be real."

Marilyn chuckled lightly. "Hey, don't fret," she said. "Look on the bright side. At least we haven't found any mice or rats."

"That thought has already crossed my mind, but I'm more afraid of ghosts."

The sudden sound of footsteps resonated from across the hall. Kennedy, Rachel, and Marilyn froze.

"Could it be Brant, or one of the others?" Rachel whispered.

"No," Kennedy said darkly, "those footsteps are too heavy to belong to any of them. I think it sounds like a man. And they sound like they're coming . . ."

She gasped and looked at the open door. She could hear the footsteps rush down the hall. She looked at Marilyn and Rachel.

"We need to hide!" she mouthed at them.

The three girls tiptoed to the closet. They hid inside, leaning against the wall. Kennedy tried to keep her heavy breathing silent. Rachel grasped her elbow. Kennedy listened. The footsteps slowed down a little bit before stopping.

Rachel looked at Kennedy quizzically, then she leaned forward a little bit. But Kennedy and Marilyn gently pushed her back. Kennedy put her finger to her lips, shaking her head as she did so. Rachel nodded with understanding. The footsteps started back up again, but they didn't sound as rushed.

With bated breath, the girls waited until the footsteps receded, then Rachel tiptoed over to the closet's doorway and peeked out. She turned to Kennedy and Marilyn.

"Coast is clear," she whispered, waving her finger.

The girls slowly tiptoed out of the closet. They made sure that the hallway was clear before they left the room and dashed back downstairs.

"Nobody's down here, right?" Marilyn asked nervously.

Kennedy shook her head. "Don't see anyone, but let's not linger."

UUUUUHHHHH!

The girls screamed and spun around. The sight before them made Kennedy's heart drop.

Hovering in the hallway were the figures of two ghostly cowboys, both of whom were glaring at the girls.

Marilyn lifted a shaking finger. "It's th-th-them," she stammered. "H-Henry Plummer and Chester M-Morris!"

Kennedy barely moved a muscle. She could only gape at the two ghosts.

They cannot really be there! This cannot be happening!

Rachel and Marilyn screamed. Kennedy felt them grab her by her elbows and pull her away. She followed them outside. Brant, Andrew, and Victoria were standing on the porch.

"Oh, good, you're finally out of there!" Victoria said in relief. "We were gonna make Brant and Andy go in after you!"

She grinned. "Did you hear those wails? Did you see the ghosts?"

"We saw them, alright!" Rachel said breathlessly.

"Awesome!" Victoria took a step toward the door.

"Oh no, you don't!" Kennedy said. She grabbed Victoria's arm. Victoria gave her a scowl.

"What happened in there?" Brant asked.

"We saw Plummer and Morris, and we heard footsteps in there!" Marilyn said.

"Maybe it was their footsteps!" Victoria said.

"Can ghosts make any sounds?" Rachel asked.

"Alright, girls, just calm down!" Brant said.

They walked down the steps to the rest of the group. Jessica wrapped her arms around Kennedy in a relieved hug.

"So what are we gonna do now?" Andrew asked.

"I'd like to poke around some more," Kennedy said. "There's got to be a rational explanation for those ghosts. Oh, by the way, I found this."

She pulled the cloth out of her pocket and showed it to Brant. He took it, looking puzzled.

"What's this?" he asked.

"I found it on a nail by the window. The one that had the ghosts."

Brant put the cloth in his pocket. "Kennedy," he said, "I agree with you that there must be some explanation for those ghosts. Let's split up. We'll cover more ground that way."

Kennedy looked over at her sisters. She then noticed that Shawn, Lydia, and Trent were not present.

"Hang on a second, where did that trio of treasure hunters go?" she asked. "You know, Shawn, Lydia, and Trent?"

Victoria sniggered. "That Trent guy chickened out and ran off," she said. "Shawn and Lydia went after him."

Kennedy nodded slowly. She did have to wonder, what were Shawn, Lydia, and Trent doing in Bannack?

"Well," she said, "I'm going to check out Skinner's Saloon. Anyone wanna join me?"

"I will." Marilyn went over to Kennedy's side. "Someone's gotta keep an eye on you."

"I'll go with you," Rachel said.

"And I will keep an eye on the three of you," Darcy said.

"I will check out the hotel one more time," Brant said. "And the area around it. Andrew, I want you to stay out here with everyone else."

Kennedy eyed Andrew. She couldn't help but allow a small, relieved smile to creep across her lips. Andrew had been outside while the screams and the ghost sightings happened inside the hotel.

Kennedy followed Darcy, Marilyn, and Rachel into the saloon. Her eyes wandered from the boards on the wall, with their writing of the history of the saloon, to the barber chair in the corner near the door, and to the counter.

"See anything odd?" she asked.

"Not really," Marilyn said.

All of a sudden, a ghostly wail rang through the saloon. The girls screamed and huddled together.

"Those ghosts must be spying on us from the hotel!" Darcy squealed. "We gotta hide!"

The girls crawled behind the counter. Kennedy held her breath.

Something caught her eye. It was a folded parchment in a shelf below the counter.

Kennedy let out a silent gasp. She leaned over and grabbed the parchment. She opened it and grinned.

The map!

Kennedy pulled her phone out of her pocket and opened her photo gallery. Sure enough, when she compared the parchment to the pictures of the map, they were a perfect match.

"Guys," she said in a hushed voice, "it's the map!"

Darcy whipped her head around. "What?"

Kennedy handed Darcy the parchment. Darcy gaped as she stared at it. Rachel and Marilyn were gaping too.

"I don't believe this!" Darcy said. A relieved smile came across her face. "Wait until Dad hears about this!"

"But how did the map come to be in Skinner's Saloon in the first place?" Marilyn asked.

"That's an excellent question," Kennedy said. "The thief probably thought it was the perfect hiding spot."

She stood up. "Come on, we need to show the map to Brant."

The girls dashed outside.

"BRANT!" Darcy bellowed.

The girls ran to the middle of the dirt road. In moments everyone else was running out of surrounding buildings and running to their sides.

Brant ran straight to Darcy and put his hands on her shoulders. "I heard you scream," he said. "Are you alright?"

Darcy waved the map in Brant's face. "We found the map in the saloon!" she said excitedly.

"The map?" Victoria exclaimed. "You mean, the one stolen from the gift shop?"

"This is a miracle!" Sierra said.

"Okay, everyone quiet down!" Brant said. "So, Darcy, you say that you, Kennedy, Rachel, and Marilyn found the map in Skinner's Saloon?"

Darcy nodded. "Behind the counter. Kennedy suggested that the thief hid it there."

"Not a bad hiding spot," Andrew said. "Who'd think to look there?"

Kennedy glanced at him.

"I should check out the saloon myself," Brant said. "Darcy, will you come with me?"

Darcy hesitated. She looked at the map. "Well," she said, "I was hoping we could check out the X on this thing."

Kennedy grinned. "You mean, try to find the treasure?" she said. "We could try. I mean, if the map was still hidden, then whoever stole this map in the first place hadn't found it yet."

"Alright!" Victoria said. "Let's go treasure hunting!"

Darcy opened the map. "It's close to here. Near the creek."

"But I need to scope out the saloon," Brant said. "And I need one of you girls with me. Alrighty, here's what we'll do. Darcy, please come with me to the saloon. We won't be long. We know where this spot on the map is. Andrew, you take the other girls to that spot. But don't do anything until Darcy and I arrive."

Darcy handed Kennedy the map, then she and Brant went into the saloon.

"You know," Sierra said, "I wonder if Brant saw either of those ghosts in the hotel."

"Yeah, maybe he needed to question them," Victoria joked.

Andrew laughed. "Well, while they're in the saloon," he said, "follow me to fame and fortune, ladies! Where to, Kennedy?"

Kennedy looked at the map. "We need to go across a bridge," she said.

"Ah, easy. There's a bridge right over there."

The girls followed Andrew away from the buildings and to a bridge over the creek. But they were greeted by the sight of countless holes in the area. Kennedy felt like her heart was in her throat.

"Holy smokes!" Sierra said. "Look at all these holes!"

"They look like they were freshly dug," Felicity said.

"Oh, great, that treasure better not have been found already!" Victoria said.

Kennedy walked around a few of the holes. "Well, none of them look like they've been holding a chest for a hundred and fifty years," she said.

"Hey, guys, I've found footprints over here!" Andrew called.

The girls ran over to where Andrew was standing. Sure enough, there were footprints leading to the bridge. At least, what was left of footprints.

"We didn't see any on the other side of the bridge," Andrew said.

"No, not at all," Kennedy said. "Whoever was digging around here didn't use the bridge. And said digger was here hours ago. These prints are pretty faded."

She studied a couple of the footprints. "I can make out a few details," she said. "These prints were made by tennis shoes. And the soles have squiggly lines."

She glanced at Andrew's shoes. They were not tennis shoes. And they were too small to match any of the footprints on the ground.

Andrew looked up at Kennedy. He stared at her, then at his shoes.

"What are you looking at me like that for?" he asked.

"Nothing," Kennedy said quickly. But she frowned when she noticed Victoria scowling at her.

"Don't tell me you still suspect him," she said coldly.

"What?" Andrew said. "I was a suspect? I'm sorry, Kennedy thought that I could've stolen that treasure map from the gift shop?"

Kennedy sighed and placed her hand on her forehead. "I just had a theory," she said. "When I saw you at Boot Hill Cemetery, I wondered if you could be a potential suspect."

"Oh, I was wandering around Boot Hill Cemetery, so that makes me the thief," Andrew said sarcastically.

"I didn't say that!" Kennedy said hotly. "And I know I was wrong. Andrew, you were with us here when the ghost appeared in the hotel and the saloon. And these prints don't match your shoe size. Ergo, I don't suspect you anymore."

"Well, what would my motive be, anyway?" Andrew demanded.

"I dunno, maybe the fact that you're so paranoid about your future and paying for college that you envy your brother's career and don't like your own job?"

"Alright, everyone," Felicity said sternly, "calm down. Andrew, please don't judge Kennedy so hastily. She's a fast thinker. She notices things and forms theories. She doesn't mindlessly jump to conclusions."

Andrew just crossed his arms and rolled his eyes.

"We're here!"

Kennedy spun around. Brant and Darcy were walking over the bridge. Andrew ran over to his brother.

"Bro," he said, "care to help me come up with some good alibis before Kennedy here gives you a reason to arrest me?"

"What?" Brant said.

Kennedy sighed. "I'll explain later," she said.

"Well, what's the explanation for all these holes?" Brant asked.

"They were here when we came," Felicity said.

Darcy groaned. "Oh, don't tell me the treasure was already found."

"No, we don't think so," Kennedy said, "and the map was hidden in Skinner's Saloon just minutes ago. These holes were dug hours ago."

She looked at the map. "Whoever was digging here gave up the search. But this spot is marked X. Gosh, I'm confused!"

"Well, Kennedy," Andrew said, "if you ask me, those annoying treasure hunters were here."

"Perhaps," Kennedy said. "But, if they were digging here hours ago, then why would they come back to Bannack later?"

"I can vouch for them," Darcy said. "Dad and Hugo saw the three of them at the gift shop's café early this morning. They hung around the shop for a little while. And I can honestly say that they'd never dig around here illegally."

"All the same, I wouldn't mind questioning them," Brant said. "But first, I'm going to snap a few pictures of these holes. Everyone, stand back."

He took some pictures of the holes. Then he led everyone away from the area and out of Bannack. He and Andrew walked to their car.

"Now, Andrew," Kennedy heard Brant say, "what exactly is your beef with Kennedy?"

58

Kennedy groaned and put her hands on her forehead. The embarrassment of having placed suspicion on Andrew, only the brother of Darcy's boyfriend, made her head hurt. The only relief she felt was when she saw Victoria get into Darcy's car. Kennedy got into Felicity's van.

"You okay, Ken?"

Kennedy glanced at Rachel, who was giving her a concerned look.

Kennedy shrugged. "I'm not sure," she said. "I wish I had a good relationship with my stepcousin like you do with your cousin. Victoria and Jessica are getting along. As usual. You know, when Mom married Isaiah, Victoria and Jessica were all for gaining a new stepfather. I took a while to adjust. Now it seems like the process is repeating itself. And Victoria and Andrew are mad at me, which is gonna make things worse."

"Hey, we'll figure this out," Rachel said. "You'll solve this."

"I hope so."

The gift shop seemed quieter than usual, even for ten in the morning. As soon as they entered, Kennedy saw Victoria go over to the café, where Andrew was working behind the counter. He gave Victoria a smile, but when he met Kennedy's eyes, his smile disappeared.

"Good morning, Hugo."

Kennedy looked over at the checkout counter. Darcy and Aunt Nora went behind the counter where Hugo was standing. He grunted but was otherwise quiet.

"Looks like someone got up on the wrong side of the bed this morning," Darcy said. Hugo just glared at her.

The bells of the front door jingled. Brant entered the shop and went to the counter. Kennedy went over to his side.

"Hey, Darcy," Brant said, "I came to share some news with you and your friends. I was able to talk to Shawn and Lydia Hudson and Trent Ross this morning."

Kennedy and Darcy fixed their eyes on the young deputy. Even Hugo lifted his head.

"And?" Darcy said.

"Well, they were indeed here yesterday. They showed me their receipts from the café."

"You mean those treasure hunters?" Aunt Nora said. "I heard all about what happened in Bannack yesterday. So scary! I'm

59

so glad you girls aren't going to Bannack again today. Anyway, I saw Shawn, Lydia, and Trent in the library here in town yesterday morning. They were there for hours, reading books about the Road Agents and the Vigilantes and that treasure. Then they went to the Alder Gulch train ride."

Kennedy frowned. It seemed that Shawn, Lydia, and Trent had not been in Bannack the previous morning.

"They let me search their hotel rooms," Brant added. "I looked at their shoes. None of them matched the footprints found at Bannack or Boot Hill Cemetery."

"So I guess they must not be the thieves," Darcy said.

Brant shook his head. Hugo eyed him. "Any clue on who the thieves could be?" he asked.

"Nope. That investigation is still ongoing."

Uncle Edward came down the stairs and went behind the counter. Kennedy winced at the sullen look on his face.

"Good morning, Brant," he said. He smiled feebly. "Nice to know that the map has been found."

Hugo turned his attention back to his phone. "Even though it still might be too late for my ancestor's treasure to help out your gift shop?" he said.

"Wait, your ancestor?" Kennedy said curiously.

Hugo looked at her. "Yeah," he said. "Truth is, I'm a direct descendant of Chester Morris. My last name is Morrison."

"No kidding!"

Hugo shook his head. "Why do you think I came here to work in Virginia City? I do lots of things here besides help out as a clerk. I'm a tour guide, and I frequently help with the Virginia City Players. I've been working with them these past few days."

"Anyway," Darcy said, facing her father, "what's going on, Dad?"

Uncle Edward sighed. "Honey," he said, "I was talking to Hugo earlier, and, well, things just aren't looking good for the gift shop."

"But we found the map!" Darcy said. "We can still turn it in or whatever we need to do with it!"

Hugo frowned.

"If we can do it quickly, we can save the gift shop. But the theft was bad for business. I'm sorry, honey. But I can't hold on much longer."

Darcy sighed.

"Oh, honey," Aunt Nora said soothingly, "you shouldn't have to worry about this with your cousin and her friends visiting. You should enjoy your time with them. What time does your play begin, anyway?"

Darcy looked at her phone. "It starts at one o'clock," she said. "We should be going, I guess. Get some lunch before the play."

Uncle Edward and Hugo left. Kennedy turned to leave too but stopped when she heard Aunt Nora's voice.

"Darcy, dear, I really would rather that you enjoy your time with your cousin, instead of trying to solve any mysteries."

Kennedy's heart skipped a few beats.

"Well, Brant has the map now," Darcy said, "so we should be fine."

"I'm talking about not letting Kennedy lead you into any more danger. You've heard about her past . . . adventures."

Kennedy held in a groan. She stomped out of the shop and leaned against Felicity's van. She crossed her arms and blinked; she was able to hold back the tears, but not her disappointment. It seemed as though Aunt Nora wasn't going to warm up to her.

"Well, here we are!" Darcy said. She led everyone into the auditorium. "Virginia City's vaudeville!"

Kennedy took a seat next to Marilyn. She looked around the auditorium. She spotted Hugo sitting a few rows behind them. She also saw Shawn, Lydia, and Trent sitting in the row in front of Hugo.

"I'm so glad that the performance the other day wasn't cancelled," Shawn said. "I would've been really disappointed if that ghost play hadn't shown."

"Me too," Lydia said. "Who'd want to miss a play about Hotel Meade's ghosts?"

"Even after we saw them in the hotel?" Trent asked.

"Hey, that was after the play. Why was the ghost play nearly cancelled anyway?"

"I heard a few actors saying that one of their projectors went missing. They were also missing a white sheet. Luckily, they had backups. They use those props to display the ghosts, I guess."

Kennedy raised her eyebrow. A smile crept across her lips.

"I sure love this play," Darcy said. "Of all the plays this place puts on, this one's my favorite. It's a fictional comedy based on the legends of the Road Agents. It even has Chester Morris in it."

61

"Wonder if the play will give us some good clues on Chester's booty," Victoria said.

Darcy's smile faded a little. "Wouldn't mind if it did."

Kennedy held in a sigh. She turned to look at the stage only to notice Andrew coming into the auditorium. He smiled timidly at Kennedy.

"Hey," he said. "Thought I'd pop in. You don't mind, do you?"

"It's fine," Kennedy said. She was sure that her own smile was meeker than Andrew's. "You still stalking my sister?"

"Say what now?"

Kennedy chuckled. "I just noticed a few things. You can sit next to her if you'd like."

Andrew's smile broadened. He walked past Kennedy and a few seats. Victoria smiled when she noticed him.

Everyone took their seats, and the lights dimmed. Only the stage, with its cliché Wild Western saloon background, glowed. A woman dressed as a saloon girl flounced onto the stage. The bright magenta and black colors of her costume seemed to glow.

"Chester!" she called in a dramatic voice. "Are you here?"

A man dressed in a baggy cowboy costume ran onto the stage. "Dearest Claudia," he said, "I am here! And I come with good news. Our latest stagecoach robbery found its victim a rich man. I can fill my chest, and we can flee this territory together forever!"

"But what of Henry Plummer?"

"Do not mind that old goat!"

Laughter filled the auditorium. Even Kennedy let out some chuckles. Despite her worries about Aunt Nora and the gift shop, she found herself enjoying the play. The Wild Western music coming from under the stage seemed to lift her spirits.

Two actors, one portraying Henry Plummer and the other Chester Morris, came onstage. The actor playing Plummer held up a fake gun.

"Alright, Morris," he said, "I know your schemes."

Morris's actor remained calm. "What schemes, may I ask?" he said.

"Don't play dumb with me, you traitor! I know you've been hidin' your own treasure chest from the rest of us!"

Morris's actor smiled playfully. "Whatever makes you ponder that?" he asked coolly.

"Because I found yer map!"

Morris's actor lifted an eyebrow. "Oh?"

Plummer's actor sneered. "I reckon one could not be more obvious with a treasure map. I will find the X, find the loot you have stolen from me, and then I will return to take care of you at high noon!"

Plummer's actor pocketed his gun and stomped offstage. Morris's actor stood up and faced the audience.

"He ain't gonna find nothing," he said. "Because X don't mark the spot this time. It's my own symbol that marks the spot."

That line.

It was like a lightbulb in Kennedy's head went off and burst. She held her hand up to her mouth to stifle a gasp, but she could not hide the grin that was slowly forming across her lips, nor could she keep from squirming a little in her seat. She glanced at the others. They were too engrossed in the play to notice her sudden realization.

Now all she had to do was wait for the play to be over. Kennedy still enjoyed the play, but she could only partially focus on it. As soon as the play ended, and the actors and actresses finished bowing, Kennedy jumped to her feet.

"Darcy," she said, "remember when you told us that Chester Morris was rumored to have his own secret code?"

Darcy gave her a confused look. "Yeah," she said. "Why?"

"Because I don't think that code was the riddle on the map," Kennedy said.

"What's Kennedy talking about this time?" Victoria asked.

"She's up to something again," Rachel said with a smile.

Kennedy grinned at them. "I need someone to call Brant," she said, "and tell him to meet us in Bannack. And to bring the map with him."

"Why?" Andrew asked. He gave Kennedy a suspicious look. But Kennedy did not let her smile waver.

"Andrew," she said, "I know I suspected you, and we've had our differences, but now I trust you. Can you call your brother?"

Andrew still looked confused, but he smiled a little as he pulled out his phone and began dialing.

"Hey, there!"

Kennedy spun around. Shawn, Lydia, and Trent were approaching her. She also saw Hugo rushing out of the auditorium. He paused to give Kennedy a nervous look, then he ran for the door. Kennedy stared after him.

"Alrighty, you."

Trent's voice distracted Kennedy from Hugo. She faced him.

"Sorry to be bugging you like this so much," Trent said, "but Shawn and Lydia here wanted to try to ask Miss Wilson about the map."

Kennedy glanced over at Darcy, who was smiling at her. Smiling herself, Kennedy turned to Shawn.

"Truth is, we found it," she said. "In Bannack."

Shawn grinned from ear to ear. "That's wonderful!" he said. "So, uh, might we be able to talk to someone now about finding the treasure?"

"I'm sure it wouldn't hurt," Darcy said. "Meet us in Bannack."

Kennedy could hardly contain her excitement when she saw Brant's car pull into the parking lot near Bannack. Just behind him was a car driven by Shawn. Lydia and Trent were in the car with him. They parked and got out of their cars. Kennedy and Darcy gathered everyone together. Kennedy's smile grew when she saw the map in Brant's hand.

"Alrighty," Brant said, "what's this all about?"

"I need to see the map," Kennedy said.

Brant handed Kennedy the map. She opened it up. Shawn, Lydia, and Trent gazed at it as though it were a precious diamond on display in a fancy museum.

"It's real!" Shawn said in a hushed voice. "And we're finally seeing it!"

"There's the *X*!" Lydia said, pointing to the map. "That's it, right?"

"Nope," Kennedy said. Everyone stared at her.

"Rachel, look here."

Rachel looked over Kennedy's shoulder. Kennedy pointed to the strange *C* symbol.

"Remember seeing this on the alder tree near the hotel?" Kennedy asked.

"Yeah," Rachel said. She grinned. "Do you think . . . ?"

Kennedy nodded. "It was the play that gave me the idea," she said. "I just wish I thought of it sooner!"

"What, what?" Victoria asked.

"I think this odd *C* symbol was Chester Morris's own secret symbol!" Kennedy said. "Maybe that's why *X* didn't mark the spot!"

"I see what you're saying!" Darcy said. "But, then, why put *X* on the map in the first place?"

"Probably to throw his fellow road robbers off in case they got a hold of this map," Kennedy said. "In this case, Chester's symbol marks the spot! And it's right here!"

Darcy stared at the map. "But, that's where Hotel Meade is standing," she said.

"So you're saying the treasure's in the hotel?" Lydia said.

"No," Kennedy said, "but close. Remember that Hotel Meade wasn't even built during the time of the Road Agents."

"Yeah, that's true," Brant said. "So, what do you have in mind, Kennedy? Are we going to search for the treasure?"

"First, I want to check out Hotel Meade," Kennedy said. She rolled up the map and stuck it in her back pocket.

"The hotel?" Brant gave Kennedy a confused look. "But you just said that the hotel didn't exist during the time of the Innocents. Unless you want to try to dig under it, which I doubt you can."

Kennedy chuckled. "Trust me on this," she said. She looked at Shawn. "I actually have something to ask your trio."

"Us?" Trent said. "We didn't do anything!"

"I know. I overheard the three of you talking about missing props from a play a few days ago. Something about a projector and a sheet for the ghost play?"

"Oh, yes, that," Lydia said. "But what does that have to do with anything?"

"If my hunch is correct, you'll see. Come on."

Kennedy led everyone to Hotel Meade. She was about to walk up the steps, but then Marilyn grasped her elbow.

"I don't like being back here," she whispered.

Kennedy patted her stepsister's hand. "It's fine, girl."

"GUYS, LOOK OUT!" Felicity screeched.

Kennedy spun around. Her heart dropped. A man dressed in all black, from his ski mask down to his boots and his cape, was running toward them. But even with his mask covering his entire head, Kennedy still saw the angry determination in his eyes.

"Run, everyone!" Kennedy yelled.

Everybody scattered. Kennedy saw Brant dashing after the masked man. He reached his arm out in an attempt to tackle the man. But the man pushed Brant aside, knocking him to the ground. Then the man ran after Kennedy.

Her heart felt like it was going to burst out of her chest. Kennedy forced her legs to run faster. She dashed around a tree and ran through an open door of the building next to Hotel Meade.

Suddenly Andrew jumped out at the man from behind the tree. Yelling in alarm, the man spun around. In seconds, he and Andrew were grappling each other. Fierce glares contorted both of their faces. Kennedy stood frozen in the doorway.

"Andrew, be careful!" she yelled.

The man kicked Andrew's ankle, tripping him. Andrew fell flat on his back, but he had no time to get up; the man had him pinned to the ground.

"Andrew!" Victoria's voice shrieked.

"Get off my brother!" Brant shouted.

The young deputy ran toward the man, but Kennedy reached him first. She grabbed the man's cape, yanking him back with all her might. The man was jerked backward, gasping as he clutched his neck.

"Kennedy, what are you doing?" Andrew exclaimed.

Kennedy didn't have a chance to reply. The man turned on her, his hands outstretched. Kennedy grabbed his right wrist and slung the man to the ground. He yelled in pain. Kennedy landed a karate chop on his neck. The man fell limp.

"Wow!" Brant exclaimed. He gaped at Kennedy and the man. "You knocked him out!"

Victoria helped Andrew to his feet. "That's my sister!" she said. "Kung fu Kennedy!"

"You're not kidding," Rachel said. She grinned at Kennedy.

Everybody else, followed by a few rangers, ran over. The rangers walked up to the masked man.

"What is going on here?" one of the rangers demanded.

"This man stole the map to the Innocents' hidden treasure from the Wilsons' gift shop," Kennedy said, pointing at the unconscious man.

"Yes, we heard about that. But what makes you think it was him?"

"I'll explain as soon as I unmask him."

Kennedy bent over and pulled the man's mask off his head. It was Hugo Morrison.

"What?" Darcy's eyes were wide with surprise. "Hugo?"

Hugo began moaning. His eyes fluttered open. "What is going on?" he asked weakly.

"You're under arrest," one of the rangers snapped. "Roll over and put your hands behind your back."

The rangers handcuffed Hugo and jerked him up to his feet. Hugo scowled at Kennedy.

"You!" he growled. "You foolish girl, you stopped me from finding my rightful treasure."

"Your rightful treasure?" Shawn said. "Dude, what makes you think the treasure belongs to you?"

"Is it because you're descended from Chester Morris?" Kennedy asked.

Hugo stared. "Yes," he said. "That treasure is mine because of my lineage."

"Yeah, right!" Andrew said. "Your ancestor stole all that gold, for your information!"

"So you were the one who stole the map from Dad's office?" Darcy asked.

Hugo sighed. "Yes," he said flatly. "I confess. I stole the map."

He nodded his head at Kennedy. "I overheard this young lady with her sister and friend when she took that brick out of the fireplace. I saw everything. But I knew that I couldn't just take the map from her and create a scene. I wanted to be stealthier than that. So I knocked over that bookshelf to cause a diversion, and I picked the lock of your dad's office and took the map."

"And it was you who had been digging at Boot Hill Cemetery," Kennedy said.

"Yes. It was me. I had a terrible time deciphering the map at first. I mistook the riddle's *boot of the hill* phrase to mean Boot Hill Cemetery. I got up early in the morning to dig around the place. When I didn't find the treasure, I studied the map and the riddle some more. At least, when I had time. I still had my tourist jobs to do."

"You hardly mentioned anything about Chester Morris and the Road Agents during the Alder Gulch train ride," Kennedy said. "Is it because you wanted to keep the treasure a secret as much as possible?"

Hugo stared at Kennedy. "What are you, girl?" he snapped. "A psychic?"

"Not quite," Victoria said with a wry smile, "just a really good detective."

"Were you digging around Grasshopper Creek, too?" Kennedy asked.

Hugo nodded. "I studied the map more and learned it was a map of Bannack. I went to the spot marked X. But there was nothing."

68

"You also stole a projector and white sheets from the theater in Virginia City to make those ghosts appear in Hotel Meade, right?"

"Ah, you guessed it. I wanted to scare people away from Bannack so I could continue to dig around undisturbed."

"But how did you not know about your ancestor's secret symbol?" Rachel asked.

"Hey, I didn't know everything about my ancestor," Hugo snapped. "I actually never heard of him having his own secret symbol. I was at the play earlier today. That was when I heard of it. I grew up in a family that was ashamed to be descended from Chester Morris, okay? Why do you think my last name is Morrison instead of Morris? My parents rarely spoke of him. I was the only one who knew that the treasure belonged to us. That's why I went to Virginia City for work. I wanted to learn as much about my ancestor, the history of the Road Agents, and the lay of the land as much I could so I could search for the treasure. But, tell me, Miss Kennedy, how did you know I was the thief?"

"Easy," Kennedy said. "I saw you at the theater. The way you rushed to get out. And the terrified way you looked at us made me wonder. I suspected Andrew at first, and Shawn, Lydia, and Trent. They all had possible motives to steal the map, but no opportunities to do everything else, like set up the ghost sightings at the hotel. But you worked at the theater. You had access to the projector and other props."

"That explains the cloth you found, Ken," Marilyn said.

"Well, Mr. Morrison, you won't be stealing the gold that your ancestor stole," Brant said. "Nor will Virginia City's tourism require your services anymore. Rangers, take him away."

The rangers dragged Hugo away. Shawn and Lydia began applauding.

"That was amazing!" Lydia said. "Who knew that a teenage girl could be such an outstanding detective!"

"I'm just glad to hear that we were cleared of being suspects," Trent said.

"Alrighty," Darcy said, "so now what do we do?"

"Easy," Andrew said, grinning. "We find the treasure!"

"Can we join you?" Shawn asked eagerly.

Brant smiled at him. "I think we can get legal permission to dig around here," he said. He then frowned. "But, uh, where is the treasure buried?"

Kennedy looked around on the ground. She picked up the map and stared at it.

"Near this spot just behind the hotel," she said. "That's where the C symbol is."

She took a step forward but stopped when she felt Darcy's hand on her shoulder.

"Wait," Darcy said. "Can we please call my parents? This historic find will save our gift shop, and I feel that Mom and Dad should be present."

Kennedy smiled meekly. "Of course," she said.

Darcy got out her phone. Kennedy crossed her arms. She hadn't wanted to hurt Darcy's feelings, but what would Aunt Nora say when she heard everything?

"Hey, wait a second," Sierra said. "What about the riddle on the back of the map?"

Kennedy turned the map over and read the riddle out loud.

"Where I bury my love, locate my mark above, on the tall wooden post, which has hair that falls most, when it changes colors, nearest a fine alder, at the boot of the hill, I find my treasure fill."

She frowned. "I still can't figure this out. Though, I'm guessing that Chester's love was not that saloon girl, Claudia, but his treasure that he hid."

"Let me have a look at it," Shawn said.

Kennedy handed Shawn the map.

"Great," Andrew muttered, "we get to wait over an hour before we get any action."

Kennedy chuckled. "Patience is a virtue," she said. She smiled at Andrew. "Hey, thanks for tackling Hugo when he was chasing me, Andy."

Andrew smiled back. "Thanks for tackling him when he was tackling me. And hey, look, I'm sorry I was complaining about college the other day. And for all my other complaints."

"It's nothing. I'm also worried about going back to school in the fall."

Fall. That word fall.

Kennedy ran over to Shawn, Lydia, and Trent, all three of whom were still staring at the back of the map.

"I think I got it!" she said excitedly. "The riddle says to locate the mark, Chester's mark, on a tall wooden post that has hair that falls most when it changes colors. That would be a tree in autumn, when its leaves change colors and fall!"

70

Lydia stared at Kennedy with wide eyes. "That does make sense," she said. "You are a genius, young lady!"

"Yeah, I would never have been able to think of that!" Jessica said.

Rachel nudged Kennedy's elbow. Kennedy smiled shyly.

"We know it's an alder tree," she said. "An alder tree at the bottom of a hill. That's what 'boot of the hill' means."

She turned to Rachel. "It'll be that same tree we saw when we first came to Bannack."

Kennedy turned to look at the alder tree near the hotel. She spotted the familiar mark on its trunk. She and Rachel exchanged grins.

"We have tools for digging," Lydia said. "We can go grab them."

She, Shawn, and Trent ran off. They returned a few minutes later with shovels. After an hour of waiting, Uncle Edward and Aunt Nora arrived. Kennedy watched warily as Darcy and Marilyn told them the story. Her heart skipped a beat when Aunt Nora looked in her direction, only to feel relief when she saw that Aunt Nora was smiling.

Kennedy walked over to them. "Hey," she said, "look, Aunt Nora, I'm sorry about the danger, and fighting off Hugo—"

Aunt Nora held up her hand. "You exposed my husband's employee and my daughter's coworker for the greedy, thieving, self-entitled scoundrel that he really is," she said. "None of us had any idea that he was so wicked. And you helped us find the treasure that will save our gift shop. None of that could've been done without your mystery-solving gifts. I have you to thank. I'm sorry I was so judgmental of you, dear."

Kennedy smiled. She wrapped her arms around Aunt Nora.

"Well, let's not linger," Uncle Edward said eagerly. "Let's find that treasure!"

Everybody gathered at the alder tree with Chester Morris's symbol. Eager anticipation welled up in Kennedy as she watched Brant, Andrew, Shawn, Lydia, Trent, and a few rangers dig.

It wasn't long before Andrew gave a shout.

"I've hit something!"

Everybody gathered around Andrew. Sure enough, an old, dusty chest lay deep in the hole. Brant and Andrew pulled it out. A ranger smashed the lock. Darcy flipped it open.

The chest was filled to the brim with gold coins, which gleamed under the sunlight. But Kennedy guessed that those coins weren't sparkling nearly as much as the many pairs of eyes that gazed at them.

"I can't believe this!" Darcy exclaimed. "The lost treasure of the Innocents! And we found it!"

"An amazing, historical find!" Shawn said.

Darcy jumped to her feet and hugged her father. "We can save our gift shop!"

"Yes, indeed," Uncle Edward said. "And I'm sure there will be enough reward money to spare some for your cousins and Andrew."

"Us?" Andrew's eyes grew.

"Sure. You and the girls helped so much. You deserve it."

"Oh, it's so wonderful!" Darcy said. "We should go out and have a big celebratory dinner!"

Kennedy gazed at the treasure. She felt a hand upon her shoulder. Rachel and Sierra were standing behind her.

"What did I tell you?" Rachel said. "God gave you a knack for history, which helped you solve this treasure-hunting mystery. He also protected all of us while we were on this adventure."

Kennedy smiled at her. "Guess I have nothing to worry about anymore, do I?" she said.

She glanced back at the treasure, then at Marilyn and Darcy, who were hugging Victoria and Jessica. Kennedy's smile broadened.

Bonding with her stepfamily had been a greater treasure.

A Necklace Lost Deep in the Mine

SOMETHING WAS ROCKING her bed.

Moaning softly, Marilyn Wilson turned her head on her pillow. She opened her eyes. They rested on the beaded dangles of her lamp that stood on the nightstand next to her bed. The beads were wiggling.

CRASH!

Marilyn gasped and sat up. Fear and confusion filled her when she saw the small bookshelf lying flat on the floor. All the books were scattered. Everything in her room was trembling.

Marilyn leaped out of her bed. She attempted to run for the door, but due to the shaking, she lost her balance and fell flat on her stomach. She pushed herself up onto her hands and knees, brushed her bright red hair out of her face, and crawled under her desk. The clock fell off the wall and landed on the floor. Marilyn screamed.

"Marilyn?"

At the sound of her stepsister's voice, Marilyn turned her head to her door, which was swinging back and forth.

"Kennedy?" Marilyn shouted. "I'm under my desk!"

"Stay where you are!" Kennedy called. "Vicky! Jessie! Are you guys okay?"

Marilyn watched Kennedy's sisters Victoria and Jessica hurriedly crawl out of their own rooms and get under a table in the hallway. Victoria gave Kennedy a thumbs-up.

The grandfather clock in the hall toppled over, hitting the floor with a loud clang. The glass of the little door shattered. The pieces flew all over the hall. Victoria and Jessica covered their eyes and Kennedy's head disappeared back into her room.

Marilyn wanted to close her eyes and block out what she was seeing, but the little picture frame on her nightstand caught her attention. It was just about to fall.

"NO!" Marilyn shrieked. She slid out from under her desk and leaped over to the nightstand. She caught the picture frame right before it hit the floor. She hugged the frame against her chest as she tumbled over. She lifted herself back up on her knees and leaned against the wall, hoping that nothing would fall on top of her. Thankfully, the trembling stopped right there.

Shaking, Marilyn stood up and slowly walked out of her room. Kennedy, Victoria, and Jessica were standing in the hallway. The four girls looked at the grandfather clock with its smashed glass, the vase that had fallen from the table and now laid on the floor in pieces, and several of the pictures that were no longer hanging on the walls. Marilyn took a deep breath to steady herself.

"Is everyone alright?" Kennedy asked after a moment of stunned silence.

"I-I think so," Jessica stammered.

"The ground may have stopped shaking, but I haven't," Victoria said. "We just had an earthquake, didn't we?"

"I guess so," Kennedy said. She ran her fingers through her curly blonde hair.

Marilyn stared at the picture that she had rescued. It was a dangerous feat for her to do, but Marilyn could not lose this picture or its frame. It was a picture of her mother, Bonnie. And this very frame, this beautiful bronze frame, belonged to her mother.

"You okay, Marilyn?" Kennedy said.

Marilyn snapped out of her daydream. "Uh, yeah, sure, just fine," she said.

"What's that you got there?" Jessica asked.

"Oh, it's just a picture," Marilyn said quickly, hugging the frame to her chest.

Marilyn's father, Isaiah, came rushing up the stairs that led to the hall. He was followed by his wife, Caitlin. Jessica ran up to Caitlin and hugged her.

"Are you girls alright?" Marilyn's father asked anxiously.

"Yeah, we're fine," Victoria said, "though we can't say the same for everything lying on the floor."

Dad looked down at the broken vase and frowned. "This vase was an old antique," he said. "I doubt it can be glued back together."

He bent down and picked up the pieces. Marilyn returned to her room. She looked at her picture again. The earthquake may have stopped, but Marilyn couldn't shake these recent feelings of missing a mother she never knew.

Really, Marilyn, she admonished herself, *moping about your mom will not do you any good. She died from cancer when you were a baby, and you can't change that fact. She will not be here to see you graduate high school. Besides, I grew up without my mom. So why have I spent the last month being distressed over this?*

Marilyn held in a sigh. She and Kennedy were seniors in high school. Their graduation was just a month away. Marilyn had been excited about graduation at first. But about a month ago, she began wishing that her mother could be here to see her graduate. First she ignored those feelings. Then she tried to suppress them. But their lingering persistence was strong.

Marilyn placed the frame back on the nightstand. She fought back the tears as feelings of guilt washed over her. Caitlin was a kind and wonderful stepmother. Marilyn often said that she was the mother she never had. So why run the risk of hurting Caitlin with these new feelings that she has been struggling with for the past month? And Kennedy had already gone through a very difficult time just a couple of years ago when she had to adjust to her new life after her father's death. Marilyn did not want to risk hurting her feelings either.

Marilyn threw on a red T-shirt and a jean skirt, then she went downstairs for breakfast. The kitchen didn't look like it suffered too much from the earthquake. Caitlin, however, seemed to be refraining from using the stove.

Marilyn took a seat next to Kennedy and helped herself to some cereal and a blueberry muffin.

"I didn't know we could get earthquakes in Pine Lodge," Victoria said.

"It's rare, but not unheard of," Dad said. "I don't think this earthquake was too bad. Most everything downstairs is just fine."

"That's good," Jessica said. "I can't wait to hear what my geology teacher has to say when we go to school on Monday!"

Everyone chuckled.

"You okay there, Mary?" Dad said. "You seem awfully quiet after what just happened."

Marilyn faked a smile. "Oh, sure, I'm fine," she said. "Just a little . . ."

"Shaken?" Victoria said, grinning. "Pun intended."

Everyone except Marilyn laughed.

"I gotta admit," Victoria said, "I wish that the earthquake didn't happen today, on Saturday. If it happened on a school day, school probably would have been cancelled, but now we're gonna spend our Saturday cleaning up after some dumb earthquake's mess."

Kennedy and Jessica sniggered.

"Please do," Caitlin said, "because Isaiah, Marilyn, and I still have to work."

"No worries, Mom, the house will look like there was no earthquake to begin with," Kennedy said. "It's gonna take me awhile to believe that Pine Lodge had an earthquake. I'll bet that it'll be the talk of the town today!"

Kennedy was right. The moment that the first customers entered the Lonely Pine Eatery, the main topic of chatter was that morning's earthquake. Marilyn had wondered if the café would have to be closed for the day. Dad and Caitlin had the same idea, which was why the three of them had left early that morning to inspect the restaurant. Fortunately, the damage was minor. One stove was not working, and several dishes had been broken, but everything else in the kitchen was just fine. Even the dining area had not suffered much except that a few chairs and three tables were lying on their sides. The restaurant opened at its usual hour for business.

Marilyn put on her apron as soon as she clocked in. She helped her father in the kitchen for a few minutes, then she went out to the dining room to take orders. There, she saw several of the local miners entering the restaurant. She spotted Deputy Jonathon Shea walking over to the counter. He took off his dusty hat to fan his face.

"Hello, Jonathon." Marilyn went behind the counter. "How can I help you?"

"Hi, Marilyn," Jonathon said. He put his hat back on. "I'm ordering meals to go."

He fished out a list from his pocket and read from it. Marilyn jotted everything down in her notebook.

"How 'bout that earthquake this morning, huh?" Jonathon remarked.

"Tell me about it," Marilyn said. "At least it wasn't too big, right?"

"Well, I heard that it measured five-point-five."

"Five-point-five?" Marilyn gasped. She didn't think that the earthquake had been that serious.

"Oh, yeah," Jonathon said. "People in Prescott and Cottonwood felt it. The U.S. Geological Survey is studying our epicenter even as we speak. I helped Sheriff Rudolf and Deputy Hill set up a perimeter around the mine, and I will be helping out a little bit more today, like buying lunches for the miners. I also heard that one of the entrances is temporarily closed."

"I'm not surprised."

Marilyn closed her notebook, politely excused herself, and returned to the kitchen to turn in the orders. Caitlin immediately started on the meals and Marilyn went back out to the dining room. A few other miners had entered. Marilyn spotted Felicity Weston, the daughter of the town's mayor. She was talking to one of the miners, a lanky, black-haired man in his thirties. Marilyn recognized him as Ted Garcia. She began to walk toward the two of them.

"Ted, didn't you say that you saw something that looked like a necklace down one of the shafts?"

Felicity's words made Marilyn stop right in her tracks. She stared at Felicity.

"Yeah," Ted said. "It was quite deep too. It looked stuck. I tried to get a hold of it, but I could barely reach it. And that shaft was very close to the entrance that was wrecked by the quake. I reckon it would've been too risky for me to try anything else."

"I'll bet," Felicity said. "I can imagine that a few of those shafts and tunnels are still pretty unstable."

Marilyn's heart rate increased. She made herself approach Felicity and Ted.

"E-excuse me," she stammered.

"Well, hey there, Marilyn," Felicity said cheerfully, looking her way. "How are you?"

"Fine," Marilyn said. "I'm—"

"Glad to see the earthquake didn't disrupt business here," Ted said.

"Yeah," Marilyn said. "Uh, I'm really sorry to be listening in on you guys, but you said something about a necklace in one of the shafts? Can . . . can you describe it, Ted?"

Ted and Felicity looked at one another.

"Sorry, but I can't, hon," Ted said. "I shined my headlight on it, but it was so covered with dust and dirt that I couldn't see it very well. Though I reckon that it must've been down in that shaft for a long time. And truthfully, that particular shaft has been closed off for years because of a mining accident years ago. The one that your father was in, I believe. I think that this morning's earthquake messed up the shaft some more. Hence why I couldn't stay down there and fish out that necklace, or whatever it was. That tunnel is very unstable."

Marilyn's heart skipped a beat. "It's all good," she said. "Oh, um, can I take your orders?"

"Just a moment, please," Felicity said. "We're helping Jonathon take meals to the miners. Ted and I are still undecided."

"Of course."

Marilyn slowly walked over to the counter, staring into thin air. Memories were coming back to her. Memories that she had not thought about until recently. She was twelve years old . . .

"Dad?" Marilyn had asked.

"Yes, dear?" Dad replied.

"I was just wondering if you can, well, tell me some things about my mom."

Dad looked up from his book and stared at Marilyn. He frowned a little.

"Well," he said slowly, "you look like her."

"I know," Marilyn said, "but what was she like? We don't have any of her old stuff."

Dad sighed. "You know that I had to sell most of her belongings so I could buy the Lonely Pine Eatery, honey."

"I know. But can't you tell me just a few things?"

Dad smiled feebly. "Your mother was a wonderful woman," he said. "Kind, gentle, and very imaginative. You know that she wrote that book of yours, right? And those poetry books?"

Marilyn remembered how eagerly she had nodded.

79

"She and I knew each other all our lives. I think it was inevitable that we would fall in love. I remember proposing to her during our day trip to the Yavapai Creek Wilderness. I still remember the rangers applauding us when she said yes. I had even bought her a special wedding present: a diamond necklace from the gift shop. She wore it with pride."

"What happened to that necklace? Did you have to sell it?"

Dad's face fell. "No," he said. "The truth is, Mary, I lost it. Right before we got married."

Marilyn's eyes widened with surprise. "What happened?"

Dad sighed. "I was foolish," he said. "I had just finished mining school. Well, one day, I was taking the necklace to be fixed. Part of its clasp had been broken. I told your mother that I would get it to the jewelers as soon as I got done with my shift in the mine that day. I was showing it off to one of the other miners when there was a sudden dynamite explosion. I was lucky; all I had was a broken leg. But I lost the necklace in that tunnel, and it had collapsed. Nobody could get in there. Your mother was so gracious and forgiving, but I was devastated. Not only did I lose her necklace, but I had to quit my mining job. The doctors told me that my leg would take a long time to fully heal. I couldn't work for a long time. The miners raised money to buy another necklace. That one I sold after your mother died."

He sighed again. "Oh, Marilyn . . ."

"Marilyn?"

Gasping, Marilyn spun around. Her father was standing at the counter, looking at her.

"Something wrong, honey?" Dad asked. "Why are you just standing there, staring into space?"

"Oh, it's nothing," Marilyn said quickly. "Just thinking."

"Well, keep those orders coming while you think," Dad said. "We have a bunch of hungry miners."

"I know. Sorry."

Marilyn went back to work. But all her mind could dwell upon was the necklace. The necklace that her father had bought as a wedding gift for her mother. The necklace that had been lost in the mine for twenty years. Marilyn had to fight back tears as she worked.

She looked over at her father. He looked so happy and so peaceful, as though he had no cares in the world. She remembered how sad he was when she asked about her mother when she was twelve. She hated the thought of hurting his feelings. But she had kept quiet about her own feelings long enough.

Marilyn approached her father as he was wiping down the counter.

"Dad?" she said quietly. "Can I talk to you for a minute? Just the two of us?"

"Of course, dear," Dad said. "What's on your mind?"

Marilyn glanced into the kitchen, where Caitlin was working. She led her dad away from the kitchen.

"I heard Felicity and Ted talking," Marilyn said. "Ted said that he saw something down in one of the shafts."

"Okay?" Dad raised his eyebrow in confusion. "What's so important about this?"

"It was a necklace, Dad."

"A necklace?" Dad gasped. "Ted saw a necklace?"

"I was wondering if perhaps it could be the same necklace that you . . . well, you know."

"That I bought for your mother," Dad whispered. "But it was buried a long time ago. That shaft was closed off. Completely buried. Even after some of it got dug out, it was abandoned."

"Today's quake might've reopened it," Marilyn said. "At least, that's what Ted thinks."

Dad sighed. "Your mother had it for a very short time," he said.

"Imagine if we could get it back!" Marilyn said hopefully.

"Um, no, don't be getting ideas," Dad said, suddenly becoming stern. "You know that the mine can be dangerously unpredictable, Marilyn. An explosion caused one shaft to be completely buried for years. I was lucky that day. We all were. Even today, the miners that go into that hole know the risks they are taking, and they are highly trained professionals. You stay away from that mine, okay?"

"I understand your concern, Dad, I really do," Marilyn said pleadingly, "but we have a chance to get that necklace."

"It's probably rusty and ruined, it's been down there long before you were born. I mean, I can see why it would be important to you, hon, but I'm not risking your safety for the necklace."

"But it could be one of the last things I have of my mom."

"You still have your mother's books, Mary. The ones she wrote."

"I know, but . . ."

81

Dad put his hand on his daughter's shoulder. "Is there something about this necklace that's bothering you?" he asked gently. "Come to think of it, you have seemed pretty sad lately."

Marilyn looked down at her feet. "I've been thinking about my mom a lot," she admitted. "Look, I love Caitlin. She's a great stepmother. She truly is the mother I never had. But I couldn't help but be curious about my own mother, and how she didn't see me grow up, that she won't see me finish high school."

"Why didn't you tell me sooner? You know that if there's anything bugging you, you can tell me."

"I just didn't want to risk hurting Caitlin's feelings. But the thing is, I just wish I could've known Mom."

Dad wrapped his arm around Marilyn's shoulder. "I understand that you wonder about your mother sometimes," he said. "There's nothing wrong with that. And I'm sure Caitlin would understand. You know what her daughters went through."

"Yeah." Marilyn sighed to hold back the tears. "Look, Dad, I'm sure it's nothing. Besides, you're right, who says that necklace is still in good shape anyway? I'd better get back to work."

Marilyn pulled away from her father. She went to the counter and packed several lunches in bags and handed them to Felicity.

"Is that everything?" Marilyn asked.

"Almost," Felicity said. "We're just waiting on a few more, then we'll be ready to go."

"Okay." Marilyn began wiping the counter.

"Something on your mind?" Felicity asked.

"Come again?"

"You're not your usual cheerful self today. You haven't mentioned the earthquake, but you seemed pretty interested in that necklace Ted and I were talking about. Is there something you know about it?"

"You really are observant, Felicity," Marilyn said. "Yeah, it's just that, well, shortly before his marriage to my mom, my dad bought a necklace to give to her as a wedding gift, but he lost it in the mine. He never found it again. And I was wondering if Ted, maybe, well, you know, found it after all these years."

"I guess it's possible," Felicity said.

"But I can't go into the mine," Marilyn said sullenly.

"Of course not," Felicity said, "but I daresay that the mine will be open again soon. At least, that's what I heard when I was helping Jonathon set up the perimeter. Tell you what. I'll keep you posted about the status of the mine. I'm sure that once it's safe again, the miners can fish out that necklace and get it to you."

Marilyn smiled. "Oh, Fel, I would really appreciate that!" she said. "Thank you so much."

"Of course," Felicity said. "I'd feel the same if I were in your shoes. So don't you fret anymore. I'll keep an eye on things and let you know."

Marilyn rushed into the school gym. Several other senior students were already on the stage, ready to begin band practice.

"There you are, Marilyn!" one of the girls said. "You're late!"

"Sorry," Marilyn said sheepishly, not looking at any of them.

"It's not like you to be late," Kennedy said thoughtfully. She strummed her violin.

Marilyn glanced at her stepsister. She was right. Over the past few days, Marilyn could hardly concentrate on anything. She never heard anything from Felicity. She found herself missing her mother more than she ever had, and every reminder of her high school graduation worsened her pain.

"I sure hope we don't get another earthquake now," said the boy sitting at the drums. He tapped one of the cymbals. "Imagine how these things sounded during the quake."

"Please don't demonstrate," a girl said flatly.

"I wonder how long the mine will be down," Marilyn said. She walked onto the stage.

"Dunno," said the boy sitting at the grand piano. "Though my dad told me this morning that the mine is looking better."

"Really?" Marilyn said eagerly. "How much better?"

"Well, it's stable. Why?"

"Oh, nothing," Marilyn said. "Just curious."

She noticed that Kennedy was glancing at her with a suspicious look in her eye. Marilyn tore her eyes away. She heard the piano playing an A. Kennedy started tuning her violin. Marilyn held up her sheet music.

As soon as band practice was over, Kennedy packed up her violin and walked outside with Marilyn.

"Where are your sisters?" Marilyn asked when the two girls arrived at their pickup.

"Shopping for our graduation gifts," Kennedy said. "We'll meet them at the mall and drive home."

The girls got in the truck. Kennedy started the engine and pulled out of the school's parking lot.

"So, Mary," Kennedy said, "how come you're so interested in the mine?"

"No big reason," Marilyn said, not meeting Kennedy's eyes.

"Marilyn, I can tell that something's bugging you."

Marilyn sighed. "Seems like everyone can," she said. "Is it really that obvious?"

"I'm afraid so," Kennedy said. "I remember the morning of the earthquake, how you looked at a picture frame with such sadness in your eyes. And I could tell that you've been faking smiles lately. I used to fake smiles myself, you know, when my family first moved here. I just knew that something was troubling you."

"Well, there's something in the mine," Marilyn said slowly, "that might've belonged to my mother."

"Your mother?" Kennedy raised her eyebrow.

"You know that many years ago, my dad used to be a miner, until that one mining accident, shortly before he married my mom. You know that he had to quit mining after that. Well, shortly before that accident, he had bought my mom a diamond necklace from a gift shop in the Yavapai Creek Wilderness. It was a wedding gift. His first wedding gift to her. And he lost it in the mine when he had his accident in there. He never got it back."

"That's awful," Kennedy said. "But whatever made you start thinking about this necklace?"

"When I went to work on the day of the quake, I heard Ted talking to Felicity. Ted told her that the shaft had possibly been shaken open by the quake, and he saw a necklace deep down in the shaft. But it was too dangerous for him to get to. I told the story to Felicity, and she said that she would keep me posted. And then today I learn that the mine is possibly safer."

"I see," Kennedy said. "And that picture you were looking at right after the earthquake . . . it's a picture of your mother, isn't it?"

Marilyn nodded. Her eyes began to water. "I know I have my mom's books, but, well, them, and that picture, they're all I have left of her. In fact, one of my mom's poems is about a lost necklace. I didn't truly understand that poem until Dad told me the story of him losing the necklace. You know in *The Galloping Girls of Pine*

Gulch, the main character has a necklace given to her by the man who would be her love interest? It was probably inspired by her lost necklace."

She wiped her eyes and looked at Kennedy. "Look, Kenny," she said, "I'm happy with your mom. She's a great mom. But here I am graduating, and well, for some reason, I am sad that my own mom cannot be here for it. Dad rarely talked about her. I don't know very much about her, to be honest. It always made him so sad to bring her up in conversation."

"I know how it feels," Kennedy said. "I was devastated when my dad died. At least you're not bitter like I was. Maybe you could speak to your dad about how you feel?"

Marilyn hesitated. "I'd rather not. It makes him so sad, and I worry about hurting your mom's feelings too. But well . . . I don't know."

She stared out the window, not saying another word. In a few minutes they arrived at Mingus Mall. Marilyn stepped out as soon as Kennedy shut off the engine. She had to fight to hold back the tears, and she did not want Kennedy to notice.

The two girls entered the mall through the food court, where they spotted Victoria and Jessica talking to Felicity near the pizza parlor. Marilyn's face lit up as soon as she saw Felicity.

"We're here," Kennedy said. "Finally out of band practice."

"Good," Victoria said. "Now we can grab that pizza."

Kennedy grinned. "That sounds good."

She winked at Marilyn. "Hey Marilyn, you and Felicity find a place to sit. Vic, Jess, and I will get the food."

The three girls went to the pizza parlor. Marilyn led Felicity to a table.

"What was that about?" Felicity asked.

Marilyn looked up. "What?"

"Well, it seemed like Kennedy was trying to distract her sisters."

Marilyn smiled. "Yeah, I told her everything. You know, about the mine and my mom's necklace. So, you haven't found out anything more, have you? I was told at band practice that the mine might be safer for mining, or something. So, uh, any possibility of exploration?"

"Oh, yes, about that," Felicity said, frowning.

Marilyn's stomach churned. She felt her heart beginning to beat faster against her chest. "What is it?"

"Well, the miners are still looking at things, but I heard from Dad today that the earthquake might have been a foreshock."

"A foreshock?" Marilyn put her hand over her mouth. "You mean . . ."

"We don't know anything yet," Felicity said quickly. "The information just got out today. Nobody is certain that the earthquake was a foreshock. They just received the report from the USGS with the warning."

She placed her hand on Marilyn's. "Don't get too upset, okay? I will still keep you posted. There is still a possibility that we won't have any more quakes."

"Well, I hope so," Marilyn said defiantly, "because I want a chance to get that necklace."

"We'll see. Just try not to do anything rash, okay?"

"But what if I lose the chance to get that necklace? Another tremor could bury up that shaft again. It took twenty years for the ground to reopen that shaft. I don't wanna wait another twenty years. There might not even be another chance. It's now or never."

"Look, I know that the necklace is important to you."

"It may be one of the few possessions left from my mother. It inspired things in her own books. I can't let this chance go!"

"You know you cannot go into that mine. Nobody will let you. Not the miners, not the police, nobody."

"And how am I supposed to get them to let me inside that hole?" Marilyn demanded. "Announce a let's-go-search-for-an-ancient-necklace-in-the-mine party? I'd rather not say anything more. I don't want Caitlin to hear about this and get hurt."

"I get it. But just trust me on this, okay?"

Marilyn sighed. "Fine."

Kennedy, Victoria, and Jessica came back to the table with a couple of pizzas. Marilyn and Felicity's conversation ended right there. Marilyn remained quiet while her stepsisters and Felicity talked. All that she could think of right now was that her chance of getting the necklace was slipping away from her like sand through a colander. The very thought of the necklace being lost forever was enough to make Marilyn want to cry. And enough to keep an appetite away. The pizza right in front of her smelled good, but her stomach wouldn't rumble.

Upon arriving home, Marilyn was ready to just go to her room and sulk. But before she could turn away from the front door, she felt Kennedy's hand on her shoulder. Marilyn glanced in her direction.

"Yeah?" she said.

"If you're up for it," Kennedy said quietly, "I thought that the two of us could go on a hike in the bluffs. You look like you need a pick-me-up."

Marilyn shrugged. "Okay."

She and Kennedy went back outside. They silently walked out to the bluffs, which were the large, sandstone rock formations that loomed over the town. Marilyn gazed at the sandy-colored rocks. She always found solace whenever she hiked in the bluffs. It was a nice evening out, too.

Kennedy broke the silence. "So what did Felicity say?"

"It's not good," Marilyn said. "She told me that the earthquake might have been a foreshock."

"Billy texted me the same thing," Kennedy said. She took a deep breath. "Not sure I would like a round two."

"Neither would I," Marilyn said. "And you know what that could mean for the mine, right?"

Kennedy stopped. "Oh, no, girl, please don't tell me you're thinking of sneaking into that mine."

Marilyn faced Kennedy. "Well, it was my only chance to get the necklace."

"Yeah, with only a little more than a hint of danger," Kennedy said sarcastically.

"I didn't say I was going to take that chance," Marilyn said. "It *was* my only chance. But it's gone. I'm just saying that the necklace is gonna be lost for good now."

"Oh," Kennedy said softly. "Mary, I'm so sorry."

"Well, there's nothing that can be done." Marilyn blinked back the tears. "It's just that, well, recovering that necklace would be like recovering my mother. And just in time for her to see me graduate high school."

Kennedy nodded with understanding. Marilyn shuffled her feet and gazed off into the distance. She wondered if Kennedy knew how she felt. After all, Kennedy had lost her father. Now that she thought about it, could Kennedy have been struggling with feelings of missing her father? Was she wishing that her father was still alive to see her high school graduation?

A loud rattling sound snapped Marilyn out of her sullen thoughts. She gasped and looked around nervously.

"What was that?" Kennedy asked.

"Not good!" Marilyn said. "That's a rattlesnake!"

The two girls climbed up onto a rock, and a rattlesnake slithered away from out of a hole.

"Oh my, would you look at that guy," Kennedy said. "Man, am I glad we're up here and not down there with that thing."

"Look at how fast that snake is slithering," Marilyn said.

"Yeah, like it senses something."

"Maybe a mouse or something it can munch on. Seems to be in a hurry to catch its dinner, though."

"I guess, but it looks pretty spooked," Kennedy said. She leaned forward to look over the edge of the rock. "I think it's gone now."

She and Marilyn slid off the rock.

As soon as the family returned home from church, Marilyn went straight to her room. She plopped onto her bed, but her eyes immediately wandered over to the picture frame on her nightstand. The one she had rescued during the earthquake.

Marilyn reached over and grabbed it. She stared at it.

"Happy Mother's Day, Mom," she whispered. "I'm sorry I can't rescue your necklace like I rescued this picture I'm holding."

She then gasped and sat up.

"Mother's Day!" she said to herself. "And it's not only Mother's Day but also Caitlin's birthday!"

Marilyn laid the picture next to her. She rubbed her eyes and groaned. How could she have forgotten her own stepmother's birthday, especially since it was coinciding with Mother's Day? And she had nothing to give her.

A knock at her door interrupted her thoughts.

"Come in!" Marilyn called.

Kennedy entered, holding a gift bag. Her brown eyes rested on the picture frame lying on the bed. Marilyn grabbed the frame and quickly set it back on the nightstand.

"What's up?" she asked.

Kennedy sat on the bed next to Marilyn. "I just thought I'd show you this," she said.

She reached into the bag and pulled out a three-wick candle with light green wax. She handed it to Marilyn.

"A candle?" Marilyn raised her eyebrow.

Kennedy grinned. "Well," she said, "when I was shopping for gifts for Mom yesterday, I figured you would need something to give her. No offense, of course, but I guessed that you were too preoccupied with the necklace and the mine and the earthquake that you had yet to get something for Mom. I also knew you'd be struggling today."

"So this candle is my gift to your mom?" Marilyn said.

"Yep. It has a citrus scent, one of Mom's favorites. It was on sale too. But you don't have to pay me back."

"No, no, really, I should."

Marilyn got her wallet out of her purse and opened it. "How much do I owe you?"

"Just five dollars."

Marilyn got out a five-dollar bill and handed it to Kennedy. "So what did you get for Caitlin?"

"I got her a couple of nice blouses and lotion. And Victoria and Jessica pitched in their money together and bought her a new bathrobe and bedtime slippers. We're excited to give them to her."

"I'm sure you are," Marilyn said. "Oh, me too, of course."

Later that evening, the family sat down for dinner. Kennedy and Victoria had marinated a steak, fixed a potato salad and a small vegetable tray, and baked an apple pie.

"This looks really good," Caitlin said with a smile.

"Ken and I made it special for you, Mom," Victoria said. "Happy Mother's Day, and happy birthday!"

The girls presented Caitlin with their gifts while they ate. Kennedy presented her gift first, then Victoria and Jessica. Marilyn reached below her chair for her gift bag.

"They're all so lovely," Caitlin said. She hugged the fuzzy bathrobe close to her. "This is so soft. I'll enjoy wearing this. Thank you, girls."

Marilyn smiled shyly. It was time. She lifted her gift bag and handed it to Kennedy. She gave Marilyn a quick smile then gave the bag to Caitlin.

"Oh, look at this!" Caitlin said when she dug out the candle. "A citrus candle. I love it. Thank you, Marilyn."

Marilyn pushed a strand of hair behind her ear. "You're welcome. Happy Mother's Day, and happy birthday."

"I guess it's my turn now," Dad said with a grin. He held up a small blue box. "Happy birthday, dear."

He handed the box to Caitlin. She opened it and gasped.

"It's beautiful!" she said.

"What is it, Mom?" Victoria asked. "Show us!"

Caitlin pulled out a silver necklace. Marilyn's face fell.

"It was on sale at the jewelry store," Dad said. "It was so you."

Caitlin fastened the necklace around her neck. Marilyn noticed Kennedy glancing at her. Marilyn gave her a small smile.

After dinner, Dad asked Marilyn to help Caitlin clean up. Marilyn agreed and started putting leftover food in the fridge.

"Are you alright, Marilyn?" Caitlin asked her as she piled a few dishes in the sink.

Marilyn looked up at her stepmother. "What was that?" she said.

"You've been really quiet lately," Caitlin said. "Something on your mind?"

Marilyn paused. She did not know what to say.

"Just, uh, thinking about graduation, I guess," she said. She ignored the guilt flooding her mind. It was partially true, after all.

"Oh, I'm sure that you will do fine," Caitlin said. "You and Kennedy. But you've been so excited about graduating high school. Is there something else on your mind?"

Marilyn forced a smile. "It's all good," she said quickly. "So, um, did you have a good birthday?"

"I sure did. Thank you again for the candle. I love citrus."

Marilyn felt herself relax a little bit. She then eyed the necklace around her stepmother's neck.

"You sure got a nice necklace," she said.

"Thank you." Caitlin smiled as she twiddled the necklace with her fingers. "I love it."

Marilyn held in a sigh. She almost wanted to tell Caitlin the truth. But she didn't dare. Not on Mother's Day. Not on Caitlin's birthday.

What good would it do anyway? I've already accepted that there's no chance of getting that other necklace. My own mother's necklace. I need to buck up and be happy for my stepmother.

As soon as she clocked in, Marilyn went to the counter. School had been a drag for her. All day long her mind wanted to focus on the mine instead of her classes. She just hoped that she would be able to focus on her shift now.

"Hi, Marilyn."

Marilyn turned around. Kennedy was sitting at the counter. Her cousin, Aaron Connolly, and friends, Billy Weston and Wesley Rudolf, were next to her.

"Hi," Marilyn replied, raising an eyebrow. "Kennedy, did you follow me from school or something?"

Kennedy snickered. "I asked Billy to give me a ride here," she said. "I just wanted to check on you, you know."

Marilyn couldn't help but smile. She sure was thankful to have a stepsister who cared for her.

"Seems like you've been down in the dumps for a while," Billy said.

"Yeah," Aaron said, "so we let Kennedy interrupt our hike in the bluffs."

"Gosh," Marilyn said. "I hope you guys didn't mind."

"Nah, we wanted to be with you and try to cheer you up."

Marilyn blushed. "Oh, you didn't have to," she said.

"It's nothing, girl," Wesley said. "So, anything you wanna get off your mind?"

Marilyn shrugged. "I've just been thinking of my mom," she admitted. "And well . . . something of hers was lost in the mine years ago. I'm sad that I can't get it."

The boys frowned.

"Is that all?" Wesley asked.

Marilyn sighed. "It's complicated," she said.

There was an awkward pause. Aaron broke it by changing the subject.

"Man, it feels great to get off the ranch for a day!"

"You've been busy?" Marilyn asked.

"You won't believe it!" Wesley said. "On the day of the earthquake, Billy and I both got a call from Mr. Connolly. At the time, he needed help with calming down the animals and fixing things up. Part of the corral behind the horse stable collapsed, and we had to chase frightened livestock all over the ranch."

"Then we spend the next few days fixing stuff," Aaron said. "Not that we minded all that much. We laugh about it now."

A small group of miners, including Ted Garcia, walked in. Felicity Weston was also among them.

"Hey, hey, something must be going on at the mine," Billy remarked.

Marilyn's heart skipped a beat. "Must be," she said. "They might be ordering meals to go. Excuse me, guys."

She ran over to Ted and Felicity, who had just sat down.

"Are you ordering meals to go?" she asked. "Or, uh, is there anything I can get you to drink?"

"We just came in for dinner," Felicity said. "I've been talking to Ted here, Marilyn. I hope you don't mind, but I told him the truth about the necklace."

"It's fine." Marilyn grinned. "Any news on the mine?"

92

Ted smiled at her. "We reopened it this afternoon," he said, "because the mine and everything else seems to be much safer now. Why, we even rescheduled one of our public tours. It'll be this Saturday afternoon."

Marilyn felt like swarms of butterflies were released in her stomach. "What about the foreshock possibility?" she asked.

"The USGS said things are looking better. Of course, forecasting earthquakes is no easy task, but they've been doing their research. Anyway, I'd like some coffee. Black."

"Same here," Felicity said, "and a couple glasses of water too. I feel like I'm dying of thirst."

Marilyn rushed to get Ted, Felicity, and the other miners their drinks and meals, but soon she was finally able to go to her dad in the kitchen.

"Dad!" she said eagerly. She was practically jumping up and down. "Did you hear?"

Dad stared at his daughter. "Hear what?" he asked.

"Good news!" Marilyn said. "Daddy, please. Ted told me that the mine is safer and is open again! That earthquake may not have been a foreshock after all! Please, Dad, please, may I go to the mine and look for that necklace? I'll be sure to have plenty of supervision from the miners."

"Marilyn," Dad said slowly.

"There's even a tour on Saturday! I can go on the tour!"

"Marilyn . . ."

"I'll only search for a few minutes!"

"Marilyn!" Dad held up his hands. "Slow down!"

Marilyn stopped chattering. She noticed a lot of curious stares from the other workers. Good thing Caitlin was off today.

"Dad, seriously," Marilyn said. "The mine is safer."

"How much safer?" Dad demanded.

"Enough for a public tour this weekend."

"I am not risking your safety for a necklace that has been lost for twenty years."

"But Dad, don't you know how important this is to me?"

"Yes, I understand, honey, I really do. I wouldn't mind retrieving that lost necklace if I could. I know that I had to give away lots of things that belonged to your mother after she died. I didn't want to, but we needed that money to build our lives. The good lives that we have now. I was a single father then, and I had to do something."

"You bought this restaurant."

"I might not have been able to do so without all that extra cash. Simply working here after recovering from my mine injuries was barely good enough."

"I understand, but it was still hard for me to grow up without keepsakes from my mom. Or without her."

"And don't you think that you've risked your life enough? I mean, running away from a gang of bank robbers, then confronting cattle rustlers on Oliver's ranch, then everything that happened in Montana . . ."

"Dad, please," Marilyn said, "please. I'll be careful. Really, I will. Just let me peek into that mine. I just want to find something that belonged to my mom."

Dad sighed. He turned his back and fell silent. It seemed like an eternity to Marilyn as she stared at her father. Finally, he turned back to her.

"Alright, here's what I will do," he said in a firm voice. "If everything is okay by then, as in there are no more earthquakes, then you may search for the necklace this Saturday. Go with the tour, and have someone, like Ted, help you search. But I will only allow you the amount of time that the tour has in there."

Marilyn squealed and wrapped her arms around her father.

"Thank you, Dad!" she exclaimed. "Thank you, thank you!"

"You're welcome. Now do get back to work, Marilyn. We still have hungry customers to feed."

"Sure thing!"

Marilyn went out to the counter, where Kennedy, Aaron, Wesley, and Billy were still sitting. Kennedy's chin was resting in her palm, and she was staring at her stepsister intently.

"Oh, did you hear all that?" Marilyn asked cheerfully.

"Yeah," Kennedy admitted. "I cannot believe that Dad's letting you do it."

"I'm sure it'll be fine," Marilyn said. "I pray it will be fine!"

"I wish I can be there," Billy said, "but I work on Saturday."

Kennedy fell silent for a minute, then she smiled.

"Mary," she said, "think your dad will let me tag along?"

Saturday soon came, though not soon enough for Marilyn. Over the past few days, she could hardly contain her excitement. Every night she had gone to bed anxious, hoping and praying that there would be no more tremors, and wake up every morning flooded with relief and thanking God that the ground was still. And now her waiting was over.

At quarter to two, she and Kennedy arrived at the mine. They mingled with several other tourists.

"I must admit," Kennedy said, "you seem as ready as ever."

"Oh, I am," Marilyn said, grinning broadly.

"I still can't believe Dad's letting us do this."

The two girls walked toward the front of the mine. Marilyn stared at the entrance. Her heart was thumping against her chest.

What if I don't find the necklace? she thought, frowning slightly. *What if the tour isn't long enough for me to search? Oh, no, Marilyn, don't think that. You will find that necklace! You must!*

She took a deep breath to calm her nerves. "Ken," she said, "thank you for coming with me. And for the support."

"Of course," Kennedy said. "I know how it feels. You know, I remember the time when you first mentioned your mother. I was still upset over my dad during that time. I remember feeling a bit guilty then. While I was dwelling over my dad's death, you would've been struggling with growing up without a mother, and wondering about her, and having moments of missing her. Like now."

"Anyone in our shoes would be struggling with grief," Marilyn said. "I know my dad was. Sometimes I think the grief comes back to him once in a while. That's why it was so hard for me to ask him about my mother. And the fact that Dad had to sell almost all of Mom's stuff in order to provide for me and buy the Lonely Pine in the first place. I wish he didn't. I barely have anything from my mother, other than her books and that picture. That's kind of why I'm so determined to get this necklace."

"I totally get it. I bet you I'd feel the same way if I had a chance to recover something from my dad."

"Although," Marilyn said slowly, "Dad once said to me that just having me, and my resemblance to my mother, was enough for him. That the belongings he sold were nothing compared to me."

Kennedy smiled. "Of course he'd say that."

Just then Ted Garcia and two other miners approached the group of tourists. Everyone fell silent when Ted raised his hand.

"Welcome to the Michael Williamson Mine," he greeted with a smile. "We are really excited to have this opportunity for a public tour, our first one since the earthquake."

Ted noticed Marilyn and Kennedy. He gave Marilyn a small smile and a little nod. Marilyn's heart leapt.

Ted turned his attention back to the tourists. "Follow me, please," he said. He went to his pickup and got out a box. "Everyone put on a helmet."

Ted distributed the helmets. Marilyn snatched a helmet from Ted's hand and jammed it on her head. Ted looked startled at first, then he snickered.

"So," he whispered to Marilyn, "I hear that you came along not for the ride but for a search for a long-lost necklace."

"Yes!" Marilyn said. "Can you show me where you saw it?"

"I will see what I can do," Ted said. "I've got another miner helping me with the tour so I can help you look. We'll be starting the tour in just a minute."

Everyone gathered supplies. Ted had Kennedy carry a bag with a rope, a map, and a flashlight. As soon as they were ready, Ted led the group into the mine. Almost immediately he began pointing out the rock walls and asking some trivia questions.

"Come on, come on," Marilyn muttered. "When are we going to begin my search?"

"Hold your horses, Mary," Kennedy hissed.

But Marilyn simply could not ignore the rapid beating of her heart and the constant churning of her stomach. She turned her head back and forth, searching for the shaft where her mother's necklace lay hidden.

After what seemed like an eternity, another miner took over the tour. Ted approached Kennedy and Marilyn.

"Alrighty," he said to the two girls, "you ready?"

Marilyn held her hands together. "Yes!" she squealed.

Ted led the girls down a ladder to another shaft. There was yellow caution tape at the bottom. Marilyn peered down into the narrow tunnel. The roof looked like it could collapse any minute.

"Here we are," Ted said. He shined his helmet light down the shaft. "I will take Marilyn down there just a few feet. Enough so she can see. But only the two of us."

Kennedy nodded with understanding and began climbing back up the ladder. Ted held up the caution tape. Marilyn ducked under it. Ted followed her down the tunnel.

"If you really peek down there," Ted said, "you can see something."

Marilyn stepped up. Borrowing Ted's flashlight, she shined her lights down the shaft. Sure enough, she thought she caught a glimmer. Her heart skipped several beats.

"That must be it!" she said excitedly. "A glimmer that has survived all these years!"

Ted held up his pickaxe. "And if I'm very careful," he added, "I should be able to fish it out. The miners and I have been working on this shaft since the earthquake reopened it. I must ask you to step out and let me do the work, though."

"Of course, of course!"

A clanking sound startled Marilyn. She and Ted turned around. Dust and a few small stones were falling from the rocky ceiling.

"What was that?" Marilyn asked nervously.

"I'm sure it was nothing," Ted said. He turned his attention back to the tunnel.

But before Marilyn or Ted could move, the tunnel began shaking, more rocks were falling from the ceiling, and the timbers were trembling up and down.

"What on Earth is going on?" Marilyn asked.

"Oh, this is really bad!" Ted yelled. He dropped his pickaxe. "We need to get out, Marilyn! Right now!"

"But what about that necklace?" Marilyn shrieked. She shined her flashlight upon the glimmer. She was tempted to lunge for that shine and yank it out of the rocks.

"No time for that!" Ted bellowed. "Out!"

But the shaking became more violent by the second. Marilyn had fallen to the ground as soon as she started running, and a huge boulder loosened itself from the wall and fell between her and Ted, who had already managed to run several feet ahead.

"Marilyn!" Ted shouted. "Are you alright?"

"Yeah!" Marilyn called. She jumped to her feet and tried to climb over the boulder, but it started rolling. Marilyn screamed and ran.

"MARILYN!" Ted's voice was filled with horror. "Hey, no, no, Kennedy, don't go!"

"But I've got to get Marilyn!" Kennedy's voice yelled.

"Don't worry!" Marilyn called. "I'm coming!"

She could hear the frightened screams of the tourists and the loud crumbling of rocks and timbers falling. The ladder shook violently, then Marilyn heard Kennedy scream. Marilyn leaped to the side and crouched down, covering her head with her arms, and froze. She heard the boulder crash into a wall, causing more rocks and dust to come tumbling down.

It was then that the shaking ceased. Marilyn slowly lifted her head. She tried to control her shaky breathing. She dusted the dirt off her clothes and ruffled her hair.

"Mary?" Kennedy's frantic voice called out.

Marilyn gasped and spun around. "Kennedy!" she shouted. "Kennedy, where are you?"

"Over here!" Kennedy called back. "Just follow my voice!"

Marilyn shined her flashlight down the tunnel and ran ahead. Much to her relief, she found Kennedy near the ladder, which had a few broken rungs. Kennedy had just detangled herself from the caution tape. She was dusting herself off and rubbing her elbow. She bent over and picked up her bag.

"How did you get down here?" Marilyn asked.

"I wanted to come down to get you," Kennedy said. "Ted tried to stop me, but then the shaking caused me to fall off the ladder. Lucky me. I didn't hurt myself."

"So," Marilyn said, "it's just you here, I'm guessing? Did everyone else make it out?"

Kennedy looked up. "I think so," she said.

Marilyn sighed in exasperation. "Apparently we did have another earthquake," she said. "That first one was a foreshock."

"And it completely blocked our way out," Kennedy said.

Marilyn pointed the flashlight up. She gasped in horror. Kennedy was right. The entrance above the ladder had been completely covered by a huge boulder.

The girls were trapped in the shaft.

"Dandy," Kennedy said. "Just dandy! Trapped in a mine right after an earthquake that was probably bigger than the last!"

She unfolded her map.

"We might have to try to find the mine rescue chamber."

Marilyn hardly listened to her stepsister. She turned around and began stomping away.

"Marilyn!" Kennedy said abruptly. "Where are you going?"

"I'm going for the necklace," Marilyn snapped.

"Are you kidding?" Kennedy said. "Look, I know that piece of jewelry was so important to you, but how can you think about it right now?"

Marilyn spun around. "Well, I just got us trapped in an earthquake-damaged mine, all because I wanted to find some necklace. So I'm going to make all this worth it, and I am going to get that necklace."

"But this tunnel is bound to be even more dangerous than before."

"Well, I don't see how we have anything else to do while we wait for a rescue."

"Except go to the mine rescue chamber, which is our safest and most logical option right now. Who knows what could happen to us now? The entrances could be completely blocked off. We might run out of air, or die from gas poisoning, like methane or carbon dioxide, I mean, that earthquake could've caused significant damage."

"How are we gonna get to the rescue chamber?" Marilyn demanded. "The way up is blocked, remember?"

"There might be another way out of this tunnel," Kennedy said. "Please, Marilyn, please, let's just try to find it."

But Marilyn ignored her. She went down the tunnel and shined her flashlight on the ground and the walls, even lightly tapping the walls. In a few moments, Kennedy caught up with her.

They carefully made their way down the tunnel. Kennedy flinched whenever dust and little rocks fell, but Marilyn hardly paid any attention. She waved her flashlight all over the place. But she could not catch a bit of the shine that she had seen earlier. She waved the flashlight a little more. She desperately wanted to see that shine, but every time she thought she saw something and looked back, there was nothing.

"Come on, come on, come on!" she muttered. "You've got to be here!"

"Marilyn," Kennedy said, "the earthquake really did it this time."

"No, it has to be somewhere!" Marilyn said anxiously.

"I'm sorry, but I'm afraid we've lost our chance for real this time."

Marilyn stopped. Her gut told her that Kennedy was right. She had to admit defeat.

The necklace truly was gone for good this time.

Marilyn broke into tears and fell to her knees, dropping the flashlight. She covered her eyes with her hands. Her cries echoed down the tunnel.

She felt Kennedy put her hand on her shoulder. "Mary," she whispered, "I am so, so sorry about the necklace."

Marilyn touched Kennedy's fingers. "There's nothing we can do about it now," she said through choked sobs.

Kennedy kneeled next to her. Marilyn turned her blurry, tearful vision to her stepsister.

"Ken," she said, "I am very, very sorry for luring you down here. I was so certain that we would be fine. And now here we are, trapped by the mainshock."

"You're not to blame. Everyone thought that the mine was safe again."

"Yeah, sure, but if I hadn't been so determined to find that necklace . . ."

"I would've done the same thing," Kennedy said, "if I found myself in this situation. We sorely miss our parents who passed away. It is nothing to be ashamed of."

"I should've been content with what I do have," Marilyn said tearfully. "My dad, that one picture of my mother and all her books that she wrote, you and your sisters, your mother—my dear stepmother."

She wiped her eyes. "Dad said that looking at me was enough for him," she said. "That he didn't need all those valuables that he sold. He sold those things for me. He may miss them, but he doesn't regret it. I should've felt the same contentment. I should have let go of the past and looked to my future. My graduation. Then we wouldn't be here. Now we might die down here."

"I doubt it."

Marilyn looked at Kennedy in surprise. Kennedy was smiling.

"I'm sure your dad will stop at nothing to get you. To get us."

Marilyn smiled too. "I may not have gotten that necklace," she said, "but I did get something else out of all this. That there is a part of my mom with me. And I will always have it."

"Exactly," Kennedy said. "You know, my dad was very adventurous. I imagine that I got that from him. That might even explain all those risks I've taken. You know, solving mysteries?"

"Perhaps so," Marilyn said. "Dad used to say that I have my mother's spirit."

"And that could be where your determination to find this necklace came from."

"Maybe so."

Kennedy stood up. "Well," she said, "we'd better see if we can't find a way out of this tunnel."

Marilyn stood up too. "Yeah, let's," she said. She shook her flashlight and frowned. "But I think my battery's running low. The light is dimmer."

"Ah, no worries," Kennedy said, "there's a little bit of light coming from up there . . ."

She trailed off, a broad grin forming on her face.

"Ken, what is it?" Marilyn asked, raising her eyebrows.

"I can't believe we didn't notice!" Kennedy exclaimed. "There is a light coming from the entrance above the ladder!"

101

Marilyn looked up. Sure enough, a tiny ray of light shined through a little hole. Relief washed over Marilyn.

"You're right!" she said. "That would explain why we're able to breathe okay!"

"This ladder may be rickety," Kennedy said, taking hold of an intact rung on the ladder, "but I wanna take a closer look at that little hole. Perhaps we can stick something through it, like the rope, or call out to the rescue team."

Marilyn watched with bated breath as Kennedy gingerly climbed up the ladder. Luckily the rungs did not break under Kennedy's weight. She was able to get close enough to the hole to peek into it.

"It's just big enough to get something through it," she called. "But I don't hear anybody yet."

"They'll come!" Marilyn said. "We'll just have to wait."

Kennedy slowly descended back down. "I gotta admit," she said with a grin, "it's almost intriguing to be trapped in a mine after an earthquake."

Marilyn stared. "You have got to be kidding," she said.

Kennedy shrugged. "Guess it's my adventurous side coming out," she said. "I mean, first of all, we run around the Yavapai Creek Wilderness to avoid a gang of wanted bank robbers, then we mistake a mangy gray wolf for a chupacabra while chasing cattle rustlers, we found a buried treasure in Virginia City, and now here we are on an adventure in an earthquake-damaged mine."

"I'd hope not to go insane from all that danger."

"Go insane, are you kidding me, girl? I mean, yes, I like living, I've got common sense, but my adventurous side is kinda enjoying this."

Marilyn snickered. "I wonder what's next in store for us."

"I don't know, but I'm a bit eager to find out. Maybe I should be an adventurer. Travel the world. I've always wanted to travel the world."

"That would be fun. Maybe we can evade an avalanche or something like that."

The girls looked at each other and burst out laughing.

"Mom will not like any of this," Kennedy remarked. "Dear me, I hope she's not having a panic attack."

"Okay, now you really have to be kidding me," Marilyn said, "because I'm certain that she is."

They laughed again.

"I may have grown up without a mother," Marilyn said, "but I do know that mothers tend to worry about their children a lot. And if I know Caitlin, no mine is gonna get in her way. Or my dad's. You know, Ken, I truly have appreciated your mom as my stepmother, but after this, I am sure I will appreciate her even more. She truly is the mother I've never had."

"I am thankful to have her as my mom," Kennedy said. "And I must admit, as much as I miss my dad, I enjoy having your dad as my stepfather."

"I think we've learned a lesson on letting go of the past," Marilyn said, "and moving forward in life. And about God's protection."

"Yeah." Kennedy laughed. "If anybody can testify to God's protection, it's definitely us!"

Kennedy's smile faltered a little. "Seriously, though," she said, "we should pray."

"Yes, that's a good idea," Marilyn agreed.

The girls took each other's hands. Kennedy said a brief prayer.

"Heavenly Father, we come to you this moment. Thank you for protecting us and giving us air. Please let a rescue come for us soon. Amen."

The second Kennedy said "Amen", there came a faint sound of voices from above.

"Do you hear that?" Kennedy asked.

Marilyn spun around and looked up the ladder. "Yes," she said, "I hear voices!"

She dropped her flashlight and flew up the rungs. Then she realized Kennedy was not behind her. She looked down. Kennedy was pointing the flashlight to the ground and bending over.

"Hey, what are you doing?" Marilyn asked.

Kennedy looked up at her, grinning. "I think I found—"

A familiar voice from above interrupted Kennedy.

"Hello? Anyone down there?"

"Kennedy!" Marilyn said. "It's Ted! I hear him!"

Kennedy stood up and shined the flashlight at Marilyn. "Good, good!" she called back. "Yell, get his attention!"

Marilyn did exactly that.

"TED!"

"Marilyn?" Ted's voice called. "Hello? Marilyn? Is that you? Are you alright?"

"Yes, it's me, Ted!" Marilyn replied. "Me and Kennedy, we're both down here, safe and sound!"

"Oh, thank heavens!" Ted's voice was filled with relief. "I have a rescue team with me, hon, as well as a backup team waiting outside. Your parents are here too. I'll have someone go tell them that you two are okay."

"But what about this boulder?" Marilyn asked, tapping the bottom of the rock with her hand. "How are we gonna move it?"

"Ah, shouldn't be terribly hard. It's actually smaller than you probably think it is. Just stay back while we work, okay?"

"Sure thing!"

Marilyn descended back down and ran to Kennedy's side. The two girls squealed with delight, embracing each other and praising God for His rapid answer to their prayer.

Marilyn listened to the drilling and mining of the debris on the other side, as well as the huffs and deep breaths of the men who were working to push the rock away from the entrance of the shaft. Ted even allowed a couple members of the backup team to enter and help out to make the work go faster. Marilyn silently prayed that there would be no more injuries or setbacks.

And it all proved fruitful. The rock was removed from the entrance. Light allowed Marilyn to see Ted and the other miners looking down at her and Kennedy.

"Well, what are you ladies standing down there for?" Ted asked, grinning. "Come on up!"

The girls rushed up the ladder. The men helped them climb out of the shaft. In no time, they were exiting the mine. Marilyn squinted at the bright sunlight, but she was still smiling.

Cheers and applause erupted from the other miners, the police, and the rest of the onlookers. Marilyn saw Felicity holding up the yellow tape to allow her father and Caitlin through. Marilyn and Kennedy embraced their parents.

"Oh, I'm so glad you made it out of there!" Dad said.

"Are you girls alright?" Caitlin asked anxiously. "No cuts, broken bones . . ."

"Oh, we're fine," Kennedy said. "Maybe a minor bruise or two, and we're covered in dirt and grime, but we're good."

While Kennedy was hugging her mother, Dad took Marilyn aside.

"Marilyn, dear," he said, "you mean more to me than some old necklace. Look, I am sorry that you didn't find it."

"Oh, Dad, it's okay," Marilyn said. Tears filled her eyes. "I know what's more important now."

"Uh, wait, hold on a second!" Kennedy said, running up to them. "Mary, I am so sorry, I didn't get to tell you, but I found this."

She reached into her bag and pulled out a necklace caked in old dirt and grime. Marilyn gasped. Dad covered his mouth with his hand and looked at Caitlin.

"Is . . . is that . . ."

"It might be," Kennedy said. She rubbed her thumb against the silver pendant, scrubbing off some of the gunk. A tiny white diamond was revealed to be inserted in the pendant. Kennedy then turned the pendant around.

"Look at the back," she said, handing the necklace to Marilyn.

Marilyn could hardly breathe as she looked at the inscription on the back of the silver pendant.

"'I and B,'" she said softly.

Dad gasped. "For 'Isaiah and Bonnie'," he said. He looked closer at the necklace. Tears brimmed in his eyes. "I recognize this necklace. It is indeed the one that I had given to your mother, Marilyn."

Marilyn's eyes filled with tears. She looked up at Kennedy.

"Oh, Ken," she said, her voice breaking, "you found it! Oh, how can I ever thank you?"

"No need to," Kennedy said.

Ted and Felicity came over. Felicity put her hand on Marilyn's shoulder.

"I heard everything," she said. She smiled at the necklace that lay in Marilyn's hand. "I'm so happy for you, Mary. You found your mother's necklace after all."

"Good to know our search wasn't in vain," Ted said.

Marilyn looked down at the necklace. "This can be like a graduation gift from my mom," she said. "And a symbol of what I've learned. To move forward, and leave the past be."

She then turned to Caitlin. "I take it you know all about this necklace?"

"I do, hon," Caitlin said. She was also smiling. "I'm not hurt at all. Why, if Kennedy here were in your place, oh, sweetheart, I do understand."

Relief filled the pit of Marilyn's stomach. She wrapped her arms around Caitlin.

"You're a wonderful mom."

With tears in her eyes, Caitlin patted her stepdaughter's head.

"Well," Dad said, "this calls for a celebration. Let's say we head home and get cleaned up, then we'll go to the mall and have some pizza and ice cream."

"Yeah, pizza sounds good," Marilyn said. "Anything sounds good, really. Just realized that I'm famished."

"Me too!" Kennedy said.

Marilyn stared at herself in the backstage mirror as she tugged at her braid. She was standing in line with Kennedy. They were waiting their turn to go on stage and receive their diplomas. She took her necklace out from behind her black graduation gown and looked at it.

Having been buried in a mine shaft for over twenty years, the necklace had needed a serious cleanup. But it was treated well by the local jewelers, and Marilyn was now wearing it for her graduation ceremony. Even now, she could not believe her luck or contain her relief that it had actually been found.

The principal called out another name. The boy in front of Kennedy and Marilyn walked onto the stage.

"We're next, Mary," Kennedy whispered excitedly.

Sure enough, in just a moment, the principal called out the last two names.

"Marilyn Bonnie Wilson and Kennedy Miriam Ryan, daughters of Isaiah and Caitlin Wilson!"

The two girls walked out. They heard the excited screams of Victoria and Jessica in the audience. They hugged their parents and gave them their roses, and Dad and Caitlin gave the girls their diplomas. The foursome posed for a picture. Marilyn noticed that Caitlin was wearing her own necklace, the one she had received from Dad for her birthday. But Marilyn didn't mind in the least.

After the ceremony was over, families and friends gathered in the school cafeteria for the reception. Almost immediately, Marilyn and Kennedy were bombarded with questions about their adventure in the mine. Marilyn was more than happy to show off her necklace.

"So," Billy said jokingly, "why did you ladies have this mine adventure without me?"

"Wasn't our fault." Kennedy sniggered. "Pun intended."

106

Billy laughed.

"Dude," Felicity said, "I'm glad you weren't in there. It was bad enough worrying about two of my little friends, I'd hate to see my little brother trapped in there."

"I'm not little," Billy said defensively.

Felicity chuckled. Then she turned to Marilyn.

"I'm really happy that you and Kennedy were able to recover that necklace," she said. "It's so wonderful to see you back to your old cheerful self again."

Just then Dad approached the kids. "Hate to interrupt," he said, "but Marilyn, your mom wants to see you."

Marilyn went over to Caitlin. She noticed that her stepmother was holding a tiny black box.

"What's up, Mom?" Marilyn asked.

Caitlin smiled. "Well, yesterday, while doing some last-minute gift shopping, I saw this at the jewelry store. I thought they'd look wonderful with your necklace. The one you and Kennedy found."

Caitlin handed Marilyn the box. Marilyn opened it and gasped. She stared at the pair of diamond earrings.

She smiled at Caitlin and wrapped her arms around her. "Thank you. They're perfect! You're the most wonderful mother ever!"

Escape From Under the Mendenhall Glacier

*W*ITHOUT MAKING A sound, Victoria Ryan slipped behind the boulder. She kneeled by its side, peeking her head out from behind her hiding place.

Hardly daring to breathe, she spied on the creature. It was indeed a black wolf, but it wasn't hairless. And its tracks remained in the snow.

"I knew it!" she whispered to herself. "It's not a keelut, like everyone was saying! But I, Victoria Ryan, was not fooled!"

The wolf turned its head in her direction. Gasping, Victoria tore her head away. She hoped that the animal did not see her.

That wolf was huge. Bigger than that Mexican gray wolf that Victoria had almost believed was a chupacabra . . .

No! Don't think about that! Oh, great, here come the embarrassing memories and the snide remarks of your classmates.

"Victoria, I cannot believe you actually thought that mangy gray wolf was a chupacabra . . ."

"Hey, Vicky, how does it feel to have been fooled by Facebook into thinking a gray wolf was a real chupacabra?"

"You're always chasing fantasies!"

No, NO! Alright, just push those thoughts away, Vicky. That's it. Now, we need to decide how you are going to survive your encounter with the black wolf that everyone except you believes is a keelut.

"Victoria?"

Kennedy's voice snapped Victoria out of her daydream. She turned her head to look at her older sister, who was sitting across the aisle from her.

"You okay?" Kennedy asked. "You've been really quiet during the whole ride. You and Jessica."

Victoria shrugged. "Just tired," she said.

Kennedy did not look convinced. "Well, I did expect you and Jessica to be really excited and talking nonstop," she said. "You just loved the idea of exploring Alaska. And I was certain that Jessica would be excited about studying the glacier's geology."

A pang of jealousy gnawed at Victoria's stomach. "Yeah, she is a science nerd, isn't she?" she remarked. She quickly changed the subject. "Well, I think it's almost time to get off the plane."

She stood up. Her younger sister, Jessica, who had been sitting in the window seat, also stood.

"Kennedy's not wrong," Jessica whispered. She stood on her tiptoes as though she was trying to reach Victoria's ear. "We really should be more excited. This is a family vacation, after all."

"I know," Victoria said. "And you don't need to stand on your toes, Jess."

With a sheepish look on her face, Jessica let her feet fall back. Victoria gave her sister an apologetic look.

"Sorry," she whispered. "I didn't mean it like that."

"It's fine."

But Victoria still felt a pang of guilt as Jessica brushed past her. Holding a sigh, Victoria followed her, Kennedy, and their stepsister, Marilyn Wilson, off the plane.

"Hey, everyone, look at that!" Marilyn called. She ran toward the large windows. She set her suitcase down and pressed her nose against the window, staring in awe at the enormous Mendenhall Glacier in the distance.

Jessica walked over to Marilyn's side. She smiled meekly at the beautiful view.

"I'll bet you're excited to give us a lecture on the glacier's geology," Marilyn said to Jessica.

"Well, I don't want to bore anyone," Jessica said.

"Oh, you won't, honey," Mom said. "We know how much you love science."

Jessica just shrugged. Yes, her family did know how much she loved science. And so had her envious classmates the previous spring.

"Hey, look over there," Kennedy said, pointing. "It's the Hummingbird Hollow Gifts shop. Do we have time to check it out?"

Isaiah smiled. "I think we do," he said. "But we shouldn't take too long."

Kennedy and Marilyn rushed over to the gift shop. Jessica followed them. The gift shop had a wide variety of items on sale. There were shelves loaded with jewelry, tote bags, and sweatshirts. Several dreamcatchers of bright, colorful hues hung from a rack on the ceiling.

Jessica went over to a bookshelf. On the top shelf, she spotted a book with the words MENDENHALL GLACIER GEOLOGY on its spine.

Smiling a little, Jessica stood on her toes and reached her hand up. But she was still unable to reach the book.

Sighing, Jessica lowered her hand. Her eyes wandered to the yellow price tag below the book. She frowned.

It is a little expensive. Besides, I don't suppose I need another geology book. My classmates would never let me hear the end of it.

"Hey, Jess, need a little help reaching that book?"

Jessica turned around. Isaiah was walking toward her.

Forcing a smile, Jessica waved her hand dismissively. "Nah. I don't think I really want it."

"Are you sure?" Isaiah said. He looked up at the book. "It's definitely something you'd enjoy reading."

Jessica hesitated. "Well, it's a bit spendy anyway."

But as Isaiah turned away, Jessica cast a longing look at the book. She tore herself away and crossed her arms.

At least my classmates aren't here to see my inability to reach that book. Gosh, if only I was taller!

"Hey, girls," Mom said, "we should be heading to the lobby to get our luggage. I'm sure the bus will be here soon."

Jessica glanced over her shoulder at the bookshelf as she followed her family out of the gift shop.

"Well, here we are!" Isaiah said. "Our hotel!"

Victoria shivered as she stepped out of the bus. "Finally," she said. "Can we go inside, please? It's freezing out here!"

"I agree, honey," Mom said.

They went into the lobby. Isaiah went over to the front desk to check in. Victoria sat down on an easy chair in front of the lobby's fireplace. The lobby appeared cozy with its fireplace, wooden mantel, and dark green, floral-print carpet. It also had three vending machines lined up against one wall and pictures of the Mendenhall Glacier, a woodland, and a lake hanging on other walls.

In a few minutes, Isaiah and Mom were leading the girls upstairs to the second floor.

"Alrighty," Isaiah said, "our rooms are right next to one another. They have adjoining doors. Girls, you have Room 207. Mom and I have 209."

Marilyn inserted the key card into the door's silver lock. A tiny green light flashed, and Marilyn opened it and let the girls in.

"Wow," Kennedy said, "this is a really nice room."

Victoria had to agree. The room had two queen beds and a sofa. A table with two chairs stood next to a long chest of drawers, on which a TV sat. Two easy chairs stood in front of the window.

Marilyn pulled out the sofa bed from underneath its cushions. "I'll take the sofa bed," she said.

Victoria laid her suitcase on the queen bed closer to the window.

"Jess and I can share this bed," she said.

"So," Kennedy said, "what's bothering the two of you?"

Victoria looked up from her suitcase. She and Jessica exchanged glances, then they turned around to face Kennedy.

"It's nothing," Victoria said, looking down at her feet.

"Aw, come on, I know there's something wrong," Kennedy said. "You can tell me."

"Well," Jessica said slowly, "Victoria and I were having trouble with being bullied by our classmates this past spring."

Victoria scowled at her sister.

Kennedy raised an eyebrow. "You have?" she said.

"What were they saying?" Marilyn asked.

"Well, I've been teased about being the shortest kid in my classes," Jessica said. "And some of my classmates seem to be a little jealous of my good grades in my science classes. I've been called a science nerd. But not in a nice way."

But at least you are good at science, Victoria thought glumly. *Nobody's teasing you about thinking some dumb gray wolf was a chupacabra.*

"I'm very sorry to hear that," Marilyn said. She looked at Victoria. "What about you, Vic?"

Victoria hesitated. "I've been teased about mistaking that Mexican gray wolf for a chupacabra," she admitted. She did not meet any of her sisters' eyes. "I do feel really silly about it now."

"But that was a year ago," Kennedy said. "And you weren't the only one who thought that gray wolf could've been a chupacabra, Vic. But why didn't either of you say anything to anyone? Like Mom, for instance?"

"Because the two of you were very distracted with all the drama caused by the earthquakes in Pine Lodge and Marilyn's mother's long-lost necklace," Victoria said. "The truth is, Jessica and I feel inferior to the two of you. We've just made mistakes, like thinking a gray wolf was a chupacabra while you go on exciting adventures. Like stopping a gang of criminals, saving our uncle's ranch from rustlers, and finding a lost treasure in Montana. You even got out of the Michael Williamson Mine right after an earthquake."

Kennedy and Marilyn looked at one another. Then Kennedy walked over to Victoria and Jessica and took their hands. She smiled sympathetically.

"I'm so sorry to hear this," she said. "But you two are special to me. And Marilyn. Besides, lots of people thought that the gray wolf was a chupacabra, even the kids at school. So, who are they to talk? And Jess, your height does not define who you are. You know, I've always wished to be a genius at science the way you are. Me and Victoria both."

"Same with me," Marilyn said.

"And remember," Kennedy said, "you're not alone in dealing with bullies at school. I used to have that problem too. I know how you two feel."

Jessica smiled. "Well, that is true."

Victoria forced a feeble smile. But she still did not feel better about herself.

"Oh my, the glacier is so much more magnificent up close!" Marilyn exclaimed.

Jessica smiled. She had to agree with her stepsister. The Mendenhall Glacier gleamed under the blue sky. It appeared to be perfectly wedged in between two mountain peaks. The shimmering Mendenhall Lake right in front of the gigantic body of ice added to the white and blue scenery.

"It sure is warm," Kennedy said. She took off her jacket.

"Yeah, it is warmer than I expected, even for June," Mom said. "But I would still advise that you keep your jacket with you. And we should head over to the visitor's center. Our tour begins in an hour."

"I'm really looking forward to seeing Jessica's reactions when we get into the ice caves," Marilyn said. She gave Jessica a hopeful smile.

"I'm sure the tour guide will share geological info with us," Jessica said.

"Are you okay, dear?" Isaiah asked. "You've been quiet today. You and Victoria. That's not normal for the two of you."

Jessica made herself smile wider. "Oh, sure," she said. "Just fine."

Kennedy and Marilyn stared at Jessica with their knowing looks. Jessica hoped that they would not say anything to Mom and Isaiah about being bullied in school. She wanted her family to enjoy their vacation, not worry about school problems.

At the visitor center, Isaiah and Mom went to the front desk while the girls wandered over to the gift shop. It was a small shop. There was a little table standing in the middle of the floor, just across from the checkout counter. Wooden animal toys, a box of woodland drawings, and other souvenirs stood displayed on the table. Even the windows had shelves filled with books and stuffed animals.

Jessica stared at the wide and empty room just adjacent to the gift shop. A middle-aged woman was peeking through the telescope facing the window.

"Hey, Jess," Marilyn said, "here's a book you might be interested in."

Jessica walked back into the shop. She went over to the shelves by the window. Marilyn was holding open a book.

"It's a book on the formation of Mendenhall Glacier."

Jessica looked at the book's front cover, but she did not take it when Marilyn offered it to her.

"Don't you want to look?" Marilyn asked.

"Well, it does look interesting," Jessica said. "What's in it?"

Marilyn flipped through a few pages. "They have a lot," she said. "The first chapter is on the geological history of the glacier. Ooh, they even have a chapter on avalanches near the area!"

Jessica's interest was aroused. She stood next to Marilyn to look at the pages.

"Wow, look at that picture," Marilyn said. "That avalanche looks like it was a really bad one. Close to the glacier, too! Hey, what's this?"

She turned the page and gasped quietly.

"They have lakes under the glacier?" she said in disbelief.

"Yeah," Jessica said. "Subglacial lakes. If we go under the glacier, we might see one."

Marilyn turned the book over. "This is a good price," she said. "You wanna buy it?"

Jessica shrugged. "I'll think about it."

She turned around and went over to a shelf filled with resin animal figurines. Jessica gazed at them admirably. She looked up at the taller shelf. A mountain goat figurine stood just above her, staring down at her. It was so beautifully crafted that it looked real.

Wanting a closer look, Jessica stood on her toes and reached her arm up for the figurine. But she could not reach. And she was only off by an inch or two. Jessica sighed.

"Need a hand?"

Jessica turned around to see who spoke. Standing before her was a teenage boy, probably around sixteen years old. He had neat, dark brown hair, grayish-blue eyes, and a tall and slim figure.

"Uh," Jessica stammered, forcing herself to smile awkwardly, "j-just looking at that mountain goat up there, but I can't seem to reach it. Too short, I'm afraid."

"Let me," the boy said. He walked over to the shelf and lifted his hand. With ease he took the figurine off the top shelf.

"Thank you," Jessica said shyly as the boy handed it to her. She had to keep herself from sighing, but she could not fight off her embarrassment. If only she wasn't so petite!

"No problem," the boy said with a smile. "Are you here for the tour?"

"Yeah," Jessica said. "Me and my family."

"Cool. Name's Nathan, by the way."

Jessica shook his hand. "I'm Jessica."

"Oh, there you are, Jess!"

Jessica turned around. Kennedy was walking toward her and Nathan. Jessica noticed that Kennedy had a magazine in her hand.

"Tour's about to begin," Kennedy said. "Our family's in the lobby."

Jessica looked longingly at the figurine that she was holding. She hoped that she would be able to buy it later. For the time being, though, it had to be put back on the shelf.

"Are you going on the tour too?" she asked Nathan as he replaced the figurine. For some reason, part of her hoped that he would be.

"Sure am," Nathan said. "My uncle will be leading it. I guess I'll be meeting you in a few moments."

"Yeah. See you then."

Jessica left with Kennedy.

"Who was that?" Kennedy asked.

"Uh, just a guy who helped me get that goat thing I was holding," Jessica said quickly.

Kennedy smiled. "Well, he seemed pretty nice."

Jessica glanced back. "He was."

Victoria gazed at the clock. When was the tour going to begin? It seemed like she, Marilyn, Mom, and Isaiah had been standing in the lobby for an eternity.

"Ah, here comes Kennedy with Jessica now," Isaiah said.

Victoria looked over at Kennedy and Jessica, who were leaving the gift shop. Envy filled the pit of Victoria's stomach as she stared at Jessica.

She's going to enjoy this tour for sure. Her love for everything science will come out. I just know it will. If only I was as smart as her. Then I wouldn't have thought that gray wolf was some chupacabra.

Kennedy went over to Victoria's side. "Hey, Vic," she said, smiling, "I bought this from the gift shop. I figured we'd both enjoy it."

Kennedy held up a magazine. Victoria took it and flipped through its pages. It had articles about several creatures from Alaskan folklore.

"The kushtaka and the keelut are mentioned in there," Kennedy said.

"I see." Victoria turned another page. "Hey, there's an article about the Alaska Triangle."

An older gentleman appeared from behind the front desk. He was tall with a broad figure. He wore glasses over his brown eyes and a helmet over his neat brown hair. Victoria spotted a teenage boy standing next to him. The boy was carrying a dark green backpack. Jessica smiled shyly at the boy and waved at him.

"Does Jessica know him?" Victoria whispered to Kennedy.

"She met him in the gift shop just now," Kennedy said. "His name's Nathan."

"Hello, everyone," the man greeted in a loud voice, "I'm your tour guide, Richard Bell. This is Nathan, my nephew and assistant. I'm pleased to be leading you on a tour of the ice caves of the Mendenhall Glacier. Before we leave, I would like to ask you to please stay with the tour at all times. Wandering off on your own is dangerous, especially if you have no knowledge of the surrounding wilderness. Please help us keep the area clean by appropriately disposing of your garbage items in available trash cans. Alrighty, let me take a roll call and make sure we have everyone. Nathan, will you count our guests?"

Nathan started counting. Victoria looked around to see who was going on the tour. It was a very small number of people. Other than Victoria and her family, there was a lanky, brown-haired man who appeared to be in his early thirties. Standing next to him was a willowy, gray-haired woman who was probably in her early to mid-sixties. Standing on the man's other side was a tall boy, taller than Jessica. Victoria noticed that he was wearing a black brace around his left knee.

"Everyone present and accounted for, Uncle Richard," Nathan said. He patted his backpack. "And I've got all our usual supplies in here."

Richard and Nathan led the guests out of the visitor center.

"This will be so exciting," Marilyn said. "I feel so lucky that we're gonna see the ice caves."

"I just hope my old bones can handle the long hike," the gray-haired woman said with a chuckle.

"Aw, Mom, you're still pretty spry," the brown-haired man said. "You used to teach gymnastics. You'll do just fine."

"I appreciate your confidence, Paul," the woman said with a smile.

The tall boy frowned. "You might even do better than me, Grandma," he said. He kicked his left foot forward. "You're not wearing a brace."

The man, Paul, frowned. "You'll be just fine, Colin," he said.

The woman patted the boy's shoulder. Then she looked over at Kennedy, Victoria, Jessica, and Isaiah.

"So, what are your names?" she asked.

Isaiah introduced himself and the girls.

"Good to meet you," the woman said. "I'm Gail. This is my son Paul and my grandson Colin. We're from Juneau. We came here on a day trip."

"Where are you from?" Paul asked.

"We're from Pine Lodge," Isaiah said. "It's a little town in Arizona."

"Arizona?" Paul grinned. "Wow, did the summer heat of the desert drive you up here to icy Alaska?"

Isaiah laughed. "Not exactly. Though it is nice to be somewhere cool on our family vacation."

Paul chuckled. "I've only been to Arizona once in my life." He peered down the sidewalk. "I think we're approaching a trail."

Paul was right. The group indeed arrived at a trail.

"This is the West Glacier Trail," Nathan said in a loud voice. "It'll lead us to the ice caves."

Everyone exchanged excited glances. Even Victoria had to smile. She was looking forward to seeing the ice caves.

"If you look over there," Nathan called, pointing toward Mendenhall Lake, "you can see Stroller White Mountain, just to the left of Mendenhall Glacier. And that's McGinnis Mountain."

He moved his finger in the opposite direction. "And over there is Bullard Mountain."

He paused and looked at Richard. "Did I get it right?" he asked.

Richard chuckled. "You did," he said.

Everyone laughed. Everyone, that is, except Victoria.

Of course he would've gotten it right, she thought gloomily. *I would've messed it up. I can't even tell the difference between a legendary chupacabra and a real-life Mexican gray wolf with mange.*

117

She held her hand over her eyes. The mountains on either side of the glacier were beautiful. Victoria wondered what it would be like to hike to the top of the glacier. She grinned; perhaps they would do that!

"There's plenty more mountains," Nathan said. "Thunder Mountain offers a wonderful view of the glacier. It's from the top of Thunder Mountain where Steep Creek flows. The creek empties into Mendenhall Lake and is fed by rainwater and snowmelt. The creek is known to rise dramatically during heavy rainfall. So does anyone here know how Thunder Mountain got its name?"

Victoria saw Kennedy elbowing Jessica.

"You know," Kennedy whispered. "Come on, go for it."

Jessica hesitated. "Uh," she said, "because Thunder Mountain is known for its avalanches."

"Correct!" Nathan said. He grinned; he looked impressed. Jessica blushed. Victoria sighed quietly and crossed her arms. She tore her eyes away from Jessica and looked at her feet.

Richard and Nathan led everyone deeper into the forest. The scent of fresh vegetation filled the air. On both sides of the trail stood many cottonwoods, alders, and willows.

"Break!" Richard called. "Let's take a break!"

Colin plopped down on the ground with his back to a boulder. He held his braced knee up. Victoria frowned; she hoped that he was not in any pain.

"You okay?" she asked him. She and Jessica sat down next to him.

Colin looked up. "Sure," he said. He scowled at his brace. "Just wish I didn't have to wear this brace for another two months."

"What happened?" Victoria asked. "I mean, if you don't mind me asking."

"Nah, it's cool," Colin said. "A few months ago, I was playing basketball. I'm on the basketball team at my private school, you see. I got tackled by some jerks on the opposing team after I scored a winning basket. Let's just say they were a little too rough. I tore a ligament in my knee."

Jessica clapped her hand over her mouth. "Ouch."

"Ouch is right," Colin said. He hung his head. "The doctor stuck me with this brace. Now I can't play sports until it comes off. I feel like the most important thing to me was just taken away. So far, middle school has been the worst."

"So you like playing sports?" Victoria asked.

"Like it?" Colin looked straight at her. "I love sports, girl. I was in Little League when I was six."

Victoria frowned. She felt annoyed with herself; obviously Colin loved sports.

"Wait a second," Jessica said, "you're in middle school?"

Colin nodded. "I'm eleven years old. I know, I'm tall for my age."

Victoria's eyes widened. Colin was only eleven years old? But he was almost as tall as Kennedy!

Jessica lowered her eyes. But Victoria could still see the envy in them.

"The plants are really nice," Kennedy said, "but I was really hoping that we'd see some animals."

"We still might," Nathan said.

Colin grinned. "Maybe we'll see a kushtaka," he said.

Victoria looked up, curiosity aroused.

"What's a kushtaka?" Marilyn asked.

"A shape-shifting spirit from Tlingit folklore," Colin said. "It looks kinda like an otter-human hybrid. It's said to lead sailors to their watery grave. But some kushtaka spirits are much nicer. They may save you from freezing to death by turning you into a kushtaka. In fact, some people believe the kushtaka is responsible for the many disappearances in Alaska."

"Wait, disappearances?" Jessica looked around warily. "We are safe, right?"

Nathan sniggered. "Yes, my uncle's led numerous tours with no incidents," he said. He put his hand on his chin. "Though, we are fairly close to the infamous Alaska Triangle where there's an alarming rate of disappearances per year."

"Nathan," Marilyn said playfully, "I'm not sure your uncle wants you scaring us tourists."

Everyone chuckled. Victoria smiled.

"I've heard of the Alaska Triangle," she said. "And the kushtaka."

"But why would so many vanish in that part of the state?" Marilyn asked.

"It's most likely inexperienced travelers falling prey to the wildlife and terrain," Nathan said.

"Or it could be energy vortexes that lead to other dimensions, or aliens, or other malevolent spirits," Colin said with a smirk.

Paul chuckled. "Don't mind my son," he said. "He really likes to read about Alaska's legends and folklore."

"Then maybe I should let him take over the parts of our tour on folklore," Richard joked.

"He'd like that," Paul said. "He's basically an expert."

Victoria grinned at Colin. "I really like reading folklore too," she said.

After a few minutes, the tour continued hiking up the trail. Richard droned on about animals and plant life. They took a short break every twenty minutes. After their last break, Victoria looked ahead of the trail. Just beyond the many trees, she could make out what looked like a huge wall of blue ice.

"Alright," Richard called, "if you look ahead and above all these trees, you can see the glacier itself. We will be approaching one of the ice caves very soon."

Victoria's heart leapt. The ice walls were becoming more visible. In a few minutes, the group was walking toward a huge wall made entirely of light blue ice. Just in front of the group, there was a large opening in the ice.

Richard stood in front of everyone. "Alright, now," he said, holding up his hands, "before we go in, let me be clear on one thing: stay with the group. Ice caves are fun to explore, but they can be very dangerous. Now, let's go under Mendenhall Glacier!"

Victoria cast a glance at Jessica. Her wide eyes were filled with awe. Victoria frowned.

I know what she's thinking. Glacial facts and geological history running through her mind. Man, if only I was a smart and gifted science prodigy like her.

Almost as soon as the tour entered the cave, Jessica heard the snapping of cell phone cameras. She stared in awe at the ice cave herself. It was more magnificent than she could have ever imagined. Some of the icy walls were covered in what appeared to be big, frozen blue bubbles. Jessica could barely see her own distorted reflection flicking through those bubbles. Water droplets trickled down from the large icicles hanging from the blue ceiling. Other walls were smoother, almost like mirrors.

"This is so amazing!" Kennedy said. "This place looks like it could be a magical ice castle!"

"I know!" Marilyn said. She turned to Jessica. "So why are the walls blue, Jess?"

Jessica hesitated. "Well," she said, "because they absorb all light from the color spectrum except blue. They emit the blue light, thus giving the ice its color."

"Couldn't have said it better myself."

Jessica turned around. Richard was grinning at her. Standing just behind him, Nathan was staring at her with an impressed look on his face. Jessica blushed.

"Do you know the other names for this glacier?" Richard asked.

Jessica's smile disappeared. She shook her head.

"One was Sitaantaagu," Richard said. "Another original name was Aak'wtaaksit. The current name *Mendenhall* came from Thomas Corwin Mendenhall in the 1890's. He studied physics and meteorology."

Jessica nodded. She looked over at the glassy ice walls and gazed at her reflection. She wanted to feel better about herself; after all, Richard seemed impressed with her. But she still could not stop thinking about her classmates back home.

"Pretty, isn't it?"

Jessica looked up. Nathan was standing by her side.

"Yes, very pretty," she agreed. She smiled. "So, do you do these tours often?"

"Yep. I love going on tours with my uncle. I really enjoy studying the geological history of the glacier and the mountains and everything."

Jessica's smile broadened. "I'm a bit of a science person myself," she said.

"I noticed." Nathan looked right at her. "I was impressed."

A yelp echoed throughout the cave. Jessica gasped and spun around. Colin was on his knees, having apparently tripped. Paul and Gail ran over to him, worry filling their eyes.

"Colin!" Paul said. "Are you alright?"

Jessica and Nathan walked over. The others were also beginning to gather around.

Colin brushed his father's hand off his shoulder. "Yeah, yeah, just fine," he said. "No need to get fussy, Dad."

"How's your knee?"

Colin stood up. He gingerly rubbed the brace over his knee. "It's okay," he said. "Didn't hurt too bad."

"Are you sure?"

Colin groaned. "Positive," he said defensively. "Look, Dad, I don't need a reminder that a bunch of bullies might have ruined my ability to play sports for life."

Colin pulled away from his father and walked away.

"I'm very sorry about that," Paul said to Richard. "My son suffered a torn knee ligament in school."

His worrisome eyes wandered after his son. "Colin used to enjoy playing sports in school," he said. "But, well, after he won a basketball game for his team, some sore losers ganged up on him."

Jessica heard her mother stifle a gasp.

"The doctor diagnosed his knee injury as a grade three tear," Paul added.

Jessica's eyes widened.

"Colin has a couple more months until the brace comes off," Paul said. "But as for his future in sports, well, we will just wait and see what the Lord provides."

Silence fell over the group. Finally, Richard and Nathan continued leading everyone through the ice cave.

"Think Colin will be okay?" Kennedy whispered to Jessica. "The poor guy, losing his ability to play sports because of some sore losers."

Jessica nodded. "Well, I do know that when a torn knee ligament is a grade three, it's very serious," she said. "I remember studying about those in my anatomy class."

She gazed at Colin. He seemed to be walking slowly compared to everyone else. A wave of pity washed over Jessica. To suffer because of bullies? She knew exactly how that felt.

Soon the group came out of a second cave opening. Before them was a hilly landscape with very few trees. Rocky ledges jutted out of the snow-covered hills.

"Where are we?" Marilyn asked.

"The ice cave led us to the top of McGinnis Mountain," Richard said.

He and Nathan led the tourists on another trail. Jessica looked back longingly at the glacier. She really wanted to hike on top of its icy roofs.

"If you look over there," Richard said, pointing backward, "you can see the Mendenhall towers."

Everyone looked back. Jessica smiled. Far in the distance, she saw the majestic black granite peaks that were the Mendenhall towers.

"Hey," Nathan said, bending over, "this rock is really pretty. I like the black spots. Might have to keep it for my rock collection."

"You collect rocks?" Jessica said. She had considered starting a rock collection herself, but the taunts of her classmates caused her to put it off.

"Sure," Nathan said. "Studying rocks is one of my favorite hobbies. So can you tell what kind of rock this is?"

Jessica looked at the rock in Nathan's hand. "It's tonalite," she said. "It's an igneous quartz-rich, diorite rock. Eroded by

Mendenhall Glacier itself, no doubt. They're bound to be in the glacier sediments all over the place."

"Yeah!" Nathan looked impressed. "What else?"

"Well, these rocks have magnetic minerals."

"Yep," Nathan said. He grinned. "That's why the darker sands are attracted to magnets. Sometimes I carry magnets with me so I can watch these dark sands cling onto them. Good job, Jess."

Jessica smiled a little. She wasn't blushing too much. Oddly enough, she was feeling somewhat proud of herself. At least Nathan was impressed and not taunting her.

"Look over there!" Paul called. "There's a mountain goat!"

The group looked at the towering rocks above the trail. Jessica gasped. Sure enough, a mountain goat stood on top of one of the ledges. He stared curiously at the tourists as they took pictures of him.

"Wow," Jessica whispered to herself, "that goat looks just like the figurine from the gift shop."

"It sure does." Nathan smiled at her.

Several howls pierced the air. Everyone gasped and looked around anxiously. Jessica grasped Nathan's shoulder. He gave her an odd look. Jessica quickly let go and lowered her eyes.

"Ah, wolves!" Richard said with a smile.

"Are they close?" Mom asked.

"No, I wouldn't think so," the tour guide said reassuringly.

"Let's just hope none of them are actually keeluts!" Colin said. "Vicious black dogs that leave no footprints in the snow, so we wouldn't know if one was sneaking around and stalking us!"

Victoria burst out laughing.

"Oh, please don't, I'm already nervous enough as it is," Kennedy said. "And . . . hang on, do you guys hear a rumbling sound?"

Jessica listened. She heard low rumbling in the distance. The mountain goat bleated nervously and sprinted away.

"Could it be rocks?" Victoria asked. "Falling off a ridge or something?"

"No, doesn't sound like rocks falling," Nathan said.

Suddenly Richard screamed. "Everyone, follow me! Run!"

Jessica's heart skipped several beats and her stomach churned. What was going on?

The rumbling noise became louder. Jessica looked back. And she immediately felt sick.

An avalanche was charging toward them!

Screams erupted as the tourists took off. Jessica tried not to look back. But she did, and she ended up grabbing Nathan's hand. Nathan looked at her. Jessica tried to let go, but Nathan had already tightened his grip on her hand. She plugged her right ear with her free hand. She felt like the roar of the avalanche would blast out her eardrums.

"Colin!" Paul shouted. "Where are you?"

"I'm right behind you, Dad!" Colin yelled.

Jessica saw Colin running over to his father's side. Despite his braced knee, he seemed to be running without any trouble.

Fortunately, they found a large ice opening in the glacier. Richard led everyone inside just as a massive amount of snow from the avalanche completely filled up the entrance.

Victoria's eyes were squeezed shut. She could hardly tell if she was shivering because of the cold or because of her fear. Her heart was certainly beating fast and hard enough against her chest.

"Is everybody alright?" Richard's voice echoed down the ice cave.

Victoria opened her eyes and slowly stood up. Everyone else seemed to be just fine, if not shaken. Colin was sitting down on the icy floor, rubbing his braced knee. Paul and Gail were standing over him with worried looks on their faces. Marilyn was bending over, her hands clutching her knees. Kennedy was hugging Jessica, who was hiding her face in Kennedy's coat and shivering.

Victoria felt a hand upon her shoulder. She looked up at her mother.

"Are you okay, sweetheart?" Mom asked.

Victoria nodded.

Everyone began talking at once.

"We're trapped!" Marilyn said. She nervously twiddled the necklace that she was wearing.

"Great, this is just great!" Colin said. He jumped to his feet and began to pace. "What are we going to do now?"

"Should we call someone?" Victoria asked. She pulled her phone from her pocket.

"None of us would get a signal down here," Jessica said.

Victoria frowned. Her sister was right. She put her phone back in her pocket, feeling silly for even thinking of trying to call someone in an ice cave.

"Alright, everyone just calm down!" Richard shouted, holding up his hands. "Panicking will not help. We need to get out of this cave and return to the visitor center."

"This isn't the same cave we were in before," Nathan said.

"Don't you know this one, Nathan?" Marilyn asked.

Nathan shook his head. "I haven't seen this cave before."

"I know you're all scared," Richard said, "but we'll just have to try to find another way out. Everyone, follow me."

Richard led the way down a tunnel. The group walked in nervous silence. Victoria glanced around. This cave was bigger than the other one. It also had blue walls, but unlike the other cave, it had ice stalactites and stalagmites. A few water droplets fell from the icicles. Victoria tore her eyes away from the ceiling; the very thought of one of those icicles falling on top of somebody made her shudder.

"This is just like being trapped in that mine after that earthquake back home," Marilyn said to Kennedy.

"I was thinking the same thing," Kennedy said. "I just hope we can get out of here."

I second that notion, Victoria thought. *We were lucky enough to survive that avalanche. Oh . . . oh no, oh no!*

She remembered her laughter at Colin's joke about a keelut stalking them.

What if it was too loud? What if I caused the avalanche with my laughter? What if all this is my fault?

She looked down at her feet, feeling overwhelmed with embarrassment. She was distracted from her gloomy thoughts, though, when Kennedy stopped right in front of her.

"What is it?" she whispered to her sister.

Kennedy pointed at Richard. He and Nathan were studying the walls, which had a few cracks in them. Victoria groaned.

"Dead end," Richard said. "We'll have to go the other way. Everyone, I will take Nathan and we will scout ahead. We will be back in just a few minutes. Stay right here."

Richard and Nathan went down the way they had come. Victoria slumped to the cold floor. She tightened her coat around herself, but she was still shivering.

"You okay there, honey?"

Victoria looked over her shoulder. Isaiah was standing over her.

"Oh, just scared," she said.

"I get it." Isaiah sat down next to her. "Me too."

Victoria sighed and turned her head away.

"Hey, we'll get out of here," Isaiah said soothingly. He wrapped his arm around Victoria. "There's bound to be another way outta here."

"But what if there isn't?" Victoria said. "What if the avalanche blocked the only exit to this cave? It will be my fault that we're trapped!"

"Your fault? What are you talking about? It's not like you triggered that avalanche."

"I laughed. Really loud. When Colin made his keelut joke."

Colin raised his eyebrow. Soon everyone was staring at Victoria. With a heavy sigh, Victoria hung her head between her knees. Shame knotted at her stomach.

"Victoria," Jessica said, "loud noises aren't strong enough to cause avalanches."

Victoria whipped her head up. "What?"

"That's just a myth. A movie cliché."

Victoria could feel her face flushing. Now she really felt like a total moron.

"Hey, don't beat yourself up over it," Kennedy said. "Lots of people believe that myth."

Victoria jumped to her feet. "Well," she said, glaring at Kennedy, "how many people have mistaken a mangy gray wolf for a chupacabra?"

"Chupacabra?" Colin said, looking confused.

"Yeah," Kennedy said, "about a year ago, our hometown went abuzz with a rumor of a chupacabra roaming around. It turned out to be a lost Mexican gray wolf with mange. But lots of people fell for it. I keep telling Victoria not to obsess over it. Lots of our classmates fell for it too."

Victoria scowled at her sister. "I didn't completely fall for it," she said defensively. "I just, well, I just thought the idea was cool. So I got carried away. Guess I've been reading too much Latin American folklore."

Colin sniggered. "Hey, I'd love to see a keelut or a kushtaka," he said. "Why, if I were in Pine Lodge last year, I probably would've gone searching for that 'chupacabra' myself."

"But you probably would've figured out what it really was as soon as you saw it," Victoria said flatly. "Unlike me. Golly, I wish I was smart, like my sisters! Kennedy and Marilyn are detectives who've actually caught criminals, and Jessica's the queen of science!"

"Oh, stop complaining," Jessica said. "You aren't the only one who's been teased in school. I've been wishing that I can be tall like Kennedy, or even Colin there, and that I wasn't such a science geek."

"Alright!"

All eyes turned to Gail as she stood up and walked over to the kids. "Enough of this. Arguing about useless topics will get us nowhere."

Victoria sighed and turned her back to the group. Gail put her hand on her shoulder.

"Victoria," she said in a gentler voice, "everyone makes mistakes. And based on what you said about this fake chupacabra story, it doesn't sound like you truly believed that the animal was a real chupacabra. Your love for fantasy just made you want to look."

"Yeah," Colin said, "I know how it feels. I keep wishing that I could see a keelut. Sometimes I'm tempted to go search for one. But deep inside me, I know I never will actually see one. And I believed in the myth that sound causes avalanches when I was little."

"I did too," Paul added. "I was probably ten or eleven when I first learned it was just a myth."

Victoria looked over her shoulder at Gail.

"I'm sorry," she said, "but what my classmates said to me in school . . . it just hurts."

"I'm sure it does," Gail said.

"Definitely," Mom added. She walked over to Victoria. "Why didn't you say anything? You and Jessica?"

Victoria shrugged. "We didn't want to cause more issues. This happened when Kennedy and Marilyn were graduating high school and Marilyn was worried about her mother's necklace in the mine."

"Oh, honey, I don't ever want you to feel as though you cannot come talk to me and Isaiah. Bullying is a serious issue. You shouldn't have to go through that."

"Yeah," Kennedy added. "Remember what I went through when we first moved to Pine Lodge? I think it's possible that your classmates are teasing you because they feel the same way you do. Maybe they're also embarrassed about believing the chupacabra narrative. And I'll bet you they're picking on Jessica because of her brains."

"I know how that feels," Colin said. "The reason I'm wearing this brace is because I was attacked for my athletic skills. Jessica, my height won't make a difference if my knee injury doesn't heal well enough for me to go back to sports."

Kennedy nodded sympathetically.

"But I have faith in God to take care of my grandson and his future," Gail said. She looked at Jessica. "And God created you to be good at all kinds of sciences. Your short stature does not define who you are."

She turned to Victoria. "And your mistakes do not define who you are. God created you with your own special gifts. Like your knowledge of folklore."

Victoria smiled. She patted Gail's hand. "That's true," she said. "I guess I'm still trying to figure out my place."

Gail smiled back. "God will guide you. And Jessica."

Victoria turned around and nodded at Gail to show her agreement. She then looked at her mother and stepfather, who were giving her encouraging smiles.

"Hey," Paul said, "our tour guides are back!"

Victoria turned around. Sure enough, Richard and Nathan were walking toward the group. Everyone looked at them expectantly.

"We scouted pretty far ahead," Richard said, "and we found something that looks promising. Now, let's keep going so as to keep our circulations moving."

The trek through the ice caves seemed to take forever to Jessica. She was relieved to finally arrive at a wide cavern at the end of the tunnel. One part of it was nearly filled with stalagmites, and the ceiling was covered in giant icicles.

Despite her fear, Jessica could not help but look around in awe at the cave. These walls were a light, icy blue color, lighter than any of the ice walls she had seen so far under the glacier. Toward the center of the cave, just past the tall stalagmites, some of which had funny-looking spiral forms, the ice floor was flat. Jessica could almost picture herself ice-skating right there.

"I must admit," she whispered to Nathan, "this is a very beautiful ice cave."

Nathan nodded. "I totally agree," he whispered back.

Everyone else seemed to agree too. With small smiles on their faces and awe in their eyes, they were holding up their phones to take pictures. Jessica decided to follow their lead and got out her phone.

But she was distracted when she heard low cracking noises.

"What was that?" Marilyn asked.

Everyone froze. Jessica whipped her head to look up at the ceiling. She stared nervously at the icicles. They seemed to be still.

Richard held out his right hand. "Nobody move."

A hushed silence filled the air with tension. Richard walked past the stalagmites. He took a few more steps forward and gingerly walked onto the flatter part of the ice floor.

"I think we're good," he said at last, turning to face the group. "I was worried one of those giant icicles or a stalactite from the ceiling would fall, but we—"

He was abruptly interrupted when the ice floor beneath him cracked and gave way, plunging him into blue water!

"Uncle!" Nathan exclaimed. He threw off his backpack and dashed over to the edge of the water, nearly slipping on the ice floor. Jessica remained frozen, barely hearing the screams of her mother, sisters, and Marilyn.

"Oh no, that must've been a subglacial lake!" Paul said.

"Come on, guys, help me!" Nathan yelled.

Isaiah and Paul rushed over and kneeled by the edge of the water next to Nathan.

"Where is he?" Paul demanded. "I can't see him!"

Nathan plunged his arm into the water. He shivered for a moment then waved his arm around. Paul quickly pulled it out.

"Hey, what are you doing?" Nathan said.

"You can't just freeze your arm off, Nathan!"

"But how else am I supposed to find him?"

Nathan stuck his arm back in the water. Jessica was shivering, but not from being cold.

"Hey!" Nathan shouted triumphantly. "I got his coat! Oh, no, no, it's slipping! Hurry, help me before I lose my grip!"

"Right!" Paul said. He plunged his arm into the water. Isaiah jumped to his feet and dug through Nathan's backpack. He pulled out a rope and ran back to the edge of the water. He uncoiled the rope and handed one end to Nathan. Kennedy and Colin ran over to help. Jessica felt her mother's hand upon her shoulder. Gail stood next to Victoria and Marilyn. Jessica stared at Nathan. Her heart, racing against her chest, went out to him.

After what seemed like an eternity, Nathan, Paul, and Isaiah pulled Richard from the lake. They dragged him across the ground and laid him against a stalagmite. Everyone else gathered around him just as Nathan gently took the wet coat off his shivering uncle. He began to remove his own coat, but Isaiah stopped him and took off his own. He and Nathan wrapped the coat around Richard.

"Are you alright?" Nathan asked, his voice shaking. "Uncle Richard, can you hear me?"

Much to Jessica's relief, Richard's eyes fluttered open. He looked straight at his nephew.

"Nate?" he asked, his voice shivering. "Is that you?"

"Yeah!" Nathan grinned. "It's me, your nephew."

Richard managed to smile weakly, but his eyes closed.

"No!" Nathan patted his uncle's cheeks. "Come on, man, stay with me!"

"Oh," Richard said weakly, his eyes still closed, "I m-must r-r-rest."

"How long do you think he was submerged?" Paul asked.

"Five minutes?" Kennedy suggested.

Jessica pulled away from Mom and ran over. She kneeled next to Richard and held his wrist in her hand.

"He has a weak pulse," she said. She looked at his face. His lips were turning blue. "He seems confused. I don't think he's lost full consciousness, but he seems to be fighting to keep it. I'd say he has mild hypothermia."

"And it's bound to get worse if we stay in this ice cave," Nathan said impatiently. "We need to get him out of here quick!"

"But how are we going to move him?" Jessica asked.

"We need to keep him conscious," Paul said. He kneeled by Richard and gently shook his shoulder.

"Richard? Can you move?" he asked in a loud voice.

The tour guide did not respond.

"Richard?" Paul said.

There was still no response.

"Well," Kennedy said, "at least he's not shivering anymore."

"Wait, he's not?" Jessica said. She took hold of Richard's wrist again and gasped in horror.

"I can't find a pulse!" she exclaimed. She immediately began chest compressions on the unconscious tour guide.

Even while doing the compressions, Jessica could see Nathan out of the corner of her eye. He had tears in his eyes. Jessica longed to go by his side and comfort him, but she forced herself to focus on pumping Richard's chest.

A few coughs escaped Richard's throat. Jessica ceased pumping his chest and looked at his face. Nathan breathed a heavy sigh of relief. He kneeled next to Jessica.

"Uncle Richard?" he said. "Can you hear me?"

Richard sputtered a little bit, but he smiled at Nathan. "I'm awake again," he said.

Nathan smiled. He took his uncle's hand. Jessica smiled too.

A crashing sound resonated throughout the cave. Everyone gasped and looked around wildly. Jessica expected to see an ice stalactite sticking out from the ground, but the cave looked just as it had before. Jessica silently prayed that none of the icicles from the ceiling would fall.

"What was that?" Marilyn asked, her voice shaking.

Colin peered down a tunnel. "It didn't sound too far."

"We need to get out of here," Isaiah said. "Nathan, I understand that you're just a tour guide trainee, but you might be the one with the best chance of leading us out of here. And didn't you and your uncle say earlier that there was something that looked promising?"

"There was." Nathan stood up. "Uh, down that tunnel."

He pointed down the tunnel that Colin was looking at. "But we didn't get a close look."

He sighed and crossed his arms. "Alrighty, here's what we'll do. I mean, I . . . I'd rather stay with my uncle. But he'd want me to lead the rest of you out. So I'll take a few of you down the tunnel. We'll see what we can find. But I need a few others to stay with my uncle."

"I will stay with him," Gail said. "I have some minimal nursing skills from back when I taught gymnastics. I'll stay and help him."

She looked at Jessica. "And I think I should have Jessica help me."

Mom nodded. "I will stay too," she said. She turned to Isaiah. "Watch over the other girls, will you?"

"Of course, dear." Isaiah wrapped a comforting arm around Mom.

Jessica watched Nathan as he led Kennedy, Victoria, Marilyn, Isaiah, Paul, and Colin down the tunnel. Nathan did not appear to be confident in himself, but Jessica believed he could lead them out.

"So," Kennedy's voice said, "what was so promising about this tunnel?"

"We felt a draft down here," Nathan said.

Jessica put the back of her hand against Richard's cheek. His eyes wandered over to her.

"My nephew's taking over, huh?" he whispered.

Jessica smiled at him. "Yep," she said. "He'll do great."

"I know he will," Richard said.

Nathan's alarmed yell echoing down the tunnel caught Jessica's attention. She exchanged panicked looks with her mother, Gail, and Richard.

"What could be going on now?" Mom asked nervously.

Before anyone could answer, Kennedy and Marilyn came running back to them. Jessica jumped to her feet.

"What's going on?" she demanded.

"The tunnel!" Kennedy said, waving her arms toward the tunnel. "It's blocked off! Come on, I'll show you!"

Jessica followed Kennedy and Marilyn down the tunnel. She felt her stomach drop. Her sister was right; the tunnel appeared to be almost completely blocked off.

"I think it collapsed," Nathan said. "I'll bet you that was the crash we heard earlier."

"Now we're really trapped!" Colin said.

"No, we aren't," Paul said. "Don't you feel that draft, son?"

Jessica stood next to Victoria. She indeed felt a draft of icy air.

Kennedy bent over to look more closely at the large pile of icy debris and rocks that covered the opening.

"It's not terrible," she said. "There's an opening under all these icy rocks. But I'm too big to get through."

"I know I'm tall," Colin said, "but I'm pretty skinny. I might be able to squeeze through there."

"No," Paul said, "not with your brace. We shouldn't take any chances."

"But who else could get through there?" Colin demanded. "I might have no choice, Dad. We have to get out of here. And almost everyone else is too big to crawl through."

"Yeah," Kennedy said slowly, "almost everyone, except . . ."

She faced Victoria and Jessica.

"You two can fit through there," she said.

Jessica's eyes grew wide. She and Victoria looked at each other.

"She's right, you know," Victoria said. "We can."

"So, what, we're just gonna climb through there and get help by ourselves?" Jessica said incredulously.

"Jess, we have to," Victoria said. "There's no other way."

Jessica sighed. "You're right. Guess it is up to us."

She turned to Kennedy. "We'll be careful," she said.

Kennedy hugged Jessica. "I know you will. Good luck."

Jessica and Victoria hugged their father and Marilyn. They looked at one another, nodded, and got on their hands and knees. Victoria crawled through the opening first, then Jessica crawled after her. She winced. Even for her petite size, it seemed like it was a tight squeeze. She managed to glance back. She saw Kennedy's hopeful face staring after them. Jessica gave her older sister a smile and nodded, then she continued following Victoria.

Victoria breathed a sigh of relief when she saw the other end.

"Whew!" she said. She wanted to turn her head to look back at Jessica, but she did not feel as though she had much room. "That was like crawling through an ice castle's air duct!"

She pulled herself out and slowly stood up on her feet. Jessica came crawling out. Victoria helped her sister stand up.

"Looks like we reached another cave," Jessica said. She looked around. "So, where's the air coming from?"

"Let's find out!" Victoria said.

She and Jessica raced through the cave, careful not to slip on the icy ground. In just a couple of minutes, they reached an opening through which they could see the blue sky. Victoria felt like jumping and cheering.

"Oh, good, fresh air again!" she exclaimed.

"Yes, thank heavens!" Jessica said. "Let's go, it's gonna take us a few hours to reach the visitor center!"

"Then we have no time to lose!"

The girls darted outside and raced down the trail. Victoria hoped to see other tourists, but no other people were in sight. Only a few trees, wildflowers, and the enormous ice wall to the side.

Suddenly Jessica stopped. "Vic, do you hear that?" she asked.

Victoria listened. She could hear a whirring noise. She looked at the sky and grinned.

"That sounds like a helicopter!" she said. "Quick, let's get out of the trees and see if we can catch its attention!"

The girls bounded through the thicket, but they could not find an area clear of trees.

"What do we do now?" Jessica asked. "I can still hear the helicopter, but we can't get to where it can see us!"

Victoria looked at the glacier wall behind them. "Well," she said, "it's a good thing that you can hike on top of the Mendenhall Glacier."

"I'm sorry, are you suggesting . . . ?"

"Yes, I am. Follow me, Jess!"

She turned around and ran toward the glacier.

"Vic, this is stupid!" Jessica yelled after her. "We can't hike on top of the glacier without a guide!"

Victoria stopped. She knew that her sister was right. But what choice did they have? Worrisome thoughts filled her mind. What if they did not catch the helicopter? What if Richard died from hypothermia before the rescue team could reach him?

Don't think about that, she admonished herself. *We will make it. We have to. Everyone else is counting on us!*

But her stomach was still churning with sickening doubt. After all, she had never gone on adventures like Kennedy had.

But I'm on an adventure now. If only this was a fantasy adventure. Oh! Yes, of course! Pretend you are on a fantasy adventure. Just imagine that a kushtaka is coming for Nathan's uncle, and I have to get help before it arrives to turn him into a kushtaka to save him from the cold.

It was when she thought of the folklore that courage started filling her gut, and her usual adventurous spirit returned. The idea of climbing on top of the Mendenhall Glacier gave her excitement and determination. She was not going to let her older sister down. Or her stepsister, or her friends.

As soon as she reached the glacier, she sprinted up the icy ground. Jessica was right behind her. White ice surrounded them.

They were in the clearest area they could get. And they saw the helicopter above them.

The two girls started shouting and waving their hands wildly. Victoria kept her eyes on the helicopter, as though afraid that if she blinked or looked away for one second, the helicopter would vanish.

Crackling underneath her feet did cause her to look down.

"What was that?" Victoria asked.

"I heard something, too," Jessica said. She looked down at her feet and gasped. "Vic, we need to move fast!"

"Why—?"

Victoria interrupted herself with a screech when the ice below Jessica's feet gave way, revealing a hidden crack. Jessica screamed as she fell through the opening that had suddenly appeared.

"NO! JESSIE!" Victoria screeched. She lunged forward, only to slip and slide right behind her sister.

Victoria fell down the dark crack. But only for a moment. With a thud, she and Jessica fell on a rocky ledge. Victoria gasped upon impact and took a deep breath.

"What was that?" she said. She slowly sat up and rubbed her shoulder. She rubbed her neck and looked down at the bottom of the icy gorge. She cringed when she saw the height. She quickly tore her eyes away.

Jessica groaned as she sat up. "That was a crevasse," she said. "An invisible crevasse covered by what is called a snow bridge. Oh, I should've known! I studied glaciers last winter. Now we'll miss the helicopter!"

She wrapped her arms around her knees. Victoria heard her sniffle.

"Hey, don't worry," she said. She scooted herself over to her sister and wrapped her arm around her. "We'll be fine. We just gotta do what Kennedy would tell us if she were here. You know, trust in God?"

She said these words to soothe Jessica, but she was scared herself. There was no way they could climb out of the crevasse. And all the others were depending on them. Victoria did not want to fail any of them.

Heavenly Father, she prayed silently, *please help us.*

"Hey! Hey, girls!"

Victoria looked up at the familiar voice.

"What was that?" Jessica asked.

Victoria did not dare stand up on the rock. All she could do was straighten her back and look up. "That sounded like Colin!" she said.

"But Colin's back in the ice cave under the glacier," Jessica said.

Victoria held her hand over her eyes. A figure appeared above. Despite the bright sunlight, Victoria recognized that figure.

"Colin!" she shouted. "What are you doing up there? Hey, don't fall in!"

"I convinced my dad to let me crawl out!" Colin called. "A little more of that ice blocking that tunnel fell, making just enough room for me to squeeze through!"

"With your leg brace?" Jessica said.

"It was a tight squeeze, but I made it," Colin said. "I'm sure my knee will be fine, but that's not important right now. The helicopter's landing!"

Indeed, Colin's voice was drowned out by the loud whirring of the helicopter. Victoria's heart beat faster as relief filled the pit of her stomach.

"How far are you?" Colin hollered.

"About thirty feet?" Jessica yelled.

"Hang in there!"

Victoria nodded. Then she heard an unfamiliar female voice.

"Hey, move over so you don't fall in! You say two girls fell in there?"

"Yes!" Colin's voice said.

Victoria grinned. The rescue team was finally here!

"Hello, girls!" the female voice called. "We're here to help you!"

Victoria breathed a sigh of relief.

Jessica squealed in terror.

Victoria spun her head around and gasped loudly when she saw that her sister was slipping off the rock. Victoria screamed and reached her hand out.

"OH NO!" Colin's voice bellowed.

It all seemed just a flash to her, but just in the nick of time, Victoria had caught her sister's wrist. Jessica grinned up at her.

"Is everything alright down there?" a male voice called out. "We heard screaming!"

"We're good, but my sister nearly fell farther down!" Victoria responded as she pulled Jessica back onto the ledge.

"We'll hurry, we're almost ready!" the man shouted.

Their rescuers were true to their word. Very soon, two ropes had been thrown down to them. As soon as the girls attached the ropes to themselves, they were being pulled out. Upon reaching the surface, Victoria and Jessica were greeted by rescue personnel. A tall and bulky man was holding his hand out to her. She took his hand and climbed out with his help. A blonde woman was helping Jessica out. Colin was standing just several feet away, a smile of relief on his face. He ran over to the two girls.

"Are you two alright?" the woman, whose name tag read SALLY, asked the sisters. "Did you break any bones? Are you hurt at all?"

"No, we're both okay, thanks," Jessica said shakily.

"Are you three kids alone?"

"No, we aren't," Victoria said, "the rest of our tour is trapped under the glacier. Our tour guide, Richard Bell, fell into a subglacial lake and needs immediate medical treatment."

"It all started with an avalanche," Jessica said.

"Yes, we know about the avalanche," Sally said, "that's why we were flying above the glacier. We were dispatched to make sure no hikers were hurt. Can you lead us to your group?"

"Yes, this way." Victoria turned around. She, Jessica, and Colin led the rescue team back to the ice cave. Victoria explained the entire situation along the way. Soon, but not soon enough for Victoria, they arrived at the blocked entrance to the other ice cave.

"This is where we left them," Victoria said. "We were the only two who could fit through that small opening."

"Well, I was able to crawl through later," Colin said.

"Yes, I see," one of the men said.

"Vic? Jess?" Kennedy's voice called. "Is that you?"

Victoria squealed with delight. "Yes, it's us and Colin, and we met with a rescue team!" she said. "They were in a helicopter! Are you guys okay?"

"Yes, but Mr. Bell's getting colder and weaker. Dad and a few of us were picking away at this ice in hopes of thinning it out."

"Stand back!" one of the men barked. "We have pickaxes and we're gonna knock down this ice blockage!"

The team began working while Sally escorted Victoria, Jessica, and Colin out of the ice cave. Victoria was grinning with relief and silently praising God. The rescue team was here, and they were working away. Soon they would all be safe.

Colin winced and grasped his knee.

"You okay?" Sally asked him.

"Yeah," Colin said, "but my knee had a twinge of pain just now."

Victoria looked at him sympathetically. "I hope you didn't damage it further," she said. "I know you really love your sports."

Colin just shrugged. "I just wanted to take the chance to go after the two of you and make sure things were alright," he said. He smiled. "Glad I did."

"Yeah," Victoria said, smiling back. "Hey, thanks for leading the rescue team to me and Jess in the crevasse."

"Yes," Sally said, "thank you for helping us."

"You know something, Vic?" Jessica said. "After all this, I'm actually quite glad that we live in the nice deserts of Arizona."

"Thanks again for driving us here, Mr. Foster."

Paul smiled at Jessica. He turned off the engine. "No problem. I'm also curious to know how Richard's doing."

Jessica got out of Paul's van. She looked around the hospital parking lot for Nathan, but she did not see him. She guessed that he might already be inside, sitting in the waiting room. She shivered. It was a chilly morning.

"I must admit," Kennedy said as she got out, "that was one awesome adventure!"

"You think it was awesome?" Mom said skeptically. "I keep wondering how you repeatedly find yourself in these situations."

"I'm glad I got to have my adventure!" Victoria said. "I kinda enjoyed it!"

"Well, I didn't enjoy it," Jessica said. "Who knows what would've happened if the rescue team wasn't there when Vicky and I fell down that crevasse?"

"Don't think about that," Marilyn said, "the important thing is that God made sure they were there. The team and Colin. Say, where is Colin?"

"He's coming with his grandmother," Paul said.

Mom, Isaiah, and Paul led the four girls into the waiting room. Jessica spotted Nathan, Colin, and Gail sitting in some chairs. They jumped to their feet and walked over to them. Jessica noticed that Nathan was carrying a brown paper bag.

"Hey, everyone!" Nathan said. "You're just in time. The nurse told us that Richard is doing well and he can receive visitors."

"Wonderful!" Kennedy said. "Let's go."

A nurse led them to Richard's room. Jessica smiled when she saw him. He was indeed looking much better than he had been yesterday when she and Victoria had left them in the ice cave. His face and lips had their color back, and his eyes were wide open.

Nathan gave his bedridden uncle a gentle hug. "How are you feeling?" he asked.

"Much warmer," Richard said with a chuckle. He smiled at Jessica. "I heard about your CPR, Jess. Thank you for saving me."

Jessica smiled shyly. She had a hunch that her cheeks were turning red.

"Of course," she said. "I knew that the hypothermia was getting worse when you stopped shivering."

"You know," Kennedy said, "if Jess didn't know these certain scientific facts, she may not have been able to save our tour guide."

"Indeed," Gail said. "And you, as well as Victoria, were the only ones who were able to fit through that small opening in the tunnel at first."

"So I guess being short and a science geek is useful," Victoria said, grinning at her sister.

"And you saved me from falling deeper into the crevasse," Jessica said. "Thank you for that, Vic."

"Hey," Nathan said, "anyone want a drink? I can go down to the cafeteria."

"I could use a coffee," Richard said.

Everyone agreed to a warm drink. The girls, Nathan, and Colin volunteered to go down and get them.

"So," Nathan said, "you've had your special adventure, Jess."

"I guess so. Me and Victoria, that is. I'll admit, my science knowledge really helped us. And so did my height. I won't be ashamed of who I am anymore."

Victoria smiled. "You know," she said, "I imagined that a kushtaka would come to claim your uncle and save him from freezing, and I had to beat that. A race against time, you might say. That helped me to stay focused and not be afraid."

"I love that!" Colin said. "Oh, I forgot to mention, I have good news myself. My mom insisted that I get looked at by a doctor here after crawling through that tight ice space. And the doctor said that my knee wasn't further damaged. In fact, he thinks it's healing very well, and I should be able to go back to playing sports a few months after I get my brace removed!"

"Oh, Colin," Marilyn said, "that is wonderful! I'm so happy for you."

The kids arrived at the cafeteria. But before Jessica could follow Kennedy, Victoria, Marilyn, and Colin over to the counter, she felt Nathan grab her by her elbow.

"What's wrong?" she asked him.

"Nothing," Nathan said. "I just have something for you."

He held up his paper bag and set it on a table. Jessica gasped when he pulled out the mountain goat figurine that she saw at the gift shop.

"I bought this for you," he said, handing the goat to her. "I thought you might like it. Just a little something to show you my gratitude for saving my uncle."

"Oh, thank you!" Jessica said. She wrapped her arms around Nathan. He gasped, but in a moment, he was patting her back.

Jessica's eyes wandered over to her new mountain goat figurine. It looked identical to the goat that she had seen on the tour, just before the avalanche. And that souvenir would serve as a reminder to her of her exciting adventure and what she learned about loving and cherishing the way God made her.

The Case of the Vanishing Painting

KENNEDY RYAN WONDERED if she was the only passenger from the flight free of jet lag. For the last thirty minutes of the plane ride, she had kept her nose pressed against the tiny window so she could gaze at the city of Florence, Italy. And now that she was leaving the airport with the rest of her group, she could finally see Florence up close. The city was more beautiful than she could ever imagine. Stylish Renaissance architecture dominated the city. Even from afar, Kennedy could see the round dome of the Cathedral of Santa Maria del Fiore.

"We're finally here!" she said to her stepsister, Marilyn Wilson. "I can't believe we're in Florence, Italy!"

Marilyn grinned. "It sure is gorgeous," she said.

Kennedy looked over her shoulder at her two friends, Rachel Hamilton and Susannah Anders. Rachel was wide-eyed and gazing at the sights around her, while Susannah appeared to be exhausted.

"You sure look like you're enjoying the sights!" Kennedy said to Rachel.

Susannah eyed Kennedy, frowning.

"Definitely!" Rachel said with a grin. "This trip is going to be our best college course yet!"

Kennedy turned her gaze back to the cathedral. That dome looked so inviting.

"Now, Kennedy, don't go wandering off!"

Kennedy turned around. Lloyd Jennings, who taught most of her music and art classes at Grand Canyon University, was grinning at her.

"I see that excited look in your eye," Lloyd said. "But no, you won't be allowed to wander Florence all by yourself. Sorry."

Kennedy smirked. "I'm not planning anything."

Lloyd's grin broadened. "You? Not planning anything? If there's anything I know about you, Kennedy, it's that you're always investigating something, especially when a crime is involved. Why don't you just investigate our bus? It just arrived."

Kennedy rolled her eyes. She followed everyone to a bus parked along the curb. Kennedy stared at the big red letters on the side of the bus: ACCADEMIA EUROPEA DI FIRENZE.

Susannah stood next to Kennedy. "Think we'll get a chance to rest once we get to our hotel?"

"Yeah, I'm sure," Kennedy said. She looked at her friend. "You alright, Susie? You used to be so excited about this college trip. Now you're really quiet."

Susannah smiled and shrugged. "Just the jet lag, I'll bet."

Kennedy nodded slowly. She wasn't convinced.

Everyone boarded the bus. Kennedy couldn't keep her eyes away from the window. They darted back and forth to catch glimpses of every building and every street.

Kennedy and Marilyn had enrolled at Grand Canyon University just months after they graduated from high school. Much to Kennedy's delight, Rachel and Susannah were attending the same university. The four girls rented a house in Phoenix. Kennedy was studying for a double major in music and art.

The bus parked along the curb. Everyone got off. Kennedy looked up at the bright yellow words high above the hotel's oval-shaped entryway.

"So this is Hotel Gioia," she said.

"Yep," Rachel said.

Everyone went inside. They walked down the hallway, past a stairwell, and began forming a few lines in front of the reception desk.

"Alrighty," Lloyd said, "let's all get checked in, then we'll begin our first orientation meeting."

Marilyn and Susannah went over to the front desk. Kennedy smiled at Rachel. "So glad that the four of us will be sharing a room," she said.

"I know!" Rachel said. "Glad Marilyn's checking us in. She's the only one who actually knows how to speak Italian."

Kennedy laughed. Susannah glanced over her shoulder and smiled meekly. She and Marilyn turned and went over to Kennedy and Rachel.

"Okay," Marilyn said, "I got us all checked in. We're in 233."

"Before we go," Susannah said, "I wanna get some coffee."

The four girls went to the breakfast room. Kennedy, Rachel, and Marilyn sat down while Susannah got her coffee. The three of them looked up at the TV on the wall. A news station was on, but everything, from the wording on the TV to the language being spoken, was in Italian.

"Can you understand any of that?" Kennedy asked Marilyn.

Marilyn gazed at the TV. "Oh," she said, frowning a little, "seems like they're talking about a theft at an art museum that happened about a month ago."

"Really?"

"Yeah. Probably an update. That lady just said the police still haven't caught the thief."

"Which museum was robbed?" Rachel asked.

"I think they said it was the Palatine Gallery of the Palazzo Pitti."

"That's awful," Kennedy said.

Susannah snapped a lid on her cup. "Ken?" she said quietly.

Kennedy turned to her friend. "Yeah?"

Before Susannah could speak, everybody else gathered into the breakfast room. Lloyd was holding a clipboard.

"Looks like our meeting's about to begin," Kennedy said. She gave Susannah an apologetic look.

"Well, here we are in lovely Florence, Italy!" Lloyd said. "Tomorrow's our first big day. Our first stop will be the famous Uffizi art gallery."

Kennedy and Rachel grinned at one another.

"We'll also check out our temporary school, the Accademia Europea di Firenze," Lloyd said. "That's where we'll be having most of our classes. It's the perfect school for our trip since the lot of you are majors in art, music, Italian studies, and culinary skills. And it's very close to this hotel."

Kennedy noticed Rachel elbow Marilyn. But the noise of the TV seemed to be fighting for her attention. Kennedy glanced up at it; she wished she could understand Italian better.

"Kennedy?"

Kennedy whipped her head back. Lloyd was grinning at her.

"I can translate the news," he said. "They're discussing an art theft from the Palatine Gallery."

"Marilyn already translated," Kennedy said.

Lloyd's grin only grew. "If you catch the thief, let us know."

Everyone burst out laughing. Even Kennedy smiled, despite the mild embarrassment floating in her stomach. If there was anything her teacher loved to tease her about, it was her reputation as an amateur detective. She was glad when the laughter died down and Lloyd started going over the syllabus. After twenty minutes, the orientation meeting ended and everybody dispersed to go to their rooms. Kennedy followed Marilyn, Susannah, and Rachel to the elevator. They stopped on the second floor.

"Alrighty, 233," Marilyn said. She held up her key card. "Where's that?"

"Right here." Rachel walked over to a door. Marilyn inserted the key card and the four girls entered the room.

"Hey, this is nice," Rachel said. "Lots of space."

Kennedy nodded. There were two queen beds and one twin bed with a nightstand in between. Across from the beds stood a wooden desk with a flatscreen TV sitting on top of it. Right next to the desk was a cabinet with a pair of glass doors.

Kennedy sat on the bed closest to the window. She looked over at Susannah, who had just plopped herself on the twin bed.

"You tired?" Kennedy asked.

Susannah turned her head. She smiled at Kennedy. "Very."

Kennedy paused. She still didn't think Susannah seemed as excited as she had been before. "Are you sure there's nothing bothering you?"

Susannah shrugged.

"It's really too bad about that one art museum," Marilyn said. "The Palatine Gallery. I know the robbery happened a month ago, but I certainly hope nothing ruins our chances of visiting it."

"Totally," Rachel said. "At least we're still visiting other art museums. Which one are we going to tomorrow?"

"The Uffizi," Kennedy said. She grinned. "I can't wait."

"Oh, yeah, we'll have so much fun!" Rachel said. "Unless the Uffizi gets robbed too!"

"Don't say that!" Kennedy said with a laugh.

Kennedy stood in the narrow courtyard of the Uffizi, gaping and swinging her head in different directions, not wanting to miss anything. On both sides, round pilasters appeared to be holding up the upper floors of the two wings. Several other pilasters were wider and square-shaped and had statues standing in large niches.

"This is the Loggiato," Lloyd said in a loud voice. "The courtyard between the two wings of the Uffizi."

He pointed to a few of the statues. "Who can tell me the names of these statues? What famous people do they represent?"

Kennedy raised her hand. Lloyd nodded at her. Kennedy pointed at one of the statues.

"That's Andrea di Cione di Arcangelo," she said. "He was a painter, sculptor, and architect."

"Excellent!" Lloyd said. "Anyone else?"

Rachel's hand shot up. She smiled when Lloyd pointed at her.

"Over there is Giotto di Bondone," she said, pointing at another statue. "He was an Italian painter and architect during the Late Middle Ages."

Kennedy gave Rachel a high five. "Us art majors are rocking our art history!"

"We sure are!" Rachel said.

Kennedy's eyes wandered to the other statues, but they rested on Susannah, who was staring at Kennedy with a sorrowful and envious look in her eyes. Kennedy frowned. She wanted to ask Susannah what was wrong. But then Lloyd and the other teachers began leading the group inside the gallery.

Kennedy's eyes darted all over the place as she followed her group down the hallway. Even the hallways were fancy, decorated with black-and-white square tile floors, sculptures displayed along the walls, and even paintings on the ceilings.

"This is awesome!" Marilyn whispered.

"I know!" Kennedy said. "I can't wait to begin exploring!"

"Well, you won't have to wait long. I think that's our tour guide over there."

Kennedy looked to where Marilyn was pointing. A slender woman was approaching the students. She wore a white blouse and a pair of gray slacks over black dress shoes. Her curly brown hair was up in an elegant twist. She went over to Lloyd and spoke to him in Italian. Lloyd whistled at the students. Their chatter died down, and they turned to Lloyd and the woman.

The woman smiled. *"Buongiorno,"* she said. "My name is Rosa Morelli. I am a curator here at the Uffizi. I'm pleased to be your tour guide today. I spent a year studying abroad in the United States of America at Grand Canyon University."

Her smile broadened. "I know you're from the very same university," she said. She motioned her hand to the hallway. "Let's begin our tour."

Rosa led the group up a flight of stairs. They came to a room with several paintings hanging on white walls. Kennedy grinned; she could hardly believe she was actually seeing these famous, lifelike paintings with her very own eyes.

"This is the Leonardo da Vinci room," Rosa said. She pointed to a painting. "Over here is the *Annunciation*. This piece of art is dated around 1472. Note how the angel Gabriel kneels before the virgin Mary, who is alluded to be pure by—"

"*Ciao, Rosa!*"

Kennedy whirled her head around at the unfamiliar voice. A tall, broad-shouldered man was walking toward the front of the group. His amber skin complemented his hazel eyes and dark brown hair. He was grinning at Rosa, but she only scowled at him.

"Excuse me a moment," Rosa said to Lloyd. She turned to the man and spoke to him in Italian. Her voice sounded slightly stern. The man's smile disappeared. He replied to Rosa in Italian. His voice had a pleading tone mixed with a little bit of gruffness.

Kennedy and Rachel exchanged concerned glances. A few people were staring. Kennedy noticed a thin, black-haired man pushing a cleaning cart into the gallery. Judging by his professional black uniform and hat, Kennedy guessed that he was a janitor. His face fell when he noticed Rosa talking to the man. The janitor looked away and began sweeping a corner.

"*Per favore scusami,*" Rosa said brusquely.

The first man turned from Rosa and walked away from the group. He gave the janitor a scowl before he left the room.

Rosa turned back to the students and forced a smile. "Sorry about that. Just . . . a coworker of mine. Let's move on."

Rosa lectured on the paintings in the Leonardo da Vinci room for twenty minutes before she led the group away. Kennedy noticed that Rosa was eyeing the hallway warily.

They entered another room with white walls and a bright brown hardwood floor. Rosa approached a painting of a woman holding a baby boy on her lap and surrounded by five angels.

"Who here knows what this is?" she asked.

Kennedy raised her hand. "That's *Madonna of the Magnificat*," she said. "By Sandro Botticelli. It's dated from 1481."

"*Eccellente,*" Rosa said. "Do you know any of its interpretations?"

"Well, Mary is supposed to be writing the *Magnificat* in the right-hand page of the book. The left-hand page has the *Benedictus*. The infant Jesus is guiding Mary's right hand as she's writing. She's holding a pomegranate in her left hand. Two of the five angels are crowning her."

Rosa grinned. "You really know your art history," she said.

After lecturing on other paintings, Rosa allowed everyone to disperse around the room. Kennedy and Rachel took pictures of the paintings.

"I sure hope I can be like these artists!" Kennedy said. "Talent that matches that of Leonardo Da Vinci and Sandro Botticelli, being remembered throughout history, and maybe even having my artwork displayed in an art gallery . . ."

"Well, I'd say your talent is pretty dang close," Rachel said.

Kennedy looked over her shoulder at the other paintings. She saw Rosa talking to Marilyn and Susannah. Kennedy and Rachel went over to them.

"Hey there," Marilyn said. "Rosa's giving me and Susie a lecture on *Pallas and the Centaur* here."

Kennedy approached the painting of a woman with light brown hair rustling the shaggy hair of a centaur.

"Another one of Botticelli's masterpieces," Kennedy said. "It depicts either Pallas Athena, also known as Minerva, the Roman goddess of wisdom and warfare, or Camilla, a virgin warrior. The proud female figure represents chastity. And the centaur represents humanity's feral instincts. Oh, and the three-ring decoration on the woman's dress is also the insignia of the wealthy Medici family."

"We were looking at *The Birth of Venus* just a moment ago," Rachel said. "Venus is the Roman goddess of love and beauty, counterpart to the Greek Aphrodite. Venus is arriving on the island of Cyprus. She was born of sea spray. Venus is celebrated as a symbol of love and beauty. In fact, that painting may have been suggested by the poet Agnolo Poliziano."

"Wow," Rosa said, "you two are really good."

"We're art majors from Grand Canyon University," Kennedy said. "You said you went there?"

Rosa nodded. "That's pretty much why I speak English so well. I studied art, music, and history in college."

"That's cool," Kennedy said. "I'm actually a double major in music and art."

"And I'm a music major," Susannah said. "I'm going for teaching and music performance. Kennedy and I take lots of our classes together."

"And Kennedy takes a lot of art classes with me," Rachel added.

"That sounds so cool," Rosa said. "And all of you are here to study at *Accademia Europea di Firenze*?"

"We sure are," Susannah said. "We haven't been there yet. We're going later today."

"It was the perfect academy for all of us," Kennedy said. "You know, since we're music and art majors. Well, my stepsister here is studying culinary arts. She loves cooking."

Marilyn smiled. "My dad owns a restaurant back home. I'm going for minors in Italian and Spanish too."

"What instruments do you play?" Rosa asked.

"I play the violin and piano," Kennedy said.

"I play the piano too," Susannah said. "But I really love singing and opera. I'm a soprano one."

"Oh, I love opera," Rosa said. "One of my favorite operas is *La Traviata*."

"I love *La Traviata*!" Susannah said. "Our university's choir participated in a production of *La Traviata* last fall."

"Yeah, that was a lot of fun," Kennedy said. "Marilyn helped Susannah with the Italian lyrics. And I got to play my violin for the performance."

"Oh, you are a quartet of talented young ladies!" Rosa said. She grinned at Kennedy. "And I also know that you are quite the detective."

"Really? Oh, you heard about all those crazy adventures my friends and I had back in Arizona?"

"Yes. I heard everything about you on the news when I was an exchange student at Grand Canyon. You caught bank robbers."

"Yeah. Then six months later, my friends and I ran afoul of cattle rustlers on my uncle's ranch."

"Then Kennedy and I escaped from a mine damaged by a couple of earthquakes," Marilyn added.

Rosa laughed. "Wow, you are quite the adventurers!"

"I guess so," Marilyn said. "So, what other paintings are here?"

As Rosa showed the four girls some of the other paintings, the janitor entered from the other room. He grabbed a spray bottle from his cart and turned around. Almost immediately, he bumped into a bulky security guard who had just entered the room. The guard glared at the janitor and snapped at him in Italian.

"*Mi scusi!*" the janitor said quickly. He had an embarrassed, apologetic look on his face.

The guard didn't reply. He turned and walked briskly out of the room.

Kennedy and Rosa frowned at one another. Rosa politely excused herself from the four girls and went over to the janitor. His brown eyes twinkled when he saw Rosa. They smiled at one another and shared a hug. They had a brief conversation in Italian. Rosa gave the janitor a quick peck on his cheek before returning to the girls.

"Sorry," she said, "I just wanted to give my boyfriend a little comfort."

"No problem." Kennedy smiled at the janitor. "He's your boyfriend, you say?"

Rosa glanced over her shoulder. The janitor smiled at her and tipped his hat at her. Rosa chuckled.

"He sure is," she said. "His name's Lorenzo. He and I went to college together. Well, he's still got one year left. I already graduated. Poor guy, fell a little behind. But neither of us mind. He's going to become a curator like me."

"I'll bet you two are looking forward to that," Rachel said.

Rosa nodded. "We sure are." She frowned. "Just as long as that other guy stays out of our way."

"Other guy?" Kennedy said. "You mean that guard?"

Rosa shook her head. "No, I meant my coworker who had interrupted our tour earlier. I'm sorry about that, by the way. That man was another curator. Alfonso Martini. He's from a wealthy family. And believe me when I say rude, stuck-up, and entitled attitudes run through that family. They own a winery in Calenzano called *Viti Reali di Calenzano*. Alfonso works there part-time. He came here mainly just to stalk me."

"Stalk you?"

Rosa shrugged. "At least I feel like it. Alfonso and I met in college. He's been wanting to date me ever since. He doesn't give up easily, it seems. He keeps inviting me to his family's winery. But I wouldn't date him in a million years. He's rude and arrogant. I've never been to his family's winery, and I don't plan to go."

Rosa smiled. "But let's forget about him," she said. "In fact, I think it's about time we continued our tour."

Rosa went over to Lloyd and the other teachers. They gathered the students together and led them to a room filled with sculptures and paintings.

"That's Medici Venus," Rosa said, pointing to a statue.

Sudden movement in the corner of her eye distracted Kennedy from the Medici Venus statue.

Kennedy whipped her head around. She spotted a tall, broad-shouldered man behind another statue. He was dressed in a black trench coat. He wore a black bowler hat over untidy black hair. Sunglasses covered his eyes, but even so, Kennedy could feel him staring at her. He turned and briskly walked out of the room.

Kennedy raised her eyebrow. She shrugged and turned her attention back to Rosa and the statues.

"Alright, everyone, here we are at *Accademia Europea di Firenze*. This is where we'll be doing most of our studies."

Lloyd led everyone off the bus. Several of the students, including Kennedy, were carrying instruments. Kennedy looked up at the pastel yellow building. Fancy, dark brown trim decorated the door and windows. Just next door, Kennedy spotted a sign hanging over a white awning that read SHAKE CAFÉ AND JUICE BAR.

The group went inside and stopped at the front desk, where a middle-aged woman with brown hair up in a braided bun was sitting. She smiled cordially. Lloyd spoke to her in Italian, and then he turned back to the students.

"We're going to separate now," he said. "Culinary students, you will follow Betty Driscoll down that hallway. The rest of us will take the music and art students."

Kennedy watched Marilyn walk down a hallway with a willowy woman, who was Marilyn's culinary teacher, and a few other students. Lloyd took everyone else down another hallway.

Kennedy ran to her teacher's side. "Professor Jennings?"

"Yeah?" Lloyd looked down at her.

"What am I supposed to do? I'm studying both music and art. How should I bounce back and forth?"

"Just focus on one subject per day. Like today, you can choose either a music or art class."

Susannah ran over to Kennedy. "Wanna join me in music class?" she asked hopefully.

Kennedy smiled. "Sure."

Susannah grinned.

"Hey, girl, I'll miss you," Rachel said.

Kennedy chuckled. "I'll be with you tomorrow."

Kennedy and Susannah followed several of their classmates into a classroom. A large, black-and-white photograph of Florence hung on the wall. A piano stood near the center of the room. Lloyd went over to the piano and sat down. He played a scale and smiled.

"Alright, everyone," he said, "get out your instruments and tune them up good."

Kennedy kneeled by the wall and got her violin out of its case. She plucked the two middle strings.

"Glad you're here with me for our first music class, Ken."

Kennedy looked up at Susannah. "You feeling nervous?" she asked.

"Oh, maybe a little."

Kennedy stood up. "So, what's bothering you?"

Susannah raised her eyebrows. "Nothing."

"Hey, come on, I know something's up. You used to be so excited about this trip. Now you're all quiet."

Susannah sighed. "Guess I just really miss you in Dallas."

Kennedy frowned. "I miss Dallas too. But we're here together now. And we're in college together, and we share a house in Phoenix with Marilyn and Rachel. Come on, what is it really?"

Susannah crossed her arms. "I worry about our friendship."

"Why?" Kennedy said. "We're still friends, girl."

"Yeah, but before we moved in together, it had been ages since we had seen one another. I just hope our friendship doesn't, well, you know, continue to dwindle."

Kennedy patted Susannah's shoulder. "It hasn't been, and it won't," she said. "I can promise you that."

Susannah smiled feebly.

"Is there anything else?" Kennedy asked.

Susannah shook her head. But Kennedy had a hunch there was more. Before she could say anything, Lloyd called everyone to gather around. All Kennedy could do was give her friend an encouraging smile.

"You gals almost done?" Rachel asked. She had just thrown away her paper plate. "We need to be on the bus soon."

"Just about," Kennedy said.

"The breakfast room is quiet this morning," Susannah said. She looked up at the silent black television screen. "Wonder why the TV's not on."

"I heard the people at the front desk say it wasn't working earlier," Marilyn said. "I'm sure they'll get it fixed."

"No matter." Kennedy stood up. "Let's get ready to go."

156

The four girls went to their room and grabbed their bags. They met everyone else in the lobby. Soon they boarded the bus. Kennedy knew that they would arrive at the art gallery soon, but the ride still seemed to take forever. As soon as the Uffizi came into view and the bus pulled into a parking garage, Kennedy stood up.

"Ken, sit down." Marilyn tugged at Kennedy's backpack to pull her back on the seat. "We'll be back at the Uffizi soon enough."

Kennedy plopped down next to her stepsister. "Sorry," she said with a sheepish smile, "I'm just so excited!"

As soon as the bus was parked, the teachers led the students off and they began their trek to the gallery. Excited chatter filled the air.

"I hope Rosa leads our tour again," Kennedy said. "She was really good and very nice."

"I know, right?" Rachel said.

"And I hope we explore the other art galleries too!"

"What about the opera houses?" Susannah asked. "I mean, we'll still visit them, right?"

"Of course," Kennedy said. "That's on the syllabus."

Susannah smiled.

"What's going on up ahead?" a girl whispered.

Kennedy looked up. She frowned. She could see the Uffizi gallery up front. Yellow caution tape was set up around the entrance and police officers were walking around.

"What is this?" Lloyd asked. He stopped and held his hand up. Everyone stopped.

Kennedy made her way to the front of the group. Marilyn, Susannah, and Rachel were right on her heels.

"Alright, stay back, everyone," Lloyd said. He went over to one of the police officers and spoke to him in Italian.

Two policemen exited the gallery. One of them was speaking over a walkie-talkie.

"What's going on?" Susannah asked. "Mary, can you translate?"

"One of the paintings has gone missing," Marilyn said.

Kennedy's heart picked up its pace.

"Let me listen," Marilyn said. She stepped forward.

A policeman hurried out of the gallery. He was carrying a black hat.

"Hey," Rachel whispered, "that looks like Lorenzo's hat. The one he was wearing yesterday."

A yell captured Kennedy's attention. She whirled her head around. Two policemen were dragging a pleading Lorenzo out of the gallery. Kennedy shuffled out of the way.

"Per piacere! Non ho rubato nulla!"

Just then Rosa dashed out of the gallery. She ran after the officers who were taking Lorenzo to their car. A policeman grabbed her arm.

"No!" Rosa shouted. *"Non l'ha fatto! Per piacere!"*

But the policeman retained his grip on Rosa. All she could do was watch with tearful eyes as Lorenzo, his watery eyes filled with fear and confusion, was pushed into a police car. Just as the car drove away, Rosa broke free of the policeman holding her. But she could only stand on the curb and watch helplessly as the car disappeared from view.

Kennedy and Rachel exchanged horrified looks. Lloyd tapped Kennedy's shoulder.

"Come on," he said. "The police want the crowds to leave. We need to go."

Kennedy reluctantly turned around. Marilyn ran to her side. Kennedy looked at her inquisitively.

"We'll talk later," Marilyn whispered.

Kennedy nodded. She ignored the chatter of the students around her. Her head was swimming. She felt horrible for Rosa. And why was Lorenzo arrested?

Soon they arrived back at the bus. Everyone piled in. As soon as they took their seats, Lloyd stood up front and whistled. The excited chatter died down as everyone looked at Lloyd.

"I found out what happened," he said in a loud voice. "The *Pallas and the Centaur* painting had been stolen during the night."

Gasps erupted from the students. Kennedy and Rachel gaped at one another.

"Apparently one of the officers found a hat and a name tag that belonged to the janitor who had been working the night shift," Lloyd said. "As we've just seen, he has been arrested. Needless to say, we won't be touring the Uffizi today. I'm sorry for any inconvenience all this drama has caused us. We'll be going to the academy instead. Please write a two-page essay on one of the works of art that you viewed yesterday."

Disappointment knotted at Kennedy's stomach. She stared out the window. She barely listened to the chatter of the other students, but Kennedy didn't doubt that every one of them had the same thoughts on their minds as she did. Well, except for one thing. Kennedy's mind was flooded with the images of Lorenzo's desperate confusion as he was being arrested and Rosa's pleading with the police to not take him away. Kennedy fidgeted in her seat; she couldn't shake the feeling that there was something really wrong.

Soon they arrived at the academy. Everyone got off the bus and went inside. Kennedy followed Rachel, Marilyn, and Susannah to a student lounge.

"Wow, what an interesting day!" Rachel said.

"I'll say!" Marilyn said. "I hope this doesn't ruin our trip."

"Ditto. Poor Rosa. She seemed so distressed."

"I think she was trying to convince the police that Lorenzo would never do a thing like that," Marilyn said. "Though, she was speaking so fast, I had a hard time catching everything she said. But apparently, that black hat that the cop found was Lorenzo's janitor hat. It was found right where the missing painting had been. Same with his name tag."

"That's awful," Susannah said. "I feel bad for Rosa."

"Yeah," Kennedy said thoughtfully, "but did you see his face as he was being taken away by the police? He seemed so confused and scared. I can't shake the feeling that something is wrong."

"Uh, don't tell me that you're gonna try to meddle in this," Susannah said dryly. "Lloyd would never allow that."

"I don't plan to," Kennedy said. "But it's just that . . ."

She sighed. "I don't know. You know what, maybe we should just get started on our assignments."

But when she sat down, all Kennedy could do was open her notebook and point her pencil to the paper. She lacked all motivation to write. She wondered which painting she should write about. The first one that came to mind was *Pallas and the Centaur*.

No way. I'd never be able to focus. Maybe I can write about the Annunciation *by Da Vinci.*

"Hey, that was a very good workshop," Rachel said.

Kennedy shrugged. Yes, she did enjoy the art workshop. She would've enjoyed it even more without thoughts of the Uffizi robbery hiding in the back of her mind.

Kennedy and Rachel left the classroom. They met Marilyn and Susannah in the hall.

"How was your workshop?" Marilyn asked.

"It was fine," Kennedy said.

"Missed you in music class," Susannah said. "You should've heard my solo."

Kennedy nodded slowly. Marilyn peered at her. "Are you okay?" she asked.

Kennedy forced a small smile. "Yeah, I'm fine."

"Still thinking about the theft?"

Kennedy shrugged. She looked down at her feet. Her stepsister was right. She couldn't take her mind off the theft of the painting. Or Lorenzo and Rosa.

"Hey, what's Rosa doing here?" Rachel said.

Kennedy looked up. Much to her surprise, Rosa was walking down the hallway toward them. Her pleading eyes met Kennedy's.

"*Ciao, Rosa,*" Marilyn said, smiling a little. "How're you doing? What brings you here?"

Rosa smiled meekly. She wiped her eyes. "I'm glad to see the four of you," she said. She looked straight at Kennedy as she spoke.

"Us?" Susannah said. "How come?"

Rosa took a deep breath. "I was allowed to visit Lorenzo last evening," she said. "He told me that he didn't steal the painting. He wasn't even wearing the janitor's hat that the police had found at the crime scene. He told me that he took his own hat off before he started his night shift. I believe him. And I know him. He'd never steal anything, especially not from the very gallery where he's hoping to work as a curator. But the police wouldn't listen to either of us."

"Well, okay," Kennedy said, "but why come here to us?"

"Because I know of all your adventures back in America," Rosa said. "All those mysteries you've solved. You're basically an amateur sleuth. The police won't listen to me, Kennedy. But you're so good at spotting clues. I . . . I was hoping that you'd be willing to come to the Uffizi with me tonight. It reopened today. We can go and look at the area just before closing. I mean, uh, it's still a crime scene, but we can take a peek at it. And I will make sure to keep you girls anonymous."

Rosa sighed. "I don't wish to put you in any danger or get you in trouble with your teachers. But I am desperate to prove Lorenzo innocent, Kennedy."

160

Kennedy nodded. "I understand," she said. She glanced at Marilyn, Rachel, and Susannah. All three of them stared at her with wide eyes.

"I'm not entirely sure we can sneak away without any of the teachers noticing," Rachel said.

Kennedy crossed her arms. "I think Rosa might be onto something," she said. "We all saw Lorenzo when he was being taken away. He was so confused. And Rosa here is so sure that he's innocent."

She looked at Rosa. "Do you know if the police checked the security cameras?" she asked.

"The cameras were down," Rosa said.

"What? Down? In a famous art gallery like the Uffizi?"

Rosa nodded. "That was one of the first things the police discovered. And it's weird because when the cameras go down, an alarm goes off. But no alarm had been reported at all."

Kennedy put her hand on her chin. "Interesting."

Susannah glanced at Kennedy. "We're supposed to go to the opera house later," she said.

Kennedy nodded slowly. "But we won't be there for long." She turned back to Rosa. "Come get us at our hotel tonight at six."

Rosa smiled. "Oh, thank you!"

Even though it was only quarter after six, the sun was already beginning to set, making the evening appear dark. Rosa led Kennedy, Marilyn, Rachel, and Susannah across the Loggiato. Kennedy felt like the statues were staring at her.

"I still don't think we should be here," Susannah hissed.

"We'll just peek at the crime scene and get out," Kennedy said.

Rosa stopped at a door. She unlocked it and let the girls inside.

"It's so empty in here," Rachel whispered. "And quiet."

Kennedy hardly agreed; she felt like their footsteps were echoing too loudly down the hallways.

Rosa led them straight up the stairs toward the Sandro Botticelli room. The dark room was blocked off by a chain.

Kennedy's eyes wandered to the yellow caution tape on the wall. She remembered seeing the *Pallas and the Centaur* painting in that very spot. Now the wall was empty.

"*Ragazze,*" a stern voice said, "*cosa ci fate qui?*"

161

Kennedy gasped and whirled around. A tall, broad-shouldered man was glaring at them. He wore a navy blue police uniform with a matching hat over his dark brown hair.

The girls exchanged nervous glances. Rosa took a step toward the man and spoke to him in Italian. The man's expression softened a little. He tipped his hat at Rosa.

"Is this man a police officer?" Kennedy asked Rosa.

"Sì," the man said. "Mi chiamo Nicoli Parisi."

Kennedy glanced at Marilyn.

"He says his name is Nicoli Parisi," Marilyn said.

"Ah, my apologies," Nicoli said. "I am a detective for the Carabinieri Command for the Protection of Cultural Heritage, or the Carabinieri Art Squad."

"Oh, nice!" Susannah sounded relieved. "Well, then, you can help Rosa prove her boyfriend's innocence. The rest of us can go back to the academy."

Kennedy grasped her friend's shoulder. "Not so fast."

Nicoli narrowed his eyes. "What is this now?"

"Per favore, Ispettore," Rosa said, "but we need to look at the crime scene. I am certain that Lorenzo is innocent."

"Our prime suspect?" Nicoli said. He tapped a finger on his chin. "He did seem like he had no idea what was going on, did he?"

"That's just what I thought!" Kennedy said.

"But even so," Nicoli said, "we did find his hat and name tag at the scene of the crime. We have our suspect. I'm just here to guard the crime scene."

He turned to Rosa. "Why did you bring these young ladies here, anyway?"

"This is Kennedy Ryan. I've heard about her roles in solving mysteries in the United States."

Nicoli looked at Kennedy. "Oh, so you are a detective? And these girls too?"

Kennedy shrugged. "Not officially. I just seem to find myself chasing criminals. Me, Marilyn, Rachel, and Susannah."

"Yeah, we can't seem to avoid it," Rachel added.

Nicoli smirked. "So you think you can just look at a crime scene and determine if our main suspect is innocent or not?"

Susannah sighed and crossed her arms. "We don't have time for this," she said.

"I know you don't," Rosa said. She turned to Nicoli. "Just let Kennedy try. You can even help her."

Nicoli hesitated. "You're certain," he said quietly, "that there is a chance this Lorenzo might be innocent?"

Rosa nodded. She appeared to be holding back tears.

Nicoli sighed. "*D'accordo.* But don't touch anything."

He pulled the chain away. Kennedy walked straight over to the yellow caution tape. She saw a few large footprints on the floor. Kennedy pulled out her phone and took a few pictures of the footprints.

"That's all there is?" she asked.

Nicoli nodded. "We dusted for fingerprints but found none," he said. "So I think the thief was wearing gloves. And those footprints were here when the police came. We guessed that the thief walked on the floor when it had been mopped, and the prints dried. Lucky for us."

Rosa stared at the footprints. "Those are too big to be Lorenzo's," she said.

"Oh, really?" Nicoli said.

"Yes. Lorenzo wears a size eleven in shoes. Those look like they have to be a twelve."

Nicoli crossed his arms. "That may be so," he said in a gentle but firm voice, "but that doesn't change the fact that Lorenzo's hat and name tag were found here. And no alarm went off even when the cameras went down."

"But Lorenzo's a janitor," Rosa said. "He doesn't know how to handle any of the security cameras or computers or anything."

"Can we look at the security room?" Kennedy asked.

"We've already done that," Nicoli said impatiently. "I can tell you why the alarm didn't go off. The wire between the alarm and the cameras had been cut."

Kennedy raised her eyebrow. "Cut?"

"*Sì.* Lorenzo would've been able to at least do that."

"But he had no key to the security room!" Rosa said. "He had no reason to go in there at all!"

Nicoli paused. "Well, the lock on the security door hadn't been picked. But Lorenzo still could've taken a key."

Rosa sighed. She turned away from Nicoli and crossed her arms.

"Wait a minute," Kennedy said.

Everyone looked at her. Kennedy turned to Rosa.

"You said that the footprints looked too big to be from Lorenzo, right?"

Rosa nodded.

"And you told us that Lorenzo said he wasn't wearing the hat that had been found here?"

"That's right," Rosa said.

Kennedy grinned. "Does this place have a closet where they keep spare uniforms?"

"Yes."

"I'd like to check it out."

Rosa stared. "Why?"

"Just trust me on this," Kennedy said.

"*Ehi!*" a gruff voice shouted. "*Cosa stai facendo lì dentro?*"

Kennedy spun around. A man was stomping toward them. Kennedy recognized him as the security guard who had snapped at Lorenzo the other day.

Nicoli approached the man. Holding up his badge, he responded in Italian. The guard lowered his flashlight and nodded respectfully. Rosa ran over to them. She spoke to the guard in Italian. The guard just smirked and gave her a reply that sounded snarky. Rosa sighed and turned away from him. The guard left the room.

"Sorry about that," Nicoli said as he walked over to the four girls. "Just a gruff security guard."

"What's his deal?" Rachel asked.

"His name's Matteo," Rosa said, "and he says that we're wasting our time looking for clues here."

"Yeah, apparently he's convinced Lorenzo is guilty," Nicoli said. "Unlike you ladies."

Rosa turned her glare to the hallway. "I'm sure he'd love to visit Lorenzo in prison just to gloat," she said sourly.

"Why?" Kennedy asked. "Does he have something against Lorenzo?"

Rosa nodded. "Matteo started here as a janitor," she said. "Lorenzo tried to train him. But Matteo slacked off, hardly did any work, and played on his stupid phone a lot when he shouldn't have been. Lorenzo complained about him several times. Matteo was finally written up for his poor work. Then the head of security asked that Matteo become a security guard. Said he could keep a better eye on him. Matteo didn't exactly mind the job switch, but he still felt like Lorenzo got him in trouble."

Kennedy nodded slowly.

"Nothing more to be done here," Nicoli said. He turned to Rosa. "So, are you going to show us the uniforms?"

Rosa nodded. She led Nicoli, Kennedy, Marilyn, Susannah, and Rachel out of the room. Kennedy shivered as she gazed at the dark hallways; she tried not to imagine a bulky man jumping out at them. Even while walking on her tiptoes, she felt like she was making too much noise. Kennedy glanced over her shoulder.

Movement at the end of the hall caught her eye. A feminine figure ran past and disappeared down another hall.

"What was that?" Kennedy gasped.

Everyone else stopped and turned around.

"What's wrong?" Nicoli asked.

Kennedy pointed toward the end of the hall. "I thought I saw someone running over there, down that other hall."

"Probably just one of our security guards?" Rosa said.

Kennedy shook her head. "It looked like a woman."

Nicoli stepped forward. He held his hand out toward the girls. "Stay here," he said.

He slowly walked down the hall. Kennedy's heart pounded against her chest, and her muscles were tense. She hardly dared to even breathe as she watched Nicoli with wide eyes.

A quiet clink echoed from the other hall. Kennedy stifled a gasp. Nicoli stopped in his tracks. He glanced back at the girls, and then he went to the other hall. He disappeared from view. His voice echoed.

"Who's there?"

Silence filled the halls. After a few minutes, Nicoli came back from the other hall. He walked toward the girls. Kennedy noticed that he was holding something.

"Did you see anyone?" Susannah asked.

Nicoli shook his head. "No one."

"What's that you've got?" Kennedy asked, pointing at his hands.

Nicoli showed them. A tiny hair comb decorated with white pearls and rhinestones lay in his palm. Part of it looked broken, as though it had been snapped in half.

"This is a hair comb," Nicoli said, not meeting Kennedy's eyes. He sighed and stared longingly at his hands.

"What's wrong?" Kennedy asked.

Nicoli shook his head and hastily put the comb in his coat pocket. "Nothing," he said. "Whoever was wandering back there dropped this. I'll be sure to let the police know."

"Well, if someone is sneaking around here," Susannah said, "then maybe we should leave."

"Let's at least check out the uniforms," Kennedy said.

"Right," Nicoli said. "Rosa, lead on."

They continued down the halls. Soon they arrived at a closet. Rosa unlocked the door and let everyone in. Kennedy went over to a rack. Several black uniforms hung from it.

"How many janitor's uniforms are there?" Kennedy asked.

"We counted extra uniforms just the day before the theft," Rosa said. "There had been six. Not including Lorenzo's uniform. He always takes his uniforms home with him."

"Well," Rachel said, "unless I'm bad at basic arithmetic, there are only five here."

"What now?" Rosa ran over to the rack.

Kennedy counted the uniforms. Rachel was right; there were five uniforms on the rack.

"I see what you mean now," Rosa said.

"Would Lorenzo have a reason to take an extra uniform?" Marilyn asked.

"No, not that I know of." Rosa looked at the tag on one of the uniforms. "And he'd take his own size."

"What do you mean by that?" Nicoli asked.

Rosa went over to a small desk and picked up a notebook. "When we counted the extra uniforms, we recorded the sizes. We had two larges, a medium, and three extra-larges. But there's only two extra-larges here."

Kennedy looked at the tags herself. She found a medium, two larges, and two extra-larges. A wry smile crept across her lips.

"Rosa," she said, "does Matteo, by chance, wear an extra-large?"

Rosa smiled. "I think he does," she said. "But I wouldn't know his shoe size."

Nicoli's eyes widened. "This is odd," he said. "Seems like the painting isn't the only theft this gallery has experienced. And you're certain there were six uniforms the day before the theft?"

"Positive. Here, take a look."

Rosa handed the notebook to Nicoli. He flipped through the pages and nodded.

"You're right," he said. "This might be worth mentioning to the police. I'll talk to them tomorrow morning, Rosa."

He handed the notebook back to Rosa. "In the meantime, you'd better take these young ladies back to wherever they came from. Oh, and I'll be sure to mention the hair comb too."

He patted his pocket.

"Thank you," Rosa said. She looked at Kennedy. "You too."

Kennedy smiled. "Glad to do what little I could. Oh, one more thing."

She turned to Nicoli. "Mind if I take a picture of the hair comb? I'd like to have one on me, just in case."

Nicoli shrugged. "I'm fine with that."

He pulled the comb from his pocket and held it out. Kennedy took a picture of it.

"Thanks," she said as she put her phone away.

They went downstairs and left the gallery through a back door. Nicoli walked Rosa and the girls back to the parking garage, where Rosa's car was waiting.

Marilyn looked up at the sky as she opened one of the car doors. "Glad we made it to the car in time," she said. "Those clouds sure are dark."

Kennedy looked up. Her stepsister was right; gray clouds were gathering in the sky.

"I'll keep you updated on everything, Rosa," Nicoli said.

Rosa nodded. "Thank you, Detective."

She drove off. Kennedy remained silent the entire time. Thoughts swam through her mind. Matteo was definitely a suspect, no doubt about that. But was his grudge against Lorenzo a good enough motive to frame the janitor for a theft? Kennedy's mind wandered back to the two men's interaction the other day. Matteo didn't seem to like Lorenzo, that was certain.

Rosa dropped the four girls off at the academy. She thanked Kennedy again for her time before she drove away. The four girls rushed down the hallway toward the classroom where they had left their stuff.

"I hope we weren't missed," Rachel said.

"Hey, there you are!"

Kennedy nearly jumped. She and the other girls spun around. Lloyd was walking toward them. He looked relieved.

"I was wondering where the four of you ran off to," Lloyd said. "We're leaving for the opera house in twenty minutes."

He stopped and crossed his arms. "So, how are you ladies doing?"

Kennedy hoped she didn't look too guilty. She tried not to wince at Lloyd's smile. His suspicious smile that matched the suspicious look in his eyes.

"Oh, we weren't doing anything!" Marilyn said.

Lloyd looked at her. "You sure?"

Kennedy kept herself from groaning. Her stepsister's eyes were full of guilt. Then Lloyd looked over at her. Kennedy kept eye contact with him.

"I know you were quite distraught over the robbery at the Uffizi," Lloyd said.

Kennedy nodded. "We were," she said. "Very much so. But I'll bet you spending time at the opera house will help us take our minds off the Uffizi."

Lloyd nodded. "I hope so. Now, why don't you ladies gather your stuff? Bus leaves soon."

Kennedy, Marilyn, Susannah, and Rachel turned to leave. Rachel tried to rush down the hall, but Kennedy grasped her elbow to slow her down. The foursome found their classroom and collected their stuff.

"Is it just me, or did Professor Jennings seem a little suspicious?" Susannah asked nervously.

Kennedy frowned. "I sure hope not," she said.

Kennedy closed her sketchbook. The little student lounge was empty and quiet, but Kennedy still couldn't focus on her artwork. Her time sneaking around the Uffizi with Marilyn, Rachel, Susannah, Rosa, and Nicoli occupied her mind the entire morning.

She heard her phone vibrating in her purse. She pulled it out. Seeing that she had a text, she swiped the screen to read it.

The text was from Rosa.

Kennedy raised her eyebrows. Rosa must have an update for her and the others! She grinned; she had been waiting for this since the previous evening. She read the text.

CAN WE MEET? I HAVE NEWS TO SHARE.

Kennedy tapped her phone's keyboard.

SURE. WE'RE GOING TO THE GRAN CAFFÈ
SAN MARCO AT NOON. MEET US THERE.

She put her phone away and gathered her stuff. She met Marilyn, Susannah, and Rachel in the hall.

"Hey, there," Rachel said. "Get anything done?"

"Not really," Kennedy said. "But we need to go to the Gran Caffè San Marco right away. It's almost noon."

169

"Hey, true," Rachel said. "I'm getting hungry."

"I'm afraid I have another reason we need to go there," Kennedy said in a hushed voice.

She ran for the door and it held it open for Marilyn, Rachel, and Susannah. She looked up at the sky. The sun peeked out from behind the remaining gray clouds.

"Did it finally stop raining?" Rachel asked.

"I guess so." Marilyn smiled. "That's a relief. Now we don't have to worry about walking in the rain."

She turned to Kennedy. "So what's going on?" she asked.

"I got a text from Rosa," Kennedy said.

Susannah stopped. "What does she want?" she asked.

"She wants to meet with us. Probably to give us an update. I told her we'd meet her at the Gran Caffè San Marco at noon."

"But a lot of our teachers and classmates will be there too," Marilyn said.

"Then we'll just have to not look too suspicious," Kennedy said. "We've wandered away once. We shouldn't do it again."

The four girls walked away from the academy. They walked around a puddle on the sidewalk and came to a crosswalk.

"Ow!" Marilyn exclaimed.

Kennedy whirled her head around. A bulky man wearing a black trench coat and bowler hat had apparently bumped into Marilyn. The man gave her a startled look before bending over to pick up a pair of sunglasses.

"Mi scusi," he said.

Kennedy gaped at the man as recognition settled in her mind. He had been in the Uffizi the day before the theft!

The man met Kennedy's eyes as he slowly stood up. She caught a hint of fear in his gray eyes. The man hurriedly put his sunglasses on and walked briskly in the opposite direction. His feet made the puddle splash around him.

"Wow, that guy's in a hurry," Rachel said. "He didn't even go around the puddle. Walked right through it."

"He seemed afraid of me," Kennedy said. She placed her fingers on her chin. "And I'll bet it's because I saw him in the Uffizi the day before the theft of the painting."

Marilyn stared. "Are you serious?"

Kennedy nodded.

"But why be so afraid of you?" Susannah asked. "He has nothing to hide."

"Maybe he does," Kennedy said darkly.

She looked down at the sidewalk. The footprints on the cement made her eyes shoot up in surprise.

"Guys, look!"

Kennedy pointed to the footprints that led away from the puddle. The girls ran over to get a closer look. Kennedy squatted.

"These footprints are the same as the ones we saw at the Uffizi!" she said.

"At the crime scene?" Susannah said. "But Kennedy, surely a lot of guys wear this kind of shoe."

"True," Kennedy said, "but not only was he the same guy I saw in the museum, but he's wearing the same coat, the same hat, and he was really spooked to see me standing here."

"But why?" Susannah demanded.

Kennedy stood up and got her phone out. "That's a new piece to this puzzle. Right now, I'm gonna snap a few pictures of these footprints. Then we'll head to the restaurant."

As soon as Kennedy finished taking pictures of the footprints, she and the other girls continued on. In a few minutes, they arrived at the Gran Caffè San Marco.

"Wow," Marilyn said as she opened the door, "this place is fancy!"

Kennedy had to agree with her stepsister. All thoughts of the man and his footprints were pushed aside as she gazed at the elegant white walls, the counters displaying food and pastries, and the tables with stylish granite tops surrounded by white and dark green cushioned chairs.

Kennedy spotted Lloyd standing in line with two other teachers and a few students. He looked in her direction, smiled, and waved. Kennedy waved back, hoping that her own smile didn't look too guilty.

"Hey, Rosa's over there."

Kennedy turned her head. Marilyn was pointing to a table next to a window. Indeed, Rosa was seated at that table. The four girls ran over to her.

Rosa stood up. "Thank you for coming," she said quietly. She crossed her arms.

Kennedy frowned. "You said you had news," she said. "I take it that it's not good news?"

"I'm afraid not." Rosa sighed. "Nicoli and I went to the police this morning and shared everything with them. They said that the uniform sizes don't provide enough evidence that Lorenzo is innocent. They said they'd look into it, but not soon enough for me."

"What did they say about that woman I saw?" Kennedy asked. "Oh, and then there's that guy."

Rosa raised her eyebrow. "Nicoli's investigating the case about the woman," she said. "But what's this about a guy?"

Kennedy told Rosa about the man she had seen in the Uffizi the day before the robbery, and about how she and the other girls had seen him on their way to the restaurant.

"His footprints matched the ones from the crime scene?" Rosa asked in a hushed voice. "And he seemed wary of meeting up with you?"

"Yep," Kennedy said.

"Hope you guys don't mind," Susannah said, "but I'm getting hungry. Mind if we order something?"

"Oh, of course not," Rosa said. "Sit down."

They picked up the menus just as a waitress came to their table. Rosa gave everyone's orders to the waitress. She took the menus and left. As soon as Kennedy was sure the waitress was out of earshot, she pulled out her phone to show her photos to Rosa.

"See?" she whispered. "All those footprints match. They're even roughly the same size."

"I suppose," Rosa said. "But that doesn't automatically mean that this man you saw is the thief."

"I get that. But I still think we should let Nicoli know."

Rosa nodded. "Text me your pictures," she said. "I'll send them to Nicoli."

Kennedy texted her photos to Rosa. Just then, Lloyd came over to their table. Kennedy, Marilyn, Rachel, Susannah, and Rosa looked up at him.

"So," Lloyd said, putting a hand on his hip, "what are you ladies up to?"

"Uh, just getting lunch?" Susannah said with a small smile.

Lloyd nodded. "I figured you'd be talking about the Uffizi mess," he said.

Rosa looked down at her napkin. "I am very worried about this whole mess," she said.

Lloyd's expression softened. "I understand," he said. "I hope I don't sound insensitive, but I heard that you are leading our tour on Tuesday?"

Rosa smiled meekly. "It's fine," she said. "And yes, I will be."

"We really enjoyed your tour the other day," Lloyd said. "I'm glad you're leading it."

"*Grazie.*"

The waitress came with the girls' meals. Lloyd went to his own table.

"So, what are we going to do now?" Rachel asked.

"I'm not sure there's anything else that can be done," Rosa said. "I doubt there's anything more at the Uffizi to look at."

"Probably not," Susannah said. "I really don't think there's anything else we can do."

"Wow, Susannah," Rachel said, "you sound like you want to give up."

Susannah scowled at Rachel. "Maybe I do," she said.

"But we can't. Rosa might still need Kennedy's help."

Susannah sighed. "I knew you and Kennedy had a lot in common."

Kennedy stared at Susannah. "What's wrong with you?"

Rosa sighed. "I'm sorry," she said. "If I had known that getting you girls involved would be too much stress—"

"*Buon pomeriggio,* Rosa."

Kennedy whirled her head around. Alfonso Martini was standing at their table, smiling at Rosa. But Rosa wasn't smiling back.

"*Ciao,* Alfonso," she said, looking down at her plate.

Alfonso's smile faded. "Are you alright?" he asked. "I don't suppose I can cheer you up? Introduce me to your new friends."

Rosa shrugged. "Meet Kennedy, Marilyn, Susannah, and Rachel."

"I saw you ladies at the Uffizi on Rosa's tours," Alfonso said. "She leads tours well. We've known each other since college. How I missed her when she was in America! So I learned English myself."

"Just to impress me," Rosa muttered.

Alfonso glanced at Rosa. "My dear," he said, "what's wrong? Or . . ."

He scowled. "You're still pining about Lorenzo, aren't you? I told you, get over that art thief. He'll never be a curator now."

Rosa glared at Alfonso and leapt from her seat. She spoke brusquely in Italian.

"Uh oh," Rachel murmured, "this is gonna escalate."

Kennedy stood up. "I'm, uh, gonna get us dessert," she said.

"I'll go with you," Susannah said.

The two girls left the table. Kennedy noticed that a few people were staring at Rosa and Alfonso. Rosa grabbed Alfonso's elbow and pulled him to a small hallway.

"So, Susie," Kennedy said, facing her friend, "want to tell me what's wrong?"

Susannah shrugged. "I just miss our friendship," she said.

"What do you mean? We're still friends."

"Not nearly as close as we used to be."

"That's not true." Kennedy crossed her arms. "Are you jealous of Rachel?"

Susannah gave Kennedy a shocked look. "No!"

"Really? Look, yes, she is my friend and we do have a lot in common."

"Like your art," Susannah said. "You attended that art workshop and missed my solo. I felt like I didn't have my own friend's support. Even though I was touring the Uffizi with you to support you."

"You know I support you in your musical endeavors, Susie."

Susannah sighed and looked away. "I just feel like we're drifting," she said. "I mean, Rachel and Marilyn were so close to you in Pine Lodge. And I was behind in Dallas. And we don't seem to be making up for it since the four of us moved in together."

Kennedy stared sadly at her friend. She wished she knew how to make Susannah feel better. But there was no way she was going to compromise her friendship with Rachel. Why would Susannah even ask for such a thing?

Sudden movement from the corner of her eye made Kennedy turn her head. A willowy woman with black hair had just seated herself at a nearby table. Just as she pulled a wallet from her purse, something else fell out and landed on the floor with a clink.

Kennedy ran over to the item and picked it up. She meant to speak to the woman, but then her eyes rested on the item she was holding, and she had to stifle a gasp.

It was half of a hair comb with white rhinestones and pearls.

Kennedy whipped out her own phone and went to her photo gallery. She pulled up a picture of the hair comb Nicoli had found in the museum.

The comb in the picture and the comb in her hand were perfect halves. They had to be the same comb!

174

Kennedy looked back up at the woman, openmouthed. So she was the one Kennedy had seen sneaking around the Uffizi. Her eyes wandered back and forth from the comb to her phone.

"*Ahem.*"

Kennedy looked up and nearly jumped. The woman was looking right at her. Her eyes darted from Kennedy to the comb in her hand.

"Oh!" Kennedy said, forcing a smile. She was about to hand over the comb, but she hesitated. Should she give the comb to Nicoli? But she had no excuse to keep the comb with her. Not to mention that she could hardly speak any Italian.

The woman held out her hand and wiggled her fingers. Kennedy gave her the comb and a polite nod.

"*Grazie,*" the woman said. She stood up and left the restaurant. Kennedy took a step forward. The temptation to follow the woman was almost irresistible. But then Kennedy noticed Lloyd talking and laughing with a few students. She couldn't risk raising his suspicions again.

"*Basta!*"

Kennedy whipped her head around. Rosa was not in sight. But she sure sounded angry.

"*Non voglio sentire altro!*"

Several heads turned just as a fuming Alfonso came stomping through the dining area. He ignored all stares as he made his way to the entrance. He pushed the door open so roughly that Kennedy almost felt relieved that the glass wasn't shattered. Her eyes searched the dining area for her table. Rosa was sitting down next to Marilyn.

Kennedy looked over at Susannah, who was standing at the counter. Susannah was staring at the entrance with wide eyes. She glanced at Kennedy. Kennedy rushed over to the counter. The two girls paid for their pastries and returned to their table.

"What was that all about?" Kennedy asked as she sat down.

Rosa hid her face in her hands. "That Alfonso," she said, her voice breaking, "will not leave me alone. I've always known he wanted to date me, but I didn't think he was this desperate. I'm sure he's relieved that Lorenzo's sitting in jail. For a crime he didn't even commit, but not that Alfonso would care. All he does care about is that Lorenzo is out of his way."

She sighed heavily. "It's no use. We might as well give up. I can't think of anything else to do for Lorenzo."

"Oh, no!" Kennedy said. "We're not giving up yet. I've got something to tell the rest of you."

"Really?" Rachel said eagerly. "Do share!"

Kennedy told Rosa, Marilyn, Susannah, and Rachel about the woman and how she had with her the other half of the hair comb that they had found in the Uffizi.

Rosa's eyes widened. "You cannot be serious!"

"I am," Kennedy said. "I think you should try to get a hold of Nicoli and tell him."

"Yes, I have his number. I can call him now. Can you write a description of the woman for me, Kennedy?"

Kennedy grabbed a napkin from the napkin holder and wrote down the woman's description. Rosa took the napkin and went back to the hall.

"Hey, Susannah, are you okay?" Rachel asked. "You seem really down all of a sudden."

Susannah shrugged. "Yeah, I'm good."

Kennedy eyed her friend. Her stomach churned as guilt washed over her.

After a few minutes of silence, Rosa returned to the table. "I called Nicoli," she said. "But he didn't seem interested in what I had to say. He ended with a hasty goodbye and hung up on me."

Kennedy raised an eyebrow. "That's . . . weird."

"You're telling me!" Rachel said. "You'd think a private detective would be all over a new clue!"

Kennedy nodded slowly. What was Nicoli's deal? Why was he being so dismissive with this woman?

"Alright!" Rosa called. "Twenty-minute break!"

Kennedy breathed a sigh of relief. Normally, she would be enjoying a tour of the Uffizi. But today, she had been unable to focus on Rosa's lectures.

Kennedy brushed past Susannah, not even looking at her. She went straight to the café, but her stomach wasn't rumbling. She bought a drink and a cookie, and then she went out onto the terrace and stood at the edge. Her eyes wandered over the city. She spotted the Palazzo Vecchio, the town hall of Florence. She sighed. Her worrisome thoughts wouldn't let her enjoy the view of the city.

Susannah hadn't said a word to her since that morning. Kennedy wondered why Susannah was even on this tour with her. And they were no closer to proving Lorenzo's innocence. Rosa acted professional and cordial during the tour, but Kennedy could tell that she was distraught over her boyfriend. At least Alfonso had stayed clear.

Kennedy looked up at the giant clock on a skyscraper. Its second and minute hands appeared frozen in place, idly pointing at the Roman numerals on the clock.

"You know, Kennedy, simply staring at that clock won't make it go any faster."

Kennedy turned around. Marilyn was standing next to her, gazing at the city.

Kennedy chuckled. "I'm just waiting for our tour to start up again. Not so patiently, I admit."

"Is that all?" Marilyn asked. "Rachel and I have noticed that you and Susannah seem distant."

Kennedy looked at her stepsister. "Susannah just thinks I'm not being a good friend to her. She thinks I'm more interested in my friendship with Rachel."

"I see." Marilyn crossed her arms. "I'm sorry."

Kennedy shrugged. "We should probably go back in. Tour's bound to continue soon."

The two girls went into the café. Kennedy's eyes glazed over the area. Lloyd was talking to Rosa in Italian. People were chatting and laughing with one another, including Susannah and Rachel at one table.

Kennedy's eyes widened and her mouth dropped. She half-expected Susannah to be sitting at a different table. Kennedy and Marilyn glanced at one another. Marilyn smiled. Kennedy ran over to the table, her stepsister on her heels.

"What's going on here?" she asked.

Susannah's smile faded a little, but she still spoke in a cheerful voice. "Rachel and I are just hanging out and chitchatting."

"I am so going to listen to her solo on Tuesday," Rachel said. "I told her that I've been wanting to hear her sing for ages. I mean, you've told me more than once that she's a fab soprano."

Susannah's smile grew. Kennedy gave her a hopeful look.

"And I'll finally have some free time on Tuesday," Rachel added, "so I'm gonna listen to Susannah sing her heart out."

Kennedy grinned. "And I'll be there too."

"You mean it?" Susannah asked hopefully.

"Wouldn't miss it for the world."

Just then Rosa approached the table. Kennedy gave her an encouraging smile. "*Ciao,*" she said.

Rosa smiled meekly. "How are you girls doing?" she asked. "Look, I feel awful about all the drama at the restaurant yesterday. I know you're all getting stressed."

"Don't worry about it," Kennedy said, waving her hand. "I don't blame you at all. Are you doing alright?"

"Well, there is something I feel like I should tell you," Rosa said. "I was talking to one of the guys at the front desk this morning. We were talking about Lorenzo's arrest. Well, mostly him. But he mentioned that Lorenzo had two name tags."

"Okay?" Marilyn said. "Why's that important?"

"Well," Rosa said, "we know that Lorenzo's name tag was found at the scene of the crime. But my coworker at the front desk said that he had seen Lorenzo's name tag on him while he was being arrested. Apparently, someone requested a new name tag for Lorenzo. It arrived the day before the theft."

"Why would Lorenzo need two name tags?" Kennedy asked.

"Well, he certainly isn't leaving one at the crime scene for police to find," Rachel said sarcastically. "Do you know who asked for this second name tag?"

Rosa shook her head. "I asked the same question. My coworker said he doesn't remember who made the request, except that he knows for sure it wasn't Lorenzo."

Kennedy cringed. "Now that is suspicious," she said. "The theft of the painting had to have been an inside job. I mean, Nicoli had told us that the lock to the security room door hadn't been picked. And now Lorenzo randomly gets a second name tag that arrives right before the theft?"

She narrowed her eyes. "Rosa, any chance it could've been Matteo? He certainly has a motive as well as the means."

Rosa shook her head. "When I visited Lorenzo in jail, I asked him who was working the night of the theft. Lorenzo said that Matteo was off."

Kennedy held in a sigh. Rapid movement from the corner of her eye made her turn her head. Kennedy spotted Alfonso walking briskly down the hall. He looked over at Kennedy. His eyes widened, and Kennedy could see the wary look in them. Alfonso averted his eyes and disappeared from sight.

Rosa checked her wristwatch. "It's about time to start the tour back up," she said. She looked at Kennedy. "Thank you."

Kennedy nodded. "Anytime. Thank you for the new info."

Rosa went over to Lloyd's side. Lloyd clapped his hands to get everyone's attention. In a few minutes, the tour continued. Kennedy kept an eye out for Alfonso. But she didn't see him again.

"Well, here we are," Rachel said, "back at the Uffizi. Don't get me wrong, visiting the Uffizi has been amazing, but I wonder when we're going to check out those other art galleries?"

Marilyn laughed. "We will, soon enough."

Kennedy nodded a little. She was looking forward to seeing the other art galleries in Florence, but she would miss visiting the Uffizi. After a boring weekend plus a Monday that seemed to last forever, Kennedy was glad to be away from the hotel.

She turned to Susannah. "I also wanna say," she said, "that your solo was excellent."

"Oh, yeah!" Rachel said. "Susie, you were awesome! More amazing than I ever could've expected!"

Susannah smiled shyly. "Thanks, gals. I'm so glad you were able to come watch my choir this morning."

She met Kennedy's eyes. She was still smiling, but Kennedy could see an apologetic look in her friend's green eyes.

"Our tour begins in five minutes," Marilyn said. She looked around the lobby. "Wonder where Rosa is."

"Not sure where Rosa is," Rachel said, "but I think that guy at the front desk is our old friend the private detective."

Kennedy looked over at the front desk. Rachel was right; Nicoli was speaking with Alfonso and two front desk employees. Kennedy frowned; Nicoli's voice had a serious—almost grave—tone. And the look in his eyes matched that tone. The two desk employees appeared concerned. Alfonso had his arms crossed and his head down.

"I think there's something wrong," Kennedy whispered.

The other students and the teachers seemed to sense that something was amiss. Lloyd went over to the front desk and spoke to Nicoli and the employees.

"Gosh," Marilyn said, "I sure hope Nicoli doesn't tell Lloyd about us."

Kennedy nodded. Her stomach churned as Lloyd looked in her direction. The next ten minutes seemed like a silent eternity. Finally, Lloyd and Alfonso approached the students.

"Everyone," Lloyd said quietly, "this is Alfonso Martini. He is leading our tour today. Miss Rosa Morelli, is, um, unavailable."

Kennedy, Marilyn, Rachel, and Susannah exchanged nervous glances. What was going on? Kennedy's eyes fell on Nicoli. He gave her a grave nod.

"Mr. Martini isn't quite ready to begin yet," Lloyd added. "We'll wait for just another few minutes."

The students dispersed around the lobby, whispering curiously to one another. Kennedy eyed Lloyd. He was talking to the other teachers.

"Think we can chance talking to Nicoli?" Marilyn asked in a hushed voice.

"I think we should try," Kennedy said.

She, Marilyn, Susannah, and Rachel went over to Nicoli. He turned his gaze to the four girls.

"Nicoli," Kennedy said, "hey, it's us. Uh, is there something going on that we need to know about?"

Nicoli hesitated. "I suppose you should know," he said, "given how much you've gotten yourselves involved."

He breathed deeply. "Rosa had been kidnapped from her home during the night."

A sudden wave of nausea washed over Kennedy, and her heartbeat took off. She and the other girls exchanged horrified looks.

"You're kidding!" Rachel hissed.

"No, I am not," Nicoli said. "We received a phone call from an anonymous witness. We've been investigating the house since early this morning. I came here to inform the Uffizi staff."

He turned his gaze to Kennedy. "I suggest the four of you watch your backs," he said. "Who knows what might happen next."

"We understand," Susannah said. "Thank you."

"Nicoli," Rachel said, "what did Rosa say to you on the phone? When she told you about Kennedy meeting that lady with the hair comb at the restaurant?"

Nicoli frowned. "That woman is nobody to worry about," he said shortly.

"No one to worry about? But she was sneaking around this place right after the theft of that painting!"

Nicoli opened his mouth, as though he wanted to say something. But he immediately closed it and shrugged. Kennedy gave him a suspicious look. With his reluctance to talk about this mysterious woman, she wasn't sure that she trusted him anymore.

She glanced over her shoulder. Lloyd was still talking to the teachers. She noticed Alfonso walking toward them.

"You four young ladies are waiting for the tour, si?" he said. "I'm almost ready."

"Yes, we are," Susannah said, "but, uh . . ."

"We're friends of Rosa's," Kennedy said. "You remember us, right? I hope you don't mind, but we know about Rosa."

Alfonso's eyes drooped, but Kennedy could still see the worry in them.

"It's alright," he said. "I do remember the four of you. And I would like to apologize for what happened in the restaurant a few days ago. I deeply care for Rosa. I fancy her. She's kind and good with the tourists and loves her job. I truly do not know what Rosa has against me. I suppose she thinks I am a rude and entitled person simply because I am from a wealthy family. If only she would let me prove her wrong. I've often worried about her relationship with Lorenzo."

"Oh?" Kennedy hoped her voice didn't betray her growing suspicions. "How so?"

"Lorenzo was always sketchy," Alfonso said. "He was never very nice to our security guards, for one thing. Especially Matteo."

"But Matteo wasn't nice to him to begin with," Rachel said.

"That's not true. Oh, I suppose Rosa told you about Matteo always hanging out on his phone? Well, that's not true. You see, Lorenzo . . . well, he manipulates facts and twists them to make him look innocent. But he was always the one slacking off on the job. Matteo was relieved when the head of security offered him a position in the security department. Anyway, Lorenzo fell behind in college very suddenly. I believe he slacked off in his studies all the time. That's why Rosa and I finished before he did. And he can hardly afford college. I've heard him complain more than once about his college bills. I also know that he used to work for the Palatine Gallery at the Palazzo Pitti."

"The Palatine Gallery?" Marilyn said. "That's the other art museum that had been robbed, right? Just a month ago?"

Alfonso nodded. "Lorenzo quit working there because he said they weren't paying him enough. I think he just wanted to be here with Rosa. Oh, and he quit his job at the Palatine just days before their robbery. I think he was behind that theft, too."

Kennedy paused. But before she could say anything else, Alfonso decided to start the tour. He led Kennedy, Marilyn, Rachel, and Susannah to the center of the lobby.

Kennedy caught Lloyd's eye. The suspicious look he had was enough to make her wish she could disappear on the spot.

Kennedy held the door open for Marilyn, Rachel, and Susannah. As soon as she closed it, she plopped herself on her bed.

"I still can't believe it about poor Rosa," Rachel said.

"Yeah." Kennedy stared up at the ceiling. "I feel like we're responsible."

"No, Ken," Marilyn said gently, "it's not our fault. But we do need to be careful now. I'll make sure our door is locked and bolted tonight."

"I do think I prefer Rosa's tours over Alfonso," Rachel said. "He doesn't seem to know his stuff as well as Rosa. He even got some of his art history wrong."

"And he doesn't seem to like answering questions," Susannah added.

Kennedy just shrugged. She had paid little attention to Alfonso's lectures. Her head had been swimming with anxious thoughts about Rosa and her own personal safety. She felt like she had just been wandering aimlessly around the Uffizi's hallways.

"You know," Rachel said, "I have a hard time believing those things he said about Lorenzo."

"Same here." Kennedy sat up. "I mean, I know we haven't known Rosa or Lorenzo for long, but Rosa seems like a very smart young woman. I can't shake the feeling that something is off with Alfonso's stories."

In a whisper she added, "And with Nicoli."

"Nicoli?" Rachel said. "But Ken, he's the detective."

"Who really will not say anything about that woman," Kennedy said.

A loud knock made all four girls turn their eyes to the door. They looked at each other. Then Kennedy got up and went to the door.

She didn't expect to find Lloyd, Nicoli, and the woman from the restaurant standing there.

Kennedy held in a gasp. Once again, she wished she could just vanish into thin air. She didn't think Lloyd's stare could get any sterner even if she had disrupted his class in the worst way possible. Nicoli had his arms crossed and a grumpy look on his face. Only the woman was smiling.

"Good afternoon, Kennedy," Lloyd said. "I'm glad to see that you and your friends are here. Mind if we step in? It seems like there's some interesting stuff that we need to chat about."

Kennedy's heart skipped a beat, but she held the door open. Lloyd, Nicoli, and the woman entered. Kennedy could only give apologetic looks to her friends, all three of whom appeared just as surprised and nervous as she felt.

The woman turned to Kennedy. Her smile grew. *"Ciao,"* she said. "You are Miss Kennedy Ryan, *sì?*"

Kennedy nodded. "I reckon you remember me from the Gran Caffè San Marco?"

"I do," the woman said. "And from the Uffizi."

"I'm sorry," Rachel said, "who are you?"

"That's what I would like to know," Lloyd said. He sat on a chair and crossed his arms. "Among a few thousand other details."

The woman chuckled. "My name is Arianna Farina," she said. "I'm a detective for the Carabinieri Art Squad."

She reached into her black jacket and pulled out a badge. She gave it to Kennedy. But everything on the badge was written in Italian. Kennedy could only read the name: *Arianna Farina*.

She showed the badge to Marilyn. "Can you translate?"

Marilyn took the badge. "Yep," she said, "she's a detective, alright."

She handed the badge back to Arianna. "So what brings you to us?"

"I hope this doesn't ruin my reputation," Arianna said with a grin, "but it appears that I need your girls' help."

"And I need your girls' explanation!" Lloyd said.

"Yes, yes, we do owe you an explanation," Kennedy said. She looked back at Arianna. "Is this about Rosa Morelli?"

"I'm afraid it is," Arianna said.

"Wait, I'm really confused!" Rachel said. "If you're another art squad detective, Arianna, then why were you sneaking around the Uffizi the other night?"

Nicoli sighed and crossed his arms. "Apparently, she was investigating the theft as well," he said.

Arianna glared at him.

"I think everyone owes everyone an explanation." Kennedy glanced at Lloyd. "I'll begin. The truth is, Professor Jennings, I may have been doing some sleuthing."

"Sleuthing!" Lloyd jumped to his feet. "Excuse me?"

He put his hand on his forehead. "Oh, what am I saying? I should've known. I've been suspicious all this time."

"Yeah, we could tell," Rachel said flatly.

With a sigh, Kennedy told Lloyd everything. She told him about going to the Uffizi after Rosa asked her and her friends to help. She told Lloyd about meeting Nicoli at the Uffizi and looking at the uniforms. She also mentioned how she met Arianna at the restaurant after she found the second half of the broken hair comb.

184

"I didn't know who she was at the restaurant," Kennedy said. She glared at Nicoli. "But I wondered why Nicoli here was so reluctant to talk about her."

Nicoli groaned. "So you want the truth?" he said. "Fine. Arianna is my ex-girlfriend."

"Your ex-girlfriend?" Kennedy said.

"Yeah, we used to date," Arianna said. She scowled at Nicoli. "But things, well, they fell apart after he falsely accused my brother of robbing the Palatine Gallery last month."

"It was a mistake!" Nicoli said, raising his hands. "Those clues had been planted very cleverly. Anyone could've fallen for it!"

"Yeah, as though Angelo would ever rob from the art museum where he works as the head of security!"

"Alright," Lloyd said impatiently, "can the two detectives please stop arguing and get on with their explanations?"

Arianna sighed. "My apologies," she said. "A month ago, the Palatine was robbed. Nicoli and I both took the case. Nicoli found evidence against my brother, Angelo, who is the head of security at the Palatine."

She and Nicoli exchanged scowls.

"But," Arianna continued, "after I investigated a little more, I found, much to my relief, that Angelo was innocent. I discovered that the real culprit was Gerardo Greco, an art thief who is infamous throughout Florence for his cunning. And when I heard about the robbery at the Uffizi, I decided to investigate."

"And you suspect that this art thief Gerardo Greco robbed the Uffizi?" Marilyn asked hopefully.

"Very much so," Arianna said. "Gerardo is a tricky thief. He knows how to plant the most convincing false clues to cover up his own tracks and keep all evidence away from himself. Nicoli told me about the four of you girls helping Rosa."

"Well, this is the first time I'm hearing about this Gerardo Greco," Kennedy said. "Rosa never mentioned him."

"Then you've already answered my question," Arianna said with a smile. "I'm certain Rosa would've heard of Gerardo, given his infamy, but I wanted to ask you if Rosa gave any indication of knowing Gerardo personally. But I guess not."

"Wait, hold on," Kennedy said, holding up her hands, "even if Gerardo did rob the Uffizi, why would he kidnap Rosa days later?"

"That's what we're trying to find out," Nicoli said.

"What about that guy Rosa was yelling at in the restaurant the other day?" Lloyd asked.

"That was Alfonso Martini," Kennedy said. "A coworker of Rosa's at the Uffizi. He really wants to date her, but she does not like him. I think he was relieved when Lorenzo was arrested."

"And Alfonso was the one who told us that Lorenzo was behind the theft at the Palatine Gallery!" Susannah said.

"But why would he lie to us?" Marilyn said. "Unless he didn't know about Gerardo?"

"I dunno, girls," Lloyd said, "what you're saying sounds pretty suspicious if you ask me."

"What does Gerardo look like?" Kennedy asked. "Just in case, you know. I wouldn't mind keeping an eye out for him."

"I have a photo," Arianna said. She reached into her pocket. She pulled out a little photograph and handed it to Kennedy. Her heart dropped and she let out a gasp when she saw the man in the photograph.

It was the man who had bumped into the four girls on the sidewalk. Who left the footprints on the sidewalk. Who Kennedy saw in the Uffizi the day before the theft of the painting.

"What's the matter, Kennedy?" Rachel asked.

Kennedy showed her the photo. Rachel's eyebrows shot up in surprise. She showed the photo to Susannah and Marilyn, both of whom looked every bit as astonished as Kennedy felt.

"You girls know him?" Arianna asked.

"I'm sorry!" Lloyd exclaimed. "We've only been here from another country for what, a week? How can four of my students already have met an infamous criminal?"

He slapped his forehead in disgust. "What am I saying, this is Kennedy Ryan I'm talking about."

Kennedy snorted and told her teacher about her and her friends meeting Gerardo on their way to the Gran Caffè San Marco.

"I promise you, we didn't know who he was at first," she said. "But when he walked through that puddle, the footprints he left matched the ones in the Uffizi."

Nicoli pulled out his phone. "You mean this picture? The one Rosa sent me the other day?"

Kennedy looked at his phone. She compared his photos to the pictures on her phone. The footprints were identical.

"So this means that Gerardo was at large in the city after the theft," Arianna said.

186

Lloyd sighed. "This isn't good," he said. He looked at Kennedy. "You need to be careful. After what happened to Rosa, who knows what danger you might be in?"

Kennedy's stomach flipped. Her teacher was right. Why else would Gerardo kidnap Rosa, unless he somehow figured out everything that was going on? How much did he already know about the four girls, for that matter?

"Is there anything else that you want to share with us?" Lloyd asked Nicoli.

Nicoli shook his head. "I don't believe so. But I will be keeping an eye on these four girls until we catch Gerardo, or until Rosa is found."

"What about Arianna?" Rachel asked.

"I will be investigating the *Viti Reali di Calenzano,*" Arianna said.

"The what?" Rachel said.

"It's a winery," Arianna said. "We found a receipt from that winery at Rosa's house this morning."

"What?" Kennedy gasped. "But that winery is owned by Alfonso's family!"

"I know. I planned to go there, and after what you girls told me about Alfonso, I really need to."

"But Rosa's never been there," Kennedy said. "She told us the day we met her. She also said she wouldn't go there. What's the date and time on the receipt?"

Arianna pulled a small piece of paper from her pocket. She looked at it.

"2:05 PM on Thursday, May 7th," she said.

"Yeah," Kennedy said, "Rosa was at the Gran Caffè San Marco with us then. That was when she yelled at Alfonso. After we left the restaurant, we all went to the Uffizi. Rosa included."

"So you're saying she wasn't at this winery in Calenzano on this date?" Arianna said.

Kennedy nodded.

"Then how did this receipt get into Rosa's house?" Arianna asked.

"The only other person would've had to have been the kidnapper," Nicoli said. "It's very important that we go to this winery now."

"And I'm going with you," Kennedy said. She met each pair of shocked eyes with a defiant stare.

187

"I don't think so," Nicoli said. "Why would you want to go anyway?"

"Because I'm already too involved," Kennedy said. "We all are. You say this winery's in Calenzano, right? Well, we'll be in Calenzano."

She looked at Lloyd. "The syllabus calls for the attendance of an outdoor concert in Calenzano, right? At 11:30?"

Lloyd groaned. "I'm afraid it does. And we do need to leave for that concert shortly."

"The winery doesn't open until noon." Arianna smiled. "It might not hurt to keep you posted on everything, Kennedy. Alright, we'll all go to Calenzano. Nicoli and I will follow you. After your concert, we'll check out the winery."

"I might as well go too," Lloyd said. "As a teacher, I'm responsible for the safety of my students."

Under normal circumstances, Kennedy would've enjoyed an outdoor concert. The rolling hills covered in lush green grass, glowing under a cloudless blue sky, seemed to match the string quartet's cheerful and lively music. But Kennedy couldn't push back the guilt clouding her mind. While she was sitting around watching a concert, Rosa was still being held prisoner somewhere. Was she okay? Was she even still alive?

No, Kennedy! she admonished herself. *You've got to have faith in God. He's guided your friends before. Just think of Susannah's cousin, Alec. And your friend Tiana Flores. They've suffered from kidnapping, but they're alright now. Just trust in God to protect Rosa now and that she'll be alright like Alec and Tiana turned out to be.*

Kennedy took a deep breath.

After what seemed like an eternity, the four musicians stood up and bowed. Even the applause seemed to take forever to Kennedy.

"That was really good," Susannah said.

"Yes, it was," Kennedy said. "But now we've got to meet up with Nicoli and Arianna."

"We don't need to," Lloyd said. "They're over there."

Kennedy turned around. Nicoli and Arianna were walking over to them.

"Enjoy the concert?" Arianna asked.

Kennedy just nodded.

"Nicoli and I are ready. The winery is only a five-minute drive from here."

"Let's go, then," Lloyd said, "and get this over with."

Nicoli and Arianna led Lloyd and the girls to their police cars. Kennedy, Susannah, and Lloyd got into Arianna's car. As soon as Arianna started the engine and pulled out, Kennedy looked over her shoulder. Nicoli was close behind them.

It truly was only a five-minute drive. They didn't even leave the countryside. Arianna pulled the car into the parking lot of a fancy winery. She parked right in front of the building. Nicoli parked his car next to hers.

Everyone climbed out of the cars. Kennedy gazed at the winery. It was a big building made of a beautiful, off-white stone. An elegant brown trim decorated the windows and main entrance. There was a wide patio in front of the winery. It stretched out to the side of the building. A pergola made of fine wood sitting upon the patio could be seen on the side of the winery. Under the pergola was a black outdoor table surrounded by cushioned outdoor chairs. Kennedy spotted hanging flowerpots within the pergola, larger flowerpots sitting on the patio, and a small fountain in one corner.

Nicoli turned his gaze to Arianna. He spoke to her in Italian. Judging by the longing and hopeful look in his eyes and voice, Kennedy wondered if he was asking Arianna on a date at this very winery. Well, if he was, Arianna didn't seem interested; she looked down on the ground and responded in a low voice. Nicoli's face dropped.

Kennedy quickly turned her attention away from the two detectives. She looked up at the wooden sign hanging above the main door. In purple calligraphic lettering, the sign read VITI REALI DI CALENZANO.

"So, what does that say?" Rachel asked Marilyn.

Marilyn looked up at the sign. "That translates to *Royal Grapevines of Calenzano*," she said.

Nicoli held the door open. Everyone entered. The tasting room looked like a fancy restaurant. The floor was made of shiny, oak brown tile. Dark green sofas stood under the large windows near the front of the tasting room. The main counter had a beautiful brown top that seemed to match the floor. Just below the top, golden yellow curlicue patterns decorated the gray siding of the counter. Stools were placed under the countertop. Behind the counter, Kennedy could make out shelves of different kinds of wine, all of which appeared to be kept in glass bottles of various hues of red, green, purple, orange, yellow, pink, and blue. The wall against which the shelves stood was a solid olive green color. Kennedy caught whiffs of floral and citrus scents as she approached the counter.

Kennedy took a step forward, intending to sit on one of the stools. But she hesitated. She turned to the other girls.

"You know," she whispered, "should the four of us be in here? None of us are of age. At least not if we were in the United States."

Rachel shrugged. "We can just sit down over there."

She pointed her thumb over her shoulder to the sofas near the windows.

"I'll stay with you," Lloyd said.

He led the four girls to the sofas. Kennedy and Susannah sat on one sofa. Lloyd, Rachel, and Marilyn sat on the other sofa. Kennedy watched Nicoli and Arianna go to the counter. Nicoli had the receipt in his hand. All Kennedy could do was stare at them and exchange a few nervous looks with the other girls, all the while twiddling her thumbs in her folded hands.

A middle-aged woman came to the counter. She smiled cordially at Nicoli and Arianna and greeted them in Italian.

Kennedy frowned. She came to listen to Nicoli's questions. She even expected to see Alfonso. But Alfonso was absent, and she wouldn't be able to understand Nicoli and Arianna's conversation. She laid back and shrugged in defeat.

Lloyd stood up. The four girls turned their eyes to him. He smiled and nodded at Kennedy. Then he went over to a small table and sat down.

Kennedy stared at her teacher. She smiled. Was he really going to translate for them?

She looked back at Nicoli and Arianna. Arianna handed the receipt to the woman. The woman looked at it, and then she began speaking.

Lloyd turned in his seat to face Kennedy. "Alright," he said in a hushed voice, "that lady is saying that a man did come into this winery on Thursday."

Arianna spoke in Italian.

"Arianna's asking for his description," Lloyd said. "Ah, she's describing the customer as a man about six feet, two inches, broad-shouldered, uh, with a pale and pointed face, shaggy black hair, and gray eyes."

Arianna pulled the photo out of her pocket and showed it to the woman. She continued speaking in Italian, but abruptly stopped when the woman gasped and covered her mouth with her hand. Kennedy didn't need Lloyd to translate.

Susannah grinned. "Seems like Gerardo was in here!"

"Hush, there's more," Lloyd said, waving his hand.

Kennedy gazed at her teacher. His eyes were fixed on the counter, and he sat as still as a statue on display at the Uffizi. Kennedy couldn't stop fidgeting. When was Lloyd going to speak?

Lloyd's eyes widened in surprise, and he nearly jumped out of his seat. Kennedy leaned back, her fingers clutching the arm of the sofa.

"What's wrong?" she asked.

Lloyd spun around to face her. "Alfonso was with that guy when he came in on Thursday."

Kennedy stifled a gasp. Alfonso met an infamous art thief right here in this winery?

"Apparently there was nobody else here when Gerardo came in on Thursday," Lloyd said. "Just that lady and Alfonso. The guy was wearing a black trench coat, a black bowler hat, and a pair of sunglasses."

Kennedy's eyes widened. Gerardo was wearing those very things when Kennedy saw him in the Uffizi and on the sidewalk.

"He and Alfonso went outside to talk. After about an hour, the man left. He seemed to be in a hurry to get out."

"*Grazie,*" Nicoli said.

Kennedy stood up. She knew what that meant. Nicoli had just thanked the woman. Which meant he and Arianna were done asking their questions. They walked over to Lloyd and the girls.

"We heard you whispering back here," Arianna said with a smile. "You're good, Lloyd."

Lloyd shrugged.

"But if the woman recognized Gerardo from your photo," Susannah said, "why didn't she recognize him when he came in to meet Alfonso?"

"His hat and sunglasses covered his face," Arianna said. "The woman said that she thought Gerardo looked familiar when he came in. But she couldn't figure out why. She just assumed he was a friend of Alfonso's."

"But why would Alfonso meet with an art thief in his own parents' winery?" Kennedy asked. "At a very calm moment when there are no customers and only two employees on the job? One of which happens to be Alfonso himself."

"Yes, that is suspicious," Nicoli said.

"You know what else is suspicious?" Kennedy said. "Both Alfonso and Rosa work at the Uffizi. Alfonso likes Rosa, but Rosa doesn't like him. The Uffizi gets robbed. Rosa's boyfriend Lorenzo is arrested for the crime. Then Rosa is kidnapped days later. And Alfonso meets with an infamous art thief."

All eyes turned to Kennedy. She smiled. Nicoli and Arianna exchanged glances.

"Well, Arianna and I learned that Alfonso is coming for his shift in just a few minutes," Nicoli said. "We want to question him. I suggest that the rest of you wait outside."

"I like that idea," Lloyd said dryly.

He waved his index finger at the girls, motioning for them to follow him outside. Kennedy reluctantly stood up. She wanted to be present for Alfonso's questioning. She had so many questions herself. But then again, how well would Alfonso cooperate with her? And it did make sense that Nicoli and Arianna wouldn't want anyone else present when Alfonso arrived, given that he had been meeting with an infamous art thief.

Lloyd and the girls went outside. But before any of them could walk off the patio, a red Ferrari pulled into the parking lot of the winery. Kennedy narrowed her eyes; Alfonso was the driver.

"Well, look who's here," Rachel said. She stepped to the side. "I suppose we'd better get out of here before there's trouble."

Alfonso parked his car and got out. As he walked toward the patio, Lloyd stood in front of the four girls.

"Stay behind me," he said sternly. "Just let him pass. We'll let Nicoli and Arianna ask their questions."

Kennedy's heart rate went up as Alfonso approached them. He stared at them with wide eyes.

"What are you all doing here?" he asked.

"Uh," Rachel said, her voice and awkward smile betraying her anxiety, "we were just at a lovely countryside concert."

Alfonso turned to Lloyd. "Aren't your students a little young to be hanging around a winery?"

He looked over at the windows. Kennedy's heart dropped when she saw Alfonso's eyes widen in horrified astonishment. She eyed the windows; she saw Nicoli and Arianna staring expectantly at Alfonso through the clear glass.

"What are the *polizia* doing here?" Alfonso demanded.

He spun around and glared at the group. Then he pointed a finger at Kennedy.

"You!" he exclaimed. "What is going on here?"

Kennedy winced. She felt Lloyd's hand against her chest, as though urging her to step back.

Suddenly Alfonso lunged forward. He grabbed Lloyd's arms and flung him away from the girls. Lloyd fell flat on his stomach on the pavement.

"Lloyd!" Marilyn squealed. She ran over to him.

Kennedy froze, staring at her teacher. She was distracted from him when, out of the corner of her eye, she saw Alfonso advancing on her.

Kennedy let out a startled yell. Nicoli and Arianna burst out of the winery. Both of them pointed their guns at Alfonso.

"*Fermo!*" Nicoli shouted.

Arianna ran over to Kennedy's side. "Run!" she said. "All of you must get away from here!"

Kennedy felt Susannah grab her elbow. She allowed her friend to pull her away. Lloyd was back on his feet and leading the four girls away from the patio. Kennedy winced when she noticed the scrape on Lloyd's cheek.

A yell from Nicoli made Kennedy whip her head around. She gasped. The detective was grappling with Alfonso. Arianna was screaming. Her Italian sounded so rapid that Kennedy didn't think that Marilyn or even Lloyd could understand what Arianna was saying.

"Come on, Kennedy!" Lloyd said impatiently.

Kennedy took a step back, only to be frozen on the spot again when she saw Alfonso bash Nicoli's head against the wall. Nicoli slumped down to the patio.

"Nicoli!" Arianna shouted.

Brief nausea washed over Kennedy. Alfonso scooped up Nicoli's gun and turned to Arianna. The detective screamed and raised her gun. Alfonso stopped in his tracks. He didn't wince. He just held his gun on Arianna.

"What should we do?" Marilyn exclaimed.

Kennedy wanted to run forward. But Lloyd's grip on her arm wouldn't let her move. Alfonso and Arianna stood still, guns pointed at one another. Angry, determined looks contorted their faces.

"Drop your weapon," Arianna snapped.

"Oh, no, ladies first," Alfonso shot back.

Kennedy felt like her heart was beating faster than any bullet could fly. Was Arianna going to do something? She and Alfonso couldn't just stand there, glaring at each other with guns, waiting for the other to surrender.

BANG!

The girls screamed. Glass shattered. Arianna yelled in pain. Kennedy felt like she nearly had a heart attack. She put her hand over her mouth as she watched Arianna drop her gun and grasp her arm. Kennedy didn't have to guess who fired.

"Arianna!" Rachel exclaimed.

Alfonso took the moment to attack. He knocked Arianna over and grabbed her gun. Then he turned and ran toward Lloyd and the four girls.

"Stay back, girls!" Lloyd shouted. "I'll try to tackle this guy!"

The girls took several steps back. Lloyd snatched up a stick and went after Alfonso.

BANG!

Kennedy turned her head away. The gunshot made her feel lightheaded. But at least she didn't hear Lloyd yelling in pain, only in alarm. Kennedy took a step forward.

"Kennedy, no! Don't!" Marilyn shouted. She and Susannah grabbed Kennedy's arms.

"Let go!" Kennedy said, struggling against the girls' grasps.

"Yeah, we can't leave our teacher to the mercy of that crazy dude!" Rachel said.

A yell from Lloyd made all the girls look up. Alfonso had pushed Lloyd aside. Then he ran toward the girls. Before any of them could react, Alfonso grabbed Susannah and yanked her aside. Susannah shrieked. Alfonso covered her mouth with his hand and pointed the gun at her head.

"No!" Kennedy screamed. "Let her go!"

"Stay back!" Alfonso shouted. "Or this *signorina* gets it!"

Kennedy moaned. The fear in her friend's green eyes made her feel like she was going to faint.

Lloyd dashed over, but stopped in his tracks when Alfonso turned his glare to him. Lloyd raised his hands as he slowly walked toward Kennedy, Rachel, and Marilyn.

"Do something!" Kennedy hissed at her teacher.

Lloyd glanced at her. "What do you expect me to do?" he hissed back. "Alfonso's got two guns on him."

"Alfonso!" Arianna screamed.

Alfonso looked over his shoulder. Arianna was walking toward them, grasping her bleeding arm. Her eyes held no fear. Only a fierce look. Kennedy's eyes wandered to the patio. Nicoli was still lying unconscious. Kennedy could only hope that he would be alright, but was it possible that he had a serious head injury?

"Let the girl go," Arianna snapped.

Alfonso laughed. "Who's armed here?" he said. He pointed his gun at Arianna. She raised her good arm in the air.

"Alright," Alfonso said, "you all are coming with me as my hostages. Can't have you sharing anything."

"Oh?" Kennedy said. "Like the fact that you are involved in Rosa's kidnapping? And that you know that Lorenzo is innocent? And you don't want Rosa to find out anything?"

Alfonso glared at Kennedy. "Smart girl," he said.

"Well, you're outnumbered," Lloyd said. "And there's a policewoman behind you."

"But the policewoman is injured," Alfonso said coolly, "and I have two guns. Not to mention that if you don't do as I say, I will blow this girl's brains out."

He pressed the gun harder against Susannah's head. She moaned quietly.

Lloyd sighed. "Have it your way," he said. "But promise me you will not harm any of the girls if I go with you."

Alfonso smiled deviously. "I suppose a deal is in place," he said. "Yes, if you and the lady cop come with me, I won't harm any of your precious students. But first, ditch the cell phones."

He waved the gun. Everyone dug through their pockets and dropped their phones on the grass.

Everyone, that is, except Kennedy.

Under the cover of Lloyd, Susannah, Rachel, and Marilyn in front of her, Kennedy slipped her phone in a pocket in the inside of her jacket. She looked at Alfonso; he didn't seem to have noticed.

"Phones all down?" Alfonso said. "Alright, everyone to my car."

"What about Nicoli?" Arianna demanded. "After what you did to him, he might need treatment."

"He can suffer from a traumatic brain injury for all I care," Alfonso snapped. "He'll be one less witness for me to worry about. Now, all of you, to the red Ferrari!"

Alfonso marched everyone to his Ferrari. Arianna looked over at Nicoli. Kennedy thought she saw tears stemming from her eyes. She turned her own eyes to the Ferrari and stared at the numbers and letters on the license plate. They read AM-503LA. Kennedy took a mental note to remember that number. Too bad she couldn't write it down; all she could do was silently repeat that number to herself.

Alfonso pointed his gun at Lloyd. "You!" he barked. "You take shotgun." He sneered. "I wanna keep my eye on you so that I don't have to give anybody else here a shotgun to the head. The rest of you will have to make do with the back."

He turned to Arianna. "I hope you enjoy rolling around in a trunk," he said. "Can't risk you causing any trouble."

Arianna reluctantly crawled into the trunk. The four girls climbed into the backseat.

"Oh, we're going to be so cramped," Rachel muttered.

"Deal with it," Alfonso snapped.

As soon as everyone was loaded up in the car, Alfonso drove away as fast as he could. Kennedy could only stare at the winery wistfully. She saw Nicoli lying on the patio. Guilt flooded her mind.

A tense, fearful silence permeated the entire ride. Kennedy kept her eyes out the window. Alfonso had made a right turn onto the road when he left the winery. In just five minutes he made another right turn onto the highway. They were still in the countryside. Hardly any buildings around. License plate number? AM-503LA. Good, Kennedy still remembered it. A left turn onto a dirt road now.

Kennedy looked ahead. Alfonso was driving down the hill and toward a two-story chalet. It looked like it could be a nice little log chalet, with its front porch and surroundings of hills and numerous evergreen, cypress, and laurel trees. Kennedy held in a sigh. This place looked so peaceful. It was almost hard to believe that her current situation was anything but peaceful.

Alfonso parked the car in front of the cabin. He turned off the engine and pointed his gun at Lloyd.

"Get out," he said harshly.

Lloyd snapped off his seatbelt. "Care to say where we are?" he demanded.

"Just get out."

Everyone got out of the car. Alfonso went around to the trunk and let Arianna out. Kennedy shivered. She felt Susannah's hand upon her shoulder.

"It'll be okay, Ken," Susannah whispered. She sounded like she was trying to be encouraging, but her voice was quivering.

Alfonso marched everyone up the porch and to the front door. Kennedy glanced at the golden number plate to the right of the door. It was 12.

Still holding one gun toward the group, Alfonso went up to the door and kicked it.

"*Gerardo!*" he shouted in a gruff voice. "*Aprite!*"

The door opened. Kennedy's heart sank. It was him. That man whom she had seen at the Uffizi and the crosswalk. But he wasn't wearing his sunglasses or his bowler hat this time, allowing Kennedy to recognize him as Gerardo Greco.

Gerardo's eyes widened in shock when he saw the number of people on the porch. He spoke harshly to Alfonso in Italian. Then his eyes turned to Kennedy. They widened even more. Gerardo reached out for her and grabbed her arm. Kennedy gasped.

"I remember you." Gerardo sneered at her. "You were in the Uffizi. And we saw each other on the street. Have you and your friends been following me?"

"Leave her alone," Arianna said coldly. "I knew it was you all this time, Gerardo."

Gerardo turned his sneer to the detective. "You are one clever lady, you know that?"

He pushed Kennedy aside. "The lot of you get inside."

Kennedy rushed inside behind Arianna. She looked around the chalet. There was a small square area of tile floor in front of the front door. It was hard to tell that the tile was white; it was covered in dark gray dust and specks of dirt. Just across from the front door were sliding double doors, probably the front closet. One door was slightly ajar, allowing Kennedy to see the mess of coats and mismatched shoes and boots on the closet floor. The living room had a light tan carpet that looked like it hadn't been vacuumed in weeks. A dark green sofa and matching easy chair, as well as a glass coffee table standing on top of a black rug with ornate gold designs, stood in front of a stone fireplace. The glass table had several coffee stains. Framed pictures sat upon the wooden mantel above the fireplace. On both sides of the fireplace, there were shelves filled with books and figurines, a few of which were lying on their sides. The bay window had a cushioned seat and curtains with a crimson hue that matched the seat. The kitchen and dining area were separated from the living room by a white tile floor that matched the floor of the front entrance. A small chandelier hung above the dining room table, which was cluttered with books, newspapers, and notebooks.

Alfonso and Gerardo were still arguing in Italian, but in hushed voices.

"—*signora Rosa Morelli qui in cantina*—"

Kennedy whipped her head around. She didn't understand everything that Gerardo had said, but she did hear him say Rosa's name. Was Rosa here at this chalet?

Kennedy, Marilyn, Susannah, and Rachel huddled behind Lloyd and Arianna, who was clutching her arm. Her sleeve was covered with dried blood stains.

Gerardo finally barked at Alfonso. Alfonso turned to the group and held up his gun.

"The lot of you are going up in the attic," he said. "Move!"

He marched them up the stairs and to an empty room. The only light was from a ray of sunlight shining through a small window. As soon as Lloyd, Arianna, and the four girls were inside, Alfonso slammed the door. Kennedy heard a click; they were locked in.

Arianna pressed her ear against the door. She stood still for a few minutes, then she turned to everyone else. She held her finger to her lips.

"Alright," she said in a hushed voice, "they're gone, but if we want to talk, we should keep our voices low."

"How's your arm?" Marilyn asked.

"It's fine for the most part," Arianna said. "No bullet got under my skin. My arm was just grazed."

"Did you catch anything they'd been saying?" Rachel asked.

"Alfonso told Gerardo everything," Arianna said. "And I heard Gerardo say that Rosa Morelli is here in the basement."

Kennedy's heart leapt. She knew it!

"Gerardo told Alfonso to put us up here so that Rosa wouldn't know we were brought here," Arianna added. "And so that we wouldn't know about the other stuff hidden in the basement."

"Other stuff?" Kennedy said. She grinned. "You don't think that other stuff could be paintings that Gerardo had stolen?"

"Like perhaps *Pallas and the Centaur*?" Rachel said. "Looks like Gerardo is the thief after all."

"And Alfonso's working with him," Kennedy said. "It's my guess that Alfonso hired Gerardo to steal the painting from the Uffizi and make it look like Lorenzo was the thief."

"Possibly," Arianna said softly. She crossed her arms and lowered her eyes. "Gerardo's a crafty art thief. He did know how to throw the law off his trail when he robbed the Palatine last month. That is why Nicoli almost arrested my brother."

She sighed. "I hope Nicoli's okay."

Susannah placed her hand on the detective's shoulder. Arianna gave Susannah's hand a gentle pat.

"I should've kept a better eye on my amateur detective student," Lloyd said.

"I am sorry to have gotten you into this mess, Lloyd," Kennedy said. She smiled and unzipped her jacket. "But I might be able to get us out."

All eyes turned to her. Kennedy put a finger to her lips and slowly pulled her phone out of her jacket's interior pocket. She held it in her palm.

A flurry of quiet gasps arose. Kennedy grinned, only to gasp herself when she looked down at her phone.

"I have two missed calls and a text message!" she said.

She opened the message. "It's from Nicoli!"

Arianna dashed over to Kennedy's side. "I must see it!" she said, reaching for the phone.

"Wait, everyone gather around," Kennedy said.

Everybody huddled so closely together that Kennedy was sure that all their noses could almost touch each other. She looked at her phone and read the text message aloud.

"'Kennedy, this is Nicoli. Other than my head aching, I am alright. I regained consciousness just as Alfonso's red Ferrari drove away. The waitress had called the police, but they arrived minutes after Alfonso's escape. We found the cell phones on the grass. After studying them, we determined who the phones belonged to. We determined that none of them belonged to you. I concluded that you still had yours. So I risked sending you this text. Can you tell me anything about your whereabouts? And is Arianna alright? I'm coming after you!'"

Kennedy saw the hope in each and every eye that she looked into. She rapidly began texting. She mentioned Alfonso and Gerardo. She included all the information she could about the chalet and its surroundings, the directions from the winery, the chalet number, and the license plate number of Alfonso's Ferrari.

"Whoa, you remember all that?" Arianna said.

Kennedy smiled. "Let's just say I've got a good memory."

"She does, actually," Marilyn said. "And I am glad for it!"

Kennedy shrugged. "I'm going to tell him that I don't want him calling me. I can't risk Alfonso or Gerardo finding out that I still have my phone on me. Anything else I should say?"

"Sì." Arianna placed her hand on Kennedy's shoulder. "Tell Nicoli that I am alright."

Kennedy nodded. She finished typing her text and sent it.

"Great, so what do we do now?" Marilyn asked.

Gruff voices from outside made everyone fall silent. Lloyd went over to the window and peeked out. Kennedy, Marilyn, Rachel, and Susannah gathered around him.

"Alfonso and Gerardo are outside," Lloyd said. "But why?"

"Probably discussing what to do with all of us," Arianna said darkly. "And Rosa."

"And I can imagine Alfonso doesn't want Rosa to know he's here," Kennedy added. She faced the door. "With those two outside, do we dare break out and try to find Rosa?"

"Are you kidding?" Lloyd put his hand on his forehead. "It's way too risky. If any of us make it home alive, whatever am I going to tell my wife? In fact, what are we going to tell all the other students, and all my colleagues?"

Kennedy chuckled. "I have a knack for getting out of bad situations."

"But Alfonso's got the guns," Susannah said. "And Gerardo probably has weapons too."

"But not on his person right this minute," Kennedy said. "Which means there might be weapons hiding somewhere in this chalet."

"I can pick locks," Arianna said. "Kennedy could be right. We might need to try this. We outnumber Gerardo and Alfonso. I do have my training. And if we can find any weapons, our chances of getting out of here in one piece would look better."

Lloyd groaned. He turned to the four girls. "You ladies stay up here," he said. "With the phone. And keep an eye on the guys."

"No, I'm going down with you," Kennedy said.

"Uh, absolutely not."

"We don't have time to argue," Arianna said. "Let's just all go. We will find the weapons and Rosa and get out of here."

The detective went to the door. She pulled a few hairpins out of her hair, allowing her bun to come apart and her hair to fall to her shoulders. In a few minutes that seemed like an eternity, Arianna had the lock undone. But even the turning of the knob and the slow opening of the door was too creaky for Kennedy's ears.

"Are they out there?" Rachel whispered.

"No, they're still outside," Marilyn said.

Arianna motioned for everyone to follow her. They tiptoed out of the room. Arianna quietly closed the door behind her. Lloyd insisted on going first. He checked downstairs. He nodded and led everyone down the stairs. As soon as they reached the living room, Arianna made everyone get on their hands and knees so they could avoid the windows. But even so, Kennedy still wished for some sort of darkness; the bright sunlight shining through the windows made her feel vulnerable. And the chalet was so messy with stuff cluttered all over the furniture and floors that Kennedy was worried she could stumble over something and cause a noisy ruckus that would attract Alfonso and Gerardo.

Arianna kept an eye on the windows while the others searched the rooms for weapons. Kennedy crawled over to the front closet, but her eyes were fixed on the front door. She desperately hoped it wouldn't open. She checked the closet but found nothing useful. In a few minutes, everyone met back in the living room.

"Alright, what next?" Susannah asked.

"The basement," Arianna said. "Rosa's down there."

Everybody turned their eyes to the stairs that led down into the basement. Kennedy thought that the stairwell looked dark, as though it were a dungeon. Well, it was basically a dungeon for Rosa.

Lloyd and Arianna led the girls downstairs. They came to the main den. Somehow this area appeared even messier than upstairs. Most of the floor was plain gray stone. A small area was covered in a brown carpet with a few stains. There was an old, tattered sofa sitting on the carpet, just across from a small, dusty fireplace. A short stand with a few pokers stood on the right of the fireplace. The wooden walls seemed to be peeling in a few spots.

"Hey, what's that over there?" Marilyn asked.

Kennedy looked to where her stepsister was pointing. She squinted her eyes. Just wedged in between the white washer and dryer machines, she saw something odd. Like a large picture frame.

Kennedy gasped. She ran over to the washer and dryer. She reached her arm in between the machines and pulled out a picture frame. Her eyes widened when she saw that it was the *Pallas and the Centaur* painting from the Uffizi.

Kennedy whirled her head around. She and Arianna exchanged smiles.

"We were right, the other stuff was here." Arianna turned around. "But where are—"

"*Salve?*"

Everyone froze. For a split second, Kennedy thought that either Alfonso or Gerardo had come into the chalet. But then she realized that the voice that had interrupted Arianna was female.

"Guys!" Rachel said. "That sounded like Rosa!"

"And it came from over there!" Lloyd said, pointing to a small door.

He led everyone to the door and pushed it open. They entered what appeared to be some sort of dusty storage cellar with a splintering wood floor and racks filled with canned goods lining up the gray walls.

"Hey, look here!" Arianna said. She ran over to an open trunk. "There's a bunch of rifles in here."

Kennedy stood next to Arianna. Sure enough, the trunk was filled with rifles and other guns. Arianna took a few out and distributed them.

"Rosa?" Susannah called. "Where are you?"

"Over here!" Rosa's voice called back.

Arianna and Kennedy ran around a corner. Kennedy gasped. There was Rosa, sitting on a chair toward the back of the wall. She had her arms behind her. Her ankles were tied together, and she had a black blindfold over her eyes.

"Rosa!" Kennedy said. "It's okay! It's us."

Rosa smiled. Even without seeing her eyes, Kennedy could tell that Rosa was beyond relieved. But before any of them could approach Rosa, Marilyn and Rachel screamed.

Kennedy whirled around and ran back around the corner. Her stomach flipped. Gerardo was standing at the open doorway, pointing a gun at them.

"Girls, get behind me!" Lloyd shouted.

Arianna jumped in front of the group. She pointed her gun at Gerardo.

"Game's up, Gerardo," she said. "You are surrounded. You are under arrest for the theft of the *Pallas and the Centaur* from the Uffizi art gallery and the kidnapping of Rosa Morelli. Hands up!"

"You forget I'm not alone," Gerardo said.

"Oh, I didn't," Arianna said. "I know your accomplice is here. I know he is—"

"You will not say his name!" Gerardo shouted.

"Alfonso Martini!" Kennedy said. She looked at Rosa. Even with the blindfold covering her eyes, Kennedy could tell that Rosa was shocked. Her mouth hung open as Marilyn and Rachel began untying her.

As if on cue, Alfonso entered the storage area. He pointed his gun at Kennedy, as well as a fierce glare. Kennedy raised her own gun.

"Yes, Alfonso," she said hotly, "we figured it all out. Every little detail. You were in league with an infamous art thief. You were so angry that Rosa would not date you. That she was dating Lorenzo instead. So you hired Gerardo to steal a painting from the Uffizi and make it look like Lorenzo stole the painting. Then you would have Rosa all to yourself. But you did not count on Nicoli. Or even me, the amateur detective from the United States of America butting in! Nor did you count on Rosa's faith that Lorenzo was innocent. Then, when she yelled at you in the restaurant—rightfully, I might add—that was the last straw for you. You just had to fool and manipulate Rosa into adoring you. So you cooked up another job for Gerardo. You had him kidnap her so that you could rescue her. And Rosa would have to date you."

"You are a smart girl." Alfonso took a deep breath. If he had been a dragon, smoke probably would have snuffed out of his nostrils. "But you are also foolish. You just blew everything for me. My plans. My love for my coworker. Now you will pay!"

He lunged. Lloyd lunged back at him and pushed him against a rack. Alfonso fell against it, bringing it down to the ground with him. His gun flew out of his hand. The jars fell on top of him, almost all of them shattering against the ground. Alfonso was covered in orange and green slop.

Alfonso slowly sat up. Sputtering, he glared at Lloyd. "You will pay for that!" he shouted.

He jumped to his feet, but he still grasped his arm and hands, which had several cuts on them from the broken glass. Lloyd ran over to where Alfonso's gun had landed. He snatched it up and pointed one gun at Alfonso and the other at Gerardo. The art thief gasped, but he didn't drop his gun. Alfonso took a step toward Lloyd.

BANG!

The gunshot's deafening echo made Kennedy want to plug her ears. She gaped at her teacher, who was still holding his guns. But neither of them was smoking. Lloyd's eyes were wide with astonished confusion.

"Another step, Alfonso," a familiar voice said, "and I will make sure my next bullet hits its target."

Kennedy gasped. She recognized that voice.

"Nicoli?" Arianna said.

Nicoli walked into the storage area, holding two guns. He nodded at Arianna.

"I finally got here." Nicoli smiled at Kennedy. "Couldn't have done it without your help."

"Her help?" Alfonso glared at Kennedy.

BANG!

The girls screamed. Lloyd yelled in pain. Nausea washed over Kennedy when she saw her teacher's bleeding shoulder and Gerardo's sneer.

"No!" Kennedy screamed. "Lloyd, no!"

Lloyd fell to his knees. Alfonso lunged at him, but Nicoli fired at him. His bullet missed, but it was enough to make the curator stop in his tracks. Arianna kicked Gerardo's back as hard as she could. The art thief fell flat on his stomach. His gun flew out of his hand. Arianna held her gun on him.

"Girls!" she shouted. "Get Rosa and Lloyd out of here!"

Kennedy spun around. Rosa was untied and the blindfold removed from her eyes. Susannah and Marilyn were helping her toward the door. Kennedy, still holding onto her rifle, ran over to Rachel and Lloyd. The two girls helped him up. They followed Rosa, Susannah, and Marilyn out of the storage room. Rosa squinted at the sunlight streaming out from the window.

"Where are we?" she asked.

"Some countryside chalet," Kennedy said. "If Nicoli's here, then hopefully other cops won't be far behind."

Rosa looked over her shoulder. Horrified astonishment filled her eyes.

"So it's true," she said. Kennedy could hardly hear her due to the gunshots and crashing against the walls in the storage room. "Alfonso is behind all this."

"Guess he was pretty desperate to date you," Rachel said loudly. "After this is over, you should get a restraining order. You doing okay?"

"My legs feel like jelly," Rosa said, looking down at her wobbling knees.

Suddenly Gerardo barged out of the storage room. His face was bloody, and his shirt was torn. He turned his angry gaze to the girls. With a growl, he lunged at them.

Marilyn screamed. Kennedy lunged back at Gerardo. She pushed him against the sofa and the art thief toppled over it.

"Yeah!" Rachel cheered. "Kung Fu Kennedy at her finest!"

Suddenly there was another gunshot, screams from Nicoli and Arianna, and then Alfonso burst out of the storage room. Gerardo clumsily stood up, breathing hard. He and Alfonso looked at one another. They both glanced at Kennedy. Her heart leapt. The two men each grabbed a fireplace poker. Then they ran toward Kennedy, their pokers raised.

"Look out!" Susannah shrieked.

Kennedy held up her rifle. She whacked the pokers right out of the men's hands. Then she struck Gerardo's stomach with the rifle. Gerardo screamed in pain and fell to his knees, clutching his stomach. Alfonso went after Kennedy, but she whacked his knees. Alfonso also fell. Kennedy pointed the rifle at them. Just then Nicoli came out of the storage room, supporting a limping Arianna.

"Is everyone alright?" Nicoli called.

"As alright as we'll ever be!" Rachel said.

"Guys, do you hear sirens?" Marilyn said.

Kennedy listened. Sure enough, she heard police sirens outside.

Susannah dashed upstairs. Nicoli and Arianna held their guns on the fallen criminals. In just a few minutes, Susannah came back downstairs with several policemen behind her. The police surrounded Alfonso and Gerardo and held up their guns. One officer barked orders in Italian. Alfonso and Gerardo raised their hands in defeat. Nicoli and Arianna handcuffed them, then a few policemen led the two men upstairs. Alfonso glanced over his shoulder at Rosa. Rosa gave him a brief glare, then turned her eyes away.

Nicoli and Arianna spoke to the remaining officers in Italian. Nicoli smiled at Kennedy and held out his hand to her.

"Come on, Kennedy," he said. "We should get everyone to the hospital. I'll get a statement from you later."

Kennedy, Marilyn, Rachel, and Susannah followed the officers as they helped Lloyd and Arianna up the stairs and out of the chalet.

"Whew!" Rachel gasped. "Am I glad we're finally outta here!"

Kennedy, Marilyn, Susannah, and Rachel followed their teachers and classmates down the halls of the Uffizi. Kennedy ran forward, unable to contain her excitement. There was so much she wanted to see on their final tour of the Uffizi. She wanted to see the *Pallas and the Centaur* back in its rightful spot. But more importantly, she wanted to see if Rosa and Lorenzo were back.

"Hey, hey," Lloyd said, grabbing her shoulder, "slow down, Miss Detective. We'll be seeing the fruits of your sleuthing labor before you know it."

Kennedy nodded. She smiled at her teacher. The other day, when Lloyd had arrived at the hospital, he, Kennedy, and the other girls had been greeted by all the other teachers and students, who had apparently received the news of the hostage situation from the police and had been ordered to stay at their hotel. And then they received news that their heroic art and music teacher, and his four students, had escaped from the chalet where they had been hostages, and they were at the hospital. Lloyd had been hailed a hero by all the other teachers. Then, just yesterday, Lloyd was discharged from the hospital. He and Arianna both had been picked up by Nicoli.

"*Buongiorno!*"

Kennedy turned around at the sound of Rosa's cheerful voice. She grinned. Rosa and Lorenzo stood before the group, both of them grinning. Much to Kennedy's surprise, Nicoli and Arianna stood behind them.

Kennedy, Marilyn, Susannah, and Rachel ran forward and hugged Rosa.

"It's so good that you're back so soon," Kennedy said. "How are you doing?"

"I'm well," Rosa said. Her grin broadened. She took Lorenzo's hand. "And Lorenzo was released. We're both back at work. And Lorenzo received permission to join our final tour."

"That's wonderful!"

"How are you feeling, Arianna?" Rachel asked.

Arianna smiled. "Much better," she said. *"Grazie."*

"We also received full confessions from Alfonso and Gerardo last night," Nicoli added. "And we felt that we should share them with you."

Kennedy grinned. "Let's hear them!"

"Well, you were right about Alfonso's motive," Nicoli said. He glanced at Rosa. "He was desperate to date Rosa. But she wisely said no to his every advance. And she was dating Lorenzo. She refused to break up with Lorenzo for Alfonso."

Rosa hugged Lorenzo and buried her face in his chest. Lorenzo gently patted her head.

"So Alfonso decided to get Lorenzo out of his way," Nicoli said. "He heard about the robbery at the Palatine and how Arianna suspected Gerardo was behind it. Well, because Gerardo's father was an art appraiser, Alfonso managed to contact Gerardo. They met in late April at the chalet, which, by the way, belongs to Gerardo. He inherited it from his father and used it to hide all the artwork he had stolen. Anyway, Alfonso and Gerardo made a deal. If Gerardo stole a painting from the Uffizi, and made it look like Lorenzo was the thief, Alfonso would pay him a rich sum of money. Alfonso ordered a second name tag for Lorenzo. He also cut the wire between the security cameras and the alarm so that no alarm would go off. He didn't want Gerardo to be recorded stealing the painting."

"And he stole a uniform for Gerardo," Kennedy said with a smile. "But Gerardo's size is extra-large."

Nicoli grinned. "You are correct. You saw Gerardo in the Uffizi the day before the theft, right? Gerardo was scoping out the area, planning his crime and his steps very carefully. And he was watching Lorenzo. He left the janitor's hat and the new name tag at the scene of the crime. But he also left his footprint."

"And he left one for me and the gals to see at the crosswalk after it rained," Kennedy said.

Everyone laughed.

"Yes, well, Alfonso didn't count on Rosa's determination," Nicoli said. "She truly didn't want to put the four of you girls in any danger, but she knew of your detective skills. She figured that you could act as anonymous witnesses to the crime scene, figure out a few new clues, and share those clues with the police. But, as we know, it all went much further than that. When Rosa yelled at Alfonso at the restaurant, Alfonso decided to take more action. He asked Gerardo to kidnap Rosa and hold her at his chalet. Then Alfonso would rescue her and make up a story about Gerardo and Lorenzo being in league."

"Is that why they were at the winery?" Kennedy asked. "To discuss that plan? And Gerardo lost his receipt at Rosa's house when he went after her?"

"All correct." Arianna grinned. "You should be a detective when you finish college, Kennedy."

Kennedy shrugged. "I'm just glad everything worked out."

"And we have you to thank," Rosa said. She took Kennedy's hand. "Without you, Lorenzo might still be in prison for a crime he didn't commit."

"Well, we have Nicoli and Arianna to thank too," Kennedy said, smiling at the two detectives. "Nicoli allowed us to search the Uffizi the first time."

"Why, though?" Susannah asked.

Nicoli smiled meekly. "I saw how determined you ladies were," he said. "And I knew how confused Lorenzo was when he was arrested. I was reminded of the time when I nearly arrested Arianna's brother. Angelo, from that other art gallery. I didn't want to make the same mistake of allowing an innocent man to suffer for a crime he didn't do. I want to be a good detective."

Arianna slipped her hand into Nicoli's. "You are," she said. "You truly are. Even my brother said so. He never blamed you for the mistakes you made. Gerardo tricked you with his false clues. The other cops too. I mean, Angelo and I, we're both glad that he didn't get arrested. But he keeps telling me that he forgives you. I should've adopted my brother's attitude on the matter. He thanks you now, actually. All the paintings found at Gerardo's have been returned to their rightful spaces in the art galleries."

Nicoli's smile grew. He spoke softly in Italian. Arianna grinned. "*Sì!*" she said in an eager voice.

"What did they say?" Kennedy whispered to Marilyn.

Marilyn chuckled. "Nicoli asked her out on a date."

Just then Lorenzo walked over to Marilyn and Rachel and took their hands. He smiled warmly at them.

209

"Grazie," he said. *"Per tutto."*

Kennedy placed her hand over her heart. Seeing Lorenzo's gratitude was so heartwarming. Susannah tapped her shoulder.

"Ken," she whispered, "I'm sorry."

"For what?" Kennedy whispered back.

"For my recent attitude toward you and Rachel," Susannah said. "I don't want to be like Alfonso. You know, wanting what I can't have. I wanted to go back to the past, when you and I were best friends. I was so worried that you would forget about our friendship since we had been apart for so long. But I really do like Rachel and Marilyn. I'm glad they're our friends and housemates. I don't ever want to lose any of you now."

Kennedy grinned. She wrapped her arm around Susannah.

"It's all cool," she said. "I'd never let our friendship go down the drain, Susie. Yes, I have new friends in Arizona, but we're always besties."

Just then Rosa clapped her hands. "Are we ready for our final tour of the Uffizi?" she asked. She smiled at Kennedy. "And we will stop by the Sandro Botticelli room first."

Kennedy smiled back. "Sounds good."

"Well, I reckon we're all ready," Lloyd said. He looked at Kennedy. "Ready to go back to boring old school and homework? Oh, and please, try to stay out of any more mysteries for the rest of this trip."

Kennedy laughed. After facing the danger of chasing an art thief and his accomplice—danger for which Kennedy was thankful to the Lord for protecting her and everyone else from—she was glad to be returning to her college trip.

The Volcanism of Lake Virunga

KENNEDY. HEY, KENNEDY, wake up! You're missing the sights!"
Kennedy Ryan felt a hand shaking her shoulder. She blinked a few times and looked over at her stepsister, Marilyn Wilson, who was sitting next to the window of the plane.

Kennedy yawned. The strong smell of sulfur reached her nose. She coughed a little.

"Ugh!" she muttered, waving her hand in front of her nose. "What is that?"

"Look out the window," Marilyn said.

Kennedy leaned over her seat. The sights below pushed all remaining sleepiness out of her.

Jungle territory covered the earth below, surrounding a mountain. At the top of that mountain was a round, orange lake. Kennedy widened her eyes; that smoking orange lake seemed to glow against the dark mountain and jungle.

"Attention, passengers," the pilot's voice said over the intercom, "we are approaching Goma, the capital city of the North Kivu Province in the eastern region of the Democratic Republic of the Congo. We are flying over Virunga National Park, universally known for its endangered mountain gorillas. That mountain is Mt. Nyiragongo, an active volcano. That orange spot that many of you undoubtedly see is the volcano's lava lake. Mt. Nyiragongo is infamous for its unusually speedy lava flows."

"Isn't this amazing?" Marilyn whispered.

"It sure is," Kennedy said. "If only Jessica could be here."

"She'd be geeking out by now!"

Kennedy leaned back in her seat. She couldn't wait to land. For months now, her church in her hometown of Pine Lodge had been collaborating with a church in Prescott to plan a mission trip in the Democratic Republic of the Congo. The objective was to plant a new church in the city of Goma. Kennedy recalled the final meeting at her church. Cameron Shea, the pastor, had mentioned Mt. Nyiragongo during the meeting. The thought of being so close to an active volcano was both fascinating and terrifying.

"Ew, this rotten eggs odor is getting worse!"

Kennedy and Marilyn eyed one another. Kennedy tried not to snicker as she glanced over the aisle at a teenage girl sitting in between a woman and Kennedy's friend, Rachel Hamilton.

"Of course," Rachel said with a grin. "It's sulfur, you know."

The girl ruffled her long, light brown hair and plugged her nose. "I can't stand it. I just hope it doesn't suffocate all of us before this stupid mission trip is over."

"Annice," the woman chided, "can you please try to keep your complaining to a minimum?"

The girl rolled her eyes. "If you don't want me complaining, then why did you make me come, Mom?"

Kennedy silently agreed. Whose bright idea was it to let Annice Carrington, only a spoiled rich seventeen-year-old girl from Rachel's church, join this mission trip? How did Annice even agree to join?

Marilyn nudged Kennedy's elbow. The two girls exchanged grins. Marilyn let out a quiet snort and quickly covered her mouth. Kennedy wondered how well she could hold back her own smirk.

"We are now flying over Lake Kivu," the pilot said, "one of the African Great Lakes."

Kennedy and Marilyn turned back to the window. Kennedy stared in amazement at the enormous lake far below them, reflecting the bright blue sky.

"Lake Kivu is saturated with carbon dioxide," the pilot said. "Geologists worry that it could be capable of a limnic eruption."

"A limnic eruption?" Marilyn said. "Do you know what that is?"

"Jessica mentioned it to me recently," Kennedy said. "It's when a lake filled with carbon dioxide is disturbed and sends out the gas. It's called a lake overturn. Two instances of lake overturns happened in Cameroon in the 1980s, first with Lake Monoun, then with Lake Nyos. The second lake's overturn was much more deadly. Carbon dioxide suffocated a whole village."

Marilyn grasped her neck. "That sounds awful."

"Please fasten your seatbelts," the pilot said. "We will be landing shortly."

Kennedy and Marilyn snapped on their seatbelts. In a few minutes, the plane landed. As soon as Kennedy stepped through the passenger door of the airplane, her brown eyes wandered to the mountain in the distance. Mt. Nyiragongo appeared to loom over the city of Goma.

Kennedy looked over at the airport. It was smaller than she had imagined it to be. The most she could make out around the building was the control tower and the runway. Further away, she saw tropical trees towering over rundown buildings.

The loud sound of clapping hands distracted Kennedy. She spotted Pastor Cameron Shea standing on the pavement. Kennedy and Marilyn ran down the stairs. They followed Pastor Cameron over to the sidewalk. They were joined by Kennedy's cousin, Aaron Connolly, his two friends Billy Weston and Wesley Rudolf, Rachel Hamilton, Annice Carrington, and her mother Della.

"Where's Dad?" Rachel asked.

"He's coming," Mrs. Carrington said. "He's with Brody and Francis."

Kennedy looked at the airplane. She spotted Rachel's father, Logan, who was the pastor of Rachel's church in Prescott, walking toward the group. Two men, whom Kennedy recognized as Brody Campbell and Francis Allen from Pastor Logan's church, were walking behind him. As soon as the three men approached the group, Pastor Cameron spoke.

"Here we are in Goma," he said with a smile. "Good to finally be here after that long and boring plane ride."

"You're telling me," Francis said. He stretched out a leg. "I think I've got jet lag."

"I think I have it worst of all," Annice muttered. Kennedy rolled her eyes.

"We will be meeting our hosts here soon," Pastor Cameron said. "Before we head into the airport and collect our luggage, let's say a quick prayer."

Pastor Cameron led the group in a prayer. As soon as he finished, he and Pastor Logan led everyone inside the airport and to the baggage claim. Kennedy spotted her suitcase and took it.

"Ew!"

Kennedy saw Annice holding up a bright pink suitcase and glaring at her mother.

"Look, Mom, it's smudged!" she said, pointing to the side of the suitcase. "They smudged my favorite suitcase! Why can't these people be more careful with other people's stuff?"

Mrs. Carrington sighed. "It's not that bad, Annice."

Kennedy shook her head. If Annice had not pointed out the tiny brown spot on the side of her suitcase, Kennedy would not have noticed it.

"Dudes," Aaron whispered to Billy and Wesley, "there's no way I'm gonna focus on this mission trip with that Annice girl's constant whining."

Wesley smirked. "She's on the wrong continent, that's for sure."

"Bonjour!"

Kennedy spun around at the loud French greeting. Two Congolese men and a Congolese girl were walking toward the group. The older man had a slender figure and a bald head. The other man appeared younger, probably in his early thirties. The girl, who appeared to be about seventeen years old, was nearly as tall as the younger man. Her dark brown hair was in several tiny braids. Both the men and the girl wore big smiles. Pastors Cameron and Logan greeted them with grins of their own, along with hugs.

"Everyone," Pastor Logan said, "meet Moïse Elenga Tamba, his daughter Chantal, and their friend Pierre Openda Tabu. They speak English very well and will act as our interpreters."

Pastor Logan introduced everyone to Moïse, Chantal, and Pierre.

"It is very nice to meet all of you," Pierre said. "Welcome to Goma. We are excited for our work together in growing our new church."

"We are too," Kennedy said.

"I am sure you are tired," Pastor Moïse said. "Come, we will take you to my house."

Pastor Moïse and Pierre led everyone to the doors. Two tall men dressed as flight attendants held the doors open for them.

Pastor Moïse smiled at the men. *"Merci mingi,"* he said.

The men smiled back and nodded.

As soon as she stepped outside, Kennedy turned her gaze to Mt. Nyiragongo. It still looked ominous.

Kennedy heard a couple of worried voices behind her. She glanced over her shoulder. The two flight attendants were staring at the volcano. Even from several feet away, Kennedy could see the concerned looks in both of the men's eyes. One of them pointed to the volcano, then raised his arms up in the air as though he were miming some sort of explosion. Kennedy shot a nervous look at the volcano before she turned and ran toward her group.

Pastor Moïse and Pierre led everyone to two white vans in the parking lot. Kennedy, Marilyn, Aaron, Rachel, Annice, and Mrs. Carrington followed Pierre to one van.

"Thank you for the ride, Pierre," Mrs. Carrington said as she got into the passenger seat.

"My pleasure," Pierre said. "I knew Pastor Moïse would need help getting you and your group from the airport. I am honored to help him with the planting of his new church."

Pierre turned the van out of the parking lot. Annice scowled as she gazed out the window. She leaned in her seat toward Rachel.

"Look at the city," she murmured. "It's so rundown."

Kennedy put her hand over her forehead. Yes, some of the buildings looked like they were in need of repair, but others seemed just fine. The streets were smooth, and the palm trees standing above the streets added beauty to the city.

"They're poorer than us, Annice," Rachel whispered.

"I'll say."

Mrs. Carrington glanced back at her daughter. Then she forced a smile and spoke again to Pierre.

"What do you do for a job, Pierre?"

"I am a ranger in Virunga National Park," Pierre said. "I love it. It's so wonderful to work around God's beautiful creation."

"That does sound fun!" Rachel said. She leaned forward. "I know we're here for a mission trip, Pierre, and I really am looking forward to all the work we'll do for the church and everything, but do you think we might visit Virunga?"

Pierre looked up in his rearview mirror. Kennedy noticed that his smile had faded a little.

"I think we have some activities planned for the park," he said. "But I have heard that Mt. Nyiragongo has been showing signs of activity in the past week."

Kennedy frowned. She and Marilyn eyed one another.

Pierre smiled again. "But it has not been so bad that we are not letting tourists in," he added. "I think you would enjoy the park. One of my favorite places to visit in the park is Lake Virunga."

"Lake Virunga?" Kennedy asked curiously.

"Oh, yes. It is a lake that formed in the park only a few decades ago. Isn't God's creation amazing?"

"It sure is," Aaron said.

After twenty minutes, Pastor Moïse's van turned onto a dirt road. Pierre followed him. The road led into a neighborhood. Most of the houses were small, earthen-colored houses made of stone or old, splintered siding. Only a few houses had two stories or any bright coloring.

Pierre parked the vans in front of a small house made of dark gray stone. Its white roof appeared to be missing a few shingles. Kennedy could make out a few cracks along a corner. A few guava trees and Mediterranean cypresses stood over the house.

Pastor Moïse's van parked right next to them. Annice cast a dark, disgusted look at the house.

Everyone got out of the vans. Kennedy smiled; the guavas on the trees smelled delicious. Maybe Pastor Moïse would let her pick a few later. She followed everyone else into the house.

"Welcome to my home," Pastor Moïse said.

Kennedy looked around. It had a slight musty odor. The floor was made of a thin, splintered hardwood which creaked under every step Kennedy took. There were a couple of old sofas in the main room. A small wooden table with a lamp stood next to the sofa. A tattered black rug lay in front of a small fireplace.

Pastor Moïse called out something in French. He was answered by a Congolese woman and a boy of about thirteen years of age coming into the living room. The woman smiled at Pastor Moïse and hugged him.

"Everyone," Pastor Moïse said, "this is my wife, Violette, and her son Yannick."

Violette smiled broadly. *"Bienvenue!"* she said. "We are very excited to have you here to help plant our new church. I wish I had more room in my house for you. I hope you will be well staying in your hotel."

Pastor Logan took Violette's hands and patted them. "We will be just fine," he said. "We are thankful to be spending time with your family now."

"I have supper ready," Violette said. She let go of Pastor Logan's hands. "Please, everyone, have a seat in the living room. Chantal, will you help me serve our guests?"

"Oui, Mama Violette," Chantal said. She followed her mother into the kitchen. Yannick gave her a cold look as he walked past her. She returned it with a cold look of her own. Pastor Moïse quickly motioned his hand, inviting everyone to sit down in the living room. Kennedy sat on the rug. Annice studied a sofa for a minute before sitting down on it next to her mother.

"You know, Mom," she whispered, "I'm glad we'll be in a hotel. It'll be better than sleeping in this ruined stone shack."

Kennedy shot a nervous glance toward Pastor Moïse. He didn't seem to have heard Annice's snide remark.

"Annice," Mrs. Carrington said firmly, "these people are poorer than us. I do not want to hear any more complaints from you. I really hope you learn that being rich isn't everything. That is why I brought you here."

Annice rolled her eyes. Kennedy exchanged glances with Rachel. Relief came over Kennedy when she saw Violette and Chantal come into the living room with dishes of food. They set the dishes down on the small table next to the sofa. Kennedy looked at the food. One dish appeared to be a small salad made up of crushed dark green leaves, peanuts, minced onions, and a sauce. The salad had rice and plantains next to it. A second dish had guavas, which smelled as though they had been freshly picked, and the third dish was a bowl of soup.

"It looks really good," Kennedy said. She noticed Annice giving her a repulsed look.

"Merci," Pastor Moïse said. "Let us give thanks to the Lord and then we will eat."

He prayed over the meal, then he asked Chantal to serve.

"What is this soup?" Marilyn asked. "It's good."

"That is sancocho," Violette said. "It has tubers, plantains, auyama, and meats. And the salad is a saka saka. I am grateful to God for providing us with all this food. We have good friends who are farmers. They sell their food and products at the markets. And I still have my nursing job."

"You're a nurse?" Kennedy said. "What do you mean by you still have your job?"

Violette's eyes drooped. Her smile faded. "I needed to find a job when my first husband died," she said.

"Oh," Kennedy said. "I'm so sorry to hear that."

She looked over at Yannick. He was scowling.

"Yannick was only a year old," Violette said. "I was a widow with a baby. I was attending Moïse's old church at the time. And his family was so good to me. So were many other men. Moïse helped me find a good nursing job. Other women in the church looked after Yannick while I worked. Friends visited me at my old house to see that I was good. I am always grateful to God for all He has done for my son and for me."

"Then, a few years ago," Moïse added, "my wife got sick. She died from her illness. Chantal was fifteen."

Kennedy stared at Chantal. She had her head down, but Kennedy could see the sad look in her eyes.

"Violette and I got married," Moïse said. "We felt that God was calling us to support one another through marriage. I made sure that Violette kept her nursing job. And then, on the night of our wedding, we drove by this old, crumbling chapel just outside of Goma. It was a chapel that had been destroyed by lava flows from the eruptions of Mt. Nyiragongo in 2002."

Kennedy noticed Yannick's scowl deepen, but she was more focused on Pastor Moïse's story to pay much attention to Yannick.

"When we passed that chapel, I thought, how neat would it be if that building was repaired and made a new church. Then I realized that God was calling me to plant a new church. We have been working hard toward that goal ever since."

Kennedy smiled. "That's an amazing testimony."

She looked over at Chantal. "I was also fifteen when I lost my father to an illness."

Chantal looked up at Kennedy, her eyes wide.

"Marilyn and I are stepsisters," Kennedy added. "Her father is my stepfather. We're very happy together."

"You are?" Chantal looked back down. There was no enthusiasm in her voice at all. Only resentment. Kennedy frowned. She wanted to ask Chantal more. But at that moment, Pastor Logan stood up, carrying his empty plate.

"I'm afraid we need to head over to our hotel," he said. "The meal was wonderful, Violette. What should we do with our dishes?"

Violette stood up. "Chantal and I will take them," she said.

Chantal helped her stepmother collect dishes. Pastor Moïse and Pierre led everyone out to the vans. Kennedy gazed out the windows as they drove on the dirt roads. In stark contrast to the parts of the city she had seen earlier, these neighborhoods were marked by poverty. Mud splattered on the windows. Not one streetlight or telephone poll could be seen above the houses, unlike in the city.

"Hey, Lake Kivu's coming into view!" Marilyn said.

Kennedy turned her head to look out Marilyn's window. Sure enough, she saw the enormous, shimmering, light blue body of water that was Lake Kivu. Kennedy gaped at the beautiful sight.

After twenty minutes of driving, Pierre pulled the van into the parking lot of a hotel. Kennedy gazed at the hotel as she stepped out of the van.

"Hey, hey!" Annice said. She was grinning from ear to ear. This was probably the first time Kennedy had seen her look so happy. "Now this is much more like it!"

"Hey, it's not a luxury hotel," Marilyn said.

"It could be, compared to where the residents live in this city," Rachel said. She glanced at Pastor Moïse. Kennedy didn't think that Pastor Moïse was paying much attention to the hotel. He and Pierre hugged Cameron and Logan, and then they got into their vans and drove away.

Cameron and Logan led the group into the lobby. Kennedy went over to the windows while the men checked in. She stared out at the terrace, which was made of flagstones. In the middle of the terrace, there was a kidney-shaped swimming pool. Its light blue color seemed to match that of Lake Kivu, which Kennedy could see beyond the terrace's white fencing. The pool was surrounded by lawn chairs and tables, many of which had white umbrellas.

"Alrighty," Pastor Logan said, "everyone gather around."

Everyone sat down in the lobby. Pastor Logan led the group in a prayer before speaking.

"This is our hotel. I know, we are privileged to have made the money to stay here, where we have comfortable beds, a pool, a breakfast bar, and other stuff. It's a lot of stuff that other people here in Goma do not have. We'll have our first big day tomorrow. We'll visit Pastor Moïse's church and attend his service."

He grinned at Brody and Francis. "Can't say enough how nice it is to have two construction guys on this team. It'll make the repairing of the chapel that much easier."

Brody and Francis laughed.

"The men will focus on the construction," Pastor Logan said. "The women will help with childcare and preparing meals for the workers."

"Meal preparation and other culinary stuff is my specialty," Marilyn said.

"But how are we going to take care of children when we don't even speak the same language?" Annice demanded.

"That's what Chantal is for," Pastor Cameron said. "She'll be your interpreter. Trust me, Annice, you will learn a lot from this trip."

Annice's only response was to sit back and cross her arms. Pastor Cameron didn't seem to have noticed. He and Pastor Logan assigned rooms for everyone then dismissed the group. Everyone left the lobby to go to their rooms.

"Here's 108," Billy said, stopping by a door.

"Our room," Kennedy said. She, Marilyn, and Rachel stepped forward. Pastor Logan gave Kennedy a keycard.

"If you girls need anything," he said, "just let us know. All our rooms are right next to one another."

Kennedy, Marilyn, and Rachel entered their room. Kennedy thought that this room was fit for a king. The light brown hardwood floor was smooth and shiny. The two queen beds were covered in clean white linens. The nightstand in between the beds had a lamp. A flatscreen TV sat on the dresser. And the sofa looked inviting.

"Does anybody else feel guilty for staying here?" Kennedy asked. She set her suitcase on one of the beds.

"I sure know the feeling," Rachel said. She smirked. "I hope Annice is happy now."

"I'm sure she is," Marilyn said. "It's nice to have a break from her constant complaining. Why is she here?"

"Her parents made her come," Rachel said. "I think this mission trip will be good for her."

Kennedy peeked out the window. She saw Mt. Nyiragongo hovering over the city. Her thoughts wandered back to those two airport attendants.

"I'm excited for this trip," she said. "I just hope that volcano behaves itself."

"Yeah, Pierre did say that volcano was acting up, didn't he?" Rachel said.

"But it should be okay," Marilyn said.

"Hey, hey," Rachel said, "you know what my dad would say if he heard us now? He'd tell us to trust in God."

Kennedy smiled. "You're right, Rachel. Let's get some rest. We've got a big day ahead of us."

WHACK! WHACK! WHACK!

The sounds of drilling and pounding were loud, but they didn't bother Kennedy. Nor did they seem to bother anybody else. Except Annice, who kept glaring in the direction of the construction.

"Is that chapel really worth all this work?" she asked. "Why not just build a new, better building? And they'd do well to shorten their services by a couple of hours."

Kennedy held in a sigh. Yes, yesterday's church service had been longer than a service from her church back home. And yes, the chapel was an old, rundown building that did indeed look like it had been burnt nearly to a crisp years ago. But Kennedy didn't care about the decrepit chapel with a ground of dirt instead of a floor and pews made out of carved logs with splinters. No, she had enjoyed yesterday's worship service. She didn't mind humming along with hymns sung in French. And she and everyone else in her group had been provided with English translations of Pastor Moïse's sermon.

A young boy bumped into Kennedy, interrupting her thoughts. She gasped as she stumbled, but she didn't fall over. The boy gave her an apologetic look.

"Pardon!" he said quickly.

Kennedy smiled and waved her hand. "It's alright," she said soothingly.

The boy grinned at her, his white teeth shining against his dark face. He appeared to be about six years old. He wore a pair of worn khaki pants and a black T-shirt. He had no shoes on his dirty feet.

The boy grabbed Kennedy's hand. She found herself being pulled away toward a group of kids. One of them, an older girl, was holding a red ball. Kennedy spotted Chantal among the kids. Chantal laughed and walked over to Kennedy.

"I see you have met Saleem," she said. "He is a playful boy with lots of energy."

"I noticed," Kennedy said. "I think he wants me to play."

Chantal laughed again. She waved at the girl with the ball. The girl nodded and threw the ball. Chantal caught it and tossed it to Kennedy. Kennedy caught it and threw it to Saleem. Saleem laughed and threw it back to her. It wasn't long before Marilyn and Rachel joined the game. Cheers went up for anyone who caught the ball, and laughter for those who missed it.

"Are you kidding me right now?" Annice said as she walked to Kennedy's side. "You're engaging in a boring, childish game of catch?"

Chantal scowled at Annice. *"Elle me complique,"* she whispered. Kennedy just stared at Chantal.

"I said she's giving me a tough time," Chantal said.

"She's been giving all of us a tough time," Marilyn said.

"But we shouldn't judge her," Rachel said. "I mean, yeah, her whining is getting on all of our nerves. But she grew up in a rich family. She's had it easy most of her life. That's why her parents had her come with us. They felt like she has a lot to learn. Just give her a chance. She really does have a sweet side to her."

Kennedy looked from Rachel to Annice. She could hardly picture Annice as being sweet.

222

Saleem ran over to Annice and grabbed her hand. Annice ripped her hand away and scowled at him. But the boy didn't seem to notice. He grabbed Annice's hand again and pulled her toward the group.

Kennedy smirked. "He wants everybody to play," she said.

"Yes, he is a social child," Chantal said.

Kennedy didn't know how Saleem was going to convince Annice to play. Hesitation was written all over her face. But then, much to Kennedy's surprise, her gaze toward Saleem softened. She actually smiled at him. Saleem threw the ball at her. Annice gasped and held up her hands. The ball dropped to the ground as soon as it hit her. Saleem laughed and pointed at the ball, speaking incoherently. Annice hesitantly picked up the ball. Saleem raised his hands and spoke again. Annice paused, then threw the ball to him. Saleem caught it and cheered with the rest of the kids.

Just then Yannick came running over to the kids. Saleem rushed over to welcome him, but Yannick ignored him and went straight to Chantal. Kennedy grimaced; she didn't like the glare on Yannick's face. He spoke to her in French, his voice filled with irritation. Chantal glared back at him and snapped at him. The playful chatter and laughter ceased as all eyes turned to Chantal and Yannick.

"Chantal! Yannick!"

Kennedy spun around. Pastor Moïse and Mrs. Carrington were walking toward the kids. Pastor Moïse took Chantal and Yannick aside and spoke to them sternly. Chantal hung her head and crossed her arms. She said something to her father, probably an apology, but Yannick only scoffed and turned to join some of the other boys. Pastor Moïse sighed.

"Hey." Mrs. Carrington put her hand on the pastor's shoulder. "It'll be okay. I'm sure things have been hard for them. If you want, I can start our story time."

Pastor Moïse nodded. Chantal faced the kids. She clapped her hands and called loudly to get their attention. All the kids gathered around her and Mrs. Carrington and sat on the ground.

Mrs. Carrington sat down on a big rock and held up her children's Bible storybook. "We are going to read some Bible stories," she said in a loud and clear voice.

She began reading, with Chantal translating for the kids. Kennedy watched the kids in awe. They sat so still, all their eyes on

Mrs. Carrington and Chantal, as though they were mesmerized by the story.

That wasn't all. Annice's actions also surprised Kennedy. She sat on the dusty rock next to her mother with Saleem at her feet. He was raised upon his knees, his hands resting on Annice's lap, so he could see the storybook better. But Annice didn't brush him off. She laid her hand on his shoulder, as though he were her little brother. Kennedy couldn't help but smile at them. Maybe Rachel was right; maybe Annice did have a sweet side.

"Man, do I feel like a courageous safari hunter on a top-secret mission!"

Wesley whacked a low branch out of his way with his stick. Kennedy laughed. She knew Wesley had been excited about visiting Virunga National Park. She had been too. She loved seeing the lush green jungle. The trees smelled of fresh dew. Mud squelched beneath her boots. She heard the songs of crickets in the foliage and birds chirping in the trees.

Annice looked down at her boots. "I hope these nice hiking boots don't get ruined," she said.

"Well, they are for hiking," her mother said.

"I don't even go hiking," Annice said. She wiped her brow. "It's so hot out here, anyway! I'm sweating so much!"

Kennedy fanned herself. She didn't like to hear Annice's complaining, but she had beads of sweat on her forehead too.

"Hey, look!" Marilyn said. "There are elephants over there!"

Kennedy spun around and gasped. Her stepsister was right. A small herd of elephants was crossing the trail. Pierre, who was leading the group, stopped and held out his arms. Everyone held up their phones and snapped photos of the animals. One elephant raised its long nose and let out a loud trumpet.

"Whoo!" Wesley exclaimed. "Do that again, buster!"

Kennedy lowered her phone. Was it just her, or did that elephant sound agitated? It seemed to be trying to herd the little elephant next to it to hurry into the trees.

"They all seem on edge," Pastor Cameron said.

"Yes, they do," Pierre said. "Keep a good distance."

Kennedy kept her eyes on the elephants. In a few minutes, the entire herd disappeared into the trees.

"That was so awesome!" Billy said.

"Yeah," Wesley said. "I hope we see a lion!"

Rachel ran over to Pierre's side. "Hey, Pierre," she said, "do you think we can hike to the top of Mt. Nyiragongo?"

Kennedy noticed Yannick scowling at Rachel. She looked up at the volcano, which seemed to be looming over the jungle. It had a bigger and more menacing appearance than when Kennedy saw it from Goma.

Pierre frowned. "That's a very long hike," he said. "Besides, the rangers haven't been comfortable with taking tourists up to the volcano. We've been finding a few dead animals and plants on the slopes. A few volcanologists are studying Mt. Nyiragongo."

Kennedy felt a few butterflies flutter in her stomach. She glanced back at the volcano.

Yannick looked relieved. "I do not mind. I would rather we not hike up there."

"But it is a beautiful hike, Yannick," Chantal said in a hard voice. "You would let the past stop you from enjoying nature?"

Yannick glared at Chantal. He briskly walked toward the front of the group. Kennedy heard Pastor Moïse sigh. She and Marilyn eyed one another. The two of them went over to Chantal's side.

"Yes?" Chantal said.

"We were wondering if you'd like to talk," Kennedy said. "Is Yannick just an annoying little brother? Uh, stepbrother?"

Chantal chuckled lightly. "He is," she said. "He thinks I miss my mama too much to love his mama. I miss my mama, yes. But I do like Violette. I hope Yannick likes my father. He is the first father figure that Yannick has had."

"Really?" Marilyn said.

"*Oui.* Yannick's real father died from asphyxiation when Mt. Nyiragongo erupted in 2002. Yannick was only a baby."

Kennedy glanced at Yannick. No wonder he didn't seem to like the idea of hiking up Mt. Nyiragongo.

"My dad hopes to be the father Yannick never had," Chantal added.

"My mother died from cancer when I was a baby," Marilyn said.

"And I told you that my dad died from an illness when I was fifteen," Kennedy added.

"Yes," Chantal said, "so you probably do know how I feel, but at least you two love each other. I can't stand Yannick. He never listens to me. He thinks I act like a second mother."

225

"Oh, I wasn't happy at first," Kennedy said. "My mom's marriage to Marilyn's dad was very difficult for me. What helped me was the fact that Marilyn and I were friends before we became stepsisters. She was always so kind to me. I'm very glad God put her in my life. But I do know what you're going through, Chantal. I know how hard it must be to adjust."

"So," Chantal said, "you are saying I should accept God's plan to bring Yannick into my life?"

"I know it's hard. But yes, I am saying that."

Chantal smiled feebly. "I might need your help."

Kennedy patted Chantal's shoulder. "We'd be glad to help. Me and Marilyn."

"Hey, everyone!" Pierre called, waving his hands. He had an excited look on his face. "I want to show you Lake Virunga!"

He led everyone onto another trail. The trail led to a beautiful landscape that had Kennedy gaping. There was a round lake, which Kennedy assumed was Lake Virunga. The lake's crystalline waters, which had hues of light blue surrounding a darker blue middle, shimmered under the sunlight. Enormous palm leaves dangled over the water. Tall hills covered in green grass and tropical trees and flora surrounded the lake. Lily pads dotted the surface of the lake.

"This is one of my favorite areas in the park," Pierre said.

"I can see why," Marilyn said. "This is so beautiful. Look at that lake shimmering! Why, I almost want to go swimming in it!"

"A cool dip does sound good." Billy waved his hand over his face. "It's mighty hot out here!"

Pierre frowned a little. "I wouldn't recommend it," he said. "Lake Virunga is saturated with carbon dioxide."

"It is?" Aaron said.

Pierre nodded. He held his hand over his eyes as he peered at the hills. "We need to move on. It is almost time for the picnic."

The ranger led everyone toward the hills. Kennedy was looking forward to the church picnic.

"Hey, look!" Aaron said. "A gorilla!"

Kennedy spun around. Sure enough, her cousin was pointing at a black mountain gorilla on the next hill over. The gorilla didn't seem to notice the tourists staring, pointing, and taking pictures of it. It was more focused on pounding the ground while making nervous grunts.

"Boy, that big ape seems agitated," Billy said.

"Yeah," Kennedy mused, "just like those elephants."

Pierre ushered the kids to keep moving. Kennedy kept her eyes on the gorilla until it was out of sight.

They crossed the hills to a wide clearing, where there was a white tent set up. Kennedy saw Pastor Logan help a few women set food on the tables under the tent.

"Hey, hey, we're back," Pastor Cameron said.

"Great," Pastor Logan said. "How was the hike?"

"Very good. We saw some elephants, one gorilla, and Lake Virunga. It's just over those hills."

Pastor Moïse clapped to get everybody's attention. He said a prayer, then everyone started forming lines at the tables.

"Think this food is any good?" Annice muttered.

Mrs. Carrington sighed. "It looks fine," she said. "Please, just eat, Annice."

Annice lowered her eyes. She awkwardly tugged at the blue bandanna in her hair. Kennedy couldn't understand why Annice felt like she needed to complain. The food looked just fine. Baskets were filled with fresh apples, bananas, guavas, tomatoes, and oranges. There was bread, cheese, saka saka, stews, and fufu on the tables, and two jugs full of clean water and cups of palm juice. Why, this picnic would be a luxurious feast to the majority of Goma's population!

"Where are we sitting, Mom?" Annice asked.

"We'll sit next to Pastor Logan," her mother said.

"Is Saleem here?" Annice looked around. "You know, that energetic little boy?"

"I don't think so. His father's helping with the chapel."

Annice bit her lip. She and her mother sat next to Pastor Logan. Kennedy watched Annice study her fufu. She hesitantly took a bite. She smiled and took another bite.

Kennedy helped herself to some fufu, bread, and a few fruits and vegetables. She spotted Billy standing on the hill, gazing into the distance. She walked up and stood next to him. Not far from the hill, she saw Lake Virunga, its blue waters glittering under the evening sun.

Billy smiled at her. "Hey there."

"Hi." Kennedy smiled shyly. "This place is so beautiful."

"Sure is," Billy said. He bit into his apple and pointed to the orange light in the sky. "Don't you just love how Mt. Nyiragongo's lava lake can light up the sky?"

"It's gorgeous," Kennedy said. "So, how did you guys do on the chapel work?"

"I reckon we did just fine," Billy said. "It's sure tougher than repairing fences on your uncle's ranch, though."

"I'm sure it is." Kennedy looked over her shoulder. "I don't see the others from our party. You know, Pastor Cameron, Wesley, Brody, and Francis."

"Pastor Cameron left to meet up with Wesley, Brody, and Francis. They wanted to finish up a few things at the chapel. They'll be back here soon—hey, did you feel that?"

Kennedy gasped. She did feel it. A light shaking of the ground beneath her feet. She and Billy looked at each other. He looked just as bewildered as she felt.

Suddenly the shaking intensified. Kennedy yelled in alarm. She and Billy fell to their knees, dropping their plates. Almost all their food rolled down the hill.

"What's happening?" Annice's panicked voice screamed.

"It's an earthquake!" Logan shouted. "Everyone take cover!"

Kennedy's stomach dropped. Her heart seemed to beat in sync with the shaking of the ground. Memories of the earthquakes in Pine Lodge flooded her mind.

A tree fell over. Birds flew away as fast as their wings would carry them, their frightened chirps piercing the air. Billy grasped her arms.

BOOM!

Kennedy screamed. She turned her eyes to Lake Virunga. The bubbling waters were releasing a huge wave, as though a bomb had just exploded under the lake.

Then, just as suddenly as it began, the quaking stopped. Even so, Kennedy didn't dare move a muscle. She felt Billy grasp her shoulder.

"Are you okay?" he whispered.

Kennedy looked up at his concerned eyes. All she could do was nod.

"Is everybody alright?"

Kennedy gasped and turned around on her knees. But it was only Mrs. Carrington. Rachel, Chantal, Yannick, and Marilyn were right behind her. Annice was clinging to her mother, who was stroking her hair. Kennedy's eyes wandered to each of the girls. Marilyn's eyes were filled with trauma.

Kennedy ran over to her stepsister. "You okay?"

Marilyn nodded. "It was awful," she said. "It was like those earthquakes back at home."

"Tell me about it."

Kennedy turned to Mrs. Carrington. "Where did everybody else go?"

"They scattered," Mrs. Carrington said. "They couldn't have gone far, though."

"Hello!"

Relief filled Kennedy at the sound of her cousin's voice. She looked down the hill. She spotted Lake Virunga in the distance. She raised her eyebrow; why was the lake bubbling? And what was that white mist that seemed to be seeping from the lake?

The sight of Aaron and Pastor Logan running toward the hill distracted Kennedy from the lake.

"Hey!" she shouted, waving her arms. "Up here!"

Her cousin spotted her and waved back. So did Pastor Logan. Kennedy grinned, but not for long. Aaron suddenly fainted.

"Aaron!" Kennedy screamed.

"He fainted!" Yannick said, his eyes filled with horror.

Billy ran forward, as though he wanted to run down the hill. But Rachel and Marilyn grabbed his arms. Then Pastor Logan began coughing. And with every passing second, his coughing intensified.

"Logan!" Mrs. Carrington bellowed. "Logan, get up here!"

"But my cousin!" Kennedy said.

Pastor Logan waved a hand at them. He bent over and hauled Aaron over his shoulder. His face was contorted as he appeared to be holding his breath. But he managed the feat and was climbing the hill with Aaron slumped over his shoulders. He stumbled only once, didn't even fall. He trudged up the hill to the group, then collapsed right at Mrs. Carrington's feet.

"Logan!" Mrs. Carrington said, kneeling. "Are you alright?"

Rachel ran to her father's side and grabbed his shoulders. Yannick also kneeled by the pastor.

"Dad?" Rachel whispered. The pastor didn't respond.

"Dad, wake up!" Rachel patted her father's face. Kennedy rushed over to Rachel's side. She looked at Rachel, then at Yannick. Kennedy thought she could see trauma in the young boy's eyes.

Rachel grasped her father's wrist. The look of relief on her face made Kennedy calm down a bit.

230

"He's still alive," Rachel said. "I can feel his pulse."

Kennedy crawled over to her cousin and touched his wrist. Much to her relief, he also had a pulse.

"What happened?" Annice demanded. "What's going on?"

"Lake Virunga exploded," Kennedy said. "That was a limnic eruption."

"Kennedy told me about these kinds of eruptions," Marilyn said. "They happen when lakes filled with carbon dioxide are disturbed and they release the CO_2."

"The earthquake must've triggered it," Billy said. "That's why it was bubbling. The lake unleashed carbon dioxide."

"Then this is serious," Yannick said. "The earthquake. It could only mean that Mt. Nyiragongo will erupt, right?"

"We don't know that, Yannick," Chantal said irritably.

"But what else can an earthquake mean?" Yannick said.

Annice crossed her arms. "This is unacceptable," she said. "Having a mission trip so close to an active volcano, and then being caught up in its destruction."

"I highly doubt our pastors knew this would happen, Annice," Mrs. Carrington said sternly.

Annice glared at her mother. "Well, what if we faint too?"

"We won't," Kennedy said. "The carbon dioxide isn't reaching us on this hill. CO_2 is too dense to rise very high."

"So we're trapped up here?"

Kennedy sighed. "Someone will come for us."

"Are you certain of that?"

"Yes." Kennedy sat down. She wished that she was as sure as she had made herself sound. She wanted to believe that a rescue would come soon. She gazed at her cousin. Would he be okay? What if he didn't make it? Or Pastor Logan?

Kennedy turned her gaze to Lake Virunga. Its waters were no longer blue and sparkling. It was now a murky, reddish-brown color. There was still some fog around the lake. A tense silence permeated the atmosphere. No birds singing or chirping. Not even one insect sound. It almost felt as though one more sound would trigger another earthquake, or make the lake emit more carbon dioxide.

Kennedy closed her eyes. She felt like the only thing she could do now was pray silently. *Help us, God.*

"Did you hear that?"

Kennedy looked up at Billy's sudden whisper. So did everyone else. Kennedy listened; she heard it too. Voices calling in the distance.

She smiled when she recognized Pierre's voice.

"I hear them!" Chantal jumped to her feet. "They are rangers! They are here to help! And my father is with them!"

She screamed down the hill. Kennedy heard Pastor Moïse's ecstatic reply, even though he was nowhere in sight. She breathed a sigh of relief and silently thanked the Lord.

The hospital's parking lots were overrun with cars, vans, and people running back and forth. It took Pierre nearly ten minutes just to get his van close to the emergency entrance. Kennedy wished they could have dropped her cousin and Pastor Logan off at the health care center in the park, but it had filled up by the time the rescue team had arrived there. So Pierre and Pastor Moïse had to drive everyone to the hospital in Goma.

Several doctors and nurses came out of the emergency entrance to greet their new patients. A few doctors helped move Aaron and Pastor Logan onto stretchers and wheel them inside. Kennedy, Marilyn, and Rachel ran after them. Kennedy looked up at the TV monitor in the waiting room. The TV was playing news of the earthquake and the limnic eruption.

Soon Aaron and Pastor Logan were placed in a room and connected to oxygen masks and other machines. Kennedy gazed down at her unconscious cousin. She fought back the tears. She felt Marilyn put her hand on her shoulder. Kennedy eyed the doorway; she could see Pierre, Billy, Annice, Chantal, Yannick, Mrs. Carrington, and Pastor Moïse standing in the hall.

A quiet groan made Kennedy turn her head around. Pastor Logan had opened his eyes.

"Dad!"

Rachel leaned over her father to hug him. Her smile gave Kennedy a flicker of hope. She turned back to her cousin. As if on cue, Aaron's eyes fluttered open. Kennedy could only gasp; she felt that if she made any other sounds, they would be accompanied by a torrent of tears. Aaron met her eyes and smiled weakly. He took a deep breath.

"Did I scare you?" he asked, his voice barely audible.

Kennedy leaned over to hug him. "Don't do that again, eh?" she said with a faint chuckle.

232

Just then Violette came into the room, dressed in white scrubs and holding a clipboard. Her husband was right behind her. So was everyone else.

"Is everyone alright?" Violette asked. "I heard everything that has happened."

"We are fine," Pastor Moïse said. "Are you alright?"

"Yes," Violette said. She stared at her husband sadly. "But a small part of our house's roof caved in when the earthquake came. Many buildings in the city have fallen, and many streets are closed."

Pastor Moïse frowned.

"How bad was the earthquake?" Annice asked.

"It was a 5.3 magnitude," Pierre said.

Kennedy gaped at the park ranger. Her thoughts wandered to Mt. Nyiragongo. She knew the earthquake had triggered Lake Virunga's limnic eruption; could the earthquake also be a warning for a volcanic eruption?

"I have been assigned to watch over your friends," Violette said. "I will do my best to help them."

"Do you think our hotel stood?" Annice asked anxiously.

"I don't know, honey." Mrs. Carrington's eyes wandered to the hallway. In the span of a single minute, Kennedy saw five doctors and four nurses run by the open door.

"Everyone is so busy," Mrs. Carrington said. "I feel awful. I am a nurse too, back in America."

She looked at Violette. "Perhaps I might be permitted to help you?"

Violette smiled. "I will see," she said. "You can stay with my patients whenever I am out of the room."

"Of course. I'll never leave their sides."

"What about me, Mom?" Annice asked. "Can I stay with you?"

Mrs. Carrington sighed. She took hold of her daughter's hair and brushed a few strands over Annice's shoulders.

"Pastor Moïse might need your help," she said softly. She turned her gaze to everyone else in the room. "From all of you."

"I agree with her," Pastor Logan said. He smiled weakly up at Rachel. "Go with them, Rachel. Don't worry about me. Violette and Della will be with me and Aaron."

Kennedy grasped her cousin's hand.

"Logan's right, Ken," Aaron said, his voice soft and raspy. "You should go and help others. That's why we came, eh?"

Kennedy smiled meekly. "I suppose so," she said. "You still have your phone, right?"

Aaron nodded. "Our rescuers made sure I had it by my side. And Mrs. Carrington has hers too."

"Yes, we will keep in close contact with one another," Mrs. Carrington said.

Kennedy gave Aaron one last hug, and then she, Rachel, and Annice followed everyone out of the room. Rachel wrapped an arm around Annice's shoulders.

"I've got your back, girl," Rachel said.

Kennedy almost expected Annice to respond with some snarky remark, like she didn't need a babysitter. But Annice didn't even flinch at Rachel's embrace. She just nodded.

"Oh!" Marilyn gasped. "What about the others? Cameron, Wesley, Brody, and Francis?"

"It is alright," Pastor Moïse said. "I received a call from Cameron while we were driving to the hospital. He met up with Wesley, Brody, and Francis. They are at your hotel. They say that your hotel is still standing."

Kennedy heard Annice breathe out a sigh of relief. She could hardly blame her; she felt relieved herself.

The parking lot was no less busy than inside the hospital. More cars seemed to arrive with every passing second. Kennedy heard a woman soothing crying children. She turned her gaze to the city. Even from a distance, Kennedy could make out collapsed buildings. Good thing the hospital was still standing!

Kennedy followed Pierre and Pastor Moïse to their vans. The two men paused briefly to converse with each other in French. They shared a quick hug, then Pastor Moïse motioned for everyone to get in his van.

"What's going on?" Marilyn asked.

"We will go to my house," Pastor Moïse said. "I will get my water bottles and share them with the people in the hospital."

Annice stared at Pastor Moïse with wide eyes. "You mean those whole packages of water bottles that we donated to your family? You're just going to give them all away?"

"These people need the water as much as my family does."

"What about Pierre?" Kennedy asked.

"He is going to your hotel to check on your friends," Pastor Moïse said. "We will meet with all of them later."

After ten minutes of waiting for the parking lot to be clear of frantic people, Pastor Moïse was on the road. Kennedy stared out the window in silence, ignoring the nervous chatter of everyone else. She hadn't noticed the plight of Goma on the way to the hospital, but then again, she had been too busy watching over her cousin. But now, she saw the fallen buildings, telephone lines, and lampposts. She saw the cracks along the roads, and the detours that Pastor Moïse had to take because of closed roads. She saw law enforcement trying to calm frantic crowds and people digging through the dusty rubble of ruined buildings.

"Whoa," Marilyn whispered, "even those earthquakes in Pine Lodge didn't cause this much damage."

Kennedy nodded.

Soon Pastor Moïse turned the van onto a dirt road. Kennedy cringed at the sight of the neighborhood. Almost every house had fallen. Bricks and stones covered the ground. People were digging through huge piles of dirt and rubble.

Soon they arrived at Pastor Moïse's house. It looked just as Violette had said. Most of the roof was completely caved into the house. Pastor Moïse gazed sadly at the collapse. Then he straightened himself, as though trying to adopt a more confident composure.

"Let's find those water bottles," he said.

Much to Kennedy's surprise, they were able to enter the house easily. At least for the first few steps. Pastor Moïse, Billy, and Yannick dug through the rubble of broken roof pieces to get to the living room.

"He seems more worried about those water bottles than his own house," Annice said in a low voice.

"I reckon so," Rachel said. "I mean, he's still a pastor. He's gonna have a lot of people to take care of. But I think he's prepped for it."

"Found them!" Billy's voice called.

He and Pastor Moïse climbed out of the wreckage. Each carried one package of water bottles. Yannick followed them, but as he lifted his foot, he tripped over a fallen beam and landed flat on his stomach. He coughed as dust clouded his face.

"Yannick!" Chantal rushed to her stepbrother's side and helped him up. At first Yannick appeared annoyed. Then his expression softened as he looked up at Chantal.

"Merci," he said.

"Are you alright?" Chantal asked.

Yannick nodded. He looked at his knees and elbows. Other than being smudged with dirt, they seemed fine.

"Need a water?" Billy asked. He opened his package and handed a bottle to Yannick, who accepted it gratefully.

"We should save a few bottles for ourselves," Pastor Moïse said. "And I want to leave one package here for all these people. They might need water too."

"Yes, that's a wonderful idea," Marilyn said. "Come on, let's distribute them."

Pastor Moïse put his package in his van. Billy handed out water bottles to everyone. Pastor Moïse led the kids to a large group of people gathered around a pile of stones, mud, and dirt. Kennedy had a horrible feeling that huge pile of rubble used to be a house. Maybe even two or three houses.

As soon as the people saw the kids with bottles of clean water, they rushed over, surrounding them almost immediately.

"Gosh," Kennedy whispered to Billy, "I hope we don't get a mob."

But Kennedy didn't need to worry. When she gave a bottle to a man, he took the bottle to a woman and a child. He opened it but didn't take a drink. He handed the bottle to the woman, who shared it with the child sitting on her lap. And when Yannick gave a bottle to a teenage girl, the girl turned and gave the bottle to an elderly woman sitting on the ground.

"You should give her another," Chantal said to Yannick. "Look at how she smacks her lips. She must be very thirsty."

Kennedy almost expected Yannick to respond with some nasty remark. But Yannick just nodded and handed the girl a second bottle. The girl accepted it with a grateful grin on her face and took one huge gulp.

Kennedy saw Pastor Moïse approach three kids and offer them bottles. The kids accepted them. The youngest, a little girl, had trouble opening her bottle. The oldest kid among them, a boy, helped her open it.

Pastor Moïse smiled contentedly. "I love how they are watching out for one another," he said. His smile disappeared. "But they should use their waters sparingly. I am sure we do not have enough for everyone here."

"Saleem!"

Kennedy spun around. Annice was squatting and holding out her hands to a little boy hiding behind a rock. Kennedy narrowed her eyes; she indeed recognized the boy as Saleem.

She went over to Annice. "Here," she said, holding out a bottle, "try offering him this."

Annice took the bottle and held it out. "Hey, look what we've got!" she said soothingly. "Fresh water! Come on!"

Saleem poked his head out from behind the rock. He stood up and hesitantly walked toward Annice. Then he smiled, his eyes filled with relief, and he ran over to Annice and fell into her arms. She opened the bottle for him. Saleem drank the water greedily.

"Is he okay?" Kennedy asked.

Annice looked over the young boy. "He's got an awful cut on his ankle," she said. "See?"

She pointed to Saleem's left ankle. Kennedy stifled a gasp. That bleeding cut was going to need stitches.

"Why was he hiding?" Kennedy asked.

"I think he just got here," Annice said. She ran her hand over Saleem's head. "I'm sure he's really scared."

"He must be." Kennedy's eyes glazed over the area. "I don't see his parents anywhere. He must've been so relieved when he saw you."

Kennedy turned to Pastor Moïse. "Think we can try to find out how many children are without parents?"

"I talked with some of these people," the pastor said, his voice breaking. "I . . . I am afraid there have been some casualties."

Kennedy placed her hand over her mouth. "Not Saleem's parents?" she asked softly.

The pastor shrugged. "I was told that Saleem was outside playing with some of the other kids when the earthquake came. His father is not here. He was working on the chapel. I do not know where his mama is. But I also heard that many people have been taken to the hospital. Perhaps Saleem's mama is there."

"Then we should go there." Annice stood up, her hand still on Saleem's head. "Saleem needs stitches, anyway. Please, can we take him to the hospital?"

"Yes, we will do that," Pastor Moïse said. "Maybe he can stay with Logan and Aaron if we do not find his mama."

Everyone, including Saleem, returned to the pastor's van. Due to heavier traffic, the ride back to the hospital was slow.

Kennedy saw many more police officers and construction workers on the streets.

Annice sat in the back, cradling Saleem in her arms. Kennedy noticed that Annice's bandanna was wrapped around his wounded leg. Dark red blood stained the bandanna's beautiful blue color.

"You wrapped your bandanna around his leg?" Kennedy tried to sound casual, but she wondered if her voice betrayed a little surprise.

Annice smiled feebly. "I can just get a new one when I get home."

Kennedy couldn't help but smile.

After what seemed like an eternity of driving through crazy traffic on terrible roads, they finally arrived at the hospital. Everyone followed Pastor Moïse inside. Annice was helping Saleem walk. Billy carried the unopened package of water bottles.

The waiting room was no less busy than it had been before. Billy set the package down on a table and ripped it open. He handed two bottles to Kennedy.

"Let's get started," he said.

Kennedy turned to Annice. "You should probably have Saleem sit somewhere," she said.

"Of course," Annice said. "And I will stay with him."

But Saleem grabbed two bottles from the table and limped over to two little girls sitting on a bench. Saleem opened one bottle and handed it to the girl whose arm was in a cast. Both girls smiled at him as they took the bottles.

Kennedy chortled. "He's a tough little guy," she said. "But I think he needs to sit down and rest his leg."

Annice held out her hand and whistled. Saleem ran over to her. Annice wrapped her arm around the boy and guided him to a bench. Kennedy couldn't help but chuckle. Saleem kept his wide fixated eyes on her. She saw the wistful look in the boy's eyes. Then, much to Kennedy's surprise, Annice kissed his head. Saleem smiled up at her and rested his head on her lap.

"Did I just see that?" Billy said in disbelief.

Kennedy laughed. "You sure did. Annice has really grown attached to him."

Just then a young girl tugged at Kennedy's shirt. She held her hands out. Kennedy got the message and gave the girl a bottle.

"*Merci mingi*," the girl said. She turned and ran to a nurse, who was setting up rows of paper cups on a table.

Kennedy saw Pastor Moïse talking to a couple. The woman had a cast on her knee, a pair of rickety crutches, and tears in her eyes. Kennedy went over to them and gave the couple two bottles. The man took them and thanked Kennedy.

Pastor Moïse grinned at her. "Kennedy," he said, "where is Saleem?"

"He's sitting with Annice," Kennedy said. "Why?"

"Bring him over here."

Kennedy turned and went over to Annice and Saleem. But before she could say anything to Annice, an excited squeal startled her. Kennedy spun around and saw the woman with the knee cast moving toward them. The man looked equally excited.

And then Saleem gasped. His face lit up. He jumped to his feet and ran over to the couple. The man scooped up Saleem in his arms.

Pastor Moïse smiled at Kennedy. "I found Saleem's mama and papa," he said.

Tears of joy stung Kennedy's eyes. "I can see that."

"Will they be okay?" Annice asked.

"Well, their whole house fell," the pastor said.

Annice gasped. "That's awful! What will they do now?"

"I plan to help them." Pastor Moïse smiled at Saleem. "But at least they are back together."

Annice nodded slowly. She gazed at Saleem. Even with the cut on his ankle spilling blood on his father's shirt, Kennedy didn't see the joyful grins fading from the threesome's faces. She wiped away a tear and turned to Pastor Moïse.

"I hope you don't mind me asking," she said, "could we visit Aaron and Rachel's dad real quick before we leave?"

Pastor Moïse chuckled. "There is no need to leave. I got a call from Cameron. He, Wesley, Brody, and Francis came here to see your cousin and Rachel's dad. They are with them right now in another room. Come, we will go see them."

Pastor Moïse and Kennedy gathered their party. Annice was reluctant to leave Saleem, but she followed everyone else to the hall.

"You really like that boy, don't you?" Rachel said.

"He reminds me of my brother," Annice said.

"You have a brother?" Chantal said.

Annice nodded. "Needless to say, he stayed home. He's only seven years old."

"What's his name?" Kennedy asked.

Annice smiled. "Bennett." She sighed. "Saleem is a lot like Bennett. They both have a lot of energy. Not shy at all. Wanting to make friends with everyone they meet. And Bennett is so caring, whereas I am . . ."

She trailed off and hung her head. "I had wanted to go back to the hotel and see if my stuff was alright. But, after seeing Saleem and his parents, and how they could care less that their house was destroyed, just that they are together . . . I know now that all those nice things I own, like my trendy clothes and my cell phone and my tablet . . ."

She sniffled. "I miss my family. I miss Bennett."

Chantal wrapped her arm around Annice. "Your brother sounds like he would get along with Yannick."

Annice chuckled. "I think he would," she said. She smiled at Chantal. "I do love Bennett, Chantal, but I gotta admit that I know how you feel. Sometimes my brother can be a big pain."

"Did he ever tell you that you are bossy?" Chantal asked with a grin.

Annice sniggered. "All the time."

She looked up at everyone else. Kennedy noticed that they were further down the hall. The three girls rushed ahead to catch up with them just as they all stopped. Pastor Moïse met his wife at a doorway. They hugged and spoke to each other in French. Then Pastor Moïse turned to everyone else.

"My wife will lead us to our friends," he said in a loud voice.

Everyone followed Violette down the hall. They came to a large, rectangular room. Several beds, every one of which was filled with a patient, were lined against the walls. Kennedy saw patients with IV tubes, oxygen masks, and casts on their limbs.

Violette led them toward the back of the room. Kennedy smiled when she saw Wesley, Mrs. Carrington, Pastor Cameron, Brody, Francis, and Pierre standing by Aaron and Pastor Logan's beds. Annice rushed over to her mother and embraced her. The men stepped aside to talk in private.

"Hey, man," Wesley said, patting Billy's back, "where have you and the rest of the gang been?"

"Driving all over Goma," Billy said. "Dude, you missed all the action back at the park."

"Yeah, I saw the lake overturn on the news! If all that CO_2 didn't give you a heart attack, your fear must've!"

Billy laughed. "Hey, Wes, be a gentleman and step aside, we'd better let Ken and Rachel through."

He nodded at Kennedy and stepped to the side. Kennedy and Rachel walked over to the beds. Kennedy smiled at her cousin.

"How are you feeling?" she asked. She noticed that his wrist had a light brown bruise.

"Better," Aaron said. He did sound better. His voice was much less raspy. His eyes wandered to the rest of the group. "So, I take it the gang's back together?"

"I think so."

"And that's a good thing too."

Kennedy looked over her shoulder. Pastor Moïse, Pierre, Brody, and Francis were walking toward Aaron's bed.

"We were just talking with Pierre about what we should do next," Brody said. He crossed his arms. "We did take a quick look at the chapel. It's still standing for the most part, but all that work we did, putting up the new beams and new windows . . . it's gone to waste."

Kennedy bit her lip. She glanced at Pastor Moïse. Even with his head hanging, Kennedy could see the sorrowful look in his eyes. First he lost his house. Now it seemed that he may have lost his chapel. "I'm sorry to hear that."

"There's nothing we can do about it," Francis said.

"The quakes have damaged so many buildings in Goma," Pierre added. "The hospitals are filling up. Even hotels are filling up. The city is running out of shelters for the people left homeless. I do know of areas in Virunga National Park taking in the homeless. I will need to go and help my fellow rangers take care of those people soon."

"And perhaps we can help out too?"

All eyes turned to Pastor Moïse. Determination replaced the sorrow in his eyes.

"There is nothing else that we can do here," Pastor Moïse said. "But these people, they came all the way from America to help us. Perhaps they can go to the camps in the park?"

Pierre smiled. "We have a small team from the DRC Red Cross coming in," he said. "But we can use the extra help."

He gratefully shook Pastor Moïse's hands. *"Merci mingi."*

Kennedy zigzagged around the tents that were pitched just outside of the lodge. This small, tented camp, which Kennedy heard was a tourist attraction of Virunga National Park, had basically become a fancy refugee camp. Just over the hills, Mt. Nyiragongo looked like it was looming over the campsite and the nearby jungle.

Kennedy wiped sweat from her cheeks. It felt hotter in the park than it had the previous day.

"Hey, Kennedy!"

Kennedy turned around. Marilyn was waving at her from the lodge's porch. Kennedy sprinted over to her.

"Pastor Moïse needs help with unloading," Marilyn said. "He just got back with the groceries."

Relief filled the pit of Kennedy's stomach. She and Marilyn ran around the lodge. Pastor Moïse's van was parked along the side. Billy, Wesley, and Pastor Cameron were already unloading a few bags.

"Glad we can at least purchase groceries," Kennedy said.

"I know," Marilyn said. "Good thing those markets are still standing."

Kennedy took a package of water bottles from Billy and went through the campsite. Countless people sat on the grass near their tents. Kennedy spotted Annice sitting near a large white tent with Saleem and his parents. She smiled; Saleem was as happy as ever, sitting on his father's lap. The stitches on his ankle were barely visible; Kennedy had to look closer to actually see them. She held in a sigh. She hoped her cousin and Rachel's father were okay. They were still at the hospital, having stayed there overnight. Last she heard, they would be coming to the tented camp later.

Kennedy opened the package and started handing out the bottles. Marilyn and Rachel were handing out baskets of fruits and vegetables while Chantal and Yannick distributed blankets and pillows.

"Do you think this will be enough for all these people?" Chantal asked.

"I hope so," Yannick said. He yawned.

"Are you tired?" Chantal asked. "Maybe you should rest."

Kennedy hoped Yannick wouldn't make some retort. The last thing they needed right now was quarreling from Chantal and Yannick. But Yannick didn't even glare at his stepsister.

"I did not sleep well last night," he said. "I never thought I would be homeless. My mama used to have those fears when I was a baby. It is because of your father that my mama thrived, even as a widow."

Chantal smiled. "Even before my father married your mama, he was like a father to you."

Yannick smiled back. "*Oui*. He is a good father to me."

He yawned again and spoke in French. Chantal replied in French, her voice calm and soothing. Yannick nodded and went into one of the big tents.

Kennedy ran over to Chantal. "You need any help?"

"A little help." Chantal gave Kennedy a couple of pillows. "I sent Yannick out to my family's tent to sleep. He needs to rest. He is very tired. I think he is worried about the volcano erupting."

"I'll bet lots of people are," Kennedy said. Her eyes glazed over the campsite. The chatter was dying down as people were crawling into their tents to rest. Kennedy wondered if any of these people slept last night. She hung her head. While these people were sleeping in tents, she and her party had stayed in their hotel. Pastor Moïse had insisted that Pastor Cameron take his party to the hotel where they would be comfortable, warm, and safe, but Kennedy still couldn't shake away the guilt.

"How are your parents?" she asked.

"I think they are fine," Chantal said. "But all this has been hard on them. Mama spent the whole night working in the hospital. And Father is worried about the community and his chapel."

"He doesn't show it."

"No. He says that He trusts in God to take care of Goma. And his chapel. It is all our family has left now."

She patted her stomach. "I'm hungry. We should eat."

Kennedy and Chantal went into the lodge. Much to her surprise, Kennedy spotted Pastor Logan, Rachel, and Aaron in the dining area, sitting at a table with Pierre and Pastor Moïse.

"Oh, good, my cousin and Logan are here!" Kennedy said. She and Chantal ran over to the table. As soon as Aaron saw them, he jumped up and sprinted over to Kennedy. The two cousins embraced.

"How are you feeling?" Kennedy asked.

"Much better," Aaron said. "Doctors say Logan and I should take it easy, though."

"Of course."

"Come on, join us for some lunch."

Kennedy, Chantal, and Aaron sat down at the table.

"Where are the others?" Chantal asked.

"Most of them already ate," Pastor Moïse said. "Annice and her mama went on a walk with Brody. I think all of you need to rest. You have worked very hard helping all these people."

Kennedy opened her menu. But she could only stare at it. Her stomach wouldn't growl. No, not with her worries flooding her mind. She turned to the window and stared at the tents. She felt bad for those people. Especially Pastor Moïse and his family. But at least these people had food and shelter. Kennedy wondered if those tents were better than most of the homes had ever been in Goma. But Kennedy didn't like it that this tented camp was so close to the volcano. The other tented camps in the park had been filled up.

"Hey, help!"

Kennedy dropped her menu and whirled around in her chair. That was Annice screaming!

"What's going on?" Rachel asked. She stood up and ran to the open door. Kennedy was right on her heels. She looked over Rachel's shoulder at the people clamoring near the edge of the campsite.

"What's the scoop?" Aaron asked.

"No idea," Kennedy said. "Let's find out."

She, her cousin, and Rachel ran outside. Kennedy pushed her way past the crowd, only to stop in her tracks when she saw Annice. Kennedy's heart skipped a beat. Annice was trudging toward the tents, coughing so loud that Kennedy thought she was going to throw up. Kennedy saw her sweaty face and blue cheeks. A few people had already begun to gather around her. Annice then fell to her knees and burst into tears.

Pierre rushed past Kennedy and Aaron and ran to Annice. Kennedy, Aaron, Rachel, Chantal, and Pastors Logan and Moïse ran over to Pierre's side.

"What happened?" Rachel asked.

Annice took a deep breath. Her eyes were red and puffy. "My mom," she sputtered, "she's still out there!"

"Hey, calm down," Pierre said. "Tell us what happened."

Annice sniffled and coughed. "We were hiking. We heard a hissing sound. Brody went a few feet to look for the noise. Then a yellow gas erupted from the ground, and my mom just collapsed!"

Pierre groaned. "This is not good," he said gravely. He took Annice's hands and helped her stand up. Then he looked over at the rainforest. "We need to find them. Your mama and Brody."

Everyone followed Pierre to the lodge. Much to Pierre's dismay, there was only one other ranger in the lodge. Pierre spoke frantically in French. Pastor Moïse put his hand on Pierre's shoulder and spoke soothingly. Pierre nodded.

"What are they saying?" Kennedy asked Chantal.

"Too many rangers have been hurt yesterday," Chantal said, "and there is not enough to help. So my father offered to have a small search party help find Annice's mom and Brody."

"Sounds good to me," Rachel said.

"Count me in," Aaron added.

"Uh, no way," Kennedy said. "Aaron, you've already fainted and spent a night in the hospital from exposure to CO_2. I'm not sure you should go to another area with knockout gas."

"But I want to help!" Aaron said.

Kennedy didn't think she was going to stop her cousin. Who was she to talk, anyway? Kennedy was determined to go herself. In just a few minutes, Kennedy was part of a search party with Pierre, Pastors Moïse and Cameron, Francis, Billy, Wesley, Annice, Rachel, Marilyn, and Aaron.

"Alright," Pierre said in a loud voice, "be careful. We do not know what will happen. We must stay together. Annice, lead the way."

Everyone followed Annice down a trail. The area was thick with trees. Very little sunlight penetrated the canopy above. A wet leaf brushed against Kennedy's face. She wiped the dew off her cheek.

"Hey, what's that over there?" Marilyn said, pointing to a different road. She ran over to that trail.

"Don't go too far," Pierre said.

"I don't think I will," Marilyn said. She turned a disgusted face to the rest of the group. "I just found a dead frog."

"A dead frog?" Pierre went to Marilyn's side. Kennedy was right behind him. She made a face at the sight of the frog lying with all four legs sprawled out on the ground. The frog's eyes were rolled to the back of its head and its tongue was sticking out.

"Do you think a predator got it?" Marilyn asked.

"No, it doesn't look like it's been attacked and mangled," Pierre said.

"Maybe it died from Lake Virunga's overturn."

"No, that can't be," Kennedy said. "This area wasn't affected by the lake's CO_2 release."

"Who cares?" Annice said impatiently. "We have to find my mom!"

"Yes, of course," Pierre said. "Come, girls."

The group moved on. Kennedy hoped they didn't waste too much time. Every second was precious in finding Brody and Annice's mother.

"What's with all these dead trees?" Wesley asked.

Kennedy looked ahead. Several of the trees looked more like thin, vertical logs with small, barren branches.

"That is strange," Pierre said. "Those trees were fine weeks ago."

"Hey!" Billy shouted. "Over here!"

Kennedy spun around. Billy and Annice were running toward something lying on the ground. Kennedy brushed away the low-hanging leaves to get a better view. Her heart leapt when she spotted Mrs. Carrington lying on the ground.

"Hey!" Pierre called. "Don't run in there! There may be more gas!"

Indeed, Kennedy thought that she caught a whiff of sulfur. But Billy and Annice remained conscious. Neither seemed to have any trouble breathing.

"Hello!"

Kennedy gasped. She recognized that voice. She saw Brody coming out of the forest. A look of relief covered his face.

"Oh, good, you are all here!" he said. He ran over to Annice and hugged her. "I did what I could for your mother. I tried to look for help."

"It's okay!" Annice said. She broke away from Brody and kneeled next to her mother. She shook her shoulder. "Mom, it's me, I'm back! And I've brought help! Come on, Mom, wake up!"

Annice's voice was breaking. Kennedy and Pierre ran over to her. Kennedy laid her hand on Annice's shoulder.

"We'll help her," she whispered.

Annice stood up. Pierre squatted next to Mrs. Carrington and pressed a couple of fingers to her neck.

"She is still alive," the ranger said. Annice breathed a sigh of relief. Pierre scooped up the unconscious Mrs. Carrington in his arms.

"We need to get back to the camp," he said. "This woman needs medical attention."

The ranger turned away, followed closely by a teary-eyed Annice.

"Can we get to the camp in time?" Annice asked.

"We will get to the camp as fast as we can," Pierre said soothingly.

Kennedy gazed at Annice. She was keeping her hands on her mother's dangling arm and staring at her face, as though willing her to open her eyes.

"I hope her mom will be okay," Billy said.

"Me too," Kennedy said.

"I hope that we will all be okay so we can leave."

Kennedy and Billy looked up at Pastor Cameron. He had a solemn look in his eyes.

"What do you mean?" Kennedy asked.

"I was just talking to Moïse," Pastor Cameron said. "We think that we should forget the mission trip and evacuate from Goma."

Kennedy's stomach churned. She turned her gaze back to Annice. She knew that the pastors were right in their decision.

A sudden hissing noise made Kennedy stop in her tracks. She looked at Billy, then at Pastor Cameron. Annice looked over her shoulder. Then she screamed and pointed.

Kennedy whirled around. Her stomach dropped. Yellow gas was erupting from the ground!

"It is a fumarole!" Pierre exclaimed. "Back off, everyone!"

Kennedy covered her nose as she took several steps back. She glanced at the others. Much to her relief, nobody seemed to be having trouble breathing or staying conscious.

A low creaking noise. Kennedy looked over her shoulder. "What was that?" she asked.

"What was what?" Brody said.

Kennedy listened. The creaking became a loud rumbling. Kennedy then gasped; she thought she felt the ground beneath her shaking.

"Watch out!" Francis yelled.

Kennedy spun around. She saw one of the dead trees crash onto the ground, separating the group. She screamed.

"Another earthquake!" Pierre shouted. "Get down!"

"Wait!" Annice yelled. She tried to run to the fallen tree, but the shaking knocked her off her feet. But she didn't care that she fell flat on her knees in the mud. She crawled to the tree.

"My mother!"

"We've got her, Annice!" Francis said. "Just stay where you are!"

The quaking increased. Kennedy thought that this quake felt stronger than the previous one. She latched onto Billy and Marilyn. The three of them huddled together.

BOOM!

A loud rumbling that sounded almost like an explosion made Kennedy look up. What was going on?

"The volcano!" Wesley shouted. "Look!"

Kennedy looked in the direction that Wesley was pointing. Her stomach churned. Her racing heart was in her throat.

Mt. Nyiragongo was erupting.

"This is it!" Wesley moaned. "We're gonna be cooked! We're basically human hamburgers on a volcanic grill!"

Kennedy froze on the spot. She gazed as though entranced at the dark gray smoke rising from the top and the lava streams flowing down the mountain's slopes. Billy tugged at her arm.

"Come on!" he said. "We've got to move!"

Kennedy let Billy pull her to her feet and drag her to the fallen tree.

"This tree is huge!" Aaron said. "It'll take too long for us to climb over it!"

"There are more trails!" Pierre said. "You can follow them!"

Kennedy looked over the tree at Pastor Cameron, Francis, Brody, and Pierre. The ranger was still carrying Mrs. Carrington. Annice gazed tearfully at her mother.

"Take care of her," she sobbed.

"Don't worry," Brody said. "We will."

"We'll see you at the camp," Pastor Cameron said. "And we'll wait for you as long as we can. Just pray."

The four men turned and ran off with Annice's mother. Pastor Moïse gathered the kids.

"Come," he said, stealing a nervous glance at the volcano, "we must move."

Kennedy could barely keep her eyes off the volcano. The cloud of gray smoke was already increasing in size. The only relief she had was that the ground had stopped shaking.

"Pastor Moïse," Wesley said, "do you know how to get back to the camp?"

"I will do my best," the pastor said, his voice quivering.

The kids followed the pastor into the jungle. They avoided the area where the fumaroles had erupted. Pastor Moïse led the kids to a trail.

"Look out!" Billy shouted.

Kennedy spun around. Lava was snaking its way through the jungle. Even from a short distance, Kennedy felt the heat of the lava. Arizona would feel like a breeze compared to this!

"How is that lava so dang fast?" Wesley exclaimed.

"Mt. Nyiragongo is known for its speedy lava flows!" Billy said.

"This way!" Pastor Moïse called.

Everyone ran down the trail. The lava still chased after them. Terrified birds took off from the trees. Kennedy watched them, wishing she could just fly away herself. Pastor Moïse led the kids across a stream. But the lava still seemed to be pursuing them. The stream's once calm waters released hissing steam upon contact with the lava.

"Father!"

Kennedy stopped in her tracks at the familiar voice. She and Billy looked at one another. Pastor Moïse looked horrified. And for good reason. Chantal and Yannick were running toward the group.

"Chantal! Yannick!" Marilyn said. "Where did you come from?"

"The camp," Chantal said. "We saw the volcano erupting. We had to find you."

The two kids hugged Pastor Moïse. He patted their heads.

"You should not have come," he said. "It is too dangerous here."

"We were just worried about you," Yannick said.

Pastor Moïse sighed. "I would also be worried."

A cracking noise startled Kennedy. The lava had reached another dead tree. That tree was falling. Everyone screamed and ran from the tree. It crashed onto the ground. The lava lit its barren branches on fire.

"The lava's too fast for us!" Annice cried. "We'll never make it!"

"We will!" Pastor Moïse said. "God will protect us. Come!"

They continued running. Due to the lava flows, Pastor Moïse had to lead the kids away from the trail. They rushed through the thick jungle foliage. Kennedy hoped that none of the trees would catch fire.

"Hey!" Aaron shouted. "There's more lava coming down the hills!"

Kennedy whipped her head around. Her cousin was right. Streams of lava flowed down the hills.

"Hey, stop!" Pastor Moïse yelled.

Everyone came to a sudden halt. Kennedy nearly bumped into Marilyn. She ran to the front of the group to see what was wrong. Pastor Moïse had stopped right at the edge of a small ravine. But instead of a river or a stream, lava flowed at the bottom.

"We need to find a way around," the pastor said.

"How?" Wesley asked. "There's more lava coming after us!"

Kennedy looked around the area, hoping to see a clear trail, maybe a bridge. But there was nothing. Only a huge wenge tree.

An idea popped into Kennedy's head.

"Guys!" she said. "Think we can climb that tree to the other side?"

She pointed at the wenge tree. "The branches reach pretty far out. And there's another large tree on the other side."

"Climb a tree over a ravine filled with lava?" Wesley said. He shrugged. "Guess it's our best bet."

"But what if we fall?" Annice asked anxiously. "What if we get another earthquake that shakes the tree while we're still in it?"

"We have to try!" Rachel said.

"Very well," Pastor Moïse said.

The group ran to the tree. Pastor Moïse nodded at Annice, Chantal, and Yannick. "You kids will go first."

He and Kennedy helped Annice, Chantal, and Yannick up the tree. Kennedy, Marilyn, Aaron, Rachel, Billy, and Wesley followed them. Finally, Pastor Moïse climbed up.

"We made it just in time!" Wesley said. "Look!"

Kennedy didn't want to look. But she still saw the stream of lava surrounding the tree. She tried to wiggle the branch in her hand. But it wouldn't budge. Kennedy smiled; that meant the branch was strong enough to hold them.

"Hey, keep moving!" Aaron said from behind her.

"Just checking the branches, man," Kennedy said.

She crawled forward. Even up high in the tree, Kennedy felt the heat of the lava below. She willed herself not to look down at the steaming, orange river of molten rock. Would any gases from the lava suffocate them? She couldn't stand the thought of Aaron fainting from asphyxiation again.

"I am almost at the other tree!" Chantal called. Slowly and carefully, she stood up on the branch. Kennedy grimaced; she hoped that Chantal wouldn't lose her balance. Chantal made her way to the next branch over. She leaped and grasped the branch as though she were hanging onto dear life, but she was smiling.

"Keep moving!" she shouted.

But Annice hesitated. She could only stare at the branches before her. Her hands clung to her branch. Annice glanced down at the lava. She moaned and snapped her eyes shut.

"I can't do this!" she said. "What if I miss the branch?"

"You won't!" Chantal said. "God has you, Annice!"

Annice looked over at Chantal. She whimpered, but she lifted her hand. She grabbed the branch above her and made herself stand in a squatting position. Kennedy watched with bated breath as Annice made her way to Chantal's branch. Annice used the upper branch to guide her like it was a high railing. Kennedy heard her take a deep breath before she stepped onto Chantal's branch. Chantal grabbed her arms.

"I got you!" she said. "I got you, Annice! You made it!"

Kennedy let out a sigh of relief. She was certain that Annice was more relieved.

"Is it just me," Wesley said, "or is it getting hotter?"

Kennedy glanced down at the lava. Hopefully everyone else would have the same luck as Chantal and Annice.

A snap and a yelp from Yannick and startled screams from Chantal and Annice made Kennedy snap her head back up. She gasped loudly. Yannick was dangling from his branch!

"Yannick!" Pastor Moïse shouted.

"No!" Chantal yelled. She took a step forward, but Annice grabbed her elbow.

"No, stay where you are, girls!" Pastor Moïse said, holding out his palm.

Kennedy scooted herself across the branch so she could get closer to Yannick. "Don't panic!" she said. "I'm coming!"

"Hurry!" Yannick said.

Kennedy looked up at the branch. Her heart skipped several beats. There was no way that branch was going to hold. Even now, she heard the creaking of the breaking branch.

"Everyone, stay back!" Billy yelled. He made his way to Kennedy's side. "Hang in there, Yannick!"

"What else can I do?" Yannick said. Suddenly his branch creaked. He gasped and looked up. Kennedy yelped in alarm.

"Ken, can you reach him?" Billy asked.

"Maybe!" Kennedy said.

But just as she and Billy lifted their arms, the branch snapped. Yannick screamed. So did Kennedy, even as she and Billy grabbed Yannick's wrists. Kennedy watched the branch topple all over the tree and fall into the lava.

Yannick grinned up at Kennedy and Billy. Kennedy couldn't help but smile as relief flooded her stomach. She and Billy pulled Yannick up.

"Oh, thank goodness!" Pastor Moïse exclaimed.

"I know, right!" Rachel said. "Now come on, we gotta keep moving."

They made their way across the branches and to the other tree. Kennedy wanted to whoop with joy. They had made it to the other tree on the other side of the ravine.

"We did it!" Wesley cheered. "We're almost there!"

Kennedy kept wiggling the branches. But these ones were sturdy for sure. Even so, she winced whenever she felt the branch move. She was relieved to see Chantal, Yannick, and Annice finally jump down to the ground. Then Marilyn and Rachel, then Billy,

Aaron, and Wesley. Finally she slid off the branch and tumbled to the ground. Billy helped her stand up.

"Father!" Chantal called, looking up at the tree. "Come on! Hurry!"

Pastor Moïse waved at the kids. He reached his foot across the branch, ready to come down.

SNAP!

The branch broke. Pastor Moïse let out a startled yell. Kennedy screamed as she watched the pastor tumble from the tree and roll down the ravine!

"NO!" Chantal shrieked. "Father!"

Kennedy felt sick. She was right behind Chantal and Yannick as they dashed to the edge of the ravine. Kennedy was almost too afraid to peer down over the edge. What would she see?

"Father!" Chantal yelled.

Kennedy forced herself to look down. Much to her relief, Pastor Moïse was lying on a ledge, grasping his ankle. He looked up at the kids.

"My children!" he called. He coughed. "Go! Get away from here! I broke my ankle. I cannot get back up!"

"Then we will help you!" Yannick said.

"No, you must leave me!"

But Chantal and Yannick jumped down onto the ledge. Kennedy kept herself from screaming.

"What are you doing?" the pastor yelled.

"I've already lost my father to the volcano!" Yannick said. "I will not lose you."

Even from above, Kennedy saw the determined looks in Chantal and Yannick's eyes. It was like there was a fire that was even stronger and hotter than the lava. Kennedy felt that same fire erupting in her own stomach. She looked over her shoulder.

"Guys!" she screamed. "Come help! Marilyn, you, Annice, and Rachel find branches that we can use for a splint! Billy, Wesley, Aaron, you guys will have to help lift the pastor out of here!"

The kids set themselves to work. Billy, Wesley, and Aaron jumped down onto the ledge. Kennedy helped the other girls find sturdy branches. They threw the branches down to Chantal and the boys. Billy, Wesley, and Aaron took off their belts and used them to tie the branches around Pastor Moïse's injured leg. Then they helped the pastor stand up.

"So far, so good!" Wesley said.

Chantal and the boys guided Pastor Moïse onto a trail on the edge. Kennedy gasped when Chantal slipped, but thankfully she didn't fall. Nobody slipped again. As soon as he was close enough, Kennedy and Marilyn grabbed Pastor Moïse's hands and gently pulled him up. Chantal and the boys were right behind him. Then Chantal and Yannick hugged the pastor.

"Are you alright?" Annice asked.

"Yes," the pastor said, smiling, though Kennedy could still see the pain in his eyes. He lifted them up to the sky. *"Merci mingi! Glorifions le Seigneur!"*

Kennedy smiled; she didn't need a translator to tell her what the pastor had said.

"Listen!" Rachel said suddenly. "Do you guys hear that?"

Kennedy listened. It was faint, but it was there. The sound of an engine.

"A possible rescue?" Marilyn said hopefully.

Kennedy, Rachel, and Wesley ran forward, way ahead of the others. They came out of the trees to find a dirt road. And on that dirt road, a jeep was driving toward them.

Rachel whooped. "I see him!" she shouted. "I see Pierre!"

Kennedy narrowed her eyes. Rachel was right. Pierre was driving that jeep!

Pastor Moïse stumbled out of the trees. Chantal and Yannick kept him from falling over. Billy snatched up a long stick for the pastor to use as a cane.

Pierre honked and waved at them. Kennedy waved both her arms in the air, screaming with joy.

The ranger stopped right in front of them. His relieved grin seemed to cover his entire face.

"Oh, you are all okay!" he said. "Come, into the jeep!"

The kids helped Pastor Moïse get into the front seat. Pierre was surprised to see the pastor's splint, but he didn't say anything. He drove away as soon as everyone was sitting in the jeep. Kennedy looked back at Mt. Nyiragongo. It was still spewing out lava, but not as much as it had been before.

"What happened?" Pierre asked.

Rachel, Marilyn, Annice, and Wesley began talking all at once. They told Pierre everything. The ranger looked at the four of them in amazement.

"You kids really are something else," he said.

"Protected by God," Annice said. She gave Chantal a quick smile then turned back to Pierre. "How's my mom?"

"She's doing well," Pierre said. "We got her to the hospital tent at the camp. Evacuations are underway. We will meet everyone else there."

It didn't take long for the group to reach the tented camp. It was nearly empty. Several tents had been taken down. Rangers were helping people out of the other tents. Pierre drove the jeep next to a large white tent. The kids jumped out and ran inside just as Violette ran out to greet her husband, daughter, and son.

"Dad!"

Rachel ran up to Pastor Logan and embraced him. He wrapped his arms around her. Pastor Cameron, Brody, and Francis hugged the boys. Annice ran over to her mother, who was lying in a bed with an oxygen mask. But Kennedy saw that she was awake. Annice grasped her mother's hand.

"Annice," Mrs. Carrington said weakly, "are you alright?"

"Yes, Mom, now that I'm here with you," Annice said. "Oh, Mom, I'm so sorry for being such a teenage brat. I learned so much. Almost losing you was unbearable. I'd give anything to keep you by my side. I love you, Mom."

Mrs. Carrington chuckled. "I love you too, Annie," she whispered.

Kennedy's eyes stung with happy tears. She felt a hand upon her shoulder. She looked up at Pierre.

"We are all together again," he said. "There is a tourist van ready for your group."

Kennedy followed the pastors to the tourist van. Pierre and two other rangers reeled a bedridden Mrs. Carrington inside the van. Annice sat right next to her mother. Moïse and Violette sat with Chantal and Yannick.

"Where are we going?" Kennedy asked.

"To Rwanda," Brody said. He smiled. "Francis and I were just talking to Logan and Cameron. Other than praying hard for the rest of you, we did come across some interesting news. The refugee camp in Rwanda might need some assistance with all these evacuees. The lava flows only reached some outlying villages, but stopped right at the outskirts of Goma."

"Everyone ready?" Pierre called. He started the engine and drove away. Kennedy looked out the window at the volcano. It was still smoking, but it had fewer orange stripes on its slopes.

The drive out of the park was smooth. They didn't get too close to the city, but they did drive past a familiar sight.

"The chapel!" Pastor Moïse exclaimed. His eyes lit up and he smiled with joy. "It still stands!"

Kennedy looked out the window at the chapel. Indeed, the building stood. Kennedy never thought that she would imagine an old, ramshackle building with broken windows as a symbol of hope. Even the grass around the area appeared to be its usual bright green color and unburnt. No lava in sight.

Pastor Logan smiled. "Our mission trip is on pause for now," he said. "We might not have been able to help out much in Goma, but we might find some open doors in Rwanda."

Kennedy smiled. She looked back at the volcano. Like her anxious spirit, it appeared to be simmering down.

Thank you, Heavenly Father, she prayed silently, *for your protection and deliverance.*

Mystery on the Military Base

KENNEDY RYAN GAZED at the yellow house as her grandfather pulled the car into the driveway. As soon as Grandpa turned off the engine, Kennedy opened the door and stepped out. Even the pavement felt familiar. Conflicting memories—nostalgic joy and terrible grief—swarmed her mind.

"So, girls," Grandma said with a smile, "how does it feel to be back at your old house?"

Kennedy and her sisters, Victoria and Jessica, exchanged glances. "Well," Kennedy said, "it looks the same."

That was the best response she could come up with. She didn't know what to think or how to feel. She simultaneously loved and hated this house.

It was the house where she spent the first fifteen years of her life. The house where she shared birthday parties, Easter egg hunts, Thanksgiving dinners, and Christmas parties with her family and friends. The house where she and her sisters played together with their toys or played games like hide-and-seek.

It was the house associated with heartbreaking memories of the time Kennedy's father fell ill with meningitis. It was a battle that he had lost. Kennedy remembered how her mood was darker than the black dress she had worn at the funeral. And her mood remained dark for many months. As dark as death.

Kennedy glanced at Victoria and Jessica. The looks on their faces matched that of their older sister's. Only their stepsister, Marilyn Wilson, was smiling at the house.

"It's lovely, Grandma," Marilyn said. "I really like the pastel yellow color."

Of course Marilyn would be cheerful. Out of all four girls, she was probably the most excited about this visit.

"Man, I haven't been here in years."

Aaron Connolly, Kennedy's cousin, was smiling at the house, but his smile wasn't as broad as Marilyn's.

"Looks just as I remember it," Aaron said.

Kennedy held in a sigh. When she, her sisters, and their cousin had boarded the plane back in Phoenix, they were excited about visiting their grandparents for spring break. Now Kennedy was trying to push back all the bad memories.

A taxicab pulled into the driveway next to Grandpa's car. Kennedy smiled a little when she saw her friend, Susannah Anders, jump out of the passenger seat. Susannah's cousin Alec McFarlane and his girlfriend Nicole Hawkins got out of the backseat. Alec, Susannah, and Nicole had accompanied Kennedy, Victoria, Jessica, Marilyn, and Aaron on the plane from Phoenix.

"Hey, hey, the gang's back together again!" Alec said.

Susannah rushed over to Kennedy. "Hey, girl!" she said. She and Kennedy wrapped their arms around each other.

"Taxi was good?" Kennedy asked. "Grandma and Grandpa felt bad that they didn't have room in their car for you, Alec, and Nicole."

"No worries," Susannah said. "The taxi worked out great."

Her smile broadened. "So, Kennedy, how does it feel to be back here?"

Kennedy's smile faded a little. She looked back at the house. She thought about the day her mother announced that the bank was closing in on the house. For her, it had been a nightmare come true: her mother could not find a job that would be sufficient for paying the bills. Kennedy remembered being so grief-stricken at losing the house that she had grown up in. She remembered how relieved she was when she learned that her mother's parents had decided to buy the house, that the house would be owned by people within the family and not by total strangers. Now Kennedy was almost wishing that the house had been bought by total strangers. Then she wouldn't be here with her conflicting feelings.

"Weird, I guess," she said.

Susannah frowned. "We'll have fun," she said. "I'm sure."

"Of course," Kennedy said quickly.

She and Susannah followed everyone inside. Kennedy glazed over the living room. Other than a few decorations on the mantel over the fireplace and pictures on the wall that Kennedy didn't recognize, the living room seemed pretty much the same. She stared at the easy chair that her father used to sit in so often. It appeared untouched. Kennedy tried not to picture her father sitting in it, but ever since the day of his death, she couldn't look at that chair without seeing her father relaxing in it, reading a newspaper or a book on Christian apologetics. She remembered how, as a little girl, she would sit on her father's lap while he sat in that chair. He would read stories to her. He even let her take her first sip of coffee while she sat on his lap.

Kennedy's eyes wandered to the three steps that led from the living room and into the kitchen. Her father used to tease her mother about her cooking, only to enjoy the meal the moment he sat down at the table.

And of course, there was the balcony behind the sliding glass door. The balcony built by her father's own hands.

"Pizza will be here soon." Grandpa smiled meekly at Kennedy. "Welcome home, girls."

Kennedy forced herself to grin. "Nice to be back," she said. She truly wanted to mean it.

"Why don't you girls get settled in?" Grandma said. "I'll show you to your rooms."

Kennedy recognized her old bedroom the moment she stepped foot in it. It now had two twin beds instead of one. But one of those twin beds was the very bed that Kennedy used to sleep in every night. She put her suitcase on that one.

"This is nice," Marilyn said.

"Thanks." Kennedy hoped she sounded cheerful. "This was my room back in the day."

"Aw, how sweet! You get to stay in your old bedroom!"

"And so do Victoria and Jessica," Grandma said.

"But where will Aaron sleep?" Marilyn asked.

"We have an air mattress for him in the living room. He assured us that he didn't mind. Now, you girls get settled in."

Grandma, Victoria, and Jessica left. Marilyn opened her suitcase while Kennedy stared at her old bed. The bed in which she cried herself to sleep for who knows how many nights after her dad died. Kennedy quickly began unpacking; she wasn't going to make everyone go through the tedious work of switching rooms.

Kennedy peeked out the window. The backyard had more trees than she remembered. An apple tree hung over the vegetable garden that her mother used to tend to during the summer. Kennedy guessed that her grandmother was now tending to it. That was one trait that her mother picked up from her own mother: gardening. Kennedy remembered how her mom used to make her dad help her in the garden, even though her dad hated it. He always complied, though, mainly because her mom would reward him with a large coffee from his favorite café afterwards.

"Looking out at the old backyard?"

Kennedy looked back at her stepsister. "Yeah," she said. "Just reminiscing."

260

"How does it feel to be back here after so long?"

Kennedy hesitated. "Kind of conflicting, I guess," she said. "I mean, I don't mind the nostalgia, but . . . well . . ."

Marilyn's smile faded. She nodded with understanding. "You're thinking of your dad, aren't you?"

Kennedy turned away from the window. Marilyn went to the window and looked out. She was smiling, but Kennedy crossed her arms and stared at the wall.

"Never thought that coming home would be so joyful and dismal at the same time," she said.

Marilyn looked away from the window. "I hope you'll be okay here," she said.

Kennedy forced a smile. "I'll be fine. We're here to have a good time, Marilyn."

She went back to her bedside. She wasn't going to spoil this trip with bad memories. And there was no way she was going to hurt Marilyn's feelings. As soon as she and Marilyn unloaded their suitcases, the two girls went downstairs. Kennedy's gaze floated past the balcony as she went through the kitchen.

"When will the pizza get here?" Aaron asked. "I'm hungry!"

Grandpa laughed. "Food will be here soon."

Nicole plopped down on the couch. "This is a nice house," she said.

"Thank you," Grandma said. "I really like it. I'm so glad we bought it from our daughter when she moved."

Kennedy's stomach churned a little.

"What are we gonna do tomorrow?" Susannah asked.

"Well," Grandma said, "if it's okay with the other girls . . ."

She turned her gaze to Kennedy, Victoria, and Jessica.

". . . I thought we'd go to Dallas Delicacies."

Kennedy gaped at her grandmother. "That bakery closed," she said. "That's why Mom moved onto Uncle Oliver's ranch in the first place."

"The bakery reopened last month," Grandma said. "It was a successful grand reopening. And it's doing very well now."

Jessica smiled. "Oh, Grandma, I'd like to go. It'll be nice to see that bakery again."

"Ditto!" Victoria said. "We gotta make sure to take lots of pictures for Mom."

Kennedy grasped a strand of her curly hair. Now, after all these years, the bakery where her mother once worked as an assistant manager was in business again?

"I hope nobody minds," Nicole said, "but I was planning to visit an old friend of mine who's stationed at Fort Brazos."

"What?" Victoria said. "You don't mean that old historic army base?"

Nicole chortled. "Yes, I mean exactly that."

"Well," Grandpa said, his eyes twinkling, "visiting that military base would be fascinating. We'd love to go, Nicole. We can go right after we visit the bakery."

"Sounds good," Nicole said. "I'll call tomorrow morning and set up a tour for all of us."

"Excellent. I'm sure we'll all look forward to it."

The subject changed to Fort Brazos. Kennedy eyed the sliding door that led onto the balcony. She stood up and quietly made her way to it. She slipped out the door.

Kennedy laid her hands on the railing and gazed down at the yard below. She didn't think she would ever see this beautiful balcony again. It felt familiar to her fingertips. Kennedy sighed.

"You okay out here?"

Kennedy spun around. Susannah was coming out onto the balcony, a concerned look on her face.

Kennedy smiled. "Yeah, I'm great. Um, just enjoying this balcony again."

She patted the railing.

"Your dad built this, didn't he?" Susannah said.

Kennedy nodded. She looked back down at the yard. "My dad always loved his carpentry."

"I sure hope being here won't be too stressful for you."

"Oh, no!" Kennedy looked back at her friend. "Not at all."

But that was far from the truth. She blinked to hold the tears back; she didn't want to cry in front of Susannah. Or anyone, really.

Already I wish this vacation was over and I was back in Pine Lodge, she thought, *away from this miserable homesickness fueled by negative nostalgia.*

"Here we are!"

Grandpa held the door of the museum open. Kennedy took one last look at the dome protruding from the roof. This museum had to be one big, fancy building.

"I can't wait to explore this place!" Victoria said.

Kennedy glazed over the enormous model airplanes hanging from the ceiling. Her eyes rested upon a wastebasket next to a bench. She went over to the basket and threw her napkin in it. She did enjoy that sugar cookie. But its texture was different, and the frosting wasn't as sweet as Kennedy remembered. The pastries weren't the only change either; the bakery itself had been remodeled. It looked nothing like the bakery her mother used to work in.

"Nicole?" Alec said. "Is your friend here yet?"

"I don't see her," Nicole said. "She should be coming soon. She said she'd meet us here."

Kennedy wandered into the gift shop. A few shelves were filled with history books. Military history. A few books on general American history. History of Fort Brazos.

"Hey, here's my jackpot," Alec said. "I've always enjoyed studying military history."

Kennedy bit her lip. Her dad had also enjoyed military history. Any history, really.

She noticed a portrait of a soldier hanging on the wall in between two bookshelves. Kennedy recognized the soldier as General Courtney Hicks Hodges; she remembered learning about his service in the US Army during World War II when she was in middle school. She, Victoria, and Jessica had been homeschooled at the time. Her dad taught them most of their history lessons. How he would've loved to visit this historic military base!

A small bulge at the bottom right-hand corner of the portrait caught Kennedy's eye. She peered at it for a moment. Just as she turned around, she collided with someone.

"Oh, I'm so sorry!" she said as she steadied herself. She took a few steps back. She felt embarrassed when she saw that she had bumped into a young woman dressed in army attire.

"It's alright," the woman said. She bent over to pick up the book she had dropped. She flipped her light brown ponytail over her shoulder and smiled at Kennedy.

"There you are, Lara!"

Kennedy and the woman spun around. Nicole was walking toward them. Marilyn was right behind her. The woman grinned and hugged Nicole.

"Sorry I missed you, Nicole," the woman said. She held up her book. "I got distracted looking through all these history books. Were you waiting long?"

"No, we just arrived," Nicole said. She smiled at Kennedy. "I see you've already met Kennedy."

Kennedy smiled shyly. "Yeah," she said, "that's me."

She held out her hand. The woman shook it. "It's nice to meet you," she said. "I'm Lara Peterson. You must be Marilyn's stepsister."

Kennedy raised an eyebrow. Lara turned her smile to Marilyn. Marilyn grinned back.

"You've grown up so much, Marilyn," Lara said.

"Yeah, haven't seen you since I was like, what, twelve?" Marilyn said.

"You know each other?" Kennedy asked.

"We sure do," Marilyn said. "Lara's from Pine Lodge."

Kennedy widened her eyes, but only for a moment. She nodded slowly. "That one guy who's a ranger for the Yavapai Creek Wilderness," she said, "his name's Peterson, right?"

"That would be my father," Lara said. "How's he doing? And Mom?"

"Your parents are doing great," Nicole said. "Your dad and I don't work together as often as we'd like, though."

"What's that book you got there, Lara?" Marilyn asked, pointing to Lara's book.

Lara held the book close to her chest. "Just something on World War II history," she said. "So, um, how are things in Pine Lodge? How's Felicity?"

"She's great," Nicole said. "She married Jonathon a month ago."

"Oh, yes, I heard!" Lara said. "I wish I could've made it to her wedding. Oh, Nicole, I really miss Pine Lodge."

So do I, Kennedy thought.

"Where are your other friends?" Lara asked.

"Running around here somewhere," Nicole said. "Let's go find them."

"Sure," Lara said. "Just let me pay for this book first."

She went to the counter, but a tall man who was also dressed in army attire cut in front of her. He took off his cap to smooth out his spiky, dark brown hair. As he put his cap back on, he turned to Lara. He gave her a sneer.

"Back here, I see," he said. "Studying your family's shameful legacy again?"

"What I do in my spare time is my business, Emiliano," Lara said coldly. "Now if you'll excuse me. I have friends visiting."

She stepped in front of the man. He glared at her.

"Do your visitors know about your bad blood?" he asked.

Kennedy scowled at him. What was this guy's deal?

"Hey, leave her alone, Emiliano," a new voice snapped.

Kennedy turned around. Another soldier, a tall and lanky young man, was walking toward Lara and Emiliano. He and Emiliano glared at one another.

"What's the matter, Cox?" Emiliano said.

"I've had it with you bullying Lara, that's what's the matter," the second soldier said.

Kennedy looked from the two soldiers to Lara. She noticed that Lara had lowered her eyes and seemed more interested in bagging her new book.

Emiliano shrugged. "We both know who she's related to," he said.

"Her ancestry doesn't matter. You should know that. Don't make me report you to our commanding officer again."

With a scowl, Emiliano turned sharply on his heel and stomped away from the shop. Lara breathed a sigh of relief.

"Thanks, Percy," she said.

The soldier, Percy, smiled. "Don't mention it," he said. He looked over at Kennedy, Nicole, and Marilyn. "So, I heard you've got visitors?"

"Yes." Lara held out her hand toward Nicole. "These are some of my old friends from Pine Lodge, Nicole Hawkins and Marilyn Wilson. And I just met Marilyn's stepsister Kennedy."

Lara looked at Nicole and Kennedy. "This is Corporal Percy Cox."

Nicole and Percy shook hands. Kennedy wanted to ask Lara about Emiliano, but she hesitated. She didn't think such a question would be appropriate.

Kennedy followed everyone out of the gift shop. They found Kennedy's sisters and grandparents with Aaron and Alec. All of them were staring up at the model airplanes.

"Hey, everyone, I found her," Nicole said.

Alec grinned. "Great!" he said. "Sorry I wandered off."

Nicole chuckled. She introduced everyone to Lara and Percy.

"It's our pleasure to meet you, Lara," Grandma said, shaking Lara's hand. "How long have you been here at Fort Brazos?"

"A few years," Lara said. "The army base paid for my college tuition. I've been serving since I graduated. I'm stationed under my uncle."

"Hey, Lara," Victoria said, "can you and Percy give us a tour of the museum? I'll bet you know everything there is to know!"

"I'd be happy to show you around," Lara said.

She and Percy took the group to the next room over. The walls were covered with large, black-and-white pictures, most of which depicted an old, nineteenth-century army fort. One picture portrayed a river running through a plain in front of the fort.

"This room displays the history of Fort Brazos," Lara said. "The fort was founded shortly before the Texas Revolution. That's the Brazos River, after which the fort was named."

"I remember studying the Texas Revolution with Dad when I was thirteen," Kennedy said. "The river, uh, it's called the *Río de los Brazos de Dios*, right? Spanish for the 'river of the arms of God'?"

Lara smiled. "Correct," she said.

A young woman walked past Kennedy and Lara. Like Lara, she was dressed in army attire.

"Hi, Naomi," Lara said.

The woman glanced at Lara. She didn't say anything. She just went to the next room over. Lara sighed.

"What was that all about?" Kennedy asked.

"Nothing." Lara turned her attention to another picture. "So, this we have here is the first battle fought at Fort Brazos."

Lara droned on about the picture. Kennedy glanced around the area for that other woman, but she was nowhere in sight. In a few minutes, Lara ushered everyone into the next room. It was smaller and had fewer pictures and more items that looked like antique household decorations.

"These are things that belonged to soldiers and families of soldiers who have been stationed at Fort Brazos," Lara said. "Most of these items are donations from families."

Kennedy wandered over to a wooden table. A faded gold pocket watch, a dusty pistol, and a small music box sat on the table.

"Those things are really nice," Marilyn said.

"Yes, they are," Lara said. She cast a wistful look at the items. "These things belonged to a soldier named Pete Carter. He died in the Battle of Hürtgen Forest in 1944. These belongings of his were donated to this museum by his grandchildren."

Kennedy gazed at the music box. It was dusty and had a few chips in the corners, but it was a lovely antique music box.

"Mom would like that," Jessica said.

After twenty minutes of exploring the antiques room, Lara and Percy led everyone to a café. Kennedy, Susannah, Nicole, and

Lara sat at a table. Lara opened her book and flipped through the pages.

"Are you okay, Lara?" Nicole asked. "You're really quiet."

Lara forced a smile. "I'm fine. Just looking at my new book."

"What did you buy?" Kennedy asked.

Lara showed her the front cover of her book. The title read RUMORS OF SPIES DURING THE SECOND WORLD WAR.

"What would you like to drink, Lara?" Nicole asked. "Do you want any snacks?"

Lara shook her head. "I'm not hungry."

She looked up at Nicole. "I'm sorry if I seem aloof, Nicole. I am glad you're here. You know, I've been thinking about returning to Pine Lodge."

"Why?" Nicole said. "I thought you enjoyed being in the army with your uncle."

"It's your comrades, isn't it?" Kennedy said.

Lara stared at Kennedy with wide eyes. She nodded. "Yes," she said. "The thing is, Kennedy, my great-grandfather, Rhett, was a World War II soldier. He was stationed right here on this army base. But . . . well, he was rumored to have been a spy for the Nazis."

Lara dug her hands through her hair. "I was eleven when I first heard about Rhett. I was so ashamed."

She laid her open book on the table. "This is the most recent edition of this book. I was hoping Rhett would be excluded from it. But he's in there."

Kennedy pulled the book to herself. She flipped through some of the pages. She came across a black-and-white photograph of a slender German woman wearing a silky dress, a 1940s vintage hat, and a locket. Kennedy had to squint to see the locket's engraved initials *P* and *D*. The caption under the photograph read ERNESTINE KOCH. Kennedy turned a few more pages until she came to an entry entitled RHETT CARSON.

"Is this him?" she asked Lara.

Lara nodded. She sighed. "It's only a rumor that he was a spy," she said. "I have this old letter, kept by my mom, and her mom before her, from Rhett to his family."

"Do you have it?" Susannah asked.

"I do, actually," Lara said. "I keep it on me most of the time. Call me obsessed with finding proof of Rhett's innocence."

Lara pulled an envelope out of her pocket. She took out a wrinkled piece of off-white paper and handed it to Kennedy.

Kennedy took it, careful not to tear the crinkly old paper, and read it.

> *My dearest wife and children,*
>   *I'm sure you know the story by now, that I*
> *betrayed my home country to the Nazis. You*
> *know me, honey. I only hope that our children*
> *will not be too devastated. I suffer in vain. I*
> *hope to prove myself innocent. In case I don't*
> *come home, I want you and our children to*
> *know that I love you very much. And I want to*
> *reassure you that no matter what happens to*
> *me, no matter the circumstances, heaven, in*
> *the presence of Jesus Christ, is my real home.*
>   *All my love,*
>   *Rhett.*

Kennedy handed the letter back to Lara. "Doesn't sound like the words of a traitor to me," she said.

"That's what I thought when I first read it," Lara said. "The story goes that while he was stationed in Hürtgen Forest under Omar Bradley and Courtney Hodges, papers with coded messages to the Nazis were discovered in his bed. He was accused, but not convicted, of being a spy. Bradley and Hodges believed that he was innocent, but they had little backup. Then the Battle of Hürtgen Forest happened. Due to severe setbacks in the fighting, Bradley and Hodges let Rhett fight with them. Then, well, Rhett was rumored to have given up his life in battle for one of his injured comrades."

"Are you serious?" Kennedy's eyes widened.

"I am. Even I don't know how that happened. The man who had been injured was Pete Carter, the soldier whose belongings we looked at earlier. Pete was delirious from the massive blood loss and severe blow to his head. That's why nobody believed him when he said Rhett had saved him. He died from his wounds a few hours after the battle."

Lara sighed. "That's why I buy World War II history books. And checking out the library here. This museum is connected to the Fort Brazos Library. I'm always searching for anything that might help me learn more about Rhett."

Nicole patted Lara's shoulder. "You're a history major," she said. "I reckon you'll find something."

"I don't need to stay here anymore," Lara said. "I liked serving under my uncle, but all I've gotten from most of my comrades is ridicule for my family history."

"I know how it feels to be a bullied outcast," Kennedy said. "You should've seen me when my family first moved to Pine Lodge."

Lara smiled meekly, but not for long. All of a sudden she stood and held up her hand in a salute. Kennedy turned around in her chair. She saw a man who appeared to be in his fifties walking toward the table. On his shoulders, Kennedy saw three yellow chevrons above three inverted arcs; she guessed that he was a master sergeant.

"At ease, my favorite niece," he said.

Lara relaxed and smiled again. "Hello, Uncle Gabriel."

"Hello, Lara." The sergeant glanced at Kennedy. His smile grew. "These are your visitors, I'm assuming?"

"Yes," Lara said. She turned to Kennedy and Nicole. "This is my uncle, Master Sergeant Gabriel Peterson."

Everyone else gathered at the table. Lara introduced them to her uncle. Kennedy smiled when Sergeant Peterson shook her hand. She couldn't help but salute him.

The sergeant chuckled. "At ease, Miss Ryan," he said. "So Lara's friend Nicole likes to keep my niece updated on stories of Pine Lodge. I heard you're the town's unofficial amateur detective?"

Kennedy's cheeks burned. "It wasn't my choice of hobby, Sergeant."

The sergeant laughed. "I think you should join the army," he said. "Just based on what I heard, you'd make a fine soldier. In fact, did you know that your own name means 'helmet-headed'?"

"I think I did know that."

"I'll register!" Victoria said. "I'll join the army!"

"Oh, please, Sergeant," Grandpa said, "don't encourage her. Her mother would never forgive us."

The sergeant grinned. "That's too bad," he said. "I like this young lady's spirit."

His eyes wandered to the open book on the table. His smile faded. He gave Lara a sympathetic look but said nothing. He just smiled again and tipped his hat at Lara.

"I must be off," he said. "Got the usual stuff to do. Enjoy your day."

Lara saluted and sat back down.

"Lara," Kennedy said, "have you ever spoken to your uncle about your comrades' mistreatment of you?"

"Oh, he knows," Lara said. "He's taken disciplinary action against them before. But some are more stubborn than others."

"What about your great-grandfather? What does he think about him?"

"He supports me in my search for Rhett's innocence, but he doesn't say much about it. Sometimes I wonder if he thinks I'm too obsessed over it."

"Well, if your uncle is worried about that," Percy said, "I share those worries."

Lara shrugged. "Everyone done with their drinks?" she said. "We can look around some more."

"I'd like to look at the gift shop again," Kennedy said.

"Of course," Lara said. "Anyone else?"

"I'll go," Percy said.

"I'm not done with my coffee yet," Grandpa said. "The rest of us will meet you at the gift shop."

Kennedy, Susannah, Lara, Nicole, Percy, and Alec went to the gift shop. Kennedy saw Emiliano and Naomi looking at books on the first shelf. Emiliano scowled in Lara's direction, but averted his eyes when Percy scowled back at him.

"Sapper?"

Kennedy looked at Alec. He was staring at a red badge on Emiliano's left shoulder. Emiliano smiled proudly.

"Yes, sir," he said, "you're looking at a graduate of the Sapper Leader Course."

Emiliano carefully fingered his badge, which appeared to be slightly bent in one corner. "Needs to be sewn back on before it falls off completely."

Kennedy browsed the aisles, but out of the corner of her eye, she kept glancing at Lara. Percy stood behind Lara, looking over her shoulder. Lara shot him a side glare but said nothing.

"Hey," Susannah said, "nice portrait."

Kennedy turned around. Susannah, Alec, and Nicole were staring at the portrait of the World War II general.

"That's General Courtney Hicks Hodges," Lara said. She smiled at the portrait. "Rhett served under him. This portrait was a gift to the general. He had it with him during his time at the

Hürtgen Forest in 1944. Now it hangs on this wall as one of the museum's earliest donations."

"What's with that bulge?" Susannah asked, pointing to the bottom of the portrait.

"It's been there for ages," Lara said. "Bothers a few guests. I shouldn't be touching the picture, but I doubt anyone would mind if I just smooth it out."

Just as she pressed on the bulge, a tiny, crumpled piece of paper was pushed out from behind the portrait. It fell to the floor.

Lara raised an eyebrow. "Okay, I don't know where that came from."

"The portrait, duh," Alec said with a smirk.

Kennedy picked up the paper and looked at it. There were a few tears and smudges, but the handwriting was still legible.

"Looks like half of a letter," she said. "Um . . . 'Dear Mrs. Carson, I am using the last of my strength . . . to write to you . . . your husband saved my life . . .' and that's about all I can make out."

"Hold on!" Lara said. "Did you say Mrs. Carson?"

"Yeah, it is addressed to a Mrs. Carson . . . hang on . . ."

Kennedy looked at Lara with wide eyes. They turned their smiling faces to the portrait.

"Wasn't Carson the last name of Rhett?"

Lara gasped. "Can I see that?"

Kennedy handed her the paper. Lara grinned. "The name Rhett is in here!" she said. "And the letter is dated November 1944! Oh, could it be? That the rumor that my great-grandfather saved another comrade be true?"

"You mean Pete Carter?" Percy said. "But he died of his injuries just hours after the Battle of Hürtgen Forest. How could he have had the strength to write a letter?"

"If only we had the other half of this letter!" Kennedy said. She looked at the portrait. "Think it might be in there?"

Percy fingered through the corner of the portrait, but he found nothing.

"Hey, what's going on here?"

Kennedy spun around. Emiliano and Naomi were walking toward them.

"What are you doing, Corporal, messing around with that old picture?" Emiliano demanded. "I should report you."

Lara just grinned. "I might be closer to proving my great-grandfather's innocence!" she said.

Emiliano turned his astonished face to Lara. "You've got to be kidding. That's impossible!"

"Yes, Lara," Naomi said, "you ought to give up."

Lara glared at them. "Not with this new clue!" she said fiercely, waving the letter in front of their faces. "This is half of a letter, possibly from Pete Carter himself, talking about how his comrade saved his life! This could be what I've been looking for most of my life!"

"But finding the other half of that letter would be like finding a needle in a haystack," Percy said.

"He's right, you know," Naomi said.

"We'll do what we can," Kennedy said. "I'm backing Lara."

Emiliano's face fell. Naomi crossed her arms and rolled her eyes. She turned and left the gift shop. Emiliano stared after her. He gave Lara one last doubtful look, then he hurried away.

"Come on, guys," Kennedy said, "we should tell the others."

"Oh, we won't worry about it now," Lara said. She gingerly tucked the old letter in her pocket. "Kennedy, I appreciate what you said, but you're my guest. You're here to enjoy yourself. I'll just take this old letter to my barracks."

"I'll go with you," Nicole said. "Kennedy, can you gather the others? We'll meet somewhere else."

"How about the memorial gardens?" Lara said. "Percy can take you there."

"Certainly," Percy said. "We'll see you and Nicole there."

Kennedy, Susannah, Alec, and Percy returned to the café to gather everybody else.

"So, Percy," Alec whispered, "are you going to help Lara find the other half of that letter?"

Percy shrugged. "If she wants me to," he said. "But she's so obsessed with her family history. And there's a good chance that the other half of the letter doesn't even exist. What if she ends up disappointed?"

Kennedy looked down at her feet. She had to admit, Percy's concerns were valid.

"Kennedy," Grandma said, "there you are. Victoria was wondering when we're going to move on with the tour."

Kennedy smiled at her grandmother. "Actually, Percy's taking us to meet Lara and Nicole at the memorial gardens. We've got some exciting things to tell the rest of you."

"Exciting things?" Marilyn said. "Like what?"

"Let's go, and I'll tell you."

They left the museum. Percy led the group on the sidewalk through a hilly area with several evergreen trees. Kennedy told her family all about Lara's family history, her search for proof of her great-grandfather's innocence, and the part of the old letter they had found in the portrait.

"Whoa!" Aaron whistled. "That's crazy, girl. So now Lara wants to find the other half?"

"Does it even still exist?" Jessica asked.

"I'd be curious to know how one half of that letter got into that portrait in the first place," Marilyn said.

"We might never know," Kennedy said. "Lara's going to spend the rest of the day with us, but I wouldn't mind helping her."

"Of course you wouldn't," Victoria said with a grin. "Since when did you walk away from a good mystery?"

Kennedy smiled wryly.

"And get your mother all wound up?" Grandpa said. "No way."

A scream pierced the air. Everyone froze.

"What was that?" Marilyn asked.

"That sounded like Lara!" Percy said. He dashed ahead toward the trees. Alec ran after him. Kennedy tried to follow them, but her grandfather pulled her back.

"I think we are wound up now, Grandpa," Victoria said.

Kennedy felt her grandfather tighten his grip on her shoulders. She didn't blame him; she was tensing up herself.

"Here they come!" Susannah said, pointing.

Kennedy was relieved to see Percy, Alec, Lara, and Nicole trudging up the hill and toward them. Lara's depressed and anxious face didn't escape Kennedy's notice. She pulled away from her grandfather.

"What happened?" she asked.

"W-we were attacked by someone." Lara's voice quivered. "Some guy in all black. He came running after me. And I . . . I lost the letter."

"What?" Kennedy exclaimed.

"It's true," Nicole said. "Lara was showing me the letter when the man came after us. She was startled, and she dropped it. The man snatched it up and ran off just as Percy and Alec came running."

"Did you see where he went?" Kennedy asked Percy.

Percy shook his head. "He didn't even put up a fight," he said. "Just fled through the trees. I tried to run after him, but he just disappeared. Though, he did drop something. And no, it's not the letter."

He showed Kennedy a piece of paper. It definitely wasn't Lara's letter. It was too new and whole. Kennedy took the paper and read the message on it.

Keep your nose out of searching for the second half of that old letter, or you will regret it!

Kennedy drew in a sharp breath. She handed the note back to Percy. "Did you read it, Lara?"

Lara nodded grimly.

"What's wrong?" Grandpa asked. "What did the note say?"

Percy showed him the note. He gasped and showed it to his wife. Grandma's face went pale.

"Somebody doesn't want you to find the other half of that letter," she said.

"But who, and why?" Kennedy said.

"Before we try to answer those questions," Percy said, "we should report this to Lara's uncle."

Sergeant Peterson's frown increased the longer he stared at the note. The creases on his forehead made him look more like a stereotypical stern sergeant just about ready to lead his army into battle.

"This is serious," he said. "Typewritten, too. That will make it all the more difficult to figure out who wrote this."

He looked at Lara. "Why would someone attack you over part of a World War II letter?"

"That's what we'd like to know," Kennedy said. "This person doesn't want us searching for the other half of the letter. That tells me that the other half must be important. The attacker might be searching for it himself."

"So if we find the second half," Aaron said, "maybe we'll find out why Lara and Nicole were attacked?"

"But we don't know if the other half exists," Marilyn said.

"Then why attack Lara and Nicole?"

"We may not know the motive," the sergeant said, "but I do need to address the attack. I'm making a report and putting the base on lockdown. Corporal, you are to stay with my niece and her visitors at all times."

Percy saluted. "Yes, Sergeant."

"And please, Uncle," Lara said, "let me look for the second half of the letter. I know the warning note said not to. But that is why we must. I'm not afraid."

The sergeant hesitated. He crossed his arms.

"I agree with her, Sergeant," Kennedy said. "We will stay with Percy. Just let us search for a couple of hours or so."

The sergeant nodded. "Very well," he said. "If you think it's worth looking for, then I will permit it. But be very careful."

Lara grinned and hugged her uncle. "Oh, thank you!"

"Where should we start first?" Victoria asked.

"The museum," Kennedy said. "That's where we found the first part of the letter. We'll turn it over if we have to!"

She gave the sergeant a sheepish smile. "Of course, uh, we'll be careful."

The museum seemed emptier than it had been before. Just two men at the front desk and a few soldiers wandering the lobby. Good for searching for a decades-old letter in peace. Or a good opportunity for the enemy to strike again.

"Alrighty," Kennedy said, "I'd suggest that we split up, but Percy has his orders. So just search everywhere."

"I sure hope the staff doesn't mind us rummaging through these exhibitions," Percy said. "I'm still not entirely sure about this myself."

"Where should we look first?" Victoria asked.

"Anywhere," Lara said. "Just don't break anything."

Everyone began their search. Kennedy peeked into vases, opened a grandfather clock, and climbed into a tank with Percy.

"Is anybody finding anything?" Susannah asked.

"Not a clue," Alec said. "Percy and Lara just got permission from the front desk to look into a few of the pictures."

"Glad to hear that." Kennedy turned her attention to a painting of the Alamo. "Now we just need to decide which pictures are the likeliest hiding places for half of a 1944 letter."

"Are you actually searching for that letter?"

Kennedy looked away from the painting. Emiliano stood next to Alec, staring at Kennedy in disbelief.

"We sure are," Kennedy said.

"Mind helping me with this Alamo picture?" Alec said. "I'd like to look at the back."

Emiliano hesitated. "I'm just here to guard the museum," he said. "Sergeant's orders."

"This will only take a minute."

Emiliano and Alec carefully took the picture down. But the back of the frame showed nothing out of the ordinary. Kennedy brushed her fingers on the dusty canvas. Her eyes rested on a faded signature and the year.

"1835," she murmured. "We can put this one back. Doubt the letter's behind this old canvas."

Emiliano replaced the picture. "You guys know the odds are against you, right?" he said.

"We get that," Alec said.

Emiliano shrugged. "Enjoy wasting your time."

He went toward the gift shop. Kennedy wondered if she should think about scouring the gift shop when she spotted Naomi walking toward a hall. Naomi paused to take a quick look over her shoulder, then she disappeared down that hall.

"What is she doing?" Kennedy muttered.

"What was that?" Susannah asked.

"I just saw Naomi," Kennedy said, "another soldier, one of Lara's comrades, sneaking down that hall."

"Well," Alec said, "I know what you two girls are gonna do about that. Come on, I'll tail the suspicious soldier lady with you."

Kennedy, Susannah, and Alec walked toward the hall. Alec stopped to peek around the corner, then he nodded at the two girls. The threesome walked down the hall. Naomi turned into the room that had all the antique displays. She stepped behind a round table and pulled a small piece of paper out of her pocket.

Kennedy's heart skipped a beat. She and Susannah glanced at each other with wide eyes. Then Kennedy stepped forward.

"Excuse me, Private Naomi?"

Naomi gasped and spun around. She scowled at Kennedy. "Yes?" she said.

Kennedy gazed at Naomi's paper. She frowned; it was whole, and too white and too new.

"Sorry to bother you," Kennedy said. "I just, uh . . ."

Naomi glared past Kennedy. "What is going on here?"

Kennedy looked over her shoulder. Susannah and Alec were walking toward her. Alec gave Naomi a sheepish smile. Naomi glared at him.

"Oh," she said. "I see. Yes, well, this is not the mysterious second half of a letter of dubious existence."

"You know about that?" Susannah said.

"Of course I do," Naomi said. "I'm on guard duty, like the other soldiers."

"Then why were you sneaking in here?" Kennedy asked.

"I just wanted a minute to read this letter from my family in peace," Naomi said. "I got it in the mail today. Is that so bad?"

Naomi looked down at her letter, then looked back up at Kennedy. "What are you still doing here?"

"Oh, no reason," Alec said quickly. He grasped Kennedy's shoulder. "We're just leaving. Sorry to bug you."

Alec ushered Kennedy and Susannah out of the room. Kennedy stole a glance back at Naomi; she was reading her letter with that same scowl on her face.

Alec and the two girls went back to the lobby. Kennedy saw her grandparents and her sisters sitting at a table with Lara and Nicole in the coffee shop. The dejected look on Lara's face told Kennedy that she had found nothing.

"Taking a break?" Kennedy asked as she approached the table.

"Yes, honey." Grandma looked up at Kennedy. "I'm sorry to say this, but I don't think we'll find that letter. Even if we did have a chance, it's too dangerous."

"I understand," Kennedy said, "but—"

"Kennedy," Grandpa said, "your grandmother and I were talking with your sisters. We're thinking about leaving the base."

Kennedy gaped at her grandparents.

"The last thing your mother would want us to do is let you get involved in another mystery," Grandpa added.

"But don't you think simply leaving the base would be a bit of a challenge?" Kennedy said. "I mean, Nicole was also attacked, and the base is on lockdown . . ."

"We will talk to the sergeant about it. We just think that you and everyone else would be safer at home."

Kennedy crossed her arms. Home. This new mystery had kept her mind off that yellow house that she used to call home. Off the homesickness and her renewed longing for her father.

279

"Where were you guys?" Victoria asked.

Kennedy told everyone about the unpleasant encounter with Naomi.

"Naomi?" Lara said. "I've always guessed that she didn't like me, but—"

"What is Naomi's deal with you, Lara?" Kennedy asked.

Lara shrugged. "She thinks my uncle favors me. We're both under him."

"Maybe Naomi stole your letter because she doesn't want you to prove your great-grandfather's innocence? She's just that spiteful and jealous of you?"

"But it wasn't a woman who attacked us," Nicole said. "At least, we don't think so."

Kennedy raised her eyebrow. Before she could say anything else, Percy came over to the table.

"Lara," he said, "we've looked pretty much everywhere. The museum staff has asked that we stop. At least for now."

Lara sighed. "Very well."

"I'm sorry, Lara," Percy said. "But . . . look, I doubt that we'll find anything."

"Didn't I tell you that the odds were against you?"

Kennedy turned around. She frowned when she saw Emiliano approaching their table.

"Finally giving up?" he said. He gave Lara an icy smile. "You know you can't rewrite history just to suit your own personal desires, right?"

Lara's cheeks turned red.

"You have to face the facts, Peterson," Emiliano said, "your precious Rhett was a traitor. A sympathizer for the Nazis. You can't change the fact that your family's got bad blood."

Lara stood up and turned her back to the table. Kennedy scowled at Emiliano.

"I should think you'd be expected to show your comrade more respect, Private," Grandpa said firmly.

Emiliano glanced at him. "Advising her not to chase after fantasies is bad?"

He tipped his hat. "If none of you mind, I'm going back to my post."

Emiliano walked past Naomi as he left the coffee shop. Kennedy glared after him. Much to her surprise, so did Naomi.

"Hey, Lara," Victoria said, "any chance you can request for that guy to be transferred under some other commanding officer?"

Lara didn't reply. She kept her back to everyone else.

"Lara?" Nicole said softly.

With a sigh, Lara turned around. "Maybe he's right," she said. "We're never going to find the other half of that letter. It's slim to zero that it's still around. I can't get away from my family history."

She faced Nicole. "Maybe I'll go back to Pine Lodge."

Nicole stared at her friend in shock. "But you like it here," she said.

"I used to like it here." Lara turned her gaze to the window.

"So what do we do now?" Jessica asked.

"Mind if I answer that?"

Kennedy looked over her shoulder. She turned around and saluted as soon as she saw Sergeant Peterson approaching. So did everyone else.

The sergeant raised his hand. "At ease," he said. He nodded at Lara. "Have you found what you were looking for?"

Lara shook her head. The sergeant gave her a sympathetic look.

"I am sorry to hear that your search was futile," he said, "but I can't say I'm surprised. Anyway, we have more soldiers out looking for your attacker."

"Anything on him?" Grandpa asked.

"No, I'm afraid that my search has been futile as well. We have more soldiers coming over to watch the museum. Lara, I want you and Percy to accompany your guests to the library. I just sent Private Naomi ahead. She will be watching the library with you. I trust her to protect you."

Lara raised an eyebrow. Her only response was a reluctant salute.

The Fort Brazos Library reminded Kennedy of the library at Grand Canyon University. She tried not to think of her college; she didn't want her homesickness to take over. Her grandparents had spoken to Sergeant Peterson about leaving the base. He said that he would try to arrange something.

Kennedy sat down at a table with Marilyn and Susannah. She understood her grandparents' desire to leave the base. They would be safe, after all. But Kennedy didn't want to go back to her grandparents' house. She just wanted spring break to be over. Then she would be back at Grand Canyon University, away from that yellow house and its terrible memories.

"Hey, girls," Alec called, "don't disappear into the shelves. The corporal's got to keep an eye on all of us."

Kennedy looked over her shoulder. Victoria, Jessica, Marilyn, and Susannah were roaming the library, no doubt.

Her eyes rested on Lara, Percy, and Naomi. They were sitting at a booth in the corner. Although they sat across from each other, they didn't make eye contact. Kennedy stood up and walked over to their booth.

"Lara," she said, "you wouldn't mind too much if my family and friends left the base, would you?"

Lara gave Kennedy a small but encouraging smile. "Not at all," she said. "I am grateful for your help. But your safety matters more. I just wish I could go with you to Pine Lodge when you leave."

"I know, right?" Kennedy said. "I miss Pine Lodge. I don't mind visiting Grandma and Grandpa, but . . . well, their house used to belong to my family. Then my dad died. I was only fifteen. My grandparents bought the house when my family moved to my uncle's ranch in Arizona. Being back at my old house hasn't been the best experience for me. I didn't tell my stepsister. I don't want her to think that I'm pining after my lost father again and risk hurting her feelings."

Lara patted Kennedy's arm. "I understand, hon."

"But Lara," Percy said, "you're happy here in the army with your uncle. I know there are some issues, but you've always told me how much you love serving under your uncle. Besides, you have reason to believe Rhett was innocent. Remember his letter. The one you always keep on your person? When Rhett was talking about heaven being his real home?"

Kennedy gazed at Percy. The words "real home" released a few butterflies in her stomach. She smiled. Suddenly she didn't feel so homesick anymore.

Naomi sighed. "Corporal Cox has a point, Lara," she said. "You should like it here. Serving under your uncle. He favors you."

"No, he doesn't," Lara said. "He's proud of all his soldiers. I don't get special treatment just because I'm his niece."

Naomi raised an eyebrow. "I was so certain you did."

"Well, I don't. My uncle wanted you here with me because he believed you could help protect me."

Naomi gaped at Lara. "He said that?"

Lara nodded. She sighed. "He's good to all of us. I'll miss serving under him. I just can't take Emiliano's ridicule anymore."

"I understand," Naomi said. "I heard him earlier. I thought he was so rude. I am sorry you have to deal with that."

Lara stared at Naomi. "Really?"

"Of course. I know I've been cold too. And I'm sorry. It was never your ancestry, Lara. That doesn't define who you are. I guess I just wanted to earn my commanding officer's favor, and I felt I couldn't compete with his niece."

Naomi grasped Lara's hand. "All the same, it's too bad that you and your friends didn't find what you were looking for."

"It's fine," Lara said. "And you're right, Naomi. My family history doesn't define who I am."

"Well, there is one thing I thought I could show you," Naomi said. She stood up. "I know of this neat ancestry website. It's reliable and shares a lot of facts about people's lives. Maybe we can look at it? I know it may not provide very much useful information, but it might be worth a shot."

"We could try," Lara said.

Naomi led Kennedy, Lara, and Percy to a computer. She sat down and logged on.

"Alrighty," she said, "let's look you up, Lara."

She typed in Lara's full name. The site pulled up Lara's genealogy.

"That's my dad," Lara said, pointing at the screen. "And there's Uncle Gabriel. He's Dad's older brother. Rhett is on my mother's side of my family."

Naomi traced the family line back to Rhett. She found Rhett's bio. But it had no new information, only that he served in World War II and was possibly a traitor who spied for the Nazis.

"Nothing," Lara said.

"Wait, what's that?" Kennedy asked. She pointed at the bottom paragraph of Rhett's bio. "Something about a guy named Hector finding out about Rhett's supposed treachery?"

"That's probably Hector Blewett," Lara said. "He's the one who found the spy documents in Rhett's bed. He's also Emiliano's great-grandfather."

"Really?" Kennedy said.

"Yes. It's another reason why Emiliano is so antagonistic towards me."

"Let's look him up," Kennedy said.

Naomi typed in Emiliano's name and went to Hector Blewett's bio.

"Nothing much," Naomi said. "Says here that he was a bit of a ladies' man. Hey, he had a child with an army nurse named Phyllis Doyle. Yeah, look, Phyllis Doyle is in Emiliano's ancestry."

"But we're not finding out anything useful, are we?" Percy said. With a sigh, he placed his hand upon Lara's shoulder. "This is a long stretch, Lara. I keep telling you not to worry about your own ancestry. I mean, whether or not your great-grandfather . . . well, did spy for the Nazis . . . you shouldn't listen to Emiliano."

"I know that, Percy," Lara said, "but you know how important this is to me."

"And I worry it's becoming an obsession. But, well . . . I'm gonna check on the others."

Percy turned and disappeared behind a bookshelf.

"He seems really worried about you," Naomi said.

"He always worries about me," Lara said. "He thinks I'm too paranoid about my past. I mean, I guess he's got a point. You said the same thing, Naomi."

Naomi turned off the Internet. "Lara," she said, "I hope you don't mind me suggesting this . . . but what if Percy was the guy who took that letter?"

Lara gaped at Naomi. "He'd never!"

"But what if he feels you've been too obsessed with this matter for too long?"

"But he'd never steal anything, especially from me. Not even for a good cause."

"Besides," Kennedy added, "Percy was with me, my family, and my friends when Lara and Nicole were attacked. He went after Lara right after the attack."

"He was?" Naomi said. She smiled sheepishly at Lara. "I guess my theory was wrong. Sorry."

"It's alright," Lara said. "I'm not mad."

Naomi looked relieved.

A door slammed. Then Sergeant Peterson's urgent voice echoed throughout the library.

"Corporal!"

Percy, Lara, and Naomi ran to the front of the library and saluted before the sergeant. Kennedy's heart thumped just staring at him. The sergeant appeared out of breath.

285

"Corporal," he said, "the museum was robbed. The thief is still at large."

Kennedy exchanged wide-eyed glances with everyone else.

"What was stolen, Sergeant?" Percy asked.

"Something from the antiques room. The thief was seen entering the men's barracks. I need you to lead a search over there. I radioed Private Emiliano; he's on his way to help you."

Sergeant Peterson turned to Lara and Naomi. "I want the two of you to watch your guests," he said.

Lara and Naomi saluted. Kennedy watched Percy follow Sergeant Peterson out of the library. She glazed over the room. Her grandparents were seated at a table with her sisters and Marilyn. Alec, Naomi, and Nicole stood near a doorway.

Kennedy slowly made her way to another doorway.

"Where do you think you're going?"

Kennedy spun around. Aaron was leaning against a bookshelf, his arms crossed and a grin on his face. Susannah was standing behind him. She was also grinning.

Kennedy grinned back. "Just curious to see what was stolen," she said.

Aaron chuckled. "Wait for me."

"Uh, you all wait."

Lara appeared from behind a bookshelf. "I'm supposed to keep an eye on all of you."

"I understand," Kennedy said, "but don't you think it's strange that the museum was robbed on the same day that you and Nicole were attacked and that old letter was stolen from you?"

Lara made no reply. She just stared at Kennedy.

"Ah, come on," Aaron said, "we'll just run down and see what was nicked. I reckon your comrade knows what we're up to."

He pointed behind Lara. She turned around. Kennedy saw Naomi grinning at them and nodding.

Lara gave in. She led Kennedy, Aaron, and Susannah out of the library. They ran down the hallway that connected the library to the museum. But when they arrived at the antiques room, they found the entrance blocked off with yellow tape and guarded by a couple of soldiers.

"Shoot!" Kennedy said. "I should've thought of this!"

"Hey, I can check it out," Lara said. "You three stay here."

Lara walked over to one of the soldiers. The soldier let Lara go into the room.

"Guess there's nothing else for us to do but wait," Aaron said. He, Kennedy, and Susannah sat on a bench. Kennedy's eyes hardly wandered from the entrance of the antiques room. She couldn't stop picturing Lara coming out of that room.

Her eyes rested upon the soldiers standing straight and tall, like Buckingham Palace guards. She thought about Lara's comrades. How many others had histories of bullying her? Could any of those other comrades be the culprit? But would any of them have a motive of simple spite?

Static brought Kennedy back to the real world. She saw one of the soldiers pull out his MBITR radio.

"Peterson?"

Kennedy's heart leapt.

"Where are you?"

Kennedy heard a staticky, unintelligible female voice. Then Lara appeared. Kennedy stood up. Even from the bench, she could see fear in Lara's wide eyes. She whispered something to the soldiers. They nodded at her. One soldier entered the room while the other spoke on his radio. Lara rushed over to Kennedy, Aaron, and Susannah.

"What's wrong?" Kennedy asked. "Did you find out what had been stolen? What happened?"

"I have good news and bad news," Lara whispered. "The good news is that I did find out what was stolen. It was the music box that belonged to Pete Carter."

"Okay, that's one question answered. And the bad news?"

"I saw him again. The man who went after me and Nicole!"

Kennedy covered her mouth with her hand. She exchanged shocked looks with Aaron and Susannah.

"Well," Aaron said, "I'm here to protect you ladies."

"We need to warn the others," Susannah said.

The foursome ran off. The only sounds Kennedy heard were the echoes of their footsteps. At least, she hoped they were their footsteps and not the footsteps of whoever else might be sneaking around. The eerie emptiness gave her goosebumps.

Lara had everyone stop at the entrance to the history room. She peeked around the wall. She was just about to signal to everyone to continue when Aaron put up his hand.

"Do you hear that?" he said in a hushed voice.

Kennedy listened. Running footsteps. Lara quickly pulled herself back and leaned against the wall. She held her finger up to her lips. Kennedy took a deep and silent breath to calm her nerves. They finally did settle when the footsteps receded. Lara peeked around the corner again. She nodded at the others.

"We need to be careful," she said. "This room is connected to the antiques room."

The foursome tiptoed into the dark room. Kennedy kept her eyes on the floor. Even the pictures on the walls appeared menacing.

A tiny red object on the floor caught her eye.

"Hey, guys, hold it," she said. She walked over to the red object and picked it up. She rubbed her fingers on the velvety cloth.

"What's that?" Susannah asked.

"An army badge," Kennedy said. "Looks like it had been sewn on a uniform and fallen off."

She turned it around. The white letters read SAPPER.

She gave Lara a startled look. "We must find your uncle," she said.

"Why?" Lara asked.

"I'll explain when we get back to the library. Can you radio your uncle and ask him to meet us there?"

Lara pulled out her radio. But before she could even speak into it, more footsteps resonated down the hall.

"Who's that?" Susannah said nervously.

Lara stood in front of the three kids. "Stay behind me."

"Lara?"

Kennedy let out of a sigh of relief when Percy appeared. He grinned at Lara.

"Thought I heard your voice," he said. "I've been looking all over the place for you."

He frowned. "You won't believe what we found in the men's barracks!" he said. He handed Lara a dusty diary with a patched navy blue cover. "Looks like we aren't the only ones with World War II writings."

Kennedy, Susannah, and Aaron surrounded Lara as she opened the diary. Inside, she found handwritten entries with dates from the fall of 1944. And an old letter clipped in the middle!

"These belonged to Phyllis Doyle," Percy said darkly, "but I took a look at a few of the entries, and it doesn't seem like Miss Doyle was all that she seemed to be."

"What do you mean?" Lara asked.

"Corporal," Kennedy said abruptly, "you found these in the men's barracks?"

Percy nodded. "And they were in—"

"I think I know who may have had them."

Percy's eyes widened. Then he grinned. "You do, huh?"

"Look out!" Susannah shrieked.

Kennedy whirled around. She screamed. A man dressed in all black, including a black ski mask, was running toward them!

Percy jumped in front of the group. He whipped out his gun and pointed it at the man.

"Stop right where you are!" he shouted. "Unmask yourself!"

The man ignored Percy's warning. He fired his own gun. A glass window shattered.

"Take cover!" Percy said. "Lara, radio the sergeant!"

Lara hustled Kennedy, Aaron, and Susannah into a large storage closet, then she grabbed her radio and yelled into it.

"Sergeant! Uncle Gabriel! It's me, Lara! Museum, near the history room! We're under attack!"

Another gunshot. Then Percy barged into the room and shut the door behind him. He lowered his hands, signaling to everyone to get down. Kennedy and Aaron ducked behind a shelf. The door opened slowly. From the space between shelves, Kennedy saw the masked man. She didn't dare move a muscle.

"Lara!"

Kennedy froze at the sound of Naomi's voice. The man spun around and stared at the door. Then he ran out. A scream from Naomi immediately followed.

Kennedy and Aaron dashed out of the closet and ran after the man. They grabbed him, pulling him away from Naomi. The man focused his attack on Kennedy, grabbing her arms.

"Let go of my cousin!" Aaron shouted.

"Aaron, get away!" Kennedy said. She glared at the man.

More screams. Sergeant Peterson and Percy were running toward them, the sergeant yelling on his radio. Lara and Naomi stood to the side, horrified looks on their faces.

Kennedy kneed the man in the stomach. He stumbled back and fell to the floor. Aaron stood over him with raised fists.

"Kids!"

Kennedy looked around. Grandpa, followed by Grandma, Victoria, Jessica, Marilyn, Alec, and several more soldiers, were running toward them. Sergeant Peterson and Percy roughly pulled the masked man to his feet.

"Alright," Percy said, "let's see who you really are."

"I think I know," Kennedy said. She went over to the man and pulled off his mask.

She grinned at Emiliano's startled glare.

"Emiliano!" Naomi exclaimed. A flurry of gasps arose among the other soldiers. Emiliano turned his glare to Kennedy.

"How did you know it was me?" he demanded.

Kennedy pulled the red badge out of her pocket. "Is this yours?"

Emiliano's eyebrows shot up. He ripped off his black coat to reveal his left shoulder, which was missing its red badge.

"It fell off," he groaned.

"I found it back there," Kennedy said, pointing her thumb back to the history room. "Was it you who attacked Lara and Nicole and stole the half of the letter Lara had?"

Emiliano scowled. "Yes," he said. "It was me."

"But why?" Lara asked.

"Because I wanted to hide my . . ." Emiliano trailed off.

"Your family secret?" Kennedy said.

Emiliano looked back up at her. "What makes you think I have any family secrets?"

"Would it be this diary and this letter you had hidden in a box under your bed?" Percy asked in a hard voice. He nodded at Lara. She showed Emiliano the diary with its letter.

Emiliano stared at the diary in shock. "You found that?" he exclaimed. "You were sifting through my private belongings?"

"So you admit you had them," Percy said. "Because this diary belonged to Phyllis Doyle, an army nurse. Oh, no. She wasn't actually Phyllis Doyle, was she? She was Ernestine Koch, a spy for the Nazis."

Emiliano's only reply was a gulp.

"Under the guise of Phyllis Doyle, she fooled all the other soldiers," Percy said. "Except one. Your great-grandfather, Hector Blewett. But she charmed him into keeping her secret. Yes, he loved her too much. Willing to betray his own country for her. Talk about true love! But they had to keep all suspicion away from her, didn't they? So they planted false clues against a certain Rhett Carson."

He smiled at Lara. She stared at him in surprise.

"But he was never convicted," Percy added. "Much to Hector's dismay, the generals trusted Rhett. Enough to let him join a battle. A battle in which he saved another comrade at the cost of his own life. Pete Carter. But, being a nurse, Miss Doyle, or Miss Koch, made sure that Pete did not survive his injuries. She found Pete's letter to Rhett's family and tore it up. Her confessions are in

291

this diary. One half she hid in the portrait of Courtney Hicks Hodges. And the other half in a music box belonging to Pete's wife."

Emiliano remained silent for a few moments. Then he took a big breath.

"I knew the truth all along," he growled. "Yes, I am a direct descendant of Hector Blewett and Ernestine Koch. But she was always known as Phyllis Doyle. She was a clever spy who was never caught. Faked so many papers in her day, she did. Spent the rest of her life as Phyllis Doyle, an unknown American citizen. I grew up knowing the truth. My parents knew the truth, as did my grandparents. They were ashamed. I didn't care. At least, not that much. Until recently. Think I was going to ruin my family's name? No. I kept this diary and this letter, the only leftover letter, on my person to protect our family secret. When I first came to this base and learned that Lara Peterson was also stationed here, I was so shocked. I wanted to make sure she never found out the truth. But she was so determined. I constantly guarded the portrait in the gift shop and the music box. Every day."

"Then Lara and I found the first half of Pete's letter to Rhett's family," Kennedy said, "and you just knew that you had to take action yourself."

Emiliano scowled. "Wouldn't I?" he snapped. "I stole the letter from Lara and her friend. I stole the music box too."

"Well, Emiliano," Sergeant Peterson snapped, "you are discharged from the army and under arrest. But first, do you have the half of the letter you stole from my niece?"

Emiliano reluctantly reached into his pocket and pulled out a small piece of crinkled paper. Kennedy's heart leapt with recognition. The sergeant took the paper from Emiliano. Several soldiers marched Emiliano away.

Sergeant Peterson turned to Lara. "I believe this is yours," he said, smiling warmly.

Lara eagerly took the letter from her uncle. She grinned at Kennedy, then she turned to Percy.

"Did you find that music box?" she asked.

"Yes, we did," Percy said. "It should be back in its rightful spot now. But I think we have a good enough reason to look at it."

"I will escort you to the antiques room," the sergeant said. He faced the other soldiers and stood straight. The soldiers stood at attention.

"Dismissed!" the sergeant yelled.

The soldiers departed. Sergeant Peterson nodded at Lara. They led Kennedy, her family, Nicole, Alec, and Percy to the antiques room. Soon they arrived at the table with Pete Carter's items. Kennedy recognized the music box.

Lara picked up the box and looked it over. "Might be in a secret compartment?" she said. She poked at the box until she tapped a gold button on the bottom. Suddenly a drawer popped out from the side.

Inside that little drawer was a crumpled piece of paper.

Lara snatched it up. She put the two halves of the paper together. They were perfect halves, making a perfect whole.

"What does it say?" Victoria asked eagerly.

Lara breathed deeply. "'Dear Mrs. Carson, I am using the last of my strength to write to you that your husband saved my life in battle. The fighting around Hürtgen Forest has been difficult, and our leaders allowed Rhett to fight. Good for them. I cannot see Rhett as a spy for the enemy. And him giving up his own life for mine in battle only proves where his heart lies. I know that one day, you will be reunited with your husband in heaven.'"

Lara's eyes brimmed with tears. Percy patted her arm.

"You found the second half of that old letter after all," he said. "What are the odds? And with this letter and Emiliano's confession, the world can know the truth. And you can finally rest assured that your great-grandfather was a selfless hero."

"But even so," Kennedy said, "Lara, we should remember what Rhett said in his letter. Heaven is his real home. I mean, sure, we miss Pine Lodge."

She looked over at her grandparents. "And sometimes I still miss my old life before my dad died. But both Dallas and Pine Lodge can be my home. And Pine Lodge and Fort Brazos can be your two homes, Lara. But heaven is our real home."

"Well said, Miss Ryan." Sergeant Peterson patted Kennedy on the back. "But, if you ever decide that you need a third home, well, I could use a clever and strong fighter like you. Like I said, your name means 'helmet-headed'."

Kennedy laughed.

"Oh, no more danger for her, thank you," Grandpa said with a smile. He steered Kennedy away from the sergeant. "We'll take her back to our house."

Kennedy smiled. She was looking forward to returning to her old house. But this time, with memories of happy nostalgia.

Undertakings in the Ghost Town's Undertown

T HE HAZE HOVERED over the horizon like a swarm of golden ghosts haunting the sunset. Kennedy Ryan smiled; she figured that with her palomino mare, she could outride any ghost.

Kennedy goaded Sunshine into a faster trot. As the mare picked up her pace, Kennedy caught sight of a large log to the side. Kennedy steered Sunshine off the trail.

"Kennedy!" Nicole Hawkins shouted. "Be careful! Slow down!"

"And get back on the trail!" Marilyn Wilson added.

Kennedy paid no attention to her stepsister or Nicole. She grinned as her horse approached the log. It appeared bigger than it had just a moment ago.

"Come on, Sunshine," Kennedy said, "you can jump over that log! Alley-oop!"

She tightened her grip on the reins as Sunshine jumped over the thick log. Kennedy gasped when she felt herself slipping from the saddle. She wrapped her arms around her horse's neck, and she felt a jolting thud. She tore her cowgirl hat off her curly blonde hair and waved it around, laughing.

"You were awesome, Sunshine," she said, patting her mare's neck. "Shucks, we should've saved that leap for the rodeo!"

Kennedy steered Sunshine back onto the trail. She waved at her sisters, Victoria and Jessica, and her cousin, Aaron Connolly, and rode toward them.

"Girl!"

Kennedy's smile grew at the sound of Billy Weston's voice. She faced him and her other friends, Rachel Hamilton, Gunnar Smith, Wesley Rudolf, Susannah Anders, and Susannah's cousin Alec McFarlane.

Billy was grinning from ear to ear. "That was brilliant!" he said. Kennedy blushed.

"Bet that leap would've won you the rodeo!" Wesley added.

"You should do it again!" Rachel said.

"Whoa," Nicole said, holding up a hand, "nobody else here thinks it was a little reckless?"

Alec laughed. "Oh, honey," he said, "Kennedy's fine."

"I dunno," Marilyn said, "you were going very fast, Ken. You could've fallen out of your saddle. You don't want to hurt yourself right before the rodeo."

"But I didn't fall," Kennedy said.

"No, you didn't," Nicole said. "I'll give you that. Anyway, that should be enough riding for tonight. We should return to the campground."

Kennedy's smile faded a little. For July in the Sonoran Desert, it was a pleasant evening. She was too full of energy, and she wanted to use it to ride all over these hills. But she used that riding energy to follow everyone else down the trail.

Kennedy surveyed the scenery before her. The rocky hills reminded her of the bluffs near her hometown of Pine Lodge. The only major difference was that these bluffs had numerous saguaro cacti standing tall over the sandy orange ground. With their arms outstretched, the cacti seemed like they were waving at Kennedy as she rode past them. In the distance, the Silver Bell Mountains dominated the background.

"Hey, guys," Gunnar said, "I reckon we're approaching the infamous canyon."

"You mean the Canyon of the Ghosts?" Nicole said. "That's Starwood City's most famous legend."

Kennedy grinned. When she had heard that Starwood City, a tiny tourist town not far from Tucson, was holding a rodeo, she registered almost immediately. So did her sisters and many of their friends. And even though the rodeo was the main reason for this big vacation they were all taking together, Kennedy was eager to check out Starwood City's other tourist attractions.

The canyon came into view. For a canyon that wasn't very deep, it sure was wide. Kennedy gazed at it. What exactly was stopping her from riding down to that flat canyon floor right now?

Nicole pointed down at the canyon. "See that there?"

Kennedy looked to where Nicole was pointing. She saw what appeared to be a wide cave opening.

"That's the old Starwood Mine," Nicole said.

"It's abandoned now, right?" Aaron said. "Didn't it have a tunnel that led straight to Starwood City's undertown?"

"The undertown," Kennedy whispered. She had heard of Starwood City's undertown. It was supposed to be one of the tourist town's most popular attractions.

295

"Yes," Nicole said. "Needless to say, that tunnel's closed off. Has been for decades. Mine's not safe, you know."

"What exactly is the undertown?" Jessica asked. "And what is the legend of the ghosts?"

"Well," Nicole said, "Starwood City and our own town, Pine Lodge, were both founded by Michael Williamson. Well, Michael focused mainly on Pine Lodge. Whereas Pine Lodge was peaceful, Starwood City was every bit as lawless. The undertown was built during the 1860s to the late 70s, mainly because it provided the residents with shelter from the terrible crime going on in the town. Until criminals started using it for a hideout."

"But didn't Starwood City have a marshal?" Kennedy asked.

"Yes, Gideon Torres, the son of a Mexican rancher. He was a good friend of Mr. Williamson. But, for all Gideon's heroic efforts to bring law and order to Starwood City, he had a violent temper. Ruled the town with an iron fist. Then the notorious outlaw Barton Alvord, nicknamed 'Lightning Bart' because of his speedy getaways and his penchant for avoiding capture, came into town. He basically took over the undertown for a few months. The intense enmity between Lightning Bart and Marshal Gideon began when Bart shot Gideon's wife in the undertown. The marshal became obsessed with revenge. He neglected his other duties in his relentless hunt for Bart. Then, during a torrential rainstorm one night, Gideon confronted Bart right in this canyon. Gideon fired shots but kept missing his enemy. Neither of them knew about the flash flood until it came sloshing into the canyon, drowning them both. The flash flood also caused a terrible mine disaster. That's why it was closed for good."

With a grin, Wesley spoke in a mock dramatic whisper. "And the legend is that the ghosts of Gideon Torres and Lightning Bart are still chasing each other in this canyon. Hence why they call this place the Canyon of the Ghosts."

"Well, we've already met ghosts in Bannack," Jessica said. "I don't want to go through that again!"

"Oh, Jess," Kennedy said, "they weren't real ghosts. But no matter, I think it would be neat to see the marshal and the outlaw!"

"Totally!" Victoria said.

"Count me in!" Rachel added.

Kennedy laughed. She looked back at the canyon. If only those ghosts would come out and give her a show! She pictured herself riding down at the bottom of that canyon, aiding Marshal Gideon Torres in the capture of Lightning Bart.

A green item caught her eye. Kennedy narrowed her gaze; it didn't look like any of the numerous cactus plants surrounding the area. She slid off Sunshine to take a closer look. She grinned; it was none other than a five-dollar bill.

"Hey, guys!" she shouted. "I just found five bucks!"

"What?" Gunnar said. "Out here?"

"Lucky!" Wesley said. "Maybe there's more money lying around here!"

Kennedy picked up the bill. For a split second, she thought that Abraham Lincoln looked a little cross-eyed. She shrugged and pocketed the bill. Then she mounted Sunshine.

"Let's go, everyone," Alec said, "it'll be dark soon."

Kennedy didn't want to leave, but she steered Sunshine in Alec's direction. The group rode away from the bluffs and to the campgrounds. They rode under the huge wooden sign with big white letters reading STARWOOD CAMPGROUNDS. They arrived at a circle of three log cabins and horse stables with a corral. Everyone dismounted their horses and led them into the stables. Kennedy was glad that the campgrounds provided horse stables for campers. She looked up at the sky as soon as she left the stable. She smiled; several stars were already visible.

"What a nice evening," she said to Susannah.

"It sure is," Susannah said. "For the middle of July, it's quite pleasant."

"I can't wait to explore the undertown," Rachel said.

"Yeah, the undertown!" Kennedy said. "And all the other awesome attractions in Starwood City. Like the lower town, which is the actual ghost town."

"And then there's the Starwood Tourist Express," Susannah added. "Those train rides have the most scenic views of the desert and hills and all the areas surrounding Starwood City. They've got live music and saloon girls. And they put on a staged train robbery!"

"After everything I've been through, I never thought I'd look forward to getting robbed," Kennedy said with a laugh. "Come on, let's look at the stars for a bit."

Susannah hesitated. "Should we be wandering from the cabins at this time?"

"We won't go far. It'll only be for a few minutes."

"It better," Rachel said with a smirk, "otherwise Nicole will think you're going on nighttime expeditions in the desert and give you another lecture on safety. She's already fussing over your wild horse-riding antics."

Kennedy laughed. She led Rachel and Susannah across the dirt road to the playground. They walked past the wire fence that surrounded the swimming pool.

"Maybe we should go on a midnight swim," Rachel said.

"If they'd allow that," Susannah said wryly. "Maybe we can ask her."

Susannah pointed to the young woman leaving the main building. Kennedy guessed that she was leaving for the night.

"Luciana!"

Kennedy spun around. A young man with scruffy blonde hair was running toward the woman. She stared at him in surprise. So did Kennedy, Rachel, and Susannah.

"Gosh," Rachel said, "he seems wigged out."

The man grasped the woman's shoulders. "Oh, Lucy," he said breathlessly, "you won't believe what I saw!"

"What's wrong with you, Lincoln?" the woman asked.

The man, Lincoln, stuttered before he got his response out.

"I saw them, Lucy! In the canyon!"

"Who?" Luciana raised an eyebrow.

"The ghosts!" Lincoln said.

Kennedy, Susannah, and Rachel exchanged shocked looks. Kennedy glanced back at the couple. Luciana was staring at Lincoln in disbelief.

"Lincoln," she said, "we've been working here for two years and we've never seen any ghosts."

"I'm serious, Lucy!"

Kennedy heard Luciana sigh. "It's late," she said. "Both of us should head home before our parents start worrying. You shouldn't have been out in the bluffs at this time anyway."

Luciana gently pulled Lincoln away. As she walked past Kennedy, Rachel, and Susannah, she gave them an apologetic look. Kennedy stared after the two of them until they turned the corner of the building.

"Well," Rachel said, "that was weird."

"Weren't we just at that canyon?" Susannah said. "I mean, if he was referring to the famous marshal and outlaw duo, which I can only assume he was."

"And we didn't see any ghosts." Kennedy didn't know if she should feel excited or spooked. That guy couldn't have really seen anything strange in that canyon, could he?

"We should head back and get ready for bed," Rachel said.

The three girls went back to their cabin.

Starwood City looked like an old Wild Western town even more than Pine Lodge did. Most of the buildings were made of logs or wood. Almost everywhere Kennedy looked, she saw a saguaro cactus and ground covered in bright orange sand dotted with a few green spots of grass.

"There's the visitor center!" Nicole said. She pointed at a two-story log building.

"I can't wait to explore that undertown!" Victoria said.

Kennedy shared her sister's excitement. After spending the entire morning practicing for the rodeo, she was more than ready for a tour of the undertown.

Billy ran to the door and held it open for everyone. They entered a small foyer with a black rug. Billy opened the other door. The main lobby was bigger than Kennedy thought it would be. The slanted wooden ceiling had murals of Saguaro National Park and the Silver Bell Mountains. The front desk was just across the room from the wooden staircase, which led up to a gift shop. Black-and-white pictures of the early days of Starwood City and more recent, color pictures of the Sonoran Desert hung on the walls. Three vending machines lined up against the wall near the front door.

More guests entered the lobby. It wasn't long before the lobby was crowded.

"Man," Susannah said, "looks like the twelve of us aren't the only ones going on this undertown tour."

"It'll be a full house, that's for sure," Kennedy said.

Just then, a heavyset woman carrying a big bag with orange, brown, and blue Apache symbols walked past Kennedy to the front doors. The woman swung the door open just as a man wearing a red bandanna and tan cowboy hat entered the foyer. The woman rushed past him and went outside. The man nearly bumped into the door as it was closing. He scowled after the woman as he opened the door himself.

"Sheesh!" he muttered. He looked right at Kennedy. "Some people's manners! Just can't be bothered to hold the door open for someone else."

Kennedy smiled and shrugged. "She was probably just in a hurry."

"Reckon so." The man smiled back. "You here for the tour of the undertown?"

Kennedy nodded.

"So am I," the man said. "And I'm gonna be in the rodeo."

"Me too." Kennedy held out her hand. "I'm Kennedy."

The man shook her hand. "Roy Martinez. Veteran rodeo rider and winner. Hey, you'll have to excuse me, Miss Kennedy, I need to grab my ticket."

Roy went to the front desk.

"Hey look over there," Rachel whispered, "our two young ghost whisperers from last night are here."

Kennedy looked over at a bookshelf in the middle of the room. Sure enough, Lincoln and Luciana were stocking that shelf. The fear in Lincoln's eyes made Kennedy wonder if he was nervous about going on the tour. She was tempted to ask Lincoln about his sighting of the ghosts. But she didn't want to scare him or make him think she was a nosy visitor.

A bulky, middle-aged man went behind the front desk. He scowled. "Alright, where is everyone?" he asked.

Lincoln and Luciana ran over to the desk. "We're here, Ernesto," Lincoln said. "Lucy and I were finishing up with stocking new books."

"And nobody was watching the front desk?" Ernesto said icily. "Or preparing for our next tour?"

"We had the signs up," Luciana said.

"Yeah," Lincoln said, "the one that says, 'We stepped away for a moment, we will be back'?"

"I know what it says, Lincoln," Ernesto snapped. He sighed and turned to the computer. "Luciana, be ready. I'm going to take you on this tour."

Kennedy frowned. She didn't fancy the thought of going into the undertown with that grumpy guy as her tour guide.

Luciana pulled her hair into a ponytail. "Want me to round up the guests?" she asked.

"Sure, that'll be good," Ernesto said, not taking his eyes off the computer.

Luciana left the desk and clapped her hands. "Everyone here for the four o'clock undertown tour, please gather around!" she called.

Kennedy gathered with her group. Roy Martinez and a bunch of other guests made up the back of the crowd.

"Wow, we've got a good-sized tour today!" Luciana said with a smile. She held up her clipboard. "Yeah, thirty-five people on this tour. Max number, too."

Ernesto walked over to Luciana's side. "Howdy, folks," he said in a loud voice. "I'm Ernesto, your tour guide. Luciana here is my trainee and assistant. Now, permit me to ask you, do you all really want to go down into the undertown? After all, it is rumored to be haunted by the ghosts of Gideon Torres and Lightning Bart."

Wesley burst out laughing. "We're game!" he said. "This tour would so be worth double the amount I paid if we got a good glimpse of those ghosts down there! But aren't they supposed to be out in the hills near the canyon where they drowned?"

Ernesto gave Wesley a dark look. "You know there are many reported sightings of those ghosts?"

The only response Ernesto received was a flurry of smirks and excited whispers. Even Luciana was smiling. Kennedy glanced over her shoulder. She spotted Lincoln back by the bookshelf. He eyed the crowd warily.

"Very well, then." Ernesto held out his hand. "May I have your tickets, please?"

Guests handed Ernesto and Luciana their tickets. Ernesto counted the guests as he took the tickets. As soon as he was done, he and Luciana led the group outside.

"The entrance to the undertown is just around the corner of the visitor center," Ernesto said.

He and Luciana led the crowd to the back of the building. Ernesto unlocked a rusty door and revealed a dark stairwell leading down to a cement floor.

"Everyone follow Luciana down."

Ernesto counted the guests as they went down the stairs after Luciana. She held another door open at the bottom of the stairs. The group entered what appeared to be a one-room bar.

Kennedy's head was turning. The place looked like it could be a basement, just without windows. Gray cement and wood made up the walls. The wooden floorboards created a cacophony of creaks under the crowd. There was a long table, probably the bar itself, and five tables with chairs close to the center of the room. An ornate, knitted rug lay in front of the bar. An empty doorway led into a hall lit only by lamps on the wall. The smell was mustier than the barn on her uncle's ranch.

"Alright," Victoria said, "if we see those ghosts, get those cameras snapping!"

Ernesto came down. He pocketed his key and clapped his hands. All eyes turned to him.

"Welcome to Starwood City's undertown," he said in a loud voice. "First let's go over some rules. No touching things. I've dealt with visitors breaking our antiques before. Stay near the tour. I hate looking for wanderers, and I hate rescuing tourists who get locked down here after hours. Oh, and watch out for scorpions. They lurk down here sometimes."

"Oh, great!" Rachel muttered. She cast a nervous glance at the floor. Wesley and Aaron snickered.

"The scorpions usually hide from people," Luciana said. "I was down here earlier and I didn't see any."

Ernesto gave Luciana a cold stare, then he walked around the room with his arms extended. "This is one of the bars," he said. "Many of the townsfolk, including Marshal Gideon Torres and that infamous thief and murderer, Lightning Bart, used to hang out here all the time. There were a few shootings down here, but such reckless activity was normally saved for the saloon above."

Ernesto and Luciana walked toward the doorway. "If you will follow us," Ernesto said, "we'll show you the other parts of the undertown."

The hall led to another room. With its cracked red-and-white tile floor, a white counter, and a table with two chairs, the room looked like an old, underground bakery. Kennedy saw a shelf behind the counter. Leaning over the counter, she also saw a hole in the brick wall.

Jessica ran her hand over the counter. "I like this," she said. "Looks like white pearl granite."

"It is," Luciana said. "It's a much more recent addition. I think it dates from 1965."

She pointed behind the counter. "See that hole in the wall? That served as the oven for this bakery."

"Wow, talk about old-fashioned," Victoria said.

The tour moved to another room. It was larger than the bakery. With numerous beds, some of which were behind faded curtains, dressers, and coat racks, the room looked like a basement dormitory. A black woven rug with a few tears in its seams lay near one of the beds. Several old pistols, daggers, and bows and quivers of arrows hung on the walls.

"This is the main bedroom," Ernesto said. "It was added as a shelter when crime started taking over Starwood City. Widowed women and their children often lived down here. Hence why there are weapons on the walls."

"I read that as many as twenty-seven women lived down here at one time," Gunnar said. "And that it was in this room that Lightning Bart fatally shot Gideon's wife."

Ernesto scowled at Gunnar. "That's all true," he said. "Now, do you mind if the tour guide continues giving the lectures?"

An awkward silence fell, only broken when Luciana asked the tour to move on. They entered a room with dusty shelves filled with vials and various medical tools such as nineteenth-century doctor's masks, old stethoscopes, and medicine bags.

"This is the apothecary," Ernesto said. "This place made for a decent hospital when rampant crime took over the town and gunshot wounds and the like needed treatment."

Kennedy glazed over the vials. The tiny glass bottles were filled with dust instead of medicine. Well, except for a few bottles, which appeared newer, cleaner, and even filled with a clear liquid. She wanted to get a better look at those vials, but Ernesto and Luciana were ready to move on. They walked through a room with a black forge, suggesting that this room was once a blacksmith's workplace. Other rooms appeared to be little offices, complete with wooden desks and shelves filled with dusty old books that had torn seams, covers, and pages. Yet a few other rooms were tiny bedrooms. One room was a tiny, rectangular shape with only two bunks.

The tour entered a lounge. It looked so cozy, even if the sofa and the easy chair were dusty and tattered. A rug laid in front of an old-fashioned fireplace. To the right of the fireplace was a doorway leading into a pitch-black hall.

Two black-and-white pictures hung on the wall. Each picture portrayed one man. The man on the left was dressed like a lawman from the nineteenth century. The man on the right looked like a stereotypical Wild Western outlaw with his dusty cowboy hat and curly black mustache.

"Here we have one of the main lounges of the undertown," Luciana said. She pointed at the two pictures. "I'm sure some of you recognize these gentlemen."

"Yes!" Gunnar said eagerly. "Gideon Torres and his worst enemy, Barton Alvord, also known as Lightning Bart."

"And their ghosts might be down here with us!" Roy said with a laugh. Everyone else laughed too, except Ernesto.

Luciana turned her gaze to the hall. "Now, if we can get some light, we'll go down here. This hall leads to—"

"Luciana," Ernesto said abruptly, "we're not going down that hall."

Luciana stared at Ernesto with wide eyes. "But it's on the tour," she said.

"It's closed," Ernesto said. "I haven't taken tourists down there for nearly two weeks."

"It's infested with scorpions, isn't it?" Rachel said.

"No," Ernesto said through gritted teeth, "that's not why."

"Well, I led a tour through that hall just yesterday," Luciana said.

Ernesto gasped. "You what?" he exclaimed. "You shouldn't have done that!"

"I'm sorry, I didn't know it was closed."

Ernesto just glared at his young coworker.

"Excuse me, pardner."

Roy was walking up to Ernesto with his own glare.

"We paid to explore this undertown with you," Roy said, "so can you please show your trainee a little more respect and not ruin the tour for the rest of us? If we are to go down that hall, then it's your job to take us down there."

Ernesto scowled. "Mr. Martinez," he said, "just because you're a past winner of the Starwood rodeo doesn't mean you get to act like an entitled tourist who gets to go wherever. But hey, for the rest of the undertown that I will graciously show you, I will allow my guests five extra minutes in each area to look around and take pictures and do whatever you want. I'll even offer my apologies for the confusion regarding this closed-off area."

Roy nodded. "Sounds reasonable."

The people dispersed into smaller groups. Jessica held up her phone in front of a vase standing on a pedestal near the black hallway.

"That's really nice," she said.

"Don't touch that!" Ernesto snapped.

Jessica pulled her hands back. "I wasn't going to, sir," she said, her face turning pink. She backed away and went to Victoria's side.

Kennedy frowned at Ernesto. She was glad when he went into another room. She glazed over the other tourists. As soon as they were gone, she turned her attention to the black hall.

"Uh, Kenny?"

Kennedy turned around. She smiled sheepishly at Marilyn. Victoria, Jessica, Billy, and Rachel were standing behind her.

"What are you doing?" Marilyn asked.

"Just peeking down the forbidden hall," Kennedy said.

"I hope you're not going to sneak down there."

"Well, it's odd that it would be closed to visitors with no signs or caution tape or whatever indicating that it's closed, and only one employee knows that it's closed."

"Here we go again," Billy said, "looking for another mystery to solve. Ken, we'll tackle it later. The tour's just about finished. I reckon Mr. Grumpy Guide is eager to be done."

"And I reckon the tourists are eager to be done with him," Victoria added.

"Where is the rest of the tour?" Rachel asked.

"Not sure," Billy said. "Let's catch up."

The girls followed Billy into a hall. But they ended up in the apothecary.

"Huh," Billy said, "this isn't it. Uh, let's try another way."

Billy took the girls down another hall. Only to end up in an office.

"Are we making any headway?" Rachel asked.

"Hello!" Jessica called. "Nicole? Alec? Anyone?"

Silence. Except Jessica's echoes.

"Oh no," Kennedy said, "we've lost the tour. And it would be over by now!"

"Great!" Billy said. "We're lost in the undertown. We might even be locked down here. I'd better call Alec."

"Good idea," Marilyn said.

"Well, as long as we're locked down here," Victoria said with a grin, "we might as well explore some more!"

"No, we should find the entrance," Jessica said.

"And we'll explore while looking! Come on, let's sneak into the forbidden hall!"

"No, let's not. If we're going to explore by ourselves, let's see the places open to visitors. And let's stay together."

"Right." Billy crossed his fingers. "Here's to hoping we won't have to sleep in those old rickety beds tonight."

They left the office. Soon they found themselves back in the lounge. Kennedy looked at the pictures above the fireplace. Marshal Gideon Torres's eyes held a grave, cold stare, as though he was going to arrest the six kids for getting lost in the undertown.

Rachel screamed.

"What is it?" Jessica shouted. Then she screamed. Kennedy looked down at the floor and screamed herself. A bark scorpion, probably about eight inches long, was walking across the floor. Kennedy backed away. Rachel and Marilyn jumped onto the sofa.

Billy burst out laughing. "You girls," he said, "it's just a little scorpion."

"Little?" Victoria said. "Just look at it! You call that little?"

Billy shrugged. He kneeled and reached out his hand to the scorpion.

"Dude, don't touch it!" Jessica said. "It's a bark scorpion! It's the most poisonous scorpion in the country!"

Billy ignored her. He reached out his hand further, only to pull back when the scorpion raised its tail at him. Billy stood up and watched the scorpion disappear into a crack in the wall.

"You ladies can get down now," he said with a smirk.

Rachel and Marilyn kept their eyes on the crack as they got off the sofa.

"Now I know for sure that I'm definitely not spending the night down here!" Rachel said. "Come on, let's get out of here before more scorpions show up."

"Whole undertown might be infested with them," Billy said. Rachel cringed.

"Hush!" Marilyn said suddenly. "Do you hear that?"

They fell silent. Kennedy heard footsteps. She peered down the dark hall.

"It's coming from in there," she said.

"But that hall is closed," Jessica said.

"Only to visitors," Victoria added.

"So it might be an employee down here after hours!" Rachel said hopefully. "We can finally get out of here!"

She rushed toward the hall but bumped into the pedestal with the ornate vase. The pedestal tipped over.

"The vase!" Marilyn screamed.

Kennedy caught the vase before it could hit the floor. Much to her surprise, several dollar bills spilled out of it.

"Whoa!" Victoria said. "That old vase must be a tip jar."

"But this vase is an antique," Kennedy said. "And why have a tip jar right in this spot of all places?"

"Who cares?" Billy said. "Let's put it all away."

He scooped up a handful of the bills, only to hesitate and narrow his eyes as he gazed at one of the five-dollar bills.

"What's wrong?" Kennedy asked.

Billy looked up. "Girls," he said in a hushed voice, "I think these are counterfeit bills."

"Counterfeit?" Rachel said. "How do you know?"

"Because Abe Lincoln wasn't cross-eyed."

Kennedy snatched the bill from Billy. She stared at it. Sure enough, Abraham Lincoln's eyes didn't look right. Then she remembered the five-dollar bill she had found in the hills. She searched her pocket and found it. She compared the two bills.

"They look the same," she said.

"You mean the five-dollar bill you found in the bluffs isn't even real money?" Victoria said. "Guess you weren't so lucky after all."

"We may not be so lucky!" Billy said. "We just discovered a bunch of counterfeit money in Starwood City's undertown! What if the counterfeiters are down here?"

As if on cue, Kennedy heard rapidly receding footsteps echoing from the hall. She and the others exchanged horrified looks.

"Let's get out of here," Rachel said.

"*UUUGGHH!*"

Kennedy froze.

"What was that?" Marilyn whispered.

"Someone's moaning," Jessica said. "It's coming from the hall that's closed."

She pointed at the hall. Kennedy stared into the blackness. She took a step forward, only to immediately back away when she saw two silver figures loom out of the blackness.

Her heart nearly stopped. Floating in the air, right in front of her, were the ghostly apparitions of two cowboys, both of them holding guns. Kennedy gaped with horrified recognition.

Gideon Torres and Lightning Bart.

Kennedy felt like their ghostly glares penetrated the depths of her very soul. Her mind was racing faster than her heartbeat.

No, no, no, it . . . it can't be!

The marshal floated forward. Kennedy took another step back, nearly bumping into Billy. Then the marshal let out a yell.

"*I'll catch you someday, you filthy polecat!*"

Kennedy screamed. So did her sisters, Marilyn, and Rachel. Even Billy screamed. Then, still screaming, the six kids turned and raced out of the room. They ran through the halls, not stopping until they found the large bedroom. Kennedy wanted to hide behind one of the curtains, but she just collapsed onto the floor along with everyone else.

"I can't believe it!" Victoria said after a few deep breaths. "We actually met the ghosts of Starwood City's most famous marshal and outlaw!"

"Did anybody recognize what the marshal said to us?" Billy asked. "That was the last thing he was reported to have been heard saying. He yelled it at Lightning Bart just as he chased him out of Starwood City. Their bodies were found the next morning in that canyon that had the flash flood."

"So, hopefully the marshal ghost is after the outlaw ghost and not us?" Victoria said.

Kennedy sat up on her knees. "They can't be real ghosts," she said. "You girls remember when we were in Virginia City with Marilyn's cousin Darcy? The ghosts we saw there were just images from a projector."

"Then maybe these ones are too," Rachel said.

"Yeah," Kennedy said darkly, "and those counterfeiters are playing with it."

She stood up. "We need to report all this."

"Sure," Billy said. "But we have to get out of here first. If only we—"

"Hush!" Marilyn said suddenly.

Kennedy listened. She stifled a quiet gasp when she heard footsteps. The six kids huddled together.

"Hello?"

Kennedy smiled with recognition and relief.

"Alec!" Rachel called. "Is that you?"

As if in direct answer to her question, Alec came into the bedroom, followed closely by Lincoln and Luciana. Relief covered Alec's face.

"Oh, thank goodness!" he said. "I just knew we lost a few of our party members! How Nicole and I managed to lose six of you is beyond me."

He gave Kennedy a mischievous smile. "I can't really say that I'm surprised you're one of the six."

Kennedy rolled her eyes.

"We're so sorry about that," Rachel said.

"Don't worry, we had a big tour today," Luciana said. She smiled. "It's fine. This isn't the first time tourists have gotten lost and locked down here, and it won't be the last."

"We've got more pressing issues," Kennedy said. "Luciana, Lincoln, we need to talk to the head ranger."

"My dad?" Luciana said. "Why?"

"I'll explain on the way. Come on, guys!"

Kennedy gazed at the drawings of the undertown that hung on the walls. She tried not to picture those ghosts in those drawings.

She heard the front door open and turned around. A slender man with neat, dark brown hair had just entered the ranger station. He certainly looked like he belonged in a Wild Western law enforcement office. He wore dusty cowboy boots over a pair of blue jeans and a brown vest over a white shirt. His cowboy hat matched his vest. His gold name tag read ETHAN OLSON, CHIEF RANGER.

Ranger Olson tipped his hat at Lincoln and Luciana. "I'm here," he said. "Hope you and your friends weren't waiting long?"

"No, Dad," Luciana said. "We got here a few minutes ago. Thanks for coming."

"Of course, honey." The head ranger took his seat behind the desk. Luciana introduced him to everyone.

"My pleasure to meet everyone," Ranger Olson said. "Now down to business. Tell me what's the problem."

Kennedy sat down. She told the head ranger everything, how she, her sisters, Marilyn, Rachel, and Billy found themselves locked in the undertown, how they discovered the counterfeit money in the vase, and how they encountered the ghosts.

Ranger Olson frowned. "This is serious," he said. "Must be a really good coverup too. I've heard plenty of ghost stories from tourists in the undertown and the bluffs, but never stories about a counterfeiting ring. Do you kids have anything you can show me?"

"Yeah." Billy pulled out a five from his pocket. "I saved this for evidence."

"And I found a five in the bluffs last night," Kennedy said. She handed her own five to Ranger Olson. He studied the two bills.

"They're counterfeit, alright," he said. "It's difficult to tell at first."

He put the fives in a drawer. "Seems that we have a counterfeiting job happening right here in this little ghost town," he said. "And I fear that you kids may be key witnesses."

Kennedy felt a few butterflies in her stomach, but she still smiled.

"Great," Marilyn said. "Kennedy Ryan just got caught up in another mystery."

"I may have a potential suspect," Kennedy said. "Ranger Olson, one of our tour guides, Ernesto, seemed to have been the only employee to know about that one hallway being closed."

"Yeah, and he wasn't happy when I said that I led a tour in that hall," Luciana added.

"That is weird," Ranger Olson said. "I thought more people knew about that hall. Including you, Lucy. I myself heard from a few rangers that it was closed. I'll question Ernesto. And I will conduct a search of the undertown. In the meantime, I suggest that you kids watch yourselves. I'll make sure I have rangers keeping a close eye on all activities in town. Good night and stay safe."

"Thank you, sir," Alec said. "Come on, you young rascals, I'm taking y'all back to our cabins."

Kennedy followed her party out to Alec's car. She made a mental note to keep an eye on all activities herself.

Kennedy clicked her tongue. Sunshine quickened her pace. Kennedy waved the lasso above her head. She swung the noose in the air a few times, then threw it at the tall saguaro cactus just as she rode past it. The noose caught the arm of the cactus and tightened itself around it.

"Nice one!" Billy said. "You're gonna rock this rodeo, Ken!"

Kennedy smiled. She remembered the first time she had moved to her uncle's ranch near Pine Lodge. At the time, she was a teenage city girl new to a life of ranching and country-living. It took her a long time to adjust. She remembered how terrible she had been at roping. She remembered how much she wanted to give up. But after a few years of practice, she was a natural.

"You should try out your archery skills," Billy said. "The judges are gonna love that!"

"Okay!" Kennedy said. She reached over her shoulder for her bow, then she pulled out an arrow from the quiver attached to the saddle. She goaded Sunshine into a slow trot. While the horse was moving, Kennedy nocked an arrow to her bow and aimed it at a cactus. Taking a breath, she released the arrow. It flew across the air and hit the cactus. Both arrow and cactus shook.

Billy rode over next to Kennedy. "That was neat!" he said. "It's great that we're still doing well with rodeo practice after what happened last night."

"Yeah," Kennedy said.

Billy's grin broadened. "I hope you're not gonna try to solve this mystery without me."

"Wouldn't dream of it." Kennedy smiled at Billy. "We know that Ernesto's our main suspect. He's got access to the undertown and his behavior was strange."

"Plus he shouldn't have been the only employee to know if a certain area is closed to visitors," Billy said. "And that hall didn't have any indication that it was closed. If only we could keep an eye on him."

"Billy! Kennedy!" Nicole called. "Come on, it's getting dark, and we still have a few more things to work on!"

Kennedy and Billy rode toward the rest of their group. Rachel was steering her horse in circles. Aaron and Wesley were swinging lassoes over their heads.

Marilyn rode her horse over to Kennedy and Billy. "I couldn't help but overhear," she said in a low voice, "you are talking about Ernesto being the prime suspect?"

She frowned. "Please be careful, Kennedy. You used to be wary about getting involved in dangerous situations. Now you always seem ready to run right into them."

"I'll be careful," Kennedy said. "We always get out of it. Even when we were hostages in Italy, we got out of that."

"I just worry something worse might happen to you."

"I'm just voicing my thoughts out loud," Kennedy said. "And since we're key witnesses to a possible counterfeiting ring, I wouldn't mind knowing who to watch out for."

"But what if you get hurt?" Marilyn said. "Or kidnapped?"

Kennedy frowned. "You know I've never been kidnapped," she said. "I'm usually the rescuer. But I get your concern . . ."

She turned her gaze to Aaron and Wesley. "Come on, let's practice some more before it's time to leave."

The threesome rode over to the other boys. Kennedy held in a sigh. She didn't want anyone else to notice her irritation. She knew that her friends and family cared for her. But she wished they wouldn't nag her so much. She was capable of taking care of herself while solving cases.

After twenty minutes of practicing rodeo skills, everyone agreed to ride back to the campground.

"Can we ride by the Canyon of the Ghosts on our way back?" Wesley asked eagerly.

"I don't think we should," Marilyn said.

"Aw, come on, Mary! I wanna see those ghosts too!"

"It is a quicker route," Nicole said, "but please, let's try not to wander off in search of ghosts."

She eyed Kennedy. "Or clues."

Kennedy suppressed a smile. She shared Wesley's view. And she figured everyone else must've been thinking similar thoughts; all faces turned toward the Canyon of the Ghosts as the group rode past.

"See any ghosts yet?" Wesley called.

"Nope!" Victoria said. "I'd recognize them for sure!"

Kennedy kept her eyes on the canyon floor.

"You're not gonna ride down there, are you?"

Kennedy gave Gunnar a playful smile. "Course not," she said. "At least, not if I don't see anything suspicious."

She looked back at the canyon. Just in time to see what appeared to be a silver flash fly across the sandy ground. She gasped and looked back at Gunnar. Judging by his wide eyes, he had seen the flash too.

"Did anybody else see that?" Rachel exclaimed.

All eyes, wide and fearful, turned to the canyon.

"There's only one way to find out what that was!" Kennedy said. She turned Sunshine around and rode off. Aaron and Gunnar were right behind her.

"You guys, wait!" Nicole shouted.

Kennedy tugged her reins to slow her mare down. Gunnar and Aaron rode close to her. Kennedy's eyes glazed over the bottom of the canyon. She saw the familiar sight of the old mine entrance. She half-expected to see ghosts floating out of that hole in the ground. Kennedy glanced over her shoulder at the others. They were still fairly far behind.

"What are we looking for?" Aaron asked. "It's getting dark, too. Reckon we'll even see anything?"

"Well, I see two somethings down there!" Gunnar shouted, his voice quivering.

He pointed a shaky finger down at the canyon. Kennedy looked and gasped.

Running at the bottom of the canyon were the two ghosts that she had seen in the undertown!

"It's them, it's them!" Aaron exclaimed. "Marshal Torres and Lightning Bart!"

The ghosts didn't seem to notice their audience from above the canyon. The marshal drew a pistol. Kennedy gasped when she heard a gunshot. Lightning Bart, not ceasing his running or even slowing his pace, returned fire.

"*I'll catch you someday, you filthy polecat!*" the marshal yelled.

Kennedy and the boys exchanged terrified looks.

"They'd better not be coming up here," Aaron said.

"Let's get out of here before they do!" Gunnar said.

The threesome steered their horses away from the area and back to the rest of their friends, who had nearly caught up with them.

"We heard gunshots!" Susannah said.

"Ghost gunshots," Gunnar said.

"Ghost gunshots?" Victoria asked. "Did you guys see those ghosts?"

"Down in the canyon where they drowned!"

Victoria grinned. "Are they still there?"

"Let's find out!" Wesley said. He steered his horse down a trail. Kennedy, Victoria, Billy, Aaron, and Gunnar followed him.

"Not again!" Nicole yelled. "Get back here!"

The six kids kept riding down the trail. But when they got to the canyon floor, all was still and silent. The kids dismounted from their horses. Kennedy saw the old mine entrance in the distance. The temptation to walk over to that hole rose within her.

"Where are they?" Wesley said. "I wanna see those ghosts!"

A light breeze made Kennedy's curls flicker. She gasped and spun around, a shiver running up her spine. But there was nothing there.

Okay, Kenny, she thought, *those ghosts aren't behind you.*

"Don't worry, girl," Gunnar whispered to Victoria, "it's just a little wind."

"It's still enough to make my heart flutter faster than a butterfly," Victoria said.

"Well, I don't see anything unusual down here," Billy said.

"I found something unusual!" Rachel called.

Kennedy, Victoria, Billy, Gunnar, and Wesley ran over to Rachel. She pointed at the ground. Kennedy stared in amazement at a line of boot prints.

"Where do they lead?" Billy asked.

Kennedy's gaze followed the line. She took a few steps forward. Her eyes rested upon the mine entrance.

"The footprints lead to the mine," she said.

"But it's been closed for ages!" Victoria said. "Hasn't it?"

Kennedy whipped out her phone and snapped a few pictures of the footprints. She followed the line and took pictures of the mine.

"Don't go in there, Ken!" Billy called.

"I'm not!" Kennedy said. She still cast a longing gaze at the mine before returning to the others.

"So," Wesley said, "what do footprints have to do with a couple of ghosts?"

Kennedy grinned. "Wesley," she said, "I reckon you hit on something."

"I did?"

"Yep." Kennedy looked through her pictures. "I'm gonna send these to Luciana. She can show them to her dad. I'll bet that we stumbled on a good clue!"

Kennedy gazed at the Prickly Cactus Café. With its octangular shape, deck, and small balcony above the front doors, the place looked like a miniature version of a vintage, Wild Western saloon.

Marilyn opened the door. "Hey," she said with a smile, "this place kind of reminds me of Dad's restaurant back home."

Kennedy smiled. "Yeah, it does."

The two girls went to the counter. The glass display showed off many pastries such as pieces of coconut cream pie, cupcakes with chocolate and vanilla frosting, slices of lemon and poppyseed bread, and bagels.

"Hey there."

Kennedy turned around. She grinned at Luciana.

"Hi," Marilyn said. "How are you?"

"Good," Luciana said. "Just grabbing a drink before work."

"Hey, Luciana," Kennedy said, "did you get my texts last night?"

"I did," Luciana said. "I showed them to Dad. But he says there's no way of knowing whether or not the boot prints in your pictures belong to any of the counterfeiters. Almost everyone in Starwood City wears boots, and we deal with tourists trying to sneak into that mine a lot. Dad also mentioned that he spoke to Ernesto yesterday. Ernesto cooperated. Answered all of Dad's questions. Dad even searched the undertown, including the closed area. He found nothing suspicious."

Kennedy frowned. "But we saw that vase filled with the counterfeit money," she said.

"I know. Dad's been wondering if the counterfeiters fled the undertown."

"I'd certainly hope so," Marilyn said.

Kennedy nodded slowly. Could the counterfeiters have left the undertown already? But she and her friends had still seen the ghosts in the canyon the previous evening.

Her thoughts were interrupted by a waiter at the counter asking the three girls if he could serve them. As soon as the girls paid for their beverages and pastries, they left the café and went to the visitor center.

Luciana waved at Lincoln, who was standing behind the checkout counter. "I'm here," she said. "I'll clock in and help you."

"No worries," Lincoln said, "business has been slow."

He looked over at Kennedy and Marilyn. His smile faded a little. "So," he said, "you were two of the tourists who got locked in the undertown the other day, right?"

Kennedy snickered. "We sure were. And yes, we saw those ghosts. We saw them a second time, too, in their infamous canyon."

Lincoln shivered. "It must've been terrifying," he said. "I'm still jumpy from when I saw them a few nights ago. And who knows if other tourists have seen them. Starwood City might lose a lot of business."

Luciana crossed her arms. "Lincoln," she said, "I should tell you that Ernesto asked me to go over that new projector with you some more."

"That won't be necessary," Lincoln said. "I've got it down pretty good. Ernesto was showing it to me just this morning."

"You do?" Luciana's eyes widened. "But it's a complicated, expensive, portable projector that we got only a few weeks ago. Even I'm still learning how it works."

Lincoln grinned. "I'm just a fast learner."

Luciana shrugged. She excused herself and went into an office.

"Wonder where the others are," Marilyn said.

"Probably still grabbing their goodies." Kennedy sipped her coffee. "Let's look at the gift shop."

The girls went upstairs. The gift shop was crowded with shelves and racks filled with cowboy hats, vests, shirts, cardigans, and boots. Kennedy saw a twirling shelf displaying keychains, refrigerator magnets, jewelry, and dreamcatchers standing close to the checkout counter.

But the gift shop and its cute clothing and items couldn't keep Kennedy's mind distracted from the case. Lincoln seemed a little eager to ask her and Marilyn about those ghosts. And what was this about a new projector? One that was supposed to be hard to work with, and yet Lincoln seemed to learn to work with that thing pretty quickly. And he had been taught by Ernesto.

"Hey, Ken!" Marilyn said. "The others are here. And Nicole and Alec want to take us to lower Starwood City. You know, where the actual ghost town is."

Kennedy smiled. "Sounds good."

"Welcome to the original Starwood City," Nicole said.

Kennedy gazed at the ghost town. Even in the daytime, the place looked like it could be haunted. The shadow of an especially tall and round saguaro cactus could very well have been a ghost. The log buildings looked like they could collapse at any moment.

"Looks like Bannack in the desert," Victoria said.

"Come on, let's scope out the place for the ghosts!" Wesley said. "They might be in one of these buildings!"

He ran into the first building, followed closely by Victoria, Jessica, and Susannah. Kennedy followed Marilyn, Rachel, and Billy to the next building over.

"Anything in here?" Marilyn asked. She winced when the wooden floors creaked beneath her feet.

"Nothing," Billy said. "Just a tiny house."

"At least it doesn't have ghosts."

Kennedy smirked. The foursome left the little house and walked over to what appeared to be an old, two-story farmhouse.

"Look at that," Kennedy said. "Wes and Vic should've gone in there."

"I'm not sure I want to," Billy said.

"Aw, don't be such a scaredy-cat. Come on!"

The four friends entered the farmhouse. The front room was wider than those of the other old buildings. A staircase stood to the right.

"Guys!" Marilyn said. "Do you hear that?"

Kennedy heard footsteps creaking upstairs. She smiled. "Probably other tourists," she said. "Nothing to be scared of. Come on."

She ran up the stairs, Billy, Rachel, and Marilyn close behind her. But just as they came into the hallway before them, a cell phone rang. Kennedy looked at her friends quizzically.

"Not mine," Billy whispered. Marilyn shook her head. So did Rachel.

Just then a door opened, and Lincoln came out of a room. He didn't seem to have noticed the four tourists near the stairs. He was too busy talking on his phone.

"Yeah, Ernesto," he said, "it's me. I'm in the ghost town. Yes, I'm getting some work done."

Kennedy raised an eyebrow. What kind of work could Lincoln be doing in this empty farmhouse?

Then again, he was talking to Ernesto.

Kennedy glanced back at her friends and held her finger up to her lips.

"I'll be there soon enough." Lincoln's voice sounded more impatient. "I have other things to do too, you know."

He sighed in exasperation and disappeared down the hall.

"What was that all about?" Billy hissed.

"No idea," Kennedy said. "But I'm going to find out."

"Why?" Marilyn asked.

"Could be important."

The foursome tiptoed down the hall. They turned the corner and went down the back stairwell, which led to the kitchen. They stopped when they found Lincoln and Luciana in the kitchen, standing in front of a pile of boxes. And this time, Lincoln noticed Kennedy, Marilyn, Rachel, and Billy. All six of them stared at one another.

"Well," Billy said, "this is awkward."

Luciana smiled. "Oh, don't mind me and Lincoln," she said. "We're just sorting through everything here."

"Yeah, and I hope this makes Ernesto happy," Lincoln said.

"Oh, was he nagging you again?"

Lincoln nodded glumly. "Working here has always been the dream life," he said. "Until Ernesto showed up."

"Why do you have boxes here?" Kennedy asked.

"We're using this old farmhouse as a temporary storage," Lincoln said. "The closets in the visitor center are full. We've got a bunch of extra rodeo stuff in these boxes."

He opened one of the boxes and pulled out a couple of lassos. "We rent out stuff to the riders if they need anything. Got a lot of new stuff in recently."

"Oh, yes," Rachel said, "when I registered, I requested to use an extra lasso. Good prices for renting things."

Lincoln handed Rachel one of the lassos. "These are fine quality ropes," he said.

"We also have costumes," Luciana said, "in case riders want to get fancy."

"Do you have any costumes of the ghosts?" Kennedy asked eagerly.

Luciana laughed. "Those were the most popular requests. You know Roy Martinez, one of our regular performers? He asked to be Marshal Gideon Torres."

She opened another box. "You guys can look if you want."

Kennedy, Marilyn, Rachel, and Billy crowded around the boxes. Sure enough, they were filled with cowboy and cowgirl costumes, lassos, fake guns, hats, even archery sets.

Luciana grinned at Kennedy. "If I didn't know any better," she said, "I'd say you're poking around."

Kennedy smiled. "I do know a few things happening on the employee side of the case," she admitted. "I've heard talk of a new portable projector, for example."

Luciana giggled. "Yeah, it's a tough thing to figure out. But Lincoln here's got it."

"Ernesto's still better at it than I am," Lincoln said. "But I'm getting the hang of it . . ."

He trailed off and turned a frown to Kennedy.

"You thinking that projector might be just the tool to make a couple of ghosts appear?" he asked. "Like, for example, if a ring of counterfeiters wanted to use it to scare people away?"

"Depends on how fancy the projector is," Kennedy said, "but yeah, it's definitely possible. And I think counterfeiters would use a famous ghost legend to their advantage."

"Our new projector is a fancy one," Lincoln said. "Come to think of it, I do remember the projector wasn't in the storage closet on the night that I saw those ghosts!"

Kennedy's eyes widened. "You mean before I saw them in the undertown?"

Lincoln nodded. A smile crept across Kennedy's lips. "So, perhaps it was in the undertown?"

"And maybe the canyon when we were there last night?" Billy added.

"What's this?" Lincoln said. "Oh, yeah, Kennedy, you said that you saw those ghosts a second time. In the canyon?"

Kennedy nodded. "You two were the ones who let us out of the undertown when we got locked down there," she said. "I don't suppose you saw anything odd?"

"Not at all," Luciana said. "Lincoln and I were too focused on helping your friend Alec look for you guys."

"Yeah," Billy said, "he told me later that you two had to go and unlock the undertown's door since Ernesto wasn't available. I think Alec felt bad since you guys were already dealing with a bunch of complaints about Ernesto's attitude."

"It was no problem to go after you guys," Luciana said with a giggle.

"That's a relief," Kennedy said. Billy snickered.

"Well," Marilyn said, "guess we'd better let you two get back to work."

"I guess so," Lincoln said. "Oh, and hey, Kennedy?"

Kennedy looked at Lincoln.

"If you need anything or have any questions, don't hesitate to come to me and Lucy. We've been pretty curious about this whole counterfeiting business too. Lucy's been bugging her dad about it."

"Yes," Luciana said. "Lincoln and I, we grew up right here. Our families have called Starwood City home for a long time. We love working with tourists, even if it means having a grumpy old coworker like Ernesto."

"And we don't want to see the ghost town of our childhood brought down by ghosts or counterfeiters," Lincoln said.

Kennedy smiled. "Don't worry," she said. "I'm good at this mystery-solving business. In fact, maybe we should see if we can't find that projector at the canyon tonight."

"What?" Billy said.

"Sure. If my hunch is right and that new projector is being used to make those two ghosts appear, then, if by chance we see the ghosts again during our rodeo lessons in our favorite canyon, then we—"

"I see!" Luciana said. "When Lincoln and I leave, we'll see if the projector is put away. If not, we'll join you in the canyon."

"I'm not sure I wanna see those ghosts again," Lincoln said.

Kennedy almost expected to see the two ghosts roaming at the bottom of the canyon. But she didn't see any silver apparitions chasing each other. Nor did she hear any ghostly wailing. Just the distant howling of coyotes.

Movement from across the canyon made Kennedy whip her head around. She recognized Roy Martinez riding on the other side of the canyon. She waved, but he didn't seem to have noticed her.

"Those Starwood phantoms keeping you waiting?"

Kennedy grinned at her cousin. "Aaron," she said, "you know me too well."

Aaron patted his horse's neck. "I sure do, cousin."

He frowned. "Billy and Marilyn want you," he said. "Those two young employees are riding here."

Kennedy's grin broadened. She and Aaron rode on a trail that led down into the canyon.

"Whoa, whoa, whoa!"

Kennedy and Aaron looked over their shoulders. Alec was riding after them.

"You're not going back down there?" Alec said. "Do you kids want to be haunted?"

Kennedy just smiled. "Just gonna see a couple friends," she said. "You can come if you want."

Alec groaned but followed Kennedy and Aaron down the trail anyway. Kennedy saw Lincoln and Luciana astride their own horses, talking with Marilyn, Billy, Gunnar, and Wesley. Lincoln was looking around, his eyes wide and fearful.

"Wow, we've got a whole posse," Alec said. "I reckon this is a posse of young detectives, huh?"

"You guessed it," Billy said. He nodded at Kennedy. "Well, Ken, turns out there's no projector at the visitor center."

"Yeah," Luciana said, "Lincoln and I checked. It's gone."

"What's gone?" Alec demanded. "A projector? What's going on here?"

Kennedy told Alec about her suspicions regarding the visitor center's new projector.

"And you think we're gonna find it in these hills?" Gunnar said. "Good luck. It's getting dark already."

Kennedy looked up at the sky. Indeed, it was covered in red and orange clouds.

"Better time to see Gideon and Bart!" Wesley said.

"So let's find them!" Kennedy said.

The group rode a little way down the canyon, then they stopped their horses to look around. But all Kennedy could see were the surrounding hills and bluffs.

A coyote howled. Sunshine let out a nervous nicker. Kennedy patted her neck. "It's alright, Sunshine," she whispered.

"Well," Marilyn said, "even if there aren't any ghosts, those coyotes' howls are spooky enough."

"Don't worry, they're far away," Gunnar said.

Kennedy stared at the trail ahead. Under the faint rays of the setting sun, she spotted a glimmer near a large boulder.

"What's that?" she said, pointing to the boulder.

Everyone turned their faces to the boulder. Kennedy slid off Sunshine and walked over to the rock. The glimmer was more obvious to her now. It was the golden handle of a suitcase.

"Guys!" she called. "I found a suitcase."

She bent over and pulled the suitcase toward her. She spotted a white tag attached to the handle. She looked at the tag. It had the initials *RM* on it.

Billy, Lincoln, and Alec kneeled next to her. "Why would a random suitcase be out here in this canyon?" Billy asked. "Maybe someone lost it?"

"Or maybe there's a more sinister reason," Kennedy said. "Only one way to find out. Glad it's not locked."

She snapped the buckles and opened the suitcase. Sure enough, it was filled with money. Lincoln took hold of a bundle and gazed at it.

"Think this is counterfeit?" he said.

Billy took out another bundle. "Yep," he said.

Marilyn screamed. So did Luciana. The horses neighed in fear. Kennedy jumped to her feet and spun around. She gasped.

The ghosts of Gideon Torres and Lightning Bart were hovering over the group.

Alec jumped in front of Kennedy, Lincoln, and Billy. He waved his hand at them, motioning for them to step back. Lincoln looked like he was about to faint.

"It's them!" Wesley shouted. "The ghosts! The infamous ghosts! I'm actually seeing the Starwood ghosts!"

"And I think the marshal wants to arrest us along with Bart!" Aaron said.

Indeed, Kennedy could see the livid look on the marshal's silvery, transparent face. She grabbed Billy's hand, only to let go when he gave her an odd glance.

"*Leave the suitcase!*" the marshal's ghost wailed. "*And leave this canyon!*"

"*Or face the same doom as I and my enemy!*" Bart's ghost added. "*And my enemy! A-and my enemy . . .*"

323

Static took over the outlaw's voice. Then the two figures glitched as though they were on an old, black-and-white TV show.

Kennedy grinned. She strolled past Alec and walked right through the ghosts. She picked up the suitcase.

"Luciana!" she called. "And Lincoln! Let's try to find that projector!"

Luciana dismounted her horse and ran to Lincoln's side. He still looked pale, but he joined Luciana, Kennedy, Billy, and Alec in searching through the nearby bushes.

"Hey!" Luciana shouted. "I found it! The projector!"

Everyone ran over to Luciana. She held up a white, square-shaped projector with a wide camera. Judging by all the buttons and the shiny lens around the camera, Kennedy guessed that this projector was pretty fancy.

"Who'd leave our nice new projector out here?" Lincoln said. "Any of the employees would get fired!"

"At least we know that our ghosts aren't real," Kennedy said. She smiled down at the suitcase in her hand. "And we've got some decent clues."

She looked up at Luciana. "We need to show these to your dad right away."

"I'll call him."

Luciana pulled out her cell phone and began dialing. Kennedy saw Victoria, Jessica, Rachel, and Nicole ride over.

"We heard screaming!" Rachel said. "I assume you guys saw those ghosts?"

"And maybe that's why you wandered off?" Nicole said.

Kennedy grinned. She told them all about finding the suitcase with counterfeit money, seeing the ghosts, and finding the projector.

"But why hide the fake money here?" Rachel said. "I can't think this place would be very safe."

Kennedy frowned. "Unless someone was coming to pick it up," she said. "The initials are *R* and *M* . . ."

She paused when she remembered seeing Roy Martinez riding earlier.

Roy Martinez.

"Guys," she said in a hushed voice, "I saw Roy Martinez riding out here earlier tonight. Before Lincoln and Luciana came."

"So," Lincoln said slowly, "you're saying that this is Roy's suitcase? I don't think—"

"Wait!" Jessica said. "If somebody might pick up this very suitcase right here, maybe we should get away from this place?"

Everyone exchanged nervous looks. Then Nicole and Alec rounded everyone up. The group rode away with the suitcase and the projector. Kennedy glanced over at Lincoln; how he managed to ride a horse while holding that projector was beyond her.

A horn honked. Kennedy smiled when she saw the chief ranger's car.

"Dad's here!" Luciana slid off her horse, still clutching onto the suitcase. She ran over to her father just as he got out of the car. She handed him the suitcase just as the others rode over.

"Howdy, everyone," Ranger Olson said. He looked over the suitcase. "So, this suitcase contains more play money, I hear?"

"That's right." Kennedy dismounted Sunshine. She nodded at Lincoln. He handed her the projector. "And this was out here in the canyon as well. Creating ghosts."

Kennedy, Luciana, and Lincoln told Ranger Olson their stories. Kennedy added that she had seen Roy riding on the other side of the canyon before Lincoln and Luciana appeared.

Ranger Olson frowned. "It's hard to imagine Roy getting involved in a counterfeiting ring," he said. "He's been one of our regular rodeo performers for a long time."

"But couldn't he still be part of the counterfeiting ring?" Kennedy said. "Being in the rodeo would be the perfect coverup for him. Maybe he was down in the undertown that night that me and the others got locked down."

"No, he wasn't," Luciana said. "I'm afraid I've got an alibi for him. That evening, he was one of the guests complaining to me and Lincoln about Ernesto's grouchy attitude. He was still in the visitor center when Alec came for me and Lincoln."

"Yes, he was," Alec said.

"Besides," Luciana added, "I've always thought he seemed nice. A little arrogant, perhaps, and he can be a little sore when he loses a rodeo, but—"

"What?" Rachel said. "Sorry to interrupt, but what do you mean when you say Roy is sore when he loses a rodeo?"

"Roy hasn't won first place in a few years," Lincoln said. "I hate to gossip, but Roy is smug about winning first place. Which, like I already said, he hasn't done in the past few years. And I did see him this morning. He seemed pretty determined to win first place. He really wants that prize money."

"Yeah, I don't blame him," Wesley said. "That prize is a lot of money. Like, five thousand dollars?"

"Then maybe he wants to switch out the prize money for the counterfeit money," Kennedy said. "Maybe he found out about the counterfeiting ring somehow, and he might be trying to switch out the real prize money with the counterfeit money? Then, if he doesn't win first place, it won't matter, he'd have the real money."

"That's not a bad theory," Ranger Olson said. "I guess I'll have to question him. I'll take the suitcase and the projector. I suggest the rest of you return to the campground."

His frown deepened. "And watch yourselves. You've found a lot of clues. You're the ones who discovered everything in the first place. I think I'll request extra security for the campground."

"Thank you, Ranger Olson," Nicole said. She turned her gaze to Kennedy. "Come on, let's all head back."

Kennedy climbed back onto Sunshine. She said goodnight to Lincoln, Luciana, and Ranger Olson, then she rode with her sisters and friends away from the bluffs.

Nicole steered her horse next to Kennedy. "Hey, Ken?" she said. "May I have a word with you?"

"Sure," Kennedy said.

"Well," Nicole said, "the truth is, I'm worried about your safety. You're being pretty snoopy. And those two ghosts appearing right when you find that suitcase? It seems like these counterfeiters know you're onto them."

Kennedy's smile faded a little. "I understand your concern, Nicole," she said. "But nothing happened to us tonight."

"Not tonight, but who knows what could happen? What if you get hurt? Kennedy, you're being a little reckless. And that could lead you into danger. What if you get hurt and then you can't be in the rodeo?"

"Oh." Kennedy lowered her eyes. "Didn't think of that."

"Maybe you should."

Nicole looked ahead. "At least we're back at the camp now. Hopefully we'll be safe."

The group rode to their cabins and put their horses away in the stable. Nicole's words resonated with Kennedy for the rest of the evening. She remained silent as she prepared for bed.

"Something bothering you, Kenny?" Rachel asked as she locked the door.

"Nicole's worried for me," Kennedy said. "I suppose I ought to be too."

"I've been worried too," Marilyn said. "I mean, it's great that we've got some good clues for Ranger Olson, but I feel like we're getting a little too involved for the counterfeiters' comfort."

Kennedy sat on her bed and yawned. "I'm beat. Let's get some sleep. Good night."

She laid her head on her pillow and closed her eyes. But sleep wouldn't come. Her head was still swimming. Was she being too reckless in her mystery-solving? But if she hadn't gone snooping herself, the chief ranger might not have found such excellent clues. And she couldn't get Lincoln and Luciana's concern for their childhood home out of her head either.

Kennedy turned on her side. Marilyn was fast asleep next to her. If only she could fall asleep like that. She slowly turned onto her back and stared up at the ceiling. In just a few minutes her eyelids became heavy.

Just sleep, girl. Just think sleep.

Thoughts of the counterfeiters still crossed her mind, but didn't seem to intrude on her sleepiness too much now.

Time seemed to pass in the darkness like a snail . . . a door creaking open . . . quick footsteps on the other side of the window above the bed . . .

Something felt like it was crawling up her arm. Kennedy flinched. She blinked her eyes a few times before actually opening them. She lifted her head slightly to see what was crawling up onto her shoulder. She blinked again to focus her vision.

An orange bark scorpion stared into her eyes.

All sleep left Kennedy's eyes as they widened.

"AAAAGGGGHHHH!"

Her scream pierced the cabin. She leaped onto her feet. The scorpion fell onto the quilt. Marilyn jerked awake. In the other bed, Rachel and Susannah were sitting up, gaping at Kennedy.

"Ah!" Marilyn shrieked. "Scorpion!"

"Scorpion!" Rachel exclaimed. She jumped out of her bed. "Where?"

"It's on our bed!" Kennedy yelled. She and Marilyn leaped out of their blankets. But Kennedy's feet got caught in the covers, causing her to trip backwards and land flat on her back.

"Don't move, Kennedy!"

Rachel stood over Kennedy, the suitcase rack above her head. "I'll get that thing!"

"Yikes!" Kennedy held her arms in front of her. "Rachel Hamilton, don't you dare hit me with that thing!"

"Yeah, the scorpion's still on the bed!" Marilyn said.

Rachel whacked the bed with the rack, but she missed the scorpion with every attack. Then the scorpion jumped onto Rachel. She screamed at the top of her lungs and threw the rack to the side. She was flapping her hands all over her chest and running around the room. Kennedy leaped up and chased Rachel.

"Get it off!" Rachel yelled. "Get it off!"

"Hold still!" Susannah said. She tried to brush the scorpion off Rachel's shoulder, but the scorpion leaped from Rachel and onto Susannah. Now Susannah was screaming. She grabbed the scorpion with her fingers, only to scream when she realized it was in her hand and threw it to Marilyn. Marilyn screamed and tossed the scorpion to Kennedy.

"Catch it, Ken!"

"Hey, hey, wait!" Kennedy somehow managed to catch the scorpion. "I don't want it!"

She tossed it to Rachel before it could sting her palm.

"Don't give it to me!" Rachel shouted as she juggled the scorpion in her hands. She threw it back to Kennedy, who then threw it to Susannah. Susannah screamed and threw it to Marilyn. She screamed when the scorpion landed in her hand.

"Ouch!" she exclaimed. She dropped the scorpion. "It stung my hand!"

Kennedy, Susannah, and Rachel backed off and stared at the scorpion skittering on the floor. Kennedy hoped it wouldn't come near them. She grasped Rachel's arm.

Just then the door flew open. Nicole, Alec, Victoria, Jessica, Aaron, Billy, Wesley, and Gunnar barged inside.

"What's going on in here?" Nicole demanded.

"Scorpion!" Kennedy exclaimed. "In our cabin!"

Victoria and the boys rushed toward the scorpion. The little animal raised its tail at the numerous hands grabbing at it.

"Hey, leave it alone!" Alec yelled. He jumped in front of the boys. He took off his nightcap and bent over.

"Everyone stay back," he said. He held out the cap toward the scorpion, ignoring the little animal's raised tail. With the cap wrapped around his hand, Alec grabbed the scorpion.

"Dude," Rachel said, "how, just how are you able to pick up a bark scorpion and not even flinch or bat an eye?"

"I'm not afraid of these things," Alec said. He frowned. "But I do have one question about this little guy. Did anybody notice the paper attached to its tail?"

Kennedy's curiosity overcame her fear. She walked over to Alec and looked at the scorpion's tail. Sure enough, a little white piece of rolled paper was tied to its tail with a rubber band.

Alec gingerly fingered the rubber band and pulled out the little roll of paper. He handed the roll to Kennedy. Before she could open it, Rachel spoke to Nicole.

"How did you guys get in our cabin? You don't have a key."

"Your door was already opened," Nicole said. "Just a little."

"But I locked it before we went to sleep!" Rachel said.

Kennedy's heart skipped a beat. "I thought I heard the door opening earlier," she said, "but I was half-asleep."

Nicole put her hand over her mouth. Her eyes widened with fear.

"So, Ken," Billy said, "what does the note say?"

Kennedy unfolded the tiny paper. "It says, 'Lay off the case of the secret business in the undertown and leave Starwood City, or you will face the consequences.'"

Her eyes wandered to the bottom of the note. "It's signed with the initials *R* and *M*."

"The same initials on the suitcase," Billy said darkly.

Kennedy scowled. "Someone is trying to scare us away."

"Then I'm calling the rangers," Nicole said. She looked at Billy and Wesley. "You two run to the main building and let the front desk know what's happening."

Nicole, Billy, and Wesley left the cabin. Nicole returned in a few minutes, already on her phone. Kennedy sat on her bed. She picked up her phone and took a few pictures of the note. She saw Jessica and Marilyn sitting on the other bed. Jessica was looking at Marilyn's hand. Guilt filled Kennedy's mind.

"Hello?"

Kennedy looked at the door. Ranger Olson came into the cabin, followed by Billy and Wesley.

"I hear we've got a scorpion problem," the chief ranger said. "A scorpion with a threatening note?"

Kennedy, Susannah, and Rachel told Ranger Olson what had happened. He wrote down everything in his notepad.

"And you say you locked the door before you girls went to sleep?" he said. "But, Kennedy, you think you heard the door open just before you noticed the scorpion? And footsteps outside?"

Kennedy nodded. Ranger Olson turned around and looked at the doorknob.

"No signs of the lock being picked," he said.

Kennedy took a closer look at the doorknob herself. The chief ranger was right. No scratch marks or anything.

"So if the lock wasn't picked," Kennedy said, "then whoever opened the door may have had a key?"

She stepped outside and shined her phone's flashlight on the ground. Sure enough, messy boot prints led away from the cabin. Everyone else gathered around the boot prints.

"Looks like someone was in a hurry to get away from here," Aaron said.

"Now I know I heard running footsteps," Kennedy said.

"And this person knew to avoid the extra security I asked for," Ranger Olson said. "I'll stay here at the campground for the rest of the night."

"And Marilyn," Nicole said, "let's get your hand looked at. The main building might have a first-aid kit for scorpion stings."

Nicole, Marilyn, and Alec walked to the main building. Everyone else dispersed to their cabins.

"You know," Rachel said, "after what happened, there's no way I'm going back to sleep."

"You said it!" Susannah said.

Kennedy laid down and stared at the ceiling. She couldn't help feeling that her friends were right.

Alec and Wesley held the doors of the visitor center open. Kennedy glazed over the packed lobby.

"Wow," Jessica said, "looks like there's a good turnout for the train ride."

"Yeah!" Victoria said. "The Starwood Tourist Express! I can't wait to get robbed!"

Kennedy smiled, but her excitement for the train ride waned a little when she saw Marilyn rubbing her bandaged hand. Their usual horseback riding in the bluffs had been rough on poor Marilyn. Once an excellent roper, she had been struggling with roping just like Kennedy had been when she first moved to her uncle's ranch.

"Cheer up, Marilyn," Wesley said to her. "I'm sure your hand will heal by the time the rodeo comes. And you're tough."

Marilyn smiled timidly. Kennedy hoped Wesley was right.

"Don't look now, Ken," Billy whispered, "but Roy Martinez is standing right over there."

Kennedy held in a groan. Billy was right. Roy stood in front of the vending machines. He didn't seem to notice Kennedy staring at him warily. His entire focus was on purchasing a soda.

A man rushed past Kennedy and Billy. Kennedy whipped her head around and stared at him. She instantly noticed that the man was holding a familiar bag. It was identical to the bag with brightly colored Apache symbols that Kennedy had seen that one woman holding only a few days ago. Right before her group toured the undertown.

A phone rang. The man dug into his pocket and pulled out his cell phone. Kennedy's eyes widened when she saw that both of the man's hands were bandaged.

"Hello?" the man said. "Yeah, it's Ruben. Where are you? I've got your stuff."

The man turned around. Kennedy pretended to look at the books on the shelf, but she still noticed the man eyeing her. She went around the shelf.

"Gotcha," the man said. "I'm coming."

Kennedy peeked around the shelf. The man was walking toward the front door. He passed by Roy.

"Oh, sir," Roy said, holding out his hand, "that bag looks a might heavy for your mummified hands. Need some help?"

The man recoiled back. "No," he said abruptly.

Roy stared in surprise. The man sighed. "Sorry. Didn't mean to be brusque. Just, uh, in a hurry."

The man made his way to the door. Roy rolled his eyes and crossed his arms. "Some people," he muttered.

Kennedy and Billy glanced at one another. The man left the visitor center. Kennedy ran to the door.

"What are you doing?" Billy asked.

"You saw his hands. Both bandaged. Just like Marilyn's."

Billy gaped. "You don't think he's—"

"Our scorpion guy?" Kennedy said. She and Billy entered the foyer. "It's possible. And I heard him on his phone. He did say his name's Ruben."

Kennedy and Billy peeked outside. Luckily, the man was still in sight. He was standing on the deck of the Prickly Cactus Café.

The door of the café opened. Kennedy recognized the woman coming out onto the deck. The previous carrier of that Apache bag. And it seemed like she was getting it back.

"Are you kidding me?" Billy said. "He refuses Roy's offer to carry that thing, but he hands it to some lady?"

"Doubt she's just some lady." Kennedy held up her phone. "These may not be the best pictures I can get, but it's better than nothing."

Kennedy took a few pictures, then she and Billy ran back inside.

"What now?" Billy asked.

"Let's find Luciana," Kennedy said. "I want her to see these pictures. And I have another favor to ask of her."

"What's that?"

Kennedy grinned. "To peek around the undertown."

Without the noise of tourists' chatter and a tour guide's lecture, the undertown seemed creepier and darker than Kennedy's last visit. Kennedy almost expected to see the floating apparitions of Marshal Torres and Lightning Bart looming out of the black hallways. She had to remind herself that they weren't real ghosts.

"Thanks for letting Billy and I come down here," she whispered to Luciana.

Luciana smiled feebly.

"What's down here anyway that you gotta see so badly?" Lincoln asked.

"I just want to double check for any more clues," Kennedy said. "Lucy, did you send my pictures to your dad?"

"I did. He hasn't responded yet. He's out of town, meeting with a few other detectives about the counterfeiting ring."

"We can't stay down here long," Billy said. "Our train ride is soon."

"I know. We'll just scour the area and leave."

The foursome went to the lounge. Kennedy gazed at the dark hall. It now had yellow caution tape blocking it off.

"Oh," Kennedy said, "now it's blocked off."

"Yeah," Lincoln said, "Ernesto and I set it up the other day. After the tour."

"Ernesto, huh?"

"You still suspect him?" Luciana said.

"Yeah, he's still my main suspect."

Kennedy approached the pedestal with the vase. She took the vase and looked inside. There was nothing. Not a single dollar bill.

"What's that over there?"

Kennedy put the vase down. Lincoln was pointing down the hall. Kennedy narrowed her eyes. Just beyond the tape, she saw a little piece of paper on the floor.

"Probably just some litter," Billy said.

"But we cleaned in here yesterday," Luciana said, "and we haven't had any tours today."

Kennedy stepped over the tape and picked up the paper. She turned it over and grinned. She walked back over to her three friends.

"There's a message on it," she said. "To someone named Winifred. It says, 'We have enough counterfeit money to replace the real money.' And guess what? It's signed Ruben. Ruben Messer."

"Ruben!" Billy said. "The guy with the bandages! And his initials are *RM*. So Roy Martinez is innocent?"

"Guess so," Kennedy said. "He doesn't have his hands all wrapped up, that's for sure. But the guy who calls himself Ruben does. And look at this handwriting."

Kennedy pulled out her phone. She compared the note to her pictures.

"If you look closely, you'll notice that the handwriting on this note and the note that we found on our scorpion are similar. But this handwriting is shakier."

"As though the person had a hard time writing," Billy said. "Maybe because of scorpion stings?"

Kennedy nodded. "So now we know that two of our counterfeiters are named Ruben Messer and Winifred. And it looks like they're planning to switch out fake money with real money."

"How are they gonna do that?" Lincoln asked.

Kennedy paused. "Perhaps the prize money of the rodeo?"

"That makes sense," Luciana said. "The prize money is a big amount. Ken, let me keep that note. I'll take a picture and send it to my dad. This is an excellent clue!"

Just as Kennedy handed the note to Luciana, footsteps echoed down the hall. Kennedy spun around, her wide eyes gazing into the blackness.

"We'd better get out of here," Billy hissed.

The foursome tiptoed away.

"Behold!" Victoria said, sweeping her arms. "The Starwood Tourist Express!"

"Just look at it!" Jessica said. "It's gorgeous!"

Kennedy took a few pictures of the train. It looked like an old locomotive from the days of the Wild West. In large gold lettering, the words STARWOOD TOURIST EXPRESS decorated each of the cars.

Victoria and Jessica ran ahead to the caboose. Kennedy followed everyone else onto the car in front of the caboose. The car looked like a long and narrow luxury restaurant. The wooden surfaces of each table glimmered under the sunlight that shone through the windows. The walls were decorated with a border of silhouettes of horseback riders. And the pale green carpet looked like it had the treatment of a fancy vacuum cleaner.

Kennedy, Aaron, Billy, and Susannah sat at a table behind Alec and Nicole. Kennedy's eyes wandered to the bundle of play money sitting at the edge of the table. She picked it up and stared at it with a small smile. This train ride attraction was probably the only circumstance it was okay to pass out counterfeit money.

"Can you believe that caboose is an entire gift shop?"

Kennedy looked over her shoulder. Victoria and Jessica had come into the car, each holding a brown paper bag. The two of them sat at a table with Marilyn and Rachel.

Lincoln came over to Kennedy's table. He was dressed in a neat white shirt with black pants and a black bow tie.

"Hey," he said, smiling at Kennedy. "We made it."

"We did," Kennedy said. "Did Luciana send the picture to her dad?"

"Yeah. She hasn't checked to see if he answered, though. She's been too busy getting ready. She's one of the saloon girls. We'll be seeing her later."

"I still can't believe Kennedy talked you into letting her sneak down into the undertown," Aaron said. He paused. "Or, no, I can believe it."

Lincoln shrugged.

"What about Ernesto?" Kennedy asked in a low voice. "Is he here?"

"He's one of the robbers," Lincoln said. "Not that I mind too much. It's nice not to have him micromanaging me for once."

Kennedy nodded slowly. She would've liked to have kept an eye on Ernesto, though.

Just then a voice over an intercom announced that the ride was beginning. And sure enough, the train started to move. More waiters and waitresses entered the car with trays of water pitchers and glasses.

"Guess I'll take your drink orders," Lincoln said.

Kennedy, Billy, Susannah, and Aaron gave Lincoln their orders. He returned in a few minutes with a water pitcher, coffee, sodas, and salads.

"This is a good salad," Susannah said.

An enthusiastic male voice boomed over the intercom. "Howdy, folks, and welcome aboard the Starwood Tourist Express! I'm your host and engineer, Irwin Romero. You will be seeing some of the finest of Arizona's Sonoran Desert! For instance, if you look outside, you will see the bluffs that surround Starwood City."

Kennedy gazed out the window. The orange desert glowed under the cloudless sky. Kennedy squinted; she could make out a few buildings of Starwood City in the distance. She also recognized some areas in the hills as the places where she and her sisters and friends had been practicing for the rodeo.

"Alrighty, folks," Mr. Romero's staticky voice said, "we are approaching the Canyon of the Ghosts, the site of the final chase between Marshal Gideon Torres and outlaw Lightning Bart."

Flurries of excited whispers filled the car. Kennedy gazed at the familiar canyon. Even in the daytime, and from a distance, the canyon seemed haunted.

Lincoln came to the table with a tray of plates of T-bone steaks, cooked carrot slices, and baked potatoes with butter and sour cream.

"This food smells so good," Susannah said.

"Glad to hear that," Lincoln said. His eyes wandered out the window. "I may know the true nature of the ghosts, but I'm still glad to be far away from that canyon."

Kennedy shrugged. She wouldn't mind being closer. Her mind was itching to find more clues for her mystery.

The train passed by a very old two-story log building. The two pillars that held up the roof over the deck looked like they could fall at any minute.

"What's that?" Susannah asked.

"Looks like an old saloon," Kennedy said. "I think that's where the saloon girls will be when the train comes back this way."

Movement outside caught her eye. Kennedy stared at the old saloon. Even as the train moved further away from the building, Kennedy thought she saw a woman darting around to the back.

The train came to a trestle. Kennedy looked down at the ground below. Even the trees and saguaro cacti looked tiny. Over the intercom, the engineer pointed out the Silver Bell Mountains. Shortly after the train crossed over the trestle, it stopped at a little station.

"Get ready, everyone!" Mr. Romero said. "We'll be turning around shortly! The ride back will be the ride of your lifetime!"

"It sure will be!" Victoria said. She snatched the bundle of fake money from her table. "Let's do this!"

Soon the train began moving again. Lincoln came back to the tables to serve apple pie and cookies. Dessert wasn't the only thing Kennedy enjoyed. A guitarist came into the car and sang country songs. Victoria even made a request, to which the guitarist gladly obliged. He also gave Victoria a signed copy of one of his CDs before he moved onto the next car.

The train moved on, as did the sun across the sky. Kennedy noticed that it was close to the horizon. Small wonder; it was already late afternoon.

"Look!" Victoria exclaimed. "There's a guy on a horse!"

All eyes turned to the windows. Sure enough, a bulky man dressed in a dark cowboy suit was sitting astride a black horse. He watched the train as it passed by.

"There's our first robber!" Victoria squealed. She began taking pictures. Kennedy copied her sister's actions. She spotted another robber. He and the first man steered their horses toward the train.

"They're coming!" Jessica said.

A gunshot. But Kennedy didn't flinch. Neither did the horses outside. They must be used to these guys shooting blanks. More men dressed as robbers on horseback appeared, firing blanks. The train began to slow down.

"Hey, look, we're passing the saloon again," Rachel said. "There's the saloon girls!"

Kennedy looked at the old log building. Five women, including Luciana, were sitting on the deck, all of them dressed in bright and colorful dance hall costumes and hats.

The train came to a full stop. Kennedy's eyes darted outside at the men on horses. But none of them looked like Ernesto.

"Here they come!" Jessica said.

Kennedy turned away from the window. Luciana and the other saloon girls had just boarded the car. They playfully flirted with the men. Kennedy grinned at Luciana. She was wearing a bright magenta dress with a black belt, fish-net leggings and boots, and a black hat with bright pink feathers. She also had a boa with black and magenta feathers.

Aaron whistled. "Looking good there, Lucy!" he said.

Luciana smiled. "Why, thank you, cowboy." She sat on his lap. "You don't mind if I give you a kiss on your cheek, do you?"

Aaron's grin faded. His cheeks turned red. Kennedy tried in vain to control her laughter. Victoria and Jessica were already snapping pictures.

"That's going on Facebook!" Victoria said.

Kennedy snorted. But then she raised an eyebrow when Luciana moved to Billy's lap.

"Howdy, handsome fella."

Billy smirked. "You should go kiss Lincoln."

"I already did. It's your turn."

Billy blushed. He squeezed his eyes shut when Luciana pecked his cheek. Aaron, Wesley, and Gunnar burst out laughing.

Almost as soon as the saloon girls left the car, the robbers clambered aboard. Kennedy smiled. These guys were probably the only robbers she would ever be okay getting tangled with. At least, until Ernesto came onboard. Kennedy's smile faded. For some odd reason, Ernesto just seemed to look more like a real robber than the other men. But that was probably just her nerves. Ernesto looked right at Kennedy. She stopped herself from flinching. Ernesto just nodded at her and proceeded to take the play money from the other tables.

"Hey, little lady," a man said to Victoria, "how about giving me that lovely bracelet?"

"What? No!" Victoria held her arm back and grinned at the man. "It's mine."

"But I'm here for all the money and jewelry."

"Tough beans. I bought it and it's mine. But maybe we can negotiate with a tip, eh?"

Kennedy dropped a bundle of fake money into another man's bag. If only that was the only fake money being passed out!

"Thank you kindly," the man said. Under his thick black beard, his smile looked like a bushy grin. "And, uh, forgive me, but are you Kennedy?"

Kennedy's eyes widened. She, Billy, Susannah, and Aaron exchanged surprised looks.

"Yeah," she said. "Why?"

"Well, your friend Luciana Olson wants to see you outside," the man said.

Kennedy, Billy, Susannah, and Aaron looked out the window. Luciana was outside with a few of the other saloon ladies.

"Wonder what she wants," Aaron said.

Kennedy grinned. "Let's find out."

She stood up and faced the man. "Thanks for the tip." She peered at his gold name tag. "Pedro."

Pedro tipped his hat at her and turned away. Kennedy led Billy, Susannah, and Aaron to the door. Rachel stood up from her table and ran after them.

"Where are you guys going?" she asked.

"That guy said Luciana wants to see me," Kennedy said. "I wonder if she has more useful info for us."

"But wouldn't she have shared it earlier when she was on the train?" Billy said.

"Not in front of all the other people," Kennedy said.

She rushed outside, her three friends and cousin close behind her. Luciana was leaning against the railing of the saloon's deck. She looked up in surprise at Kennedy.

"What are you guys doing out here?" she asked.

Kennedy frowned. Before she could reply, she noticed the saloon woman in a black dress and black mask standing just a few feet away, her beady, hawk-like eyes gazing at the kids. Kennedy didn't remember seeing that woman onboard the train. But there was still something familiar about her.

"Didn't you want to see us?" Aaron asked.

Luciana shook her head.

BANG!

Kennedy flinched. She saw the woman in the black dress pointing a gun at them. Her heart skipped a beat.

"What's going on?" Billy demanded.

Luciana laughed. "It's probably time for the saloon ladies to attack the robbers," she said. She pulled out a gun from her belt's holster. "Don't worry, it's all just blanks."

"Yeah, Kenny," Aaron said, "I reckon you're being a little too fidgety. Look, Ernesto's right there, pretending to be dead."

Kennedy looked ahead. Sure enough, Ernesto was lying face down on the grass.

BANG!

339

Susannah screamed.

"Holy moly!" Aaron yelled. "What happened?"

Kennedy spun around. Susannah grasped her left arm and fell to one knee. Kennedy felt sick at the sight of blood trickling down her arm. Horrified gasps erupted. Aaron squatted next to Susannah.

"I thought these were just blanks!" Rachel exclaimed.

"Me too!" Luciana stared at her gun in horror, as though worried it too was more dangerous than it appeared.

"Get her back onboard!" Kennedy said.

Aaron and Rachel helped Susannah back onto the train just as another gunshot was fired. Billy yelled in alarm. Kennedy spun around, her stomach churning so much that she almost felt queasy. She was relieved to see Billy hadn't been shot. But the woman had her smoking gun on him. Then Ernesto jumped to his feet and dashed toward Kennedy and Luciana.

"Look out!" Billy yelled. He pounced on Ernesto before he could get any closer to Kennedy and tackled him.

"Luciana!" Kennedy shouted. "Get on the train!"

Luciana rushed onboard. The woman ran after Kennedy. Kennedy grabbed her wrists and locked herself into a cat fight with this saloon lady. With a tight grip, she swung the woman off her feet, dragging her in circles across the grass before releasing her. The gun flew to the side. Kennedy snatched it up just as Billy ran to her side, holding a gun himself.

"Ernesto was double armed!" he said. "I got one of his guns, but he's still coming!"

Indeed, Ernesto was aiming his gun at the twosome. Billy jumped in front of Kennedy and fired his gun. But Ernesto only had a gloating sneer for Billy. No cries of agony. Kennedy jumped onto the ladder of the train's door and grabbed the railing.

Then four more men appeared. Kennedy recognized one of them as Pedro. And his face was no longer that of the polite robber actor, but of an angry criminal. And lo and behold, another man had bandaged hands. Kennedy fired. Pedro yelled in pain and clutched his bloody hand, but he picked up his gun with his other hand. Billy let another bullet fly, and it hit one of the men's arms.

"HEY!"

Kennedy saw about a dozen men come running toward them. Roy Martinez, Lincoln, Alec, Aaron, Wesley, Gunnar, and the actor robbers were part of the crowd.

"Alright!" one of the actor robbers yelled. "We've filled our guns with real bullets this time!"

The real robbers huddled together, still pointing their own guns. The gang of criminals edged away as several shots boomed. They ducked behind the saloon. In moments, Kennedy saw all six of them riding away on horses.

"Hey!" one of the actor robbers shouted. "Those goons are taking our horses!"

"At least they're gone," another robber said. "But who were they? What did they want? In no way were we advertising actual robbers!"

Alec ran over to Kennedy and Billy. "Are you two alright?" he asked.

Kennedy took a deep, shaky breath. "As fine as ever."

She looked at the faraway hills. Already, the criminals had vanished.

The campground was still and quiet. But to Kennedy, that didn't mean peaceful. It meant an eerie silence that let her anxieties flood her mind once more.

She took in a deep breath. She had been relieved that the train was able to move on, and Susannah was taken to the hospital and looked at. Her wound was just a graze. The doctors said that Susannah should still be able to perform in the rodeo. But Kennedy still felt guilty and scared. First Marilyn, now Susannah. Their safety truly was in question. Maybe her friends had been right. Maybe Kennedy was being too reckless with her mystery-solving. As of that afternoon, Kennedy knew there were six counterfeiters. Including Ernesto. There could be no doubt now that he was part of the ring. And they would stop at nothing to ensure the safety and secrecy of their criminal activity.

"Kennedy?"

Kennedy glanced to the side. Billy walked over to her.

"You okay?" he asked.

"Just worried." Kennedy grasped a strand of her hair and twirled it. "I'm sorry, Billy."

"For what?"

"My reckless mystery-solving."

Billy smiled. Kennedy's heart thumped when he wrapped his arm around her.

"We've been in dangerous situations before because of your mystery-solving," he said. But his smile still disappeared. "I do agree with your worries, Ken. I hope you'll be alright. At least we're safe here at the camp."

"How's Susannah?"

"She's doing well. She just told me that she hopes you're not beating yourself up too much. Oh, and Luciana called."

Kennedy looked right at Billy. "And?"

"Her dad will come back to town as soon as he can. He might come here to meet with us later."

Kennedy nodded. "Sounds good," she said. "I'll see you at the cabins. I think I'll grab something from the snack bar."

Billy nodded and left. Kennedy walked through the trees. She could see the fence surrounding the swimming pool just up ahead. Kennedy pulled her phone out of her pocket, thinking that some soft country music would help calm her nerves.

A rustle in the bushes made her freeze. Kennedy stared at those bushes. Probably an animal. Maybe a roadrunner, or a mouse. Heaven forbid it was another scorpion!

She turned back around.

"You!"

Strong arms grabbed her from behind. Kennedy's gasp was cut off by a cloth being smothered against her nose. A strong scent. A relaxing scent. Her body sagged. Her vision went blurry . . . she thought she saw a woman walking toward her . . . everything went black.

Kennedy blinked. But even as her vision came into focus, the room she was in was still dark. No windows. Just the musty smell of old wood.

She must be in the undertown.

Kennedy tried to gasp. But a cloth was wrapped inside her mouth. Not only that, but she was leaning against a pole with her arms wrapped around it. Something scratched at her wrists.

She tried again to make a sound. But the gag in her mouth hindered her. Bringing her arms forward was futile; her wrists were bound behind the pole. Even her ankles had ropes around them.

Her heartbeat picked up its speed with every passing second. The last thing she remembered . . . she was outside at the campground . . . someone had grabbed her from behind. A strong scent emanating from a cloth pressed against her nose. Blackout.

Kennedy's heart leapt. It made sense.

She had been kidnapped.

Now she was a prisoner in Starwood City's undertown.

"Well, well, well, look who's finally awake."

Kennedy swung her head around. A woman sat on a chair in a corner, a sneer on her face. Kennedy hadn't noticed her at first. But now that she did notice her, she recognized her. The woman who had rushed past Roy. The woman who had taken the bag from Ruben. The woman in the black saloon girl costume.

She stood up and squatted next to Kennedy. "Permit me to introduce myself," she said. "I'm Winifred. And you are the young detective Kennedy."

Winifred tickled Kennedy's chin. Kennedy pulled back.

"Oh, you don't like that, dear?" Winifred said. "Forgive me. I understand you must be pretty uncomfortable. But we couldn't let you roam free above. Not with all the information your little mind accumulated. I must admit, I am impressed. I'd almost call myself a fan of yours. It's a bit of an honor to kidnap someone I half-admire. Glad we kept that desflurane hidden in the apothecary."

Winifred fingered a few curls of Kennedy's hair. Kennedy would've done that herself if her hands were free.

"We were nervous enough when you and those other kids first found our vase of counterfeit bills down here a few days ago," Winifred said. "We had to hide all our stuff in the mine so those rangers didn't find it. Then you had to poke your nose in our business. I tried to convince Ernesto to make it look convincing that this area was closed, but his head's full of rocks. No room for anything except thoughts of wealth. He was easy to bribe. He let my husband's little counterfeiting ring down here when we offered to switch out the rodeo's prize money for counterfeit money."

Kennedy's eyebrows shot up. Winifred sniggered.

"Yes, the unlucky winner of the rodeo will gain nothing and not even know it. And our secret tunnel is the mine. It's a risky tunnel, but at least we were never spotted going in and out of this lovely undertown. Too bad you had to blow Ernesto's cover. He's been a decent help. Sure was nice to have an employee as an insider. He had the keys to every place you can think of, including your own cabin. I must admit, you're brave. Neither ghosts nor a warning note from a scorpion could deter you. I'm not terribly happy that my poor husband's hands suffered for nothing. Nor was I happy when you swung me in circles at the train earlier."

Winifred stood up. "I should excuse myself and go help the men. Since we've got you in check, we won't have to worry about you messing up our plans for a few of our men to steal the prize money. Thiago and Pedro are not only counterfeiters. They're also fine burglars. Now be a good little girl and stay where you are."

She snickered. "Don't think that'll be a problem. Ernesto and Thiago know how to tie a knot a boy scout can't untie."

Winifred disappeared down a dark hallway. Kennedy's eyes had become more adjusted, allowing her to see the computer, the scanner, and the inkjet printer sitting on a wooden table.

Terrified thoughts flooded through Kennedy's mind. She had to escape, and she knew she didn't have much time. She rubbed her hands and wrists together. Winifred wasn't kidding. Her hands were already beginning to feel numb from the ropes. But she didn't want to give up. She had to get out and warn everyone else!

But she couldn't make the ropes budge.

Kennedy slouched in defeat. Tears stung her eyes. Could she wait for a rescue? Who would find her here? There was no doubt this room was part of the closed-off area of the undertown. No tourists would be coming down here, that's for sure. Even Luciana and Lincoln would have restrictions. The only employee who probably would come down to this area was Ernesto. And not to help her, that's for sure.

Tears slid down her cheeks. What would those criminals do to her? Take her with them? Would they go flee to the Mexican border with her? Was she possibly looking at being their prisoner for the rest of her life?

Or maybe they would trap her in the mine? Winifred did say that they had been using the mine to go in and out of the undertown. It made perfect sense. And it would make sense for those criminals to tie her up in the mine.

And let it become her grave.

She slumped even further. It was no use.

Well, there was one thing she could do, and that was pray silently.

Heavenly Father, I am in a dire situation right now. Protect me and deliver me. Please don't let these wicked criminals keep me in their hands, nor let them get away with their evil schemes. Let there be a way for me, right now, to free myself from these ropes that bind me so I may escape.

She slumped even more. That was when she felt the nail.

Despite her gag, Kennedy smiled. Relief flooded her mind, like a flash flood in that canyon. The nail might help!

She rubbed her binds against that nail. Already, she could feel it digging through the rope. She worked harder, moving her wrists faster. When would that nail do the trick and undo those ropes? Who knew how much time she had until Winifred or any one of those men came back here!

After a few minutes that seemed like an eternity, Kennedy felt the ropes fall off her wrists. She ripped the gag out of her mouth and rubbed her sore wrists, which were covered in red rope burns. Then she yanked the nail out of the pole and used it to unravel the knots binding her ankles.

Kennedy grabbed the post. Slowly and shakily, she stood up. Hopefully she would be able to walk out of here, much less run if needed.

Kennedy glanced around the room. She saw a poker near a fireplace. She grabbed it and used it as though it were a cane. It should help her walk until the blood was flowing properly through her ankles again. It might even make a good weapon, a need she hoped wouldn't arise.

Now, to find her way out of here.

Her nerves seemed to be taking over. Every step she took, the floor creaked slightly. What if those counterfeiters heard it? She tried to ensure that the poker did not make any noise every time it touched the floor.

Kennedy came to a corner. She leaned against the wall and peeked around. The coast was clear. She slowly edged her way to the end of the hall. Much to her relief, she recognized the lounge. And it was empty.

As quietly as she could, Kennedy rushed down the familiar rooms. But she didn't know where to go to get out. The last thing she needed to do was get lost in the undertown again! If only she had her phone on her. She could call someone, like Nicole or Billy. Tell them what happened to her and ask to have someone come to her rescue.

Kennedy ran into the large bedroom. Her eyes wandered over the many weapons hanging on the walls. Those pistols were unlikely to have bullets. But there were plenty of archery sets. She reached out her hand to take a bow but hesitated. These were old weapons, hung for display only. They were valuable to Starwood City. Then again, she was in danger. She needed to defend herself somehow, and the poker wouldn't be good enough. She took a bow and a quiver and arrows.

Footsteps echoed down the hall. Kennedy stifled a gasp. Looking around wildly, her eyes rested upon a curtain. She rushed to that curtain and sat on the bed. She pulled the curtain in front of her and nocked an arrow to the bow. Would those criminals look behind here?

She heard light footsteps. Kennedy paused; those footsteps sounded too light to belong to any of those men. Even Winifred. Kennedy hesitantly peeked out from behind the curtain. Her heart jumped for joy when she saw it was Luciana.

Kennedy jumped out. Luciana gasped.

"Kennedy!" she said. "What are you doing . . . ?"

She trailed off when Kennedy held her finger to her lips. Kennedy's eyes flailed around the room.

"What's wrong with you?" Luciana asked in a hushed voice.

"What are you doing down here?" Kennedy hissed.

"Um, just doing an evening inspection. It was safe enough even after what happened on the train this afternoon. What's going on? Why are you down here? We had no tours. And why do you have that bow?"

Kennedy looked right at Luciana. "Lucy," she whispered, her voice shaking, "I was kidnapped."

"What?" Luciana's eyes grew even wider. "Kidnapped? But what happened?"

"I'll explain later. Just show me the way out!"

"Oh, yeah, of course! This way!"

But before the two girls could even turn around, footsteps boomed down the hall. Then angry voices.

"She's got to be here somewhere!"

"You said you tied her good!"

"I did! I don't know how that foolish girl got away!"

Kennedy felt like fainting. She and Luciana exchanged horrified looks, then glanced around. Kennedy had her bow ready. She and Luciana rushed down another hall.

"There she is!"

Kennedy ignored the sudden nausea.

"After those girls! Stop them!"

Kennedy and Luciana picked up their speed. Kennedy was sure that her heart was racing faster than she was running.

BANG!

Luciana screamed. For a second, Kennedy thought she had been shot. But she saw no blood.

"I heard a gunshot!"

Kennedy smiled with relief. Billy's voice!

She and Luciana turned another corner. Kennedy couldn't be more relieved. Alec, Billy, Gunnar, Aaron, Lincoln, Wesley, and Rachel were in the hall. They didn't make any noise, but their eyes lit up when they returned Kennedy's grin.

"Oh, Kennedy, you're safe!" Billy said. He wrapped his arms around Kennedy. "When I found your phone on the ground back at the camp, I just about had a panic attack!"

"My phone?" Kennedy said. "Do you have it?"

347

"No, we left it at the cabin," Billy said. His eyes rested on Kennedy's wrists, and his smile vanished. He grabbed Kennedy's hands. Just the feeling of him holding her hands made Kennedy's heart beat faster.

"What happened to your wrists?" Billy's voice was filled with concern. "Did they hurt you?"

Kennedy lowered her eyes. "I was tied to a post," she said. "Bound and gagged. But there was a nail. I rubbed my bonds against it."

348

"Oh, cousin," Aaron said, "we were so worried about you. I thought I was gonna faint when Billy told us."

"Is my dad here?" Luciana asked.

"No, he's still hasn't arrived in Starwood City," Alec said. "So we came."

"And I wouldn't let them leave me behind," Rachel said.

"Come on! Find those girls!"

A horrified silence fell upon the group. Kennedy backed up against the wall. Billy, Aaron, and Wesley stood in front of her.

"We've got to get out of here," Alec whispered. "Lincoln, Lucy, show us the way."

Lincoln peeked around the corner. He nodded at Alec. The two of them and Luciana led everyone down a hall.

"There she is!"

Kennedy's heart dropped. She spun around. Ernesto was pointing his gun at them.

"GO!" Alec yelled. He drew his own gun and fired. But his shot hit the wall instead of Ernesto.

"This way!" Lincoln said.

"Hey, get out there!" Ernesto shouted. "Thiago, Pedro, you two take the other exit! Cut them off!"

Alec fired another shot before running after the kids.

"They're cutting off the exits!" he said. "There's no way we will outrun them!"

"Wait," Kennedy said. "There might be a way. But it might be dangerous."

She looked at Luciana.

"Oh, no," Luciana said, "you don't mean the mine?"

"That's how they've been getting in and out unseen. And it's probably how they got me in."

BANG!

"The mine it is then," Billy said fiercely. "We need to get Kennedy out of here!"

"I second that!" Aaron said.

Lincoln and Luciana led everyone to the lounge. Kennedy wasn't too keen on running back down the hall from which she just escaped. But at least they didn't go to her prison room. Lincoln led the group to another hall.

"They're going to the mine!" Winifred's voice yelled.

Alec stopped. "I'm going to distract them," he said.

"Then I'll help!" Gunnar said.

"And me!" Aaron said.

"Be careful!" Kennedy said.

"We will! Just go! Billy, get my cousin out of here!"

Luciana and Lincoln led Kennedy, Billy, Wesley, and Rachel away from the hall. Soon they arrived at a boarded up opening in the wall. Lincoln, Wesley, and Billy tore the wooden boards off the black opening.

"This is it," Lincoln said darkly. "Basically a cave. Be very careful, everyone. This is an old mine tunnel."

"It might be somewhat safe," Luciana said. "I mean, if those criminals and Ernesto were using it a bunch of times . . ."

"Just go!" Billy said. He pulled Kennedy by the hand and ran down the tunnel. The others were right behind them. Kennedy could still hear the shouts and gunshots behind her. Dust fell from the rocky ceiling. The timbers looked like they could collapse at just the touch of a feather.

"Guys!"

Kennedy and Billy paused at Alec's voice. Kennedy smiled when Alec, Gunnar, and Aaron ran toward them.

"They went in there!"

Kennedy gasped. Ernesto's voice.

"They're coming!" she squeaked.

"Come on!" Alec said.

The group rushed down the tunnel. Just then Kennedy had an idea. She stopped and looked at a timber halfway dangling from the rocky ceiling.

"What are you stalling for?" Wesley exclaimed.

"Someone shoot at that timber!" Kennedy said.

"That could cause a cave-in!" Alec said.

"Exactly!"

Alec drew his gun and fired. The crash of the timber was louder than an explosion. Even so, it didn't look like much of a mine collapse.

"That won't hold them for long!" Rachel said.

They ran on. Soon Kennedy saw an opening up ahead. She and Billy emerged from the mine and into the canyon. The Canyon of the Ghosts.

"Over here!"

Kennedy whipped her head around. Much to her surprise, she saw Nicole, Susannah, Victoria, Jessica, and Marilyn on their horses, leading the other horses. Including Sunshine.

"Awesome!" Alec said. "You got my text, Nicole!"

Kennedy and her group rushed to the horses. Victoria, Jessica, and Marilyn slid off theirs and embraced Kennedy.

"Oh, Kennedy!" Marilyn exclaimed. "You're alright! You're safe!"

"Not for long!" Kennedy said. "We gotta go!"

She mounted Sunshine. She saw Luciana clambering onto her horse and dialing on her cell phone. But before they could ride away, Kennedy heard a gunshot. Then a yell in the distance.

"There they are! Get them!"

Ernesto, Winifred, and Ruben barged from the mine. Kennedy was horrified when she saw them meet up with the other three men, who had six horses!

"How did they meet up so fast?" Alec exclaimed. "And get their horses?"

"Who cares!" Wesley shouted. "Ride!"

Kennedy goaded Sunshine into a run. She stayed close to Luciana, Lincoln, Rachel, Billy, and Aaron.

"Stay close to me, Kenny!" Billy said. "I will protect you this time!"

BANG! BANG!

The shots startled the horses. Sunshine neighed and ran in another direction.

"Sunshine!" Kennedy said.

"Kennedy!" Billy and Aaron yelled in unison.

Just as her group scattered, so did the six counterfeiters. Kennedy peeked over her shoulder. Ernesto was riding after her. Her heart picked up its pace. She goaded Sunshine to ride faster.

Oh, Billy, Aaron, where are you? she wondered nervously. She was way too scared to be alone.

BANG!

Kennedy yelped. But she didn't feel any bullet.

Then she saw Billy riding toward her. Relief filled her, but it didn't last long. Ernesto caught up to her horse and was reaching for her reins. Kennedy screamed. She couldn't let Ernesto take her again! She swiped an arrow at him. The arrow's tip slashed Ernesto's hand. He yelled and tore it away.

A gunshot startled Kennedy. So did another scream from Ernesto. Kennedy looked ahead and gasped. Rachel and Lincoln were nearby on their horses. Rachel was holding a smoking gun. She and Lincoln began riding forward.

Kennedy used the opportunity to whack Ernesto's head with the bow. The impact was enough to make Ernesto fly off his horse. The horse whinnied in fear and rode off. Aaron caught its reins.

Ernesto shakily stood up. He aimed his gun at Kennedy. She slid off her horse, expecting a fire. But it didn't come. Only another scream from Ernesto. Kennedy ran around her horse. She saw Aaron, Lincoln, and Billy attacking Ernesto. But she didn't want to leave her cousin and friends to fight that criminal alone.

Kennedy pointed another arrow at Ernesto. She let it loose. The arrow lodged itself in the criminal's shoulder. He yelled in pain and fell to his knees. Aaron, Billy, and Rachel, who was still on her horse, pointed their guns at him.

"You're surrounded, Ernesto," Billy snapped.

Ernesto dropped his gun and raised his hands. "You kids are smart," he seethed.

"They're over here!"

Kennedy looked up. She gasped with joyful relief when she saw Nicole and Alec leading Ranger Olson, Luciana, and several other rangers toward them.

Kennedy, Aaron, Billy, Rachel, Wesley, and Lincoln backed away. Ranger Olson pointed his gun at Ernesto. Other rangers approached him and handcuffed him.

"What about the other counterfeiters?" Kennedy asked the chief ranger worriedly.

Ranger Olson gave her a warm smile. "They have been apprehended," he said. He put his hand on Kennedy's shoulder. "Are you alright? I was horrified to learn I had a kidnapping case and I wasn't even in town."

"Yes, I'm fine," Kennedy said.

The rangers led Ernesto away. He glared at Kennedy.

"I'll never forgive you for this!" he shouted.

Billy pulled Kennedy away, returning Ernesto's glare. The rangers hustled him away even faster.

"Come on, Ken," Billy said, "it's alright. You're safe now. You've had a terrible ordeal tonight. Let's get you back to the campground."

Kennedy let Billy and her other friends lead her away.

Kennedy sat atop Sunshine. Her gaze nervously fixated on the entrance of the outdoor arena. Roy Martinez was just finishing his round. His performance had been outstanding. No wonder he was considered a veteran rodeo winner. Kennedy wondered if she could do that well. Especially after a few sleepless nights due to traumatic nightmares.

She took a deep breath. She had her friends to console her, to vent to, to counsel with. Even after a few days, she felt much better, even though the very idea of having been kidnapped was still scary.

"You okay?"

Kennedy looked over at Billy. She smiled shyly. "Yeah," she said.

Susannah gave Kennedy an encouraging smile. "Luciana told me this morning that her dad is very grateful to you," she said.

"You basically saved the rodeo winner from getting a sack of fake money. You're going to get a reward, you know."

Susannah's smile faded a little. "But I'm just glad you're out of that awful situation."

Kennedy hung her head and nodded. "Me too. I should've been more careful."

Nicole patted Kennedy's shoulder. "We're always here for you," she said.

"We're almost on," Marilyn said. She smiled at her hand, which had a fresh bandage on it. "No more pain here."

"And I'm feeling better myself," Susannah added.

Kennedy grinned. Just knowing that her stepsister and friend were still able to perform made her feel better.

Just then the announcer's voice boomed over the intercom.

"And now let's welcome our riders from Pine Lodge! First off, Kennedy Ryan!"

"That's our cue." Kennedy smiled at her sisters and friends. "Wish me luck."

"You don't need luck," Billy said.

Kennedy chuckled, then she steered Sunshine out into the arena, letting her excitement overshadow all negative feelings.

About the Author

Photo credit: Elise Williams, eMarie Photography, https://emariephoto.com/

Alicia Layne Thomason is an author, poet, and musician. She graduated from Montana State University Billings in December 2021 with a Bachelor of Arts in English and a Bachelor of Arts in Music. Alicia lives in Billings, Montana. Her website is alicialaynethomason.com.